KINGZ OF THE GAME 5

Playa Ray

Lock Down Publications and Ca$h Presents
Kingz of the Game 5
A Novel by *Playa Ray*

Lock Down Publications

P.O. Box 944
Stockbridge, Ga 30281

Visit our website @
www.lockdownpublications.com

Copyright 2020 Playa Ray
Kingz of the Game 5

First Edition November 2020
Printed in the United States of America

Lock Down Publications
Like our page on Facebook: Lock Down Publications @
www.facebook.com/lockdownpublications.ldp
Cover design and layout by: **Dynasty Cover Me**
Book interior design by: **Shawn Walker**
Edited by: **Lashonda Johnson**

Stay Connected with Us!

Text **LOCKDOWN** to 22828 to stay up-to-date with
new releases, sneak peaks, contests and more…
Thank you.

Submission Guideline.

Submit the first three chapters of your completed manuscript to ldpsubmissions@gmail.com, subject line: Your book's title. The manuscript must be in a .doc file and sent as an attachment. Document should be in Times New Roman, double spaced and in size 12 font. Also, provide your synopsis and full contact information. If sending multiple submissions, they must each be in a separate email.

Have a story but no way to send it electronically? You can still submit to LDP/Ca$h Presents. Send in the first three chapters, written or typed, of your completed manuscript to:

LDP: Submissions Dept
P.O. Box 944
Stockbridge, Ga 30281

DO NOT send original manuscript. Must be a duplicate.

Provide your synopsis and a cover letter containing your full contact information.

Thanks for considering LDP and Ca$h Presents.

Acknowledgments

I don't think it would be fair to my readers if I didn't dedicate at least one of my books to them. So, to all my readers, this one is for you. I took a whole different form with the formatting, but I promise you will enjoy it. Just as you've told me you enjoyed the others. Thanks for the support. Be sure to spread the word about Playa Ray.

If you're looking back, you can't see ahead ~Billy 'O' Olsen~

Chapter 1
June 1, 2002
Saturday, 12:17 p.m.

The scene in the parking lot of the Sun Trust bank on Northside Drive was nothing short of chaotic. It seemed as though every response team from every government agency in Atlanta had been dispatched to the scene of the post-bank robbery as if the perpetrators had left behind a trail of dead bodies. Hell, from what I was told, only the bank officer had sustained a minor gunshot wound. Everybody else was unharmed. Well, that's the information that was handed down to me by my superior before *ordering* my partner and me to this circus.

All morning, since getting to my office, I'd been going over a missing child's case I'd been working on for almost three weeks, Director Manny Hopkins summoned me and Wilma Reid into his palatial office to hand down his verdict. Trust me, as much as I love investigating bank robberies, I was about to protest this mission, and Reid who was seated beside me must have sensed it because, before I could open my mouth to tell the director he could stick his case up his ass, she kicked my foot to silence me, thanked the director, then pretty much ushered me out of the office.

Am I mad at her for encroaching? Of course not. Intermittently, whenever Hopkins and I found ourselves at odds, Reid would always step in as an intermediary. It's rather funny because she'd been keeping me out of trouble from the moment we'd met years ago at the FBI Academy in Quantico, Virginia, although after graduation, she went back to her hometown in Boston Massachusetts to carry out her dreams of being a Federal agent.

Since then, I hadn't seen, nor heard anything from her until seven months ago, when she showed up at the James P. Russell building downtown, after being transferred to the Atlanta division, which was approximately two months after my last partner was murdered right before my very eyes. At that time, I was still sore and adamant about not being appointed another partner. Yes, this was one of those times when my supervisor and I were *at odds* because I refused every person he endeavored to partner me with, but when he gave me the ultimatum to either accept a partner or resign, I quickly requested for Wilma Reid to be my tag along.

"I guess we'll dock here," Reid now said, parking the dark-blue, unmarked Ford Crown Victoria in a spot closer to the exit of the lot, which is something she has a tendency of doing.

With her dark hair parted and cascading down her shoulders, Wilma Reid was clad in a smoke-gray pantsuit and some black brogues. She may be considered small at 5'5 and 140 pounds, but she's the toughest White woman I've ever encountered. Hell, she'd even kicked my ass once, during a grappling exercise in training. Okay, it was twice, but I did manage to overthrow her in our third match, although she maintains the deposition that she tripped over her own foot.

Yeah, right.

The temperature was up in the late seventies today, and the sun seemed to be radiating at its full potential. We weren't out of the car two seconds when I began to perspire under my gray, two-piece suit and light bullet-proof vest that was ensconced between my tank top and dress shirt. I adjusted the sunglasses on my face as Reid and I traversed the parking lot, nearing the small blockade that the local police had arranged to prevent passage to the bank, which was closed for the day due to the breach.

"I'm Special Agent Reid," my partner announced to one of the locals, flashing her credentials. "And this is my partner, Special Agent Bishop."

Giving only a once-over of Reid's shield, the young male cop nodded slightly, then gestured toward the building, where a few other officers were just standing around as though they had no other way to waste taxpayers' money. Of course, they eyed us as we neared, but neither of them made any attempt to stop us from entering the bank that had its air conditioner on full blast. I couldn't help but sigh inwardly at the reprieving of the warm climate condition beyond the glass doors.

Besides the white noise emitting from various radio transmitters, the establishment was almost quiet as several police investigators moved about, questioning employees and customers who were present at the time of the robbery. Per protocol, these people were to be retained until released by the FBI, being that they are all witnesses to a federal offense. Yes, that means I can hold them here for as long as I feel like holding them.

"Reid! Bishop!"

I looked up to see the Chief of Police, Darrel Manning emerging from what appeared to be the bank manager's office, clad in a dark-brown suit and tie. A former colleague to my father, who was wounded in the line of duty over six years ago, Manning had become something like a Godfather to me. The fifty-seven-year-old, highly experienced man taught me a great deal of things I've never learned in the academy. As mutual friends, we've assisted each other with solving cases and often kept one another abreast on the process of investigations.

"How's it going?" Manning asked once we approached, extending his hand.

"I can't complain, Sir," I answered, shaking his hand, and as always, I could not stop staring at his thick, overgrown mustache that was sprinkled with gray strings of hair, and protruded over his top lip, almost obscuring it. The mustache may have been a little unkempt, but his six-inch afro was always trimmed and groomed to perfection as if he and Steve Harvey have the same barber. "How's the family?"

"Everybody's fine," he answered. "What's the old man up to these days?"

"He's still driving everybody crazy."

Manning giggled at that, then turned his attention to Reid, who he'd always found himself fawning over. In fact, it's one of the only times one would see the old man flash all twenty-seven of his coffee-stained teeth.

"And how are you today, Ms. Reid?" he cooed, practically drooling all over my partner.

"I'm fine, Mr. Manning," she answered like a little schoolgirl trying her best not to blush.

"So, what's the rundown?" I intervened. No, I wasn't jealous of this little moment they were having. I just like to get straight to business.

"At approximately ten twenty-one a.m." Manning shifted into business mode. "Three unknown subjects entered the bank, armed, and wearing ski masks. One subject shoots the stationed officer in the leg before disarming him. Then, the three subjects proceed to rob the establishment, taking money from registers, and money and valuables from employees and customers."

"Nothing from the vault?" I inquired.

He shook his head. "Nope. According to the managers, they made no mentioning of the vault."

"Witnesses?"

"Thirteen," he answered. "My people should be almost done interviewing everybody."

"Any physical evidence?"

Manning cleared his throat before responding, "Only the shell casing belonging to the bullet still lodged in the officer's leg. He was medically cleared to be transported to Grady Memorial. I assume you would like to view the surveillance footage before conducting your interviews, right?"

"You seem to know me better than I know myself," I quipped, regarding him with a crooked smile.

"Well, right this way," Manning said, leading us into the office from whence he'd come out of where a thin man in an expensive-looking suit was pacing back and forth, fidgeting with his fingers. He stopped and eyed us as we entered. "This is the bank's manager, Corey Limehouse. Mr. Limehouse, this is Special Agent Bishop, and his partner, Special Agent Reid."

"It's a pleasure," the manager said, nervously shaking our hands with both of his.

"First time, huh?" I asked, studying his clean-shaven face and pointed nose that helped to keep his wire-framed eyeglasses in place.

"Yes," he answered with too much fervor. "You can prepare, prepare and prepare yourself for something like this, but when it actually happens—" He broke off, exhaling sharply, and shaking his head in disbelief.

"Could you pull up the surveillance for me?" I interrupted the beginning of his nervous breakdown.

"Sure." He stepped behind the desk, tapped a few keys on his keypad, then stepped aside. "It's all set," he apprised. "All you have to do is set the reels in motion."

"Thank you, sir." I took it upon myself to *borrow* his chair to make myself comfortable. On the screen, the frozen image was that of the entrance, where I could clearly see three dark figures approaching from the outside. After making sure my trusty sidekick was standing behind me, looking over my shoulder, I brushed the right key, thankful I'd learned how to operate this particular function.

As it went, the three masked subjects bustled through the front doors, waving guns. One carried a sub-machine gun, and the other two had handguns. The bank's officer was about six yards away from the entrance, leaning against one of the pillars with his arms folded over his chest, watching the transactions between the cashiers and customers. Hearing the subjects come in, he quickly spun around, and immediately threw his hands up in surrender, seconds before one of the subjects with a handgun, shot him in the leg. Once he fell to the floor, and the shooter relieved him of his weapon, I switched camera views just in time to see the other handgun-carrier leap over the counter to take control of the cashiers, while the third one ordered the customers to the floor.

Leaving the officer where he laid, the shooter quick-stepped to the manager's office and entered, seconds later, shoving Corey Limehouse into view from behind, forcing him to join the others on the floor. He, then, stood guard while the one behind the counter stuffed bills into a small gym bag, and the other subject went around, relieving the hostages of their monies and valuables, then, like the snap of a finger, they were all marching toward the entrance. I switched to the only exterior camera that displayed a fuzzy view of the parking lot, considering it hadn't been cleaned recently, but that didn't prevent me from identifying the white Toyota the culprit's dove into before speeding out of the lot.

"So," I began, stopping the footage and turning to face the manager, who had a concerned look on his face. "You were in your office when they first entered the bank. I'm quite sure you heard the shot. What was your reaction to it?"

"There's a stress call button installed just beneath the desk," he answered, looking directly at the tape recorder in Reid's hand. "I immediately pressed it after looking at the monitor to make sure I heard what I heard."

"And your name is, Corey Limehouse?" Reid took the rein.

"Yes, it is."

"You're the manager of the Sun Trust Bank at Ten Eleven Northside Drive, located in the city of Atlanta, state of Georgia?"

"Yes."

"Do you still hold that position today?"

"Yes, I do." There was a hint of uncertainty in his voice.

"What's today's date?"

"The first of June. Two thousand and two."

"Could you tell me the time?"

Limehouse referred to the cheap-looking watch on his wrist. "It's twelve forty-one," he offered.

My partner nodded for me to resume.

"What happened after you pressed the emergency response button, Mr. Limehouse," I posed, blindly feeling around for the electrical device to make sure it was there. It was.

"I was really panicking at the time," he responded, now regarding me. "I mean, I was shocked. All I could do at that very moment was watch the monitor as the scene unfolded. I saw the gunman coming toward my office." He shrugged his shoulders up and down. "There was nothing I could do."

"Did you hear the voice of any of the perpetrators?"

"I heard all of their voices."

"Were they masculine or feminine

"Masculine."

"Are you sure?"

"Absolutely."

"Well, I guess that's it for now, Mr. Limehouse," I informed. "While this investigation is still pending, I advise you not to leave the Sates without notifying and acquiring consent from the Federal Bureau of Investigation. There's a possible chance that I or my partner will contact you for a written statement."

"Yes sir," the manager responded with a nod.

"What I need you to do for me now," I resumed, "is to furnish me with the surveillance disc, which is now an essential part of this investigation, and property of the FBI."

"Yes sir." He moved to the desk to free the disc from the computer's component.

I turned to my old friend. "Manning?"

"Let me hear it," he came back.

"When your officers are done," I told him, "please have them to turn their written statements over to me."

"Will do."

"Also," I said, as Limehouse handed me the disc he'd enclosed in a plastic case, "you can release the customers. Reid and I will interview the rest of the employees, then drive out to the hospital to interview the officer."

"That sounds like a plan," said Manning. "I'll notify the hospital that the officer is to be retained until you show up."

As it went, once Chief Manning's officers had turned over their reports, and released the customers, they packed up and made off themselves. By that time, our forensic people were on the scene, attempting to gather whatever evidence they could. Then, as if *commandeering* the manager's chair wasn't enough, Reid and I insisted on using his office as an interrogation room to interview the other employees, which had only taken a little over half an hour. Forensics had already gone by then, making sure to leave me with a Chain of Evidence sheet.

"A penny for your thoughts," Reid said from behind the wheel of the Ford. I can't say how long we'd been in motion, but I had been reading and re-reading the written statements gathered from the bank's employees.

"I don't know," I responded, now studying the side of her face as she kept her eyes on the road. "These thoughts may cost way more than a penny."

"So, you're suspecting this was an inside job."

"Perhaps," I said, looking out at the edifice of Grady Memorial Hospital. "I'm just anxious to hear what Officer Turner has to say."

"Do you think his statement will differ from the others?"

"Perhaps." She hates it when I persist to answer her in this manner, which is probably why she didn't say another word while looking for a place to park.

I chose this time to file the statements away in my briefcase that I really hate carrying around. Hell, I only carry it whenever I feel like purveying witnesses with statement forms and assessing physical evidence myself.

Being that Manning had already furnished us with the number to the recovery room that the wounded officer was in, my partner and I bypassed the receptionist's desk, got onto an elevator, and rode up to the eighth floor, and, no, I did not bring a statement form for him to fill out, which is one of my personal tactics. You'll learn about that later.

Getting off on the appointed floor, we moved along the corridor that was buzzing with medical personnel, moving about, tending to their patients. After traveling through two more hallways we made it to room 321, where the door was wide open. If I'm not mistaken, I think visitors are supposed to get permission from medical personnel before visiting patients. Well, lucky for us, we're 'visitors.

We're the FBI, dammit!

Officer Damien Turner, according to the employee files at the bank, was a Black male of thirty-seven years of age, which made him three years older than myself. The only alterity between his employee's photo, and his current appearance, is that he was now unshaved, and looked as if he was in dire need of a barber. Underneath the white bedspread, he looked to be physically in shape. Exposed, were his arms that were down by his sides, and his right leg that had a blood-stained bandage wrapped around the thigh. He pried his eyes away from the television set mounted up on a stand, to regard us as we entered.

"How's it going, Officer Turner?" I asked as we neared his bed. That's when I noticed his uniform was folded in a chair on the opposite side.

"I assume y'all are the feds?" he said, with a hint of attitude in his voice, using the remote in his hand to mute the television. "I was told I couldn't leave until y'all showed up. Y'all need me to write a statement?"

"Not at the moment." I glanced to make sure my partner had the recorder out before going on. "Right now, we just need a brief verbal statement on what happened at the Sun Trust bank today, which is the first day of June, and the year of two thousand and two."

"The bank was robbed by three men in ski masks," he said, matter-of-factly.

"For the record," I went on, "you're the bank's security guard, right?"

"Yes, I am."

"And what exactly were you doing when the three masked subjects entered the establishment?"

"I was watching the transactions between the cashiers and customers," he responded, looking as if he was trying to retain. "My back was to the entrance. When they came in, yelling out orders, I spun around cautiously. Seeing that I had no time to react, I threw my hands up. That's when one of 'em shot me in the thigh."

"When you fell to the ground," I took the initiative, "the shooter lifted your service weapon from your holster, right?"

"Yeah," he answered slowly, looking at me as if I just revealed something that only he was supposed to know.

"Have you ever been through this before?"

"Never."

"What about their voices?" I asked. "Could they have all been male?"

He seemed pensive for a second. "I think so."

"You don't know for sure?"

"I mean, I'm sure they were all male."

17

"Thank you, Mr. Turner," I offered with a nod. "As I said, we only needed a brief verbal statement for now. However, we'll be in touch to get a more detailed written statement from you."

He only nodded. Being that we'd called the hospital ahead of time, requesting that the bullet removed from the officer's leg to be retained, Reid and I made for the medical director's office to see if our request was honored. Sure, we're in possession of the spent shell casing, but the actual bullet could very well reveal a side of the mystery that its counterpart is reluctant to give up. However, as we made the journey to our next destination, my mind was preoccupied with Officer Damien Turner. Something just didn't add up about this character. Do I have a feeling that he was complicit in this robbery?

Perhaps.

Chapter 2

Sunday

The shrillness of my cell phone's ringer roused me from my slumber a little after ten a.m. Although I went to bed at a decent time, I still felt restless. After returning to the James P. Russell building, yesterday, Reid and I made sure that every piece of evidence obtained from the bank robbery was in order, recorded everything in the logbook, then retired to our office. Reid had to leave early for personal reasons, which is why we agreed to remit the investigation of our current case until Monday. This was great because it gave me a little more time to delve back into the missing child case I was working on before being summoned by the director.

Now, with my eyes adjusting to the sunrays beaming through the light curtains hanging in the windows of my studio apartment in Smyrna, Georgia, I stretched my limbs as far as I figured I could while intentionally making the early-morning caller wait a little while longer. Yeah, leave it to me to act as though I didn't have the slightest clue as to who the caller was. Not only did I know who the caller was, but I pretty much had an inkling as to how the inception of the conversation was going to be. Seeing no reason to prolong it any longer, I collected the device off the nightstand beside the bed, lied on my back, and stared at the screen before answering.

"Yes?"

"Oh! I like your nerves!" Monique's voice boomed through the earpiece. "You didn't call me last night, then you have the audacity to answer the phone all cool and shit? Really?"

"Good morning, Monique!" I maintained my composure. Trust me, I am not easily aroused to anger. No one controls my emotions, but me.

"Don't give me that shit!" my girlfriend of almost three years, spat. "You were probably fucking that nasty ass White bitch last night. Is that why you couldn't call me? You had your mouth full of that crab infested pussy?"

All I could do was shake my head. This girl was impossible. She'd been accusing me of having sex with Wilma Reid, ever since she found out I had a female partner, but she really pushed the levers when she discovered that Reid was a White female, and I blame it on Monique's former boyfriend, who'd actually jilted her for a White woman. Hell, you're probably wondering why I even put up with the madness. To be honest, I often wonder the same thing. Now, don't get me wrong, Monique is not a horrible person. She's just been through a lot like any other human being. I guess I can identify with her because we both came from similar backgrounds. Plus, when you love a person, you don't just leave them without just cause.

Did I put that into proper perspective?

"How's Melody?" I now asked, hoping to assuage this verbal storm.

"She's fine," answered Monique, in a more composed tone. "And don't be trying to change the subject. Why didn't you call me last night?"

"I was exhausted, baby," I told her. "I'm still working that missing child's case. Plus, I have a new case."

"You do?" There was much enthusiasm in her tone. Monique was like a little child when it came to hearing my *crime stories*.

"Yeah," I answered, stifling a yawn. "Bank robbery."

"The Sun Trust bank on Northside Drive?"

"That's the one."

"I saw that on the news last night," she said, almost conspiringly. "Brian, I want all the details!"

"There are no details right now, Monique." I was shaking my head again. "And, like I told you, the things I tell you about my investigations are confidential. Don't let me find out you're writing a Sherlock Holmes book about me. I want half of the proceeds."

She giggled. "Boy, shut up! What time will you be here?"

Not too keen on wearing shorts – no matter how hot it was – I donned a pair of khaki pants, a tan Polo shirt, and a pair of black Air Force Ones. My breakfast consisted of scrambled eggs on toasted bread, and a glass of orange juice. After cleaning the used dishes, and whatever area of my place that needed to be cleaned, I was in my 2001 BMW 745i, and on my way to College Park, Georgia.

I don't have anything against the College Park Projects, or any other housing unit analogous to them, but I'm still having a hard time grasping the reason why Monique refuses to leave an environment she'd spent her entire life in. Hell, I did. When I left from under my mother's roof of Deerfield Apartments on Campbellton Road, there was no looking back. And I bet you're probably wondering why, after being together for so long, we hadn't thought about moving in together. Well, we thought about it. Then, we thought against it. The reasons why are too many to explicate at the moment, but they were logical enough to us both to render such a consensus.

I can't remember the last time I'd been inside Monique's apartment. Lately–well, every Sunday–I'll park close enough to her unit, honk the horn and wait for Melody to come flying out of the apartment like a bat out of hell, many minutes before her mother. Just as expected, the nine-year-old came bursting out of the door as if being pursued, clad in blue jeans capri pants, a pink shirt with *GIFTED* emblazoned in glitter, and white tennis shoes. Plus, she wore a huge smile on her face that seemed to intensify when she dove into the front-passenger seat and threw her arms around my neck, prompting me to embrace her back.

"Hey, Brian!" she squealed with genuine delight.

"Hey, baby!" I planted an avuncular kiss on her cheek. No, she's not my daughter, but I'm the closest thing to a father to her, being that she'd never met her biological. Monique has always refused to talk about him, although I'm under the impression that she doesn't have a clue as to who'd procreated her only child. "How are you?" I asked Melody.

"I'm fine," she answered, a smile still lingering. "My momma was mad at you for not calling her last night."

"So, I was told," I replied, playfully narrowing my eyes at her. "Were you mad at me, too?"

She now had a bashful look on her face, though she couldn't stop smiling to save her life.

"It's okay if you were mad at me," I assured. "I mean, I was tired, but I really can't use that as an excuse for not calling to check on you two. I apologize."

"I accept your apology."

"Why, thank you!"

"You're welcome."

I looked toward the apartment, but there was no sign of Monique. "What's taking that crazy woman so long?"

"She's probably still talking to herself in the mirror," offered Melody.

"Talking to herself?"

"Yep," she answered. "She be telling herself how fine she is. Then, she'll ask herself who's the baddest *B* on the planet?"

For the third time today, I found myself shaking my head in reference to my eccentric girlfriend. She was definitely a handful, but she was quite amusing at times. Now, as she finally emerged from the apartment, Monique was ravishingly stunning in a Duke Blue Devils' jersey skirt and white Reebok tennis shoes. The excessive reddish-brown weave stacked on top of her head, seemed to be experimentally coifed by her stylist, and what was there to say about those claw-like nails she'd always been so fond of wearing? What about the earrings dangling from her earlobes? The earring in her nose that completed the one stapled in her tongue? The necklaces? The rings? The wrist and ankle bracelets?

Yes, it's fairly safe to say that this woman takes extreme pride in how she looks in the public eye, but, for some reason, she just could not come straight to the car. A neighborhood celebrity, if I may, she made it her business to stop and chat with every female neighbor she spotted. She was loud, so, of course, Melody and I could hear her yapping away. Oh, I didn't have to shake my head this time. I looked over at Melody, and she was doing it for me.

I smiled.

Finally, with her designer pocketbook dangling from her shoulder, Monique sashayed toward the car with her hips tantalizingly swaying from right to left, and her other assets causing the skirt to fit her body like a latex glove. That, plus the way her voluptuous lips glossed in the sunlight, stirred up something inside of me, which was a reminder that we hadn't *been together* in a while, and yes my occupation plays a healthy part in that, but maybe we could change that tonight.

Knowing that her mother always sits up front, Melody sucked her teeth while making the transition to the back seat.

"Hey, baby!" Monique exclaimed once she slid in beside me, clasping my face between her hands and momentarily smothering me with a passionate kiss. "What are we taking my father-in-law for lunch?"

"I don't know," I answered, staring into her dark-brown eyes that accentuated her mocha complexion, "but I'm quite sure you have some kind of suggestion."

"Melody made the suggestion this week," she said, pulling her compact disc book from her pocketbook, searching for a CD.

I looked back at Melody, who already had that shy grin on her face. "And what suggestion was that, sweetheart?"

"Applebees," she answered shyly.

"That sounds like a great idea!"

So, it happened, we journeyed out to Marietta, Georgia, ordered lunch from a nearby Applebees restaurant, then made for the nursing home that my father's housed at. The staff were familiar with us, so we didn't have to go through the headache procedure of producing ten different forms of identifications, but we did have to wait forever while our food and personal items were examined as if my father was in prison, and we were susceptible to smuggle him something that could serve as a means of escape.

Dorian Bishop's room was located on the seventh floor but, as always, we were led to the dining area like every other visitor. It's not that visitors weren't allowed in the living quarters of the visitees, because they are more than welcome to inspect – and complain about – the accommodations of their loved ones. It was just that all visits began in the dining area and, by verbal request by either party, could be moved to the living area.

As soon as we entered the dining area, Melody and I allowed our escort to show us to our table, while Monique made a B-line to the line of vending machines to purchase our drinks, being that the establishment doesn't allow visitors to bring open beverages that could easily have alcohol mixed into them. Once seated, I took stock of the vast room through the dark lenses of my sunglasses. There were, at least, nine other tables occupied with visitors. Plus, there were a handful of employees moving about like undercover agents, pretending to clean already clean places while keeping an eye on what was going on between their patients and family members. This made me smile to myself while fighting the urge to rub my arms for warmth, considering how high they always had the air conditioner, no matter what season it was.

"Aren't you cold?" I asked Monique, who approached the table with four bottled drinks.

She made a face as she placed the drinks on the table. "Why would I be cold? It's almost a hundred degrees outside."

"I'm cold," Melody insisted, rubbing her own bare arms.

"You don't know what you are," Monique told her daughter before taking a seat. "Sometimes, I think you talk just to hear yourself talk."

"Monique!" I came to the rescue. "It *is* cold in here. You have alligator skin, so it doesn't affect you. We're cold."

It's not like my girlfriend to not respond to such an insult but, before she could reply, a young female orderly wheeled my father through the entrance. We watched as she pushed his wheelchair along the walk area towards the glass doors that led to the recreation area that boasted a tennis court, miniature golf course, a swimming pool, and several concrete tables with huge umbrellas, surrounded by plastic chairs. After parking my father's chair at one of the tables, and engaging the wheel locks, the young orderly strutted back inside, and up to our table with a broad smile on her face.

"I'm sorry you all," she said, revealing the gap between her extremely white teeth, "but Mr. Bishop insisted on having his visit outdoors. I hope you all don't mind the change of scenery."

"Not at all," I spoke up, of course, I was the first to stand.

Gathering the food and drinks, we followed the woman outside, and Monique must've sensed I was enjoying the view of the woman's behind, because she quickly stepped in front of me, and began tossing her hips with a vengeance, making her juicy buttocks look as though they were going to bounce from under the skirt.

Lord, have mercy!

Dorian Bishop with his large sunglasses on his face, seemed to be looking off in a distance when we approached, placing the food and drinks on the table. I let Monique and Melody divide the family meal up while I took a seat right across from my father, who looked quite comfortable in a pair of black jeans, brown dress shoes, and a brown Izod shirt. Plus, the fifty-six-year-old still didn't have no more than twenty strands of gray hairs between his beard and head that were both groomed nicely. Honestly, no matter how jealous I am with his dark and wavy hair, my father looked as though he should've been on the box of the Duke wave kit. I inherited his good looks, but not his good hair.

"How's my father-in-law doing today?" Monique asked, after giving him a peck on the cheek.

"I'm good," he answered in his mellow tone, now looking up at her. "How's my daughter-in-law?"

"I'm fine," she answered, smiling from ear to ear. "Your granddaughter-in-law picked out this lunch for you."

He stared at the meal laid out in front of him for a moment before looking over at Melody, who was regarding him with that shy grin I'm so fond of. "Did you really pick this out for me?"

"Yes." She was still grinning but had a dubious look on her face. "Do you like Applebees?"

"I've never eaten at the place," he told her, "but I do like hugs. Or do I not get one today?"

"Yes, you can get a hug."

They were both beaming with delight as they embraced. My father's sole gold tooth gleamed brilliantly against the rays of the sun, revealing that he was as crazy about the little girl as I am. Hell, I even found myself smiling at the touching picture in front of me. As Melody and Monique took their seats, my father finally looked over at me. He was no longer smiling, which had me wondering if he was thinking of her. Well, of course, he was. He couldn't help but think of her whenever he sees me. I mean, there's no way around it. He was institutionalized for his physical condition – there's nothing wrong with his mental. Therefore, he's highly capable of distinguishing his friends from his foes.

"How's it going, my son?" he finally asked.

"I can't complain, dad. Just taking it one day at a time. How's everything on your end?"

"It won't do me any good to complain," he said. "I had to take a break from that icebox, though. In fact, this is where I've been spending most of my time."

"All by yourself?" an inquisitive Melody wanted to know.

"Sometimes." He grabbed a deep-fried shrimp off his plate and surveyed it. "There's this old White guy. He'll stop by and challenge me in chess from time to time. Right now, he's out with his granddaughter and her husband and kids."

"Why can't you go out?"

"I can go out," my father responded to Melody's query, looking across the table at me. "It just seems that no one wants to take me anywhere."

Well, damn! Now, they were all looking at me. I guess I'm just guilty of neglecting everybody. What? Am I supposed to apologize for the career I'd chosen? I'm out here trying to save the world, and people are worried about little things such as returning phone calls and spending quality time? Really?

"Dad, we're not going there," I finally spoke. "You know how busy my job has me. You've been on the force, so you, of all people, know how hard it is to maintain a household.

Dorian Bishop only nodded his understanding.

"As soon as I catch a break from these cases I'm currently working on," I resumed, "I'll do my very best to better accommodate the three of you."

Having my statement concluded, I dug into my meal, stuffing a piece of fish into my mouth. This prompted everyone else to tend to their own. It was quiet, except for the huge umbrellas flapping in the light summer breeze. While eating, I saw my father look off to his left and smile. That's when I noticed that the young orderly who'd escorted him out was seated on one of the stone benches lining the walkway, resembling a schoolgirl who was awaiting a prom date, and she was smiling back. It didn't take the special skills of an investigator to discern that there was something going on between the two of them. Hell, I *hope* there's something going on between the two of them.

"Dad, how's your food?" I inquired after another moment.

"It's delicious!" he answered, regarding Melody. Then, after removing and placing his sunglasses on the table, he fixed me with a stern look. "So, how's everything going with you two?"

Oh shit! He's making his transformation from father to relationship counselor, which is something he does at every visit. "Everything's going well," I bit the bait.

"That's good! Just don't be so quick to walk down that aisle."

Uh-oh.

"You're both still young," he went on. "Cherish what you have at this moment. Nothing lasts forever. Hell, marriage ain't nothing but a promise to divorce. It's like an automated carwash – you go in one end, knowing eventually you'll come out on the other."

Monique and I exchanged awkward glances before I, as always, took it upon myself to take the wheel. "I saw your dear old friend, Darrel Manning."

"When?" the old man perked up.

"Yesterday," I answered, omitting the reason for the encounter. "He asked about you."

"And not once has he called to check on me. Does he know why I'm really here?"

"Of course."

Dorian Bishop narrowed his dark brown eyes at me. "You probably told him I'd lost my marbles."

I couldn't help but smile. "Would that be incorrect?"

The remainder of the visit with my father went smoothly. Then, which was another Sunday ritual, the three of us journeyed out to Monique's mother's house on Gresham Road in Decatur, Georgia.

This was where we spent the rest of the day with Monique's mother, and her boyfriend, who was a few years older than me. We'd always play cards while waiting for the dinner to cook, and Gloria's an excellent cook!

You may be wondering why I hadn't said anything about visiting my own mother. Well, Brenda Bishop left my father shortly after he was discharged from the hospital, where he was diagnosed with paraplegia resulting from being injured in the line of duty. A couple of months later, she moved to Ohio with another man, who was supposedly my father's friend. Yes, that's why he's bitter, and, truth be told, I have ill feelings toward my mother for pulling such a stunt, but she's still my mother no matter what, right?

"There's my favorite special agent!" Gloria beamed upon opening her door for us, inviting us into her home, where the aroma of various cooked foods permeated the air, and *Regina Belle's Show Me The Way* played softly from the stereo in the living room.

"Momma, ain't nothing special about him," Monique chimed, playfully looking me up and down.

"Child, you're just a hater."

These two always went at it like this about me, and Gloria was just as enthusiastic about my investigations as her daughter was. She'd even insisted that I allow her to accompany me to one of my crime scenes, asserting that she could probably help me solve a case, because she'd seen enough *cop shows* to know what to look for, and, yes, she was serious. I guess those *cop shows* aren't that interesting when you actually know a real-life investigator?

Leaving mother, daughter, and granddaughter in the kitchen to gossip, I made for the living room, where Gloria's boyfriend, Rico was already seated at the folding table that was set up, playing a game of solitaire. Thirty-six-year-old, Ricardo Willis had his share of run-ins with the law for minor drug and car-theft charges and has only served three years in prison for related offenses. The light brown-skinned man wasn't gaudy. The white, newer-model Chevy Malibu he had parked out front was registered to a Connie Willis. His mother, of course.

Yes, I checked this guy out, but I only did it because I like to know who I'm in the presence of. Especially when it's consistent. I'm quite sure he's dealing drugs, but am I investigating him? Shit no! He's a fish, which is what the local authorities waste their time on. The FBI investigates such federal crimes as assault on the President, bank robbery, bombings, hijackings, and kidnappings. Sure, we'll help the locals out from time to time, but we mainly focus on individuals or organizations engaged in activities that may endanger national security, and our operations include the investigation of rebellions, riots, spy activities, treason, and threats to overthrow the government, just to name a few. Trust me, we investigate more than one hundred and eighty kinds of federal crimes. Plus, we report to the President, Congress, or the Justice Department for action. Maybe that's why we're considered *special agents.* So, if Rico somehow ends up on the DEA's radar, and I, Special Agent Brian Bishop is one of the assisting agents from the bureau tagging along, I'm going to nail his ass to the same exact cross Jesus was nailed to.

"It's about time y'all showed up," Rico said, once I'd entered. "I've been dreaming about this re-match all week."

"All week?" I asked, taking a seat in one of the metal folding chairs, and placing my cell phone atop the table. "It's a wonder you could sleep after the beat down we put on y'all."

Rico laughed. "Yeah, I guess you can call it that. Did you catch the game last night?"

"Man, the only thing I caught last night was some Zs. I was so tired I still don't remember going to bed."

"When's the last time you took a vacation?" He took a sip of his canned Budweiser that instantly caused my mouth to water, although I don't partake in such pleasures in the presence of Melody.

"It's been quite some time," I answered, eyes transfixed on the beer as he sat it back down on its coaster. "I guess I've been too busy to put in a request for one."

"Let's get this party started, y'all!" my vociferous girlfriend spouted as she entered, followed by her mother.

They were both carrying beers and wine coolers, clearly indicating that Melody had already gone over to the neighbor's house to play with the neighbor's children until dinner was ready.

"Thanks, babe!" I accepted a Budweiser from Monique, and almost swallowed half the beer in one gulp before setting it down on a coaster, and it was damn refreshing, too.

"I think we should switch it up this time," Gloria insisted, twisting the cap off her wine cooler. "We should have the women against the men. Pussy against dick."

Monique cackled at her mother's risqué remark, clearly proud to be a reflection of the forty-nine-year-old woman. This was one of those times I'd be shaking my head, but I wouldn't dare. Well, at least not in front of them, but I was doing it mentally as I glanced over at Rico, who had a smirk on his face. He'd been with the older woman for a little over a month, so he should be somewhat accustomed to her spontaneous promiscuity, as I am with Monique's. I just prayed to the high heavens that Melody doesn't grow to be a replica of these two. Good luck with that, huh?

Ultimately, everyone agreed to the battle of the sexes. *Gregory Abbot's Shake You Down* played from the stereo as we settled in for our first game of spades, in which the women won. Periodically, Gloria would journey off to the kitchen to check on the food, returning with an update on what was done. Monique had delegated herself the *beverage refresher*, making sure we all had fresh drinks. During one of Gloria's runs to the kitchen, my cell phone rang atop the table, sounding like a house phone, because of the ringtone I'd chosen. Looking down at the screen, I instantly felt this was one of those times I'd have to take a rain check on dinner and rush out to some crime scene. Monique was obviously feeling the same thing because she was shuffling the deck of cards while giving me that knowing look.

"I'm listening," I answered, phone to my ear.

"A body was found earlier on Memorial Drive," Chief Darrel Manning spoke in his all-business tone. "Male. Mid-twenties. I assume he belongs to you."

Chapter 3

"Special Agent Bishop," I announced, flashing my shield to the White, rotund man seated behind the desk banked with three monitors.

He squinted his eyes behind his extremely small spectacles as if to see me clearer. "Ah, yes. They're expecting you. Examination Room Seven."

"Thank you!"

As I made my way down the dim-lit corridor, passing steel gurneys lining the walls, I couldn't help but think of how devastated Melody was that I had to leave. Monique was a little upset, but she and her mother are empathetic to my line of work. Rico? Hell, if I'm not mistaken, I think he was a bit relieved that I had to leave so early. Or maybe I read him wrong.

Every morgue I've visited always reeked of a high volume of various cleaning agents. I never understood why until I had to sit in on my first of many medical examinations of the human corpse. It's one thing to see a body being cut open, rib cage sawed into, and organs removed, but the rank odor that exudes from the insides of a corpse was indescribable. A person with a weak stomach would definitely have to sit these sessions out, but all examinations don't go that far. Sometimes, bullets or sharp objects, such as broken off knives or glass, have to be dislodged from certain organs and documented as essential evidence. However, the odor was still something to brook with.

Examination Room Seven was on my right. After peering through one of the two rectangular windows and seeing who I expected to see, I pushed one of the double swinging doors open and entered. True to his word, Manning had left the comfort of his very own home to meet me here, dressed as if he'd been out playing golf, in lieu of watching television like he'd purported over the phone. He was seated in a metal chair across a metal desk from the medical examiner, who looked every bit of fifty-seven, with his disheveled, bleach-blond hair and matching coat, he put me in the mind of *Doc* from the movie *Back To The Future*. As if the No Smoking signs meant the total opposite, the two old men seemed to be having a field day with their cigars, resembling two college professors discussing mid-term exams.

"My friend!" Darrel Manning said as I neared the desk.

I got straight to business. "Where's the rookie?"

"I relieved him." Manning took another pull on his cigar before going on, "I didn't see any reason to hold him over past shift change. He turned over all his findings. So has the CSU. The Chain of Evidence can't be finalized until you permit the M.E. Mr. Wells, here, to conduct his postmortem of the subject."

That's when I looked over at the stainless-steel examination table. It was empty. "Where *is* the subject?"

"In the freezer," answer Manning. "Still in the bag."

"Photos? Crime scene sketch?"

Manning tapped his finger on a manila folder atop the desk. "All there. All physical evidence collected is in this box."

I eyed the small cardboard box beside the folder for a second before regarding the M.E. with my hand stretched out. "Pardon my manners. I'm Special Agent Bishop."

"Mr. Alvin Wells," he replied, eyes fixed on the camera dangling from my neck. "Is that Nikkon's limited edition?"

"It is. May we get started, sir?"

"Sure."

As the ME stubbed his cigar, rose, and made his way over to the array of steel doors lining the 'freezer', I looked down at Manning. "I assume you're staying?"

He raised an eyebrow. "Unless you're kicking me out. I mean, *I'am* out of my jurisdiction right now."

I simpered. "Very funny. And my dad said you could pick up the phone sometimes."

"He said that?" Manning asked, putting out his own cigar, then getting to his feet.

"Sure did."

"Yeah, that sounds like Hot Shot. I guess I will give him a call."

We moved over to where Mr. Wells was sliding a large steel tray from one of the slots, and onto a gurney. As Manning said, the corpse was still in the body bag. Pulling a lever to unlock the wheels on the table, the examiner rolled it to the center of the room, parking it beside the examination table where a large incandescent light shone from the ceiling. Re-applying the brakes, he handed Manning and I a pair of latex gloves before donning a pair himself.

We've been through this before, so Manning and I knew that we had to assist the ME with transferring the body to the examination table. Wells pulled the zipper from the top to the bottom of the black plastic bag, releasing the natural body odor commingled with post-death excreta that was compressed inside it. The older men took hold of the upper body while I grabbed the legs. On the count of three, we hoisted the subject onto the steel. As Wells rolled the gurney out of the way, I took stock of John Doe, and immediately recognized the attire from the footage of the bank robbery, minus the ski mask.

As far as I could tell, there was no visible damage to this side of the body. However, there was a mountain of dry blood covering the left side of his face, which, undoubtedly, came from the blood clotted eye socket, where his left eye had once reigned.

"What's your take on this?" I asked Manning as Wells rejoined us.

Manning shrugged his shoulders. "Double-cross. The other two used him for the number, snuffed him out, then split the dough two ways."

I absently nodded my agreement, still evaluating the cluttered eye socket. "I wonder what caliber—"

"Thirty-two automatic," Manning interrupted.

I spun around, regarding him with raised eyebrows. "And you're able to surmise this just by looking?"

There was a benign smirk on his face. "No, Sherlock. Inside that small evidence box that you didn't take the initiative to peer into are two handguns that were found at the scene. One's a nine-millimeter Glock. The other's a thirty-two handgun."

"So, how do you figure the thirty-two is the one used?"

"There's no exit wound."

"Which proves nothing."

"There was also an empty shell casing from the thirty-two-automatic found at the scene."

"Is that also in the box?" He nodded. "Is there anything else in this magical box I should know about?"

He shrugged again. "Black ski mask."

"Shall we begin, fellas?" the ME asked, apparently fed up with our bickering.

"Sure," I answered, powering up my camera.

I took a couple of shots of the body before Mr. Wells removed the shoes and cut the clothing off with some very sharp scissors, placing the items into a biohazard waste bag. Yes, this stuff has to go through our laboratory also. I photographed the tattoos on the upper body and arms. We turned the body over, so I could photograph the rest, which totaled up to twelve tattoos. Once the body was back onto its back, the ME pulled over an X-ray machine, so we could all see the exact location of the slug that was still lodged inside the skull.

I'm going to spare you the gory details on how he actually got that bullet out. You're welcome. However, after getting the ME to sign the Chain of Evidence document, I exited Grady Memorial Hospital, placed all evidence into the trunk of my BMW, and made for the highway. I know I should've been turning the evidence in at the James P. Russell building, but my conscience was eating at me. Therefore, I was on my way to Memorial Drive. It's not that I didn't trust the findings 0of the local investigators. I just like to make my own evaluation of a crime scene. Especially if I'm the lead investigator.

Per Darrel Manning's instructions, I found the scene where the body was found. I pulled into the lot of the nondescript mom-and-pop restaurant that was deserted. It was a little after seven o'clock. The sun had gone down, but it wasn't quite dark yet. I parked close to the wooded area that Manning told me about. Shutting off the engine, I donned my gloves, grabbed my flashlight and investigation kit off the front-passenger seat, and dismounted.

I took one look around, then slowly moved into the wooded area, probing my flashlight back and forth. The earth was soft, making it easy to see the imprint of various footprints of those who'd traveled through it. I was able to recognize the rugged imprint of the name brand of boots that are famous amongst government field agents and tactical teams. Amid the trash that was strewn about were hypodermic needles, plastic drug bags of various colors, used condoms, and empty condom wrappers.

A low growling sound to the right of me, caught my attention, prompting me to swing my flashlight in that direction where a dark-brown terrier was trotting away, tail tucked between its legs. Scared. That's when I used my elbow to make sure my Glock .40 was in its holster on my hip. It was there.

Finally, I made it to the spot where the body was found. It wasn't hard to spot the impression of the figure that had incontestably been there for hours prior to discovery. Shifting my light to where the head was, I could see the dark traces of blood melded with the dark earth. Those familiar ridges belonging to boots worn by the crime scene unit. As I looked further on, I realized that a pathway had been naturally made by the constant flow of people traversing through this area, but where did the pathway lead to? Being that the locals didn't know the story behind the body they'd found, I'm quite sure they didn't bother to see what was on the other end of the rainbow, and I don't blame them, but I know the story.

Panning my flashlight to make sure I was alone, I set my feet in motion, tracing along the muddy walkway lined with grass. After several yards, I emerged from the wooded area and found myself smiling like the Grinch that stole Christmas. What I came out to was a liquor store that was like a good half a mile from the nearest housing community. The store was closed, so there was nobody in the parking lot. Only one car and I swear I could've recognized the white Toyota Corrolla from a mile away.

Placing my investigation tool kit onto the hood of the car, I pulled out my cell phone and dialed a number while moving to the rear of it. As I waited for someone to pick up, I looked around to see if I could spot some surveillance cameras that could assist me with this investigation. There was one on the side of the building, but it was facing the front of the building, and I was on the far side of it. I could clearly see two external cameras at the gas station across the street, but couldn't determine their angles for the glass bubbles they were contained in. I made a mental note to get a closer look just as my call was answered.

"James P. Russell building," the familiar male voice announced. "Information Center."

"Chad, it's Bishop. I need you to run a license plate for me."

"Okay, my friend. Shoot."

I read the alphanumeric from the plate. "Romeo, November, Delta, two, two, three."

"Stand by."

While the device was still to my ear, I moved to the right side of the Toyota, shining my flashlight inside. As I expected, it was trashed with empty bags and containers from restaurants and convenience stores. The glove compartment was standing open. There was no alarm, and the keys were hanging from the ignition. The doors were unlocked, so I didn't have to exploit my lock-picking skills.

"Are you ready?" Chad's voice sounded off seconds later.

"I'm listening."

"It's a nineteen ninety-seven Toyota Corolla belonging to a Suzanne Hunt of Austell, Georgia," he apprised. "It was reported stolen yesterday morning at ten twenty-one A.M."

"Thanks, Chad!"

"That's what I'm here for."

"I'm gonna also need a towing truck."

"Location?"

After giving him the location, I placed the phone back into its case clipped onto my belt and paused to think for a moment. The car was reported stolen yesterday morning, at ten twenty-one. Hell, that's the same exact time the robbers entered the Sun Trust bank. Coincidence? I seriously doubt that. Reid and I will definitely have to pay a little visit to this Suzanne Hunt of Austell, Georgia.

I opened all four doors on the Toyota, then pulled the trunk-release button, which caused the trunk to spring forcibly open on its hinges. I didn't have any high-intensity Klieg lights used by crime scene units to illuminate crime scenes, so my trusty flashlight would have to do the trick.

For the second time today, I powered up my government-issued camera and took pictures of the discarded trash in the same position I'd found them. Then, I moved to the trunk, where there was only a spare tire, jack, and lug wrench. Seeing no reason to draw up a crime scene sketch, I shut the trunk and returned to my investigation tool kit, where I placed my camera and flashlight, and extracted my small notepad to jot down a few reminders.

At that time, my stomach grumbled, reminding me that I hadn't eaten anything, being that I had left before dinner was served. Plus, I was perspiring, and in need of an ice-cold beverage. So, basically, I was running on fumes. Replacing my notepad, I secured the rest of the doors on the car, leaned against it, and watched the traffic move up and down Memorial Drive, waiting for the tow truck, which took about twenty minutes.

Once the car was secured on the back of the flatbed wrecker, I journeyed back through the pathway to my BMW and followed the truck to the James P. Russell building, where I had to document all the evidence into a logbook, leave notes for the forensic scientists, and fill out a mountain of paperwork. I swear I was inside that damn building for over an hour. I was so hungry, I ended up consuming a stale tuna sandwich somebody left in the refrigerator of the break room, and it was awful!

While driving away from my workplace, I thought about calling Wilma Reid and informing her of today's findings, but then I thought against it. It's not that she'd be asleep at 8:34 P.M. I just didn't feel like going over all the details, and, trust me, she's gonna want *all* the details. Especially about the postmortem. Therefore, I called the person I was gonna end up having to call anyway.

"I'm still debating if I should be mad at you or not," Monique answered her phone, sounding calm. A bit *too* calm!

"You know it wouldn't do any good to be mad at me," I reminded her.

She exhaled sharply. "I know. I just can't say the same for Melody. No matter how many times I explain it to her, I still don't think she gets it."

"Let me speak to her."

"She's asleep. She went to her room as soon as we got home and fell asleep with her clothes on.

"I'll make it up to her."

Monique drew a breath but didn't respond.

"What are you wearing?" I asked, endeavoring to lighten the mood.

"A sad face," she replied, with a hint of attitude.

I couldn't help but smile. "Is that all? Maybe I should be on my way over there."

"Well, it's too bad you're not."

"Is it? Or are you gonna just leave me standing out here on the porch alone?"

There was a momentary pause before she recovered. "Say what?"

"You're just gonna leave me out here?"

"Boy, I know you're joking!"

There was excitement in her voice now. I could hear her moving around as if getting out of bed and heading for the front door. Then came the sound of the locks on the door being disengaged. When the door swung open, I literally had to catch my phone from falling as I gawked at my girlfriend, who was wearing a pink nightgown that clung to her body the same way the skirt she had on earlier did. She didn't have on a bra, so her nipples were almost visible through the light fabric, bulging as if they were trying to break free. Speaking of *breaking free*, I had to muster up a lot of will-power to break my eyes free from this tantalizing picture long enough to disconnect the call we were on and clip the phone back onto my waist.

"You came!" Monique exclaimed in a hushed tone.

"Of course," I said this like I was the coolest man on this side of the planet while crossing the threshold. After closing and locking the door, I gandered around the relatively dark living room as if to make sure Melody hadn't awakened and emerged from her bedroom. "You know I can't spend the night," I reminded Monique.

"Boy, I know that," she said, grabbing my hand, and pulling me toward her bedroom. "That's why I'm gonna enjoy this dick while I have the chance."

Chapter 4
Monday

"You mean to tell me you had all this fun," Reid said after I told her about the recent developments in the bank robbery case, "and you didn't call me to tag along?"

We had been in our office, seated at our desks that are contrasted in the center of it, consuming breakfast sandwiches and coffee, while mulling over our initial findings of the robbery. On my computer's monitor, was a frozen image of the robbery, whereas I purposefully paused it at the part where the bank officer immediately threw his hands up in surrender upon being approached by the trio of masked men.

"You were at home, relaxing," I now answered my partner's question. "Initially, I was called down to the morgue to view the body that was found. I didn't see any need to drag you along."

"Shit, that was all the more reason to drag me along," Reid protested, resembling a little girl with her hair pulled into a bun. "A dead body was found. A dead body means autopsy, and you know how much I love autopsies. Now you gotta give me all the details. How did the ME pull the bullet from the eye socket? A suction tube?"

I narrowed my eyes. "The bullet ricocheted off the back of the skull and lodged in the cerebrum."

"So, he peeled the skin back from the forehead and sawed into the skull," she stated slowly, an amusing look etched on her face. "And you let me miss that? I think I need to re-evaluate this partnership of ours."

I rolled my eyes just as my desk phone rang. Thankful for the interruption, I hurriedly snatched the receiver from its cradle. "Special Agent Bishop," I answered, cutting my eyes at the image on my monitor for the umpteenth time.

"We have an identification on your John Doe," our lead forensic scientist informed.

"What about the items?" I inquired. "The ski-mask? The guns? The projectiles? The car? Have you all even touched the car yet?"

"You know how proficient my team is, Mr. Bishop," she replied sternly. "The answers to all of your questions are in my analysis report, which is already on its way up."

She disconnected before I could apologize for inadvertently doubting her team's proficiency, which was pretty strange, because Heather Vaughn has a keen sense of humor, and would usually make a lighthearted joke out of such a slight insult. Maybe she's going through something at the moment. Oh, well. I hung up the receiver and looked across at my partner, who was giving me an inquisitive look.

"Well?" she prompted, holding her arms out, palms up.

"The dead guy has a name," I told her.

"Which is?"

"We'll find out when Vaughn's report gets here." I was staring at my monitor again. "He didn't have a cell phone on him, so we'll contact whoever's on his file, and have them go down to the morgue for verification."

"Will we question them there?"

"If they're up for it, but we need to question the owner of the stolen car, which would entail a trip to Austell, Georgia. Plus, I wanna poke around Memorial Drive."

Suddenly, there was a rap at our glass door. We looked up to see a white female in a laboratory coat, holding a manila folder. After exchanging glances, I nodded for Reid to collect the report. As she got up and made for the door, I couldn't help but get a look at her backside, seeing how her green pants were wedged into the crack of her ass, and how her small buttocks bounced with every step. Hell, I had to force my eyes to my computer screen to keep my manhood from responding, while hoping Reid would hurry up and sit her ass down.

However, that wasn't the case. Reid accepted the folder, but it seemed as though the women had launched into an exciting conversation. Figuring they would be a while, I began tapping keys on my keypad, toying with the picture on the screen. Switching angles, I absently zoomed in on the officer's face and studied his visage for a moment. There was something about this picture that just didn't sit well with me. Tapping more keys, I zoomed out, switched views, then rewind the footage to about five minutes before the culprits entered the bank. Then, I went to multi-view, which enabled me to view all five cameras of the bank in small frames on my monitor.

Playing it from there, I looked around for the manager who, apparently, was already inside his office. I scanned the small crowd before searching the parking lot for the white Toyota that wasn't there yet, but the moment I switched my gaze to see what the bank officer was doing, I caught a glimpse of the car pulling in. There was no need to try and zoom in to get a closer view of the occupants because the sun reflecting on the car's windows made it highly impossible.

I toyed with the keypad some more to dismiss cameras one, three, and four, which brought cameras two and five into focus at split-screen view. The car parked in one of the vacant slots, but no one got out. The officer was still standing in the same spot, casually observing the goings-on within the establishment. Then, almost a minute later, he extracted his cellular from his utility belt, flipped it open, and put it up to his ear. After speaking a few words, he snapped it shut, and returned it to his belt. Then, he made a critical mistake.

"Son of a bitch!" I muttered just as Reid made it back to her desk with the folder.

"What?" Putting the folder down, she circled around to stand beside me, the scent of both her soap and washing detergent invaded my nostrils.

"I think Officer Turner was in on the heist," I said, tapping keys, and taking her through what I'd just viewed, pausing it at the point where the officer took a furtive glance back at the entrance after concluding his incoming call. "He received a call almost a minute after the suspects arrived," I went on to explain. "Theoretically, they informed him that they were outside, and he probably told them that the manager was in his office, which was why one of them went straight to the office. Then, after concluding his call, he looked towards the entrance as if to see if they were on their way in."

"It's cogent," Reid pointed out, placing a hand on my shoulder, "but it's mere speculation. None of it is concrete, and you know how the Department of Justice is about not having concrete evidence against someone."

"Oh, I plan on coming with all the concrete," I said, shutting off my computer. "In fact, I'm gonna park a whole cement truck on their front lawn. Better yet, make that *two* cement trucks."

Chapter 5

Austell, Georgia

The house wouldn't end up on anybody's Top Ten Beautiful Homes list, but it appeared to be in good condition. The vinyl sidings were eggshell white and showed no signs of weather damage. Despite the handful of leaves sprawled about its rooftop, the gutters were clean, the lawn looked freshly cut, and the two small gardens flanking the red-brick stairs with their assorted flowers put me in the mind of something out of a children's storybook.

Instead of parking behind the red Nissan Stanza in the driveway, I placed the Ford at the curb and shut the engine off. Being that we'd been to the Austell Police Department, and were able to obtain a copy of the report filed by Mrs. Suzanne Hunt in reference to her car being stolen, Reid and I didn't see any need to have her write a statement for us. I donned my mirror-tinted Nautica sunglasses before we dismounted and moved along the concrete walkway toward the house.

The temperature was in the mid-eighties, which was a bit too hot for a blazer, so I was clad in gray dress pants, a powder blue button-down, and a dark-blue tie. My gun was secured on my hip, and my cell phone and shield were clipped to my belt. As we approached the house, I surveyed the neighborhood, seeing that there was nobody out and about. The only sound was the occasional cackle from a bird in various distances.

"Who is it?" a woman's voice answered the doorbell.

"FBI, ma'am," Reid took the initiative.

There was a momentary pause on the other side of the wooden door. Then, the knob turned, and the door squeaked slowly open to a White woman wearing short purple shorts, and a white tank top that stretched over her bulging midsection. Slightly overweight, she stood at about 5'6 and could have been in her early thirties, although she looked to be in her early forties.

My partner wasted no time shoving her credentials into the woman's face. "I'm Special Agent Reid and this is my partner, Special Agent Bishop. Is Mrs. Suzanne Hunt in?"

"Um, yeah," she stammered, revealing coffee-stained teeth, with a concerned expression on her face. She then stepped aside. "Come on in, she's in the living room."

We entered the home that reeked of mothballs and some kind of cinnamon-scented air freshener. The woman closed the door back, then gestured for us to follow her to the living room, where the sixty-one-year-old was seated in an old recliner, hand-knitting what appeared to be a sweater for a toddler. Suzanne Hunt's gray hair was pulled into an unkempt ponytail, with very large eyeglasses on her face. She had her head down, concentrating on what she was doing, and making no indications of being aware of our presence when we entered. This made me inquisitive of her mental state. Is she deaf? Myopic? Is she even capable of—

"Who are these people, Maggie?" Mrs. Hunt inquired without lifting her head, nor altering the momentum of her hands.

"The FBI, Momma." Maggie crossed her arms over her chest as if waiting for her mother to explain why criminal law enforcement agents were looking for her.

The older woman's hands finally stopped mid-stitch and she lifted her head to evaluate us through narrow eyes. "The FBI, you say?"

"Yes, ma'am," Reid responded. "I'm Special Agent Reid, and this is my partner, Special Agent Bishop. We were hoping to ask you a few questions in reference to the theft of your car."

"The FBI? she said with a mixture of intrigue and skepticism. "It wasn't a Rose Royce for Christ's sake!"

Reid smiled at the woman's humor. "Very far from it."

Mrs. Hunt gestured to the sofa that shared the same cloth as her chair. "Well, please, have a seat."

My partner took advantage of the invitation, but I chose to remain standing. I already knew she was going to handle the whole interrogation.

"I don't have much," the older woman resumed, "but I do have plenty of coffee. May I offer you guys a cup?"

"No, thank you," Reid answered, then plunged in. "Could you tell me the exact time that your car was stolen from you?"

"I can't give you an exact time, but it was stolen between Friday night and Saturday morning. I noticed it missing on Saturday morning when I was on my way out to go to the grocery store."

"So, it was stolen from your driveway?"

"Sure was." She had continued knitting.

"By any chance, Mrs. Hunt, could you have mistakenly left your keys in the car?"

"No mistake at all," Mrs. Hunt told her. "I always leave my keys in the car when I'm at home."

"And I've constantly gotten on her about that," Maggie finally chimed in.

Mrs. Hunt fixed her daughter with a stern look. "Child, I've been a resident of this neighborhood long before you were thought about. If I had any reservations about where I lay my head, I wouldn't leave my front door unlocked, nor leave my keys in my car."

"So, this neighborhood doesn't have a history of crime?" Reid intervened.

"No, it does not," the older woman answered, still regarding her daughter.

"But your car was stolen," Reid pressed. "Does that change your perspective of this neighborhood?"

"Not at all." She was knitting again. "Besides, the person who stole my car couldn't have been from this neighborhood."

"And what makes you so sure of that?"

"Because we all respect one another. We look out for one another. If anything, the person who stole my car was from Baby Land."

"Baby Land?"

"Another community not too far from here," Mrs. Hunt apprised. "Off Veterans Memorial. That's where you'll find the local criminals of Austell, Georgia."

Reid looked at me. "Baby Land?"

I shrugged my shoulders. "Never heard of it."

"It's been called that ever since I can remember," Maggie offered.

"And it definitely has a history of crime."

"There's another thing we'd like to bring to your attention, Mrs. Hunt," my partner proceeded. "On Saturday morning, your car was issued in a bank robbery."

Mrs. Hunt's eyes went wide. *"A bank robbery!"*

"The Sun Trust bank in Atlanta?" asked Maggie. "I saw that on the news. They didn't say anything about her car on the news."

"That's because we withheld that information," I pitched in. "Hoping we could catch the perpetrators in the same car. However, the car was found abandoned on the following day. As of now, it's in the custody of our forensics team. Hopefully, you'll have it back in a couple of days."

"I think they said something about finding one of the men dead," said Maggie.

"We're looking into that," I replied, which was all the information I was willing to give up. "We thank you all for your time. Whenever your car is released, Mrs. Hunt, someone will call and notify you." We quickly made our exit.

"Are we taking a drive through Baby Land?" Reid asked once we were back in the car, approaching the main road.

"That would be a waste of time," I told her. "Especially when we don't know who or what we're looking for. Right now, we have a lot on our plates, and I think we're moving in the right direction."

The next destination I chose was Memorial Drive. Turning into the gas station directly across the street from the liquor store where the Toyota was found, I gave my partner instructions before dismounting and crossing the busy street to the store that was now open. While moving along the parking lot that was occupied by four cars, I studied the camera hanging from the side of the building, and, yes, I was satisfied with its angle.

Ring-a-Ling!

Don't you just hate those establishments that have those noisy gadgets that goes off whenever someone enters or exits their doors, drawing attention from those already in attendance? I sure as hell do, and the small, ancient bell hanging over this particular door, definitely drew the attention of the store clerk, and the six people in line, waiting to place their orders from the multiple brands of alcoholic beverages secured behind the Plexiglass of the counter.

Usually, people would just give a newcomer a once-over, then go back to whatever they were doing, but that wasn't the case here. I may as well had told these people to *freeze* because they were regarding me like deer caught in an array of headlights. Truth be told, I was half expecting someone to brandish a weapon and gun me down, because they had warrants in a hundred states, and was hellbent on not being taken in alive. I mean, it's not like the average citizen knew the difference between the badge of a local cop, FBI agent, prison guard, mall security, or hall monitor. All they knew was that they were in the presence of someone they should probably steer clear of.

However, disregarding the perpetual stares, I strolled the short distance to where the last person in line stood and took my place behind her. Eventually, everyone went back to paying me no mind. I was thankful that no one else entered, because when the woman in front of me had parted with her pint of Jack Daniels, I was alone with the clerk, a Black man in his mid-fifties. The first thing I noticed was the holster on his hip, conveying a chrome revolver, in which I'm sure he has a permit for.

"How may I help you, sir?" the cashier asked, with a slight grin on his face. Obviously, he thought I was out chasing a midday drink while on the clock, but those days are long gone.

"I'm Special Agent Bishop," I told him, flashing my credentials. "From the Federal Bureau of Investigation. If you don't mind, I need to view surveillance recordings of your exterior camera."

"Of course, I don't mind," he offered. "But there are no recordings on any of my cameras."

"So, they're just up for decoration?" I asked, concealing my anger. "To dissuade criminals?"

"Not exactly. My hard drive went out a couple of months ago. I just haven't replaced it yet. Sorry!"

I exhaled sharply while diverting my attention away from the man. That's when I noticed the Missing Child poster taped to the glass, with six-year-old Bernadine Yarborough's picture on it. Smiling. An innocent child supposedly abducted from her very own bed in the middle of the night, though there's no substantial evidence to support such. Other than the fact that she was missing. That was three weeks ago, and I still haven't found the little girl.

"Is there anything else I can help you with?" the cashier asked, regaining my attention.

"Not at all."

I spun on my heels and made for the exit, surprised to see that the Ford was already out front. Exiting the building, I climbed in beside Reid and immediately hit her with a questioning look.

"I hate those damn Highway Patrols!" she voiced, referring to my sunglasses. "But I checked the angles of their outside cameras. Neither one of them points in this direction. What did you get?"

"Not a damn thing," I answered, looking back at the clerk, who was looking out at us. "His fucking cameras may as well be Christmas tree ornaments."

"So, where to? Turner's place?"

"Yeah." Just as I said that my cell phone vibrated on my hip. "Bishop," I answered.

"The aunt identified Luther Harris as her nephew," Darrel Manning's voice sounded through the earpiece. "She wants to know when the body will be released, so the family can make funeral arrangements."

"I'll fax the release over to the ME once I get back to the office and have him notify her."

"Okay. Do you need anything else?"

"Not right now. Thanks for the help, though."

"Don't mention it. And give my regards to Wilma Reid, will ya'?"

"Will do."

I hung up and did not give his regards to Wilma Reid. Why? Who knows? Hell, who cares? While she drove, I retrieved the manila folder from under the armrest and opened it up on my lap. Heather Vaughn's analysis report. I encountered the same results as I flipped through it for the second time: the bullet extracted from the bank officer's leg matched the one extracted from the cadaver's skull, both being fired from the .32 handgun found at the scene, there were no prints found on the weapon or its projectiles, prints found on the nine-millimeter recovered at the scene belonged to the corpse, particles of hair found inside of ski mask also belonged to the deceased; there were no prints found on interior or exterior of stolen vehicle, and trash found inside car produced no trace evidence. Bullshit, bullshit, bullshit.

Placing the folder back under the armrest, I leaned my head back on the headrest and closed my eyes. This was one of those times when I trusted my breathing exercise to put me in a relaxed state of mind. Inhale. Exhale. Inhale. Exhale. My partner didn't bother me, so I did this up until we entered Kirkwood Flats apartments. It was only a little after one o'clock, so there weren't that many people milling about.

Some women sat out in front of their apartments, watching their children that weren't old enough to attend school, frolic around with their contemporaries, and the community maintenance man was servicing an air conditioner unit, and it didn't take a scientist to discern that the four guys standing around the white Chevy Caprice on chrome wheels, were local drug dealers, *or wannabes.*

"We don't even know if he's here or not," said Reid, as she parked the car.

"We know he's not at the bank," I replied, pressing the trunk release button before getting out, and moving toward the trunk, where I collected my leather binder.

Of course, all eyes were on us as we moved toward the unit we were looking for. The shields and guns on our waists stuck out like sore thumbs, but the binder I was carrying probably made us look like a couple of parole officers. However, eccentric to the core, when we made it to the door, my partner pounded her small fist against it as if we were here to slap manacles on someone, in lieu of conducting a routine interview.

"Who is it?" a woman answered.

"FBI," Reid announced loudly as if to make sure the onlookers heard.

Well, so much for them thinking we were parole officers. I mean if they were actually thinking this. As always, there was silence on the other side of the door, except for the wailing of a small child, who was crying up a storm. Moments later, the woman opened the door just wide enough to wedge her 5'10, 195-pound frame between it and the jamb. Her hair was standing up on her head as if she were attempting to adopt the Don King look, and she was clad in a dark-blue Atlanta Braves shirt and denim shorts. Plus, she seemed highly peeved about something, which was probably why she was evaluating us with a detestable look, instead of questioning our impromptu visit.

"Is Damien Turner in?" Reid inquired in a tone that defied the woman to get foul at the mouth.

Instead of replying, the woman pushed the door open and took a step back. Seated on the living room sofa was Damien Turner, who was regarding us like he'd never seen us a day in his life. Plus, he was holding a small boy of no more than two years old. The same boy we heard crying who was no longer crying but now staring at us with enlarged eyes. I immediately noticed the crutches propped up beside Turner, but there was no cast on his right leg.

"Come on in, y'all!" he finally said. Once we entered, he asked, "This is about the written statement, right?"

"Of course," I answered, indicating the binder in my hand. "The Chief investigators on my back about it. I think the Department of Justice is pressing the issue about solving this case in a timely manner."

"I'll take the baby," said the woman, after closing the door back. She scooped the child out of Turner's grasp, then made off to one of the bedrooms.

The drapes were all pulled back, so the living room was bathed in sunlight, which made it much easier to see how badly stained the walls were. There were various toys piled in one corner, and several others strewn about the room, including atop the coffee table amongst empty baby bottles, and an open bag of diapers. The only other furniture in the room were two tattered, and unidentical loveseats, in which Turner occupied one of.

"Y'all have to excuse the place," Turner offered, apologetically. "Everything's been a bit off since the accident, but y'all can have a seat."

I obliged, and so did Reid, but I know she only did it so Turner wouldn't think - well, know – that she'd rather run through hell, doused in gasoline than to settle in such a pigstye. I amused myself with the thought as we settled onto the other sofa, and I pulled from my binder a plastic clipboard already equipped with a statement form and pen, handing it to Turner.

"We need as much a detailed report as you can give to the best of your ability," I explained. "And what's the condition of your leg, if you don't mind me asking?"

"I'll live," he replied with a smirk while unclasping the pen. "The doctor said it was a clean shot. No damage to the bone or tendon but being that the bullet was of a small caliber, it somehow lost its velocity and got stuck."

I nodded my understanding, although I'd already gathered that information from the surgeon before leaving the hospital that day. While he scribbled away, I found myself studying him as if I could read his thoughts. A lefty. I've come across quite a few highly intelligent left-handed people in my lifetime. Could he be such a person? A Wernher von Braun, perhaps? No, von Braun was a German-born U.S. rocket scientist. Hell, he may have been *wrong-handed* also. Whatever. I went back to analyzing Turner's abode that had all the signs of a person living from check to check and was in dire need of making some extra cash—by any means necessary.

Which reminds me. "Once you're done," I told Turner. "Leave your cell phone number at the bottom, along with your signature. You know, just in case the DOI wants to contact you for verification of the statement."

"I'll do that," he replied but continued writing.

After receiving the statement form from Turner, we ordered lunch from a near-by Long John Silvers on our way back to the office, which we didn't touch until we reached our destination. As I mechanically tended to my meal, I mulled over a lot of things that were going on in my life, from social to personal. It may not seem like it to any outsider, but I really have a lot going on. Things that'll weigh the average feeble-minded person down, but that's life, right? Well, of course. After consuming my meal, I snatched the receiver from its cradle and punched in four digits.

"Information," the familiar voice answered.

"Chad, it's Bishop."

"My friend!" he exclaimed, cheerfully. "What can I do for you this time?"

"I'm trying to get a print-out of someone's phone records."

I heard him tapping on keys. "What's the number?"

I read it out to him from the statement form.

"How far are you trying to go back?"

"Two months, at least."

"I'll give you three."

"Thanks, Chad!"

"Don't mention it."

"You're really going with your intuition on this, huh?" Reid asked once I'd hung up the phone.

"You know how I am," I told her. "And you and I both have solved cases off intuition."

"True," she responded. "What I still don't get is, why would they shoot him, if he was a part of their act?"

"To throw us off." This was the only explanation I could produce. "If I were to rob a bank, and already had it planned that I was gonna shoot the bank's officer in the leg, I would use *his* gun, in order to prevent being traced back to the one I came with. Plus, the guy used a thirty-two automatic. Not only did he intend not to kill the officer, but he intended to not inflict much pain, nor cause much damage. I can't say why—"

The ringing from my desk phone interrupted my verbal analysis. Being that I consider all in-coming calls important, I immediately snatched up the receiver.

"Special Agent Bishop," I promulgated.

"Hi, Mr. Bishop."

Uh-oh. This was a very important call, indeed, but it was of much greater importance to the sixty-year-old woman on the other end. Instantaneously, my heart began to churn. This is one of those things I complained about having going on in my life, and this call from this particular person had become routine for the past three weeks.

Inhale. Exhale.

"Hello, Mrs. Rodgers," I finally respond, knowing better than to ask her how she was doing, when I already knew the answer.

"Have you heard anything on, my grandbaby?" she got straight to the point as always, despair lingering in her tone.

"Not yet" I answered, hating to tell her something I hated telling any concerned parent about their missing offspring. "But, believe me, Mrs. Rodgers, I am working very hard to find her. I also have other cases to deal with. Right now, I just need you to continue praying for her. Are you still praying?"

She didn't respond.

"Mrs. Rodgers?"

"I've never stopped praying," she sobbed. "I want my baby back."

"I know, Mrs. Rodgers," I consoled her. "And I'm working my butt off trying to get her back to you. All I ask you to do is continue praying and be patient with me. Can you do that, Mrs. Rodgers? At least try?"

"Yes." The thought of having to adhere to her promise of not bothering me while I search for her grandchild was evident in her voice.

"Thank you, Mrs. Rodgers."

Concluding the call, I took a few seconds to reflect on how, not once, had I received a call from Bernadine Yarborough's parents, inquiring information about their daughter, who's been missing for almost a month. They made a live plea on National television for whoever responsible to return their daughter home safely, but that was it. No harassing phone calls. No surprise visits. Nothing. The only relative who seemed concerned about the little girl was the grandmother.

Fancy that!

"My heart goes out to that old lady," Reid spoke, breaking me from my reverie.

I looked over at her and said nothing.

"If something bad happened to that little girl," my partner resumed. "She would be crushed. I just hope that's not the case."

"So, do I," I said, getting to my feet. "I'll be right back." Exiting the office, I marched dutifully to Director Manny Hopkins' office, figuring that he should have something to tell me by now. I mean, I am a fairly patient guy, but there are some things I just hate making exceptions for, and this is one of them.

As always, Hopkins was on his telephone when I appeared in his doorway. How he always managed to be on the phone every time I come to his office, I do not know, but, between you and I, I think he sits there holding the receiver to his ear all day, then pretends to be holding a conversation whenever someone shows up at his door, to make himself seem of great importance. So, as the ritual stood, I waited patiently until he pretended to tell the person on the other end that he'd call them back, before hanging up and waving me in.

"How may I help you, Bishop?" he asked, leaning back in his leather chair.

"Have you heard anything from the CIA?" I was now standing in front of his desk, not bothering to sit down, knowing he didn't like for people to stand over him.

"Have a seat, Bishop!"

Well, there was no need to be defiant. That would get me nowhere at this point. Therefore, I sat. My supervisor leaned forward, resting his elbows on the desk, drilling his teal green eyes into mine. Reid dissents, but the director reminds me of the younger Christopher Reeves in *Super Man* when he doffs the nerdy spectacles. He even wears his hair in the same manner, with the exception of the *baby curl* dangling over the forehead. I can't deny that the forty-four-year-old is the finest-dressed man in our division in his expensive, tailor-made suits, custom made shoes, and Rolex watches. His salary is not that much greater than mine, which kind of makes me wonder if he's on the take. Okay, I'm kidding, but you never know.

"Bishop," he spoke as if to a little child. "I submitted your request to them. The procedure you're asking them to undertake is a general protocol when there's a threat or breach of National Security. The CIA was assembled to protect citizens as a nation – not individually. So, don't be surprised if they deny it, or refuse to reply altogether."

"Then, what am I to do?" I asked, feeling this case slip through my fingers. "I'm not closing this case without finding out what really happened to Bernadine."

"You're referring to her by her first name," Hopkins pointed out, reminding me that I'd allowed myself to become emotionally attached to the case, which is something we're strongly cautioned against. "Do I need to remove you from—"

"No," I interrupted, "You do not have to remove me from the case. I was trained to utilize all resources, and that's what I'm doing. Well, that's what I'm trying to do."

He narrowed his eyes at me. "You're a great investigator. In fact, you're one of the greatest investigators I've ever had working under me. I'd hate to see you throw your career out the window by doing something irrational. This is not your first kidnapping case involving a child, Bishop. I don't mean to throw salt on open wounds, but you've made some discoveries that most agents couldn't stomach. I've seen agents fink out and quit on the spot. I've seen some allow sentiment to cloud their better judgment. I've even seen—"

"I get it, Chief," I interrupted, feeling like he was on the verge of reciting verses from the Holy Bible.

He leaned back in his chair again, and studied me for a moment, before saying, "I sure hope so. Don't force me to do something I won't enjoy doing."

Chapter 6

Tuesday

The following day, my partner and I decided to go ahead and drop in on Grace Evans, the aunt of the deceased Luther Harris, which entailed another trip to Decatur, Georgia. In fact, Ms. Evan's house was on Settle Circle, which was not too far from Monique's mother's home. However, despite her loss, she was amiable upon inviting us inside for the interview. Although we apologized for our intrusion, she insisted that it was okay and that she understood we had a job to do. She'd even admitted to have just smoked a joint while letting us in, clearly knowing we would smell the burned marijuana still permeating the air.

Now, the three of us were seated at her kitchen table, with steaming hot cups of coffee in front of us. Reid had her notepad and pen out, being that she'd insisted on conducting the interview. I only listened, intermittently taking a sip from my cup.

"I'd never expect for him to do something like that," the forty-eight-year-old woman was now saying. "It just didn't seem like him."

"Was he in a gang?" Reid inquired.

"Not that I know of."

"Do you know any of his friends?"

"He'd brought a few of his so-called friends by the house," she answered. "But I don't remember their names."

"And how long has he been living with you?"

"Ever since his mother died," she offered with no emotion at all. "He was ten at the time, so it's been about twelve years."

"And she suffered from septicemia?" Reid was jotting something down.

"Yes."

At that time, we heard the sound of the front door being opened and closed. Reid and I exchanged glances before regarding Ms. Evans, who appeared to not have heard a thing. Then, there was the sound of keys jingling. Ms. Evans took a sip of her coffee, just as some guy entered the kitchen, carrying a large paper bag from Taco Bell. He was young – mid-twenties, maybe. His face wasn't familiar, but the medallion hanging from his gold chain that read *DROP SQUAD* was. In fact, our division is conducting an on-going investigation on the notorious group that's crossed our radar almost two years ago.

"This is my son, Joshua," the woman announced as her son placed the bag atop the table. "Joshua, these are FBI agents. They're investigating Luke's death."

"My cousin didn't rob no bank," Joshua quickly defended the deceased.

"We have substantial evidence to prove otherwise," my partner begged to differ while I sized him up behind my mirror tinted sunglasses to see if I could place him at the scene of the crime when I review the video again. "Do you know any of his associates? Anybody, he hangs out with regularly?"

He shrugged. "Not really. He didn't have friends like that."

"Did you two hang out much?"

"I thought you were investigating my cousin's death," he countered.

"We are."

"Then you need to be out there trying to find out who killed him, instead of harassing his family!" Joshua voiced, before storming out of the room.

"Boy, you don't talk to people like that in my house!" his mother yelled after him.

"It's okay, Ms. Evans," Reid insisted, folding her notepad closed. "We thank you for your time, and I want to assure you that we're doing our best to track down whoever's responsible for the death of your nephew."

She nodded.

Reid turned to me. "Did you have any questions?"

"Just one," I said, turning my attention to the woman. "Did Luther have a cell phone?"

***

Being that my partner and I had nothing else to do out in the field, we headed back to our place of business to see if we could bounce ideas off each other in an endeavor to put pieces of this puzzle together. As soon as we got off the elevator, we were met by one of our fellow agents, Christopher Count, who was wearing a broad smile and carrying a cardboard box in his hands.

"You seem to be in such a good mood," I acknowledged, stopping him in his tracks. "Are you resigning?"

"Never!" he responded, laughing. "We just got a break on the dark web case."

"How so?"

"We were able to I.D. a drug dealer out in Australia," he expounded.

"We had him send us two kilos, and the dumb fucker's fingerprints are all over the damn wrappings. Right now, they're organizing surveillance to watch him around the clock to see if they can catch his supplier."

"And you're not flying out to Australia for the bust?" asked Reid.

"Not this time, but Inman's going."

I nodded. "Well, congratulations!"

"Thanks!"

Upon entering the office there was a manila envelope on the floor that had been slid under the door while we were out. Reid was the first to enter, so she picked it up, and immediately handed it over to me, being that *Bishop* was written on it in red ink. As soon as my bottom made contact with the soft cushion of my chair, I tore the envelope open and extracted the document, which was the printout of Damien Turner's cell phone record for the past three months, just as Chad promised.

"What was Luther Harris' cell phone number?" I asked Reid, who was seated behind her own desk.

Once she read the number out to me from her notepad, I scanned the printout for it, and guess what? The phone number did appear, but it only appeared once, on the first of June, at 10:18 a.m., which was four minutes before Luther Harris and the two unidentified culprits entered the bank. Ruminating this, I pulled the video of the robbery back up on my computer screen, fast-forwarded it, then paused it at the point when Turner answered his cell phone at 10:18 a.m.

See, that's the difference between us and the local authorities. They would quickly tip their hand by bringing this discovery by Turner's attention, and threaten to charge him with conspiracy, or whatever, if he didn't tell them what they needed to know, giving him a chance to hire an attorney, and come up with a cogent defense such as the caller had the wrong number, *case dismissed.*

Us, on the other hand, we wouldn't tell Turner shit. His phone would be tapped, and he'd be followed. Eventually, we'd build a case so solid against him, the only thing a lawyer would be able to do for him is hold his hand during trial and offer words of encouragement. Next case.

Chapter 7

Saturday

June 8, 2002

Being that we had agents investigating the group known as *Drop Squad*, I relayed what I knew of Luther Harris' cousin, Joshua and, sure enough, agents were dispatched to stake out Harris' funeral – some at the church where the service was being held, and some lying in wait at the burial site. Their sole mission was to get as many photographs as they could of everybody in attendance, from vehicles parked in different locations, or anywhere they could stand or sit without being noticed.

Reid and I were offered the chance to tag along. My partner accepted the offer. I wasn't at all interested, so I took the opportunity to ask the director for the rest of the day off, to which I wasn't at all surprised he'd granted, being that he'd already acknowledged that I needed a break.

Although I was officially off the clock, I still had some official business to tend to, which was why I was now pulling up in front of the Yarborough's house, hoping the mailman had already run, because I was blocking the mailbox. I dismounted, clad in light, khaki pants, and a white Izod shirt. Yes, my ever-present *Highway Patrols* were clinging to my face.

Instead of heading for the front door, I glanced expectantly at the burgundy GMC Denali that had been trailing me. At that moment, Sandy Gringer from the FBI's Behavioral Science Unit, climbed down from the SUV, wearing a smoke-gray dress suit with his briefcase in tow. He wasn't just another agent from the BSU. Gringer was someone I could count on, as he could do the same with me, which is why I'd lobbied his assistance for this mission.

"As I said," the 5'9, 225-pound man spoke while closing the gap between us. "They're not obligated to entertain any of my interrogatories."

"I know, but they don't know that."

As we tread upon their grass front toward the shabby-looking house, I glanced at the rusty-blue, older-model Dodge Ram with its matching bed-lined camper/shed that was sitting alone in the driveway. As I recalled, Mr. Yarborough did odd jobs such as plumbing, roofing, and other miscellaneous repairs a person may need done to their homes, but it's Saturday. I'm assuming no one had any domestic issues he could assist them with. He must've been expecting company because, before Gringer and I made it to the front door, he pulled it open. Plus, he was wearing clothes that one would assume he works in.

"Are you on your way out, Mr. Yarborough?" I inquired upon approaching.

"Ah, no," he stammered, looking from me to my concomitant. "I heard you pull up. Did you come bearing news? My wife is in the sitting room if you need to speak with us both."

"No, I did not come bearing news at the moment," I apprised. "But I would appreciate it if I could get you two together."

He stepped aside. "Come on in."

The place was the same as I'd seen it on my initial visit. In fact, it felt like I'd just stepped foot inside the place on yesterday, and that was strange. Another thing I found strange was the way Mrs. Yarborough was seated on the living room sofa. Expectantly. Did she hear us pull up as well? Okay, maybe I'm reading a little too much into this. Their daughter was kidnapped so, of course, they were expecting some kind of news. For some reason, I don't know why I chose to nod, instead of verbally greeting Mrs. Yarborough. As her hands rested in her lap, she returned the gesture and her husband sat beside her and took hold of one of her hands.

"Mrs. Yarborough," I began, "As I've told your husband, I did not come bearing news. However, I'm here with, Mr. Sandy Gringer another agent from our division. He's doing a follow-up on your case and would like to speak to both of you. I, on the other hand, would like to take another look at Bernadine's bedroom, to refresh my memory of the crime scene. That's if it's okay with you two."

"Oh, it's okay," said Mrs. Yarborough.

"Thanks. Has anything been touched?"

"Not at all. We refuse to touch anything until she returns."

"Great!" I gestured to the BSU agent. "I'll leave you two in the hands of, Mr. Gringer."

"Have a seat, Mr. Gringer," Mr. Yarborough said, gesturing to the recliner.

As the big guy moved toward the chair, I was exiting the living room, but not before casting a curious glance at the work boots on Mr. Yarborough's feet. I couldn't make out their brand, but I could tell they were of a much earlier time. Steel-toed. Durable, rugged bottoms. A rara avis to myself, I must admit. This is a couple of a very low income, so I doubt if he'd had those personalized. I don't know. For some reason, they just stuck out to me.

As Mrs. Yarborough had promised, their missing child's bedroom was still the same as it was on the night, she was abducted from it. I vividly remember the unmade bed, the bookbag and toys atop the dresser, the pile of clothes in one corner, and even the open closet with only a handful of items hanging in it. Okay, maybe it wasn't 'exactly' the same way as when the child ended up missing, because it's incontestable that forensics had jostled things a bit, but it was close to it.

Figuring Gringer was already at work on the Yarboroughs, I kicked my shoes off, climbed into the small bed, and lied on my back, closing my eyes. Oh. In case you don't know what Sandy Gringer's forte is, he analyzes criminal behavior by interviewing criminals, and the use of other methods I'm not familiar with. Agents in his unit usually assist the local authorities, but I called upon him to see if he could make better sense of this than I had. Do I suspect foul play? I'm an FBI agent – everybody's a suspect until proven otherwise.

Inhale. Exhale.

Having my eyes still tightly shut, I imagined myself as sleeping, seven-year-old Bernadine Yarborough. I know it sounds crazy and arduous, but some of the greatest investigators are able to pull this off and solve many cases. Hell, it works for me. Now, opening my eyes, I slowly turned my head to the right. The window was about five feet away from the bed. Its opening seemed to be the same exact way as it was in the crime scene photos. She couldn't have heard the window as the intruder lifted it – for she would have definitely screamed to warn her parents. Unless she knew her attacker.

Getting out of bed, I slipped my shoes back on and crossed over to the window where the hot air was blowing in from. Placing both hands in the opening, I experimentally lifted it slowly. Noise. Enough noise to wake the deaf if I may exaggerate a little. Reaching its full length, the window stayed in place. I leaned my upper body out of it. The next-door neighbor's house was a skip and a hop away. I'm not doubting the culprit may have come from there, because most victims are victimized by someone they're familiar with, but my intuition wasn't accepting that possibility right now in this case.

This was a two-story house, so one would need some kind of ladder in order to reach the windowsill of this particular window. Maybe it's just me, but I can't imagine someone entering the window in the middle of the night, incapacitating a seven-year-old girl, then climbing back out of the window, and down the ladder, with her in tow. That would be a task within itself. Plus, we couldn't determine if a ladder had been used because the ground beneath the window is concrete. Then, there were no marks or dents in the already weather-damaged paint on the side of the house to indicate such.

Figuring I'd given Gringer enough time with the Yarboroughs, I pulled the window to where it was, then exited the room, pulling the door shut. Mrs. Yarborough was doing the talking when I returned to the living room, and she was emotional, dabbing at her eyes with a tissue as her husband made a show of consoling her. Upon seeing me, all her babbling ceased. Now, they were all looking at me like I'd ruined their moment.

"Pardon my intrusion," I offered half sarcastically, then looked over at Gringer. "You're needed back at the office."

"All right." He began placing notes back into his briefcase before getting to his feet. "It was a pleasure talking to you two, and rest assured that the FBI is doing everything in its powers to locate your child. I wouldn't be here if that weren't true."

After that nicely delivered speech, Mr. Yarborough saw us out. Of course, we did not compare thoughts on our way to our vehicles, which may have sparked concern in the man, who we were sure was still watching us. Instead, I let Gringer follow me to the parking lot of a nearby truck stop. Throwing my car into park, I got out and walked to the driver's door of his SUV. The cool air from his air conditioner caressed my face the moment he let the window down.

"I'm listening," I told him, noting the knowing look on his face.

"I think we've drawn parallel conclusions," he said.

"Which is?"

"Something's not adding up."

Playa Ray

Chapter 8

Upon parting ways with Sandy Gringer I drove out to Campbellton Road, which is where I grew up, but I wasn't out here to revisit Deerfield Apartment. I was out here to visit the barbershop I'd been getting my hair cut at ever since I was a teenager. Of course, I leave all traces of me being a government official in the car whenever I enter the establishment. The only person that knows about my occupation is my barber, Tyrone who'd succeeded his father. If he's mentioned this to the other barbers, they had never shown any indications of it whenever I was in their presence. In fact, they carried on with regular conversation like I was a regular customer.

"Look at what the cat drug in," Tyrone voiced the moment I entered the barbershop. His chair was the closest to the door. Seated in it was a man who appeared to be getting what they called a *temp fade*. "You didn't come in last week, so I figured you found another barber."

"Never," I said, bumping fists with him. "I put it in my will that you're the one to groom me for my burial."

"Now that's what I call a true customer. As a matter of fact, you're just in time. I'm about done with this nonpaying customer."

"Nonpaying customer!" his client bit the bait, smiling. "You know I got long money. You need to go ahead and sell me this shit, so I can turn it into a strip club."

"An all-male strip club?" Tyrone asked, garnering laughter from the other five barbers, and awaiting customers. By this time, I had taken a seat in the waiting area, I was also laughing.

"Say it ain't so, Larry," Keith, another barber, pitched in. "Tell my nigga you're not gonna have no Chippendale shit going on."

"Man, y'all niggas are full of shit," Larry replied as Tyrone pulled the smock off him to shake the loose hair from it.

Standing, he brushed his pants off with his hands before pulling a folded wad of bills from his pocket. "Should I pay for everybody's hair cut?" he taunted Tyrone, flipping through the currency.

"You can barely pay for your own shit," Tyrone chided. "And you know I'm the wrong nigga to try to stunt on. *A strip club*, I'll build a strip mall right beside your baby momma's house."

"Yeah, whatever." Larry peeled off some bills and handed them to Tyrone. "Let me get an ounce of that good shit, too."

As always, whenever one of Tyrone's customers asks to purchase marijuana from him, he doesn't cast a cautious glance at me to see if I'm listening or paying attention. Hell, he'd been selling drugs ever since we were in high school. No, I'm not sparing him because we're from the same projects. I'll bust his ass like I'd bust any other criminal, but, as I said, the FBI doesn't go after the small fish, although I don't think Tyrone knows this. He'll bet all of his chips on our friendship. After serving Larry an ounce of weed in a sandwich bag, Tyrone began sanitizing his utensils.

"Let's get it, B." His back was to me, but he regarded me through the large mirror. Once I was seated in his chair, he draped the smock over me and said, "I already know what you want. You've been wearing the same hair cut since birth."

I laughed at the comment. "Very funny. Maybe you should turn this place into a comedy club. You'd probably get more customers."

"Yeah," Tyrone replied, going back to the cleaning of his utensils. "Then, I could tell a few jokes about the girl you went to the prom with. The one with the beard and sideburns."

Of course, we went back and forth like this for some time, which was customary. Leaving there feeling like a new man, I drove out to Marietta, Georgia to visit my father. Being that he'd gotten used to me visiting on Sundays, he was surprised when I showed up at his room's door, but when he opened the door for me, it was my turn to be surprised. I had to step aside for the orderly who was leaving his room to pass, with a mysterious look on her face. She nodded at me, then moved on down the hallway. She didn't have any cleaning agents or utensils, so I assumed she wasn't doing any cleaning. Being that this was the same orderly who seemed to be crushing on my father last week, there's no telling what was going on inside the room before I intruded.

"You sure picked a fine time to show me your ugly face," my old man muttered, eyeing me through his sunglasses as I eyed him through my own.

"Ugly face?" I replied with a smirk. "Hell, I look like *you.*"

"That's an insult. You get your ugliness from that woman."

I couldn't help but smile at the way he'd always find a way to verbally thrash my mother. Quite amusing. "Well, at least I don't have to dress you," I said, as he spun his chair around and began rolling away. Entering, I closed the door and just stood there with my hands in my pockets.

"Dress me for what?" He was facing me again.

"You're always complaining about how I don't take you any-where," I reminded him. "Today, I'm taking you to see a movie."

"What about Melody and Monique?"

"You'll see them tomorrow," I promised. "We're all going to the circus. And don't tell me you're too old for the circus."

"I *am* too old for the circus," he grumbled, having to have the last word as always.

Playa Ray

Chapter 9

Monday

"What all do we have to go on so far?" I asked Reid from across the desk. We were piecing together whatever evidence we had against Damien Turner, to submit to Director Hopkins, to see if he would approve and launch an additional investigation by placing the bank officer under surveillance and obtaining a court order to wiretap his phone.

"Well," my partner began, referring to her notes, "we have the print-out of Turner's phone records with an incoming call coming from the cell phone of Luther Harris, the deceased accomplice of the bank robbery, just minutes before the actual robbery took place. Plus, we have verification from Grace Evans, the aunt of the deceased, that the phone number appearing on Turner's phone records, is the same number she uses to contact her nephew. I think we could—"

She stopped midsentence to follow my inquisitive gaze. Just then, a statuesque, blonde woman was passing our office. Her hair was professionally cut into a bob, whereas the ends curled outward. Plus, she was wearing a dark-blue blouse, matching slacks, and carrying a cream-colored clutch bag. There was only a three-second window, but it was all one needed to acknowledge that her posture demanded attention.

I turned to my partner. "Who the hell was that?"

She shrugged. "I have no idea. Whoever she is, she seems very important."

"Touché," I agreed, glad to know I wasn't the only one to notice it. "Now, where were we?"

"You mean before your eyes began to wander?" she joked. "I think I was giving you the rundown on what—"

My ringing desk phone was the cause of interruption this time.

"Agent Bishop," I answered it, thinking it was Mrs. Rodgers, inquiring about her missing granddaughter, though I implored her to not bother me while I did what I could to find her.

"I need to see you in my office," Hopkins' voice boomed through the earpiece. "Alone," he made sure to add.

Whatever the director wanted with me, had to be of great importance, because he was already standing in the threshold of his office, awaiting my arrival. As I neared, I studied his visage for any tell-tale signs of a hint but didn't see any. Hell, as far as I could tell, he still looked the same as he always looked – like a well-dressed drug dealer.

"Come on in, Bishop."

He stepped aside, allowing me entrance. You better believe I was surprised to see somebody else sitting behind the director's desk, who was none other than the uber beautiful blonde who'd just passed my office. She was poised in Hopkins' leather chair as if, not just the office, but the whole world belonged to her.

Hopkins spoke as he shut the door and moved toward the desk. "Agent Bishop, this is—"

"No names needed," the woman intervened, standing, and extending her hand to me, although I was still standing by the door. "It's bad enough I'm going against the CIA's policy by being here."

Hearing this, I quickly crossed the room and took her hand. "Nice to meet you, whatever your name may be. I assume you're here to see me?"

"Which is totally off the record, by the way." She retook her seat, but my supervisor and I remained standing. As she resumed, her green eyes never wavered as they seemed to drill holes through me. "The director received your request. It just so happened that I was in his office at the time he got it, and, if you must know, he laughed, and passed the documents off to me to shred. Well, not only am I nosey by nature, but I get paid to be in people's business.

"However, I took the documents back to my office and found your request quite interesting. Being that my position gives me carte blanche to operate a lot of our top-clearance equipment, I did a little nosing around from above – if you know what I mean. But what I did, totally went against our Code of Ethics, and could easily have me brought up on charges of espionage, which is why I will not share my discovery with you until we have an understanding about my being here."

"I'm highly aware of the consequences," I told her, anxious to know what kind of *discovery* she'd made, although my stomach seemed to be churning for some reason.

"I sure hope so," she replied, tapping keys on Hopkins' keypad. "I think you two would have to be standing on this side of the monitor to see what's on the screen."

Perhaps she was born with this sassy deportment, which had me wondering what her first word was because I seriously doubt if it was *Mommy* or *Daddy*. Hell, who cares? The director and I rounded the desk and stood one on each side of her, so we could get a look at what she was trying to show us.

On the screen was a satellite view of a house in the night- time. Immediately recognizing the rusty-blue truck in its driveway, I looked at the time and date at the bottom of the screen. It was the seventeenth of May, 11:23 p.m. Right at that moment, a male figure emerged from the house, carrying some swathed object slung over his shoulder. Of course, it was no other than Mr. Yarborough, but I was focused on the unidentified object he carried, trying to make out some form beneath what appeared to be a quilt. I wanted to ask the woman if she could zoom in a little closer, but I've been on a few missions with the CIA, being that they're not authorized to operate within the United States borders without a domestic agency attached. Therefore, I was pretty sure the satellite was showing its full potential. I have no doubt that they would be more advanced in the near future.

Yarborough deposited his burden in the rear compartment of the Dodge Ram, shut it back, then climbed into the driver's seat. Now, I'm quite aware of how being self-employed could have a person working odd hours, but this was a bit absurd for the miscellaneous jobs he did, and I'm not going to stand here and pretend as though I don't have an inkling as to what was wrapped up in that bed cover. Hell, it's not like this woman came all the way from Washington, D.C. to show me aerial footage of Mr. Yarborough on his way to unclog some old woman's toilet in the middle of the night.

I attentively watched the truck, waiting for it to pull out of the driveway, but it didn't budge. The lights never came on. It was almost like he was waiting on something or someone. Then, it was confirmed when his wife emerged from the house, moving briskly toward the truck with her arms wrapped about her as if it was cold out. Yarborough waited until his wife climbed in beside him, before backing out of the driveway and driving on with the lights off.

"It's a forty-something minute drive," the woman explained. "So, I did a little cutting and pasting."

Right after she asserted this, the scene on the screen changed. Now, we were watching the truck travel along the semi-deserted highway with its headlights on high beam. 11:58 p.m. was showing at the bottom of the screen. Just then, it jumped from 11:58 to 12:02 a.m. as the Dodge took an exit, I'm highly familiar with. 12:07 a.m. was showing on the screen when the truck turned onto a dirt road that led to a large area of trees and underbrush. Being that there were no streetlamps, or any other illuminations other than those of the vehicle, in this particular region, the night vision on the satellite adjusted to accommodate the picture.

After another minute or so of driving deeper into the dense area, the truck came to a halt. The lights went out, but we could still see the truck as clear as day. Seconds later, both doors swung open, and husband and wife dismounted, both carrying flashlights. They met up at the rear of the truck, where Mr. Yarborough opened the camper and retrieved the wrapped bundle, hoisting it upon his shoulder. His wife pulled a shovel from the compartment and followed him several feet to the left of the truck. Stopping, he dropped his load into a hole that was already dug into the earth. That's when I noticed the pile of dirt off to the side.

So, they had already prepared for this shit!

"I need three warrants and a crime scene unit, right now!" I spoke through clenched teeth, as thoughts of me doing heinous things to the couple filled my head.

"Whoa! Now you wait one goddamn minute, Bishop!" the director voiced, facing me, though I was still watching the screen. "Right now, you're thinking irrational, and I've warned you about that. You're also being inconsiderate of this woman's position. She brought this to you in confidentiality, and you're already about to betray her trust by letting sentiment overrule your better judgment."

I looked at him but said nothing. Evil thoughts still swarming.

"You know how this shit goes, Bishop," he resumed. "The Department of Justice don't want theory, and you know I'm not going to uphold or advocate anything you do if it's gonna jeopardize—"

"Stop treating me like I'm a tyro," I cut him off, regarding him with a look that probably would've scared me, had I been on the other end of it. "I know what's at stake here, and I know what I need to do, so you don't have to hold my hand like I just got off the short, yellow bus."

Hopkins exhaled and look down at his friend, then back at me. "Can I trust you to do this with a clear mind?"

"You can trust me to do this with the same mind they had when they murdered their own daughter," I replied, heading for the door.

It would have taken fifty-something minutes to arrive at the location, but I made it there in thirty-two, using the emergency lights and siren. I feel guilty for leaving without Reid, but what was I supposed to tell her? She's very smart, so she would have easily put two and two together, had I returned to the office, and insisted we drive out to a certain location, where we all of a sudden stumble upon the remains of six-year-old Bernadine Yarborough. Hell, I didn't even return to the office upon leaving Hopkins and the CIA agent. Nope. I made for the elevators and exited the building.

Now, with the satellite image burned into my memory, I managed to locate the dirt road Yarborough had taken to access the woods. While slowly moving along the path, I stuck my head out of the driver's side window and studied the tire tracks left behind by other vehicles. It didn't take long to reach the spot Yarborough had parked on that early morning, though I parked the Ford a few yards from it. Immediately, my eyes darted over to where I knew the makeshift grave laid. It wasn't visible from where I was, but it felt strange that I knew exactly where to look, as if I'm complicit in what had taken place.

Inhale. Exhale. Shutting off the engine, I climbed out of the car and instantly thought I was going to suffocate. The temperature was already in the late-eighties, but within this nature-built fortress, it felt more like one hundred and eighty. It was as though the gamut of trees were preventing even the slightest breeze from penetrating its core, which is why the air was stale, and the ground was moist and this two-piece suit I had on wasn't making it any better.

Extracting my investigation tool kit from the truck, and placing it on top of its lid, I retrieved my camera and took a few shots of the light impression of tire tracks, then some of the heavy imprints where Yarborough's truck had sat four weeks ago. There were no impressions of the shoes worn by Mrs. Yarborough, but I could see faint impressions of the distinctive rugged bottoms of the rare work boots belonging to her husband. I snapped several shots of the best ones, though I knew the images wouldn't be quite clear. Well, not until one of our technicians blow the picture up so big, we could plaster a copy on every billboard along I-285.

Now, it was time for the moment I'd dreaded while en route to this location. Turning on my heels, I gingerly moved in the direction of the small grave, stepping over fallen branches. Reaching it, and making sure to stand within six feet of it, I realized it wasn't the distance that made it appear almost invisible, but it was actually invisible, being that the soil had already begun to settle in.

As Director Hopkins had pointed out, I've made some gruesome discoveries since I'd been on the force. So, why was I having a hard time with this particular case? It's not like I knew the little girl. After taking a couple of photos of the plot, I returned to the car and replaced the camera. Slipping on a pair of latex gloves, I grabbed a Ziploc bag and one of my various size measuring scoops to gather a sample of the damp earth. Once I'd labeled it and stored everything in the truck, there was only one thing left to do.

But the moment I pulled my cellular free of its case, it vibrated in my hand. Damn! You can pretty much guess who the caller was. I'm just wondering why its taken so long for her to call and chew me out for disappearing on her the way I did without an explanation, and, truth be told, I haven't even thought about what I was gonna tell her, being that I'm not at liberty to divulge any kind of information pertaining to what led me to coming out here. Well, there's no need to prolong the inevitable.

"Let me have it," I said into the device upon answering.

"I would if you were in arms reach, right now," Reid shot back. "Hopkins told me you had to run but didn't say where to."

"There was an anonymous tip," I said, taking her pause as my cue to do so, hoping she'd believe me, but, like I said, the girl is highly intelligent. She won't just go for anything.

"And where did it lead you?" my partner inquired, sounding like she was taking my word for it.

I took another look at my surroundings before answering. "In the right direction, I'm sure."

"So, who's the blonde?"

"What blonde?"

"The one that sauntered past the office before Hopkins called you to his," she said accusingly.

See? Too intelligent for her own good.

"I don't know a thing about her," I told Reid. "She has nothing to do with this case."

"Which case?"

"The kidnapping case."

"You received an anonymous tip on the kidnapping case and didn't inform your partner?" She had become animated, and I could pretty much imagine the disappointing look on her face.

"I apologize for leaving you out of it," I tried to reconcile. "I just had to check it out for myself. However, I'll fill you in on everything once I get back. Right now, I have to call in a crime scene unit for excavation."

I heard her gasp, which made me wish I'd kept that last part to myself. "Did you—"

"I don't know yet," I cut her off, hoping she didn't start bugging. It was bad enough I was still vexed about the discovery myself. "I'll fill you in when I get back to the office."

Concluding the call, I placed one to headquarters to have the crime scene unit dispatched to my location. Knowing it would take them a little over an hour to reach me, I drove out to the Cracker Barrel restaurant that was about two miles from there, where I ordered a glass of iced tea, and copped a table to sit alone and gather my thoughts. I've already mentally prepared myself for what the excavation was going to bring about. The question that was eating at me was, what kind of death did Bernadine Yarborough succumb to?

Checking my watch, I realized I'd been sitting there for forty-seven minutes. My drink had been gulped down within the first three, being that I was a bit thirsty from being out in the extremely hot weather. Well, it was time to go back out in it. Therefore, I made sure to order a large cup of tea before making my exit.

Getting back to the area, I parked at the entrance of the forest-like setting, in order to intercept the dispatched unit when they arrived. The AC was blowing so good, I did not want to leave the confines of the Crown Victoria, but I did anyway. I just couldn't chance them driving right by without seeing me.

Instead of leaning against the car, I walked over and stood close to the road. Being that there was no sidewalk to speak of, I was standing in overgrown grass growing from uneven earth, which had me a little off-balanced. Plus, in this particular spot, the gamut of trees couldn't protect me from the torturous rays of the sun. At 6'1, and 168 pounds, my complexion is considered *paper bag* brown, but if I remain in this spot longer than I need to, Sony Pictures may call me in to be a stunt double for Wesley Snipes in his upcoming action film.

Well, lucky for me, I'll be able to retain my sexiness, because I spotted the bureau's utility truck approaching from the right of me, resembling a miniature monster truck with its large all-terrain tires, as it traveled upon the two-lane road. If the bulky tires didn't give it away, then the neon-yellow paint or its bulging, rear utility compartment would have. I stepped back as the Ford F-350 Crew Cab pulled in behind my car. It was occupied by two men and one woman. The male driver, whose name I'm not familiar with, rolled the window down.

"Should we cordon off the entrance?" he asked.

I shook my head. "No need to, it could draw unwanted attention to the scene." He nodded his consent. "Right now," I continued. "I'm chasing a lead from an anonymous tip. You know how that goes. Maybe we'll find something, maybe we won't."

"Maybe the Buccaneers will make it to the Super Bowl this year," said the female, who was seated in the front passenger seat. "Hell, it's all hit or miss. This is what we get paid for."

It was my turn to nod my own consent. I climbed behind the wheel of the Crown Victoria, and led the way, parking in the same spot I'd parked before. After waiting for the trio to dismount, I moved in the direction of the plot with them trailing behind. Of course, I didn't have to point the grave out to them. When I stopped, they immediately surrounded it like the professional forensic scientists they are, visually analyzing it with pensive expressions on their faces.

"Oh, we'll definitely find something," the female assured as she squatted down, patting the uneven earth with her bare hand. "It's not that deep, so it shouldn't take long." Standing to her full height, she turned and locked her blue eyes onto mine. "Does this have anything to do with the missing Yarborough girl?"

"It does," I answered, seeing no need to lie.

She nodded thoughtfully, then turned to her crew. "Let's suit up, boys!"

I remained in the same spot as they returned to their truck to *suit up*. All I could do was watch as the triad began pulling all kinds of equipment from the cargo area. While they were donning white Hazmat suits over their clothing, my attention was on the female forensic scientist. No, not in that way. I was thinking about her question as to if this had something to do with the missing child. Perhaps she'd been attentively following the case, hoping and praying for the little girl's safe return. Her question wasn't disturbing, but the knowing look I saw in her eyes before she broke eye contact with me, was. Maybe she'd seen the same look in my eyes. Or maybe I was just imagining all this. Being out in the sun too long could do that to a person, right?

Now, with their protective suits on, and ventilation masks poised atop their heads, they were moving in my direction, each carrying equipment, putting me in the mind of astronauts invading another planet. Of course, I moved out of their way, giving them as much room as I felt they needed to set up. Again, my attention was on the woman, as she instructed her team on how and where to set up and position the Klieg lights. While one of the men made the final adjustments to the high-intensity lights so that they shone on the grave from three different angles, the other one made another trip to the truck.

By this time, the woman had taken a camera from a black bag lying on the ground and began taking pictures of the plot. Clearly satisfied with the photos, she placed the camera back inside the bag, just as the other guy returned with three spades. Before accepting hers, the woman approached me, carrying a small camcorder.

"Would you do the honors?" she asked, holding it out to me.

I accepted the device without a word, checking it to see that she'd already had it on and functioning. Moving a little closer, I aimed it at the grave, hoping I was in the right spot.

"In the spot, we're about to breach," she spoke to the co-workers, receiving her spade. "It's my theory that whatever's buried underneath it, is not too far from the rim. So, please move with caution."

Just like that, they pulled their masks down over their faces, and immediately got to work, practically nipping at the dirt, but I know they move in this manner in order to detect and preserve any kind of trace evidence that could be melded with the earth. By this time, I had, once again, become conscious of the smothering heat within the confines of the forest. The sweat on my palm felt like oil against the plastic casing of the camera, which I tried my best to hold steady, being that my hands had begun to tremble.

But why were my hands trembling? It's not like I didn't know what to expect. Hell, to be honest, I almost regret sending that request to the CIA, hoping to return Bernadine Yarborough home safely, and hauling her abductor off to jail. I guess all fairytales don't always end how we want them to because this one definitely deferred from the one I had in mind.

"Careful!" the woman cautioned, after minutes of digging.

Although I was in my thoughts, my eyes were affixed to the plot. That's why I was able to spy the first sighting of the cloth as its gray color contrasted with the dark soil. The team switched up their tactic. Now, they were using the tips of their spades to gingerly remove dirt from the top, before digging around it. Eventually, the full quilt had finally been exposed, though it was soiled with mud.

However, it wasn't the only thing exposed.

"I think we've found her," said one of the men, clearly seeing what I was now staring at.

Though smeared with dirt and scattering bugs, there was no denying the small, and bare feet belonging to Bernadine Yarborough. Like I said, I already knew what to expect. At this time, my mind reverted to the satellite image I'd seen before driving out here. The part where Yarborough tossed his own daughter into that same exact hole like she was nothing more than the bedspread she was wrapped in. I mean, I understand that the couple was barely surviving without the dependence of a dependent, but to murder their own child?

The female investigator retrieved her camera to take pictures of the body as it was first discovered. I took that time to call it in, and to arrange for the corpse to be transported to the M.E.'s laboratory. I was back to holding the camcorder as the team pulled the deceased girl from the hole, lying her beside it. When they freed her of the quilt, all I could do was shake my head as more bugs scattered after being disturbed from feasting on different parts of her body. The most disturbing thing to me was the bugs that crawled in and out the open mouth and the ones that were damaging her pretty eyes that conveyed a terrifying look as they stared up at nothing.

The fuckers didn't even have the decency to close the girl's eyes!

Bernadine Yarborough was clad in purple pajama pants, and a pink sleeveless top that had the word *Loved* stenciled across the chest, which I found to be quite ironic. Hell, maybe they *did* love her at one point in time. Who knows? Anyway, I evaluated the girl's clothing for any traces of blood but found none. That's when I spotted the large bruise around the pale skin of her neck.

Hell, I didn't need a pathologist to point the cause of death out to me. I could clearly see the innocent child fast asleep in her bed, when her father eased into her bedroom, wrapped his large calloused hands around her tiny neck, and applied pressure. The same look that was a cross between terror and disbelief, was still displayed in her eyes. Her mouth was still agape as if she died asking her father why was he hurting her? I'd bet anything her mother had stood by and watched the whole thing.

Chapter 10

Tuesday

It had been three days since the discovery of six-year-old Bernadine Yarborough's body. Besides the imprint of the tire tracks, and those of the boots allegedly worn by Kenneth Yarborough, the crime scene unit didn't find any substantial evidence at the scene. It was confirmed that the little girl had been strangled by hand, although there was no impression of prints left on her neck, indicating that her assailant had worn gloves of some sort, but there were particles of rust and sawdust stuck to her skin in that region which, undoubtedly came from fairly used work gloves.

Unfortunately, this was all the evidence I had to work with, being that I couldn't mention anything about the CIA agent and how she aided the discovery. Therefore, I drew up my report the best I could and submitted it to the director, who'd given me all kinds of flak before turning it over to the DOJ. Surprisingly, the Department of Justice approved, giving their okay to proceed in the case, which is why I was now standing at the drawing board of the FBI's war room, laying out the plan of action to the elected participants, which consisted of Wilma Reid, two deputies from the Fulton County Sheriff's Department, two agents from the Georgia Bureau of Investigation, and two officers from the Cobb County Police Department, all clad in tactical gear as well as myself. Plus, Director Hopkins was present, dressed in one of his expensive suits, which made me wonder if he had any of them bullet-proofed.

"I want Alpha Two to branch off here," I was saying, using my pointer to indicate a street on the large, geographical satellite view of the Yarborough's neighborhood that was taped up on the board, right next to two enlarged photos of the husband and wife. "Your destination will be here, putting you at the target's six. You are to immediately clear this house, which will bring you directly to the target. There are no fences or guard dogs. Take locus and wait for the go-ahead. Again, this is a no-knock warrant. Therefore, we are not obligated to play nice. Any questions?"

"I hope you're right about those boots," Hopkins voiced. He was leaning against the rear wall with his arms folded over his chest.

"That's not a question, sir," I responded, raising one eyebrow for emphasis. "But, to mitigate your worries, Mr. Yarborough is still in possession of the same boots that left those impressions at the crime scene. Just as he's still in possession of those same tires that did likewise. Again, are there any questions?"

One of the GBI agents raised his hand.

"Yes, sir?"

"What are the rules of engagement?" he wanted to know.

"Good question!" My pointer shot out like a striking snake at the photo of Kenneth Yarborough. "As you already know, this is our main target. He's a murderer and should be treated as such. If he shows any signs of aggression, all weapons are free. Take him down by any means necessary. If his wife attempts to assist him, take her down also. Now, let's gear up and get going!"

While everyone was doing a last-minute artillery check, I made a show of checking my service weapon, at the same time still fuming over the fact that I had no evidence to link Tonya Yarborough to the crime. The only way she'd be joining her husband in confinement is if he decides to sing like a canary, implicating her. I seriously doubt that, however.

"By any means necessary, huh?"

Sliding the cartridge back into my gun, I turned to face Hopkins, who was now standing within arm's reach, hands in his pants pockets.

"He should be treated like a murderer?" the director pressed.

"He's wanted for the murder of his own daughter," I pointed out. "Should we treat him like a shoplifter?"

"Treat him like a human being," my supervisor asserted, then lowered his voice. "If you do anything irrational, I will crucify your ass!"

Our convoy of two black SUVs made it to Marietta, Georgia, at 4:55 p.m. The spot we'd chosen was the parking lot of a Starbucks, which was just up the street from the Yarborough's residence. Reid and I were accompanied by the two Fulton County deputies in the heavy-tinted Chevy Suburban, in which we occupied the rear seats. As instructed, the deputy operating the truck, turned into the parking lot, and parked farther away from the vehicles of the customers, leaving the engine running for the sake of the A.C. that reprieved us of the agonizing heat on the other side.

The other SUV – a GMC Denali – that was occupied by the Cobb County police officers and GBI agents, pulled alongside us. Of course, we couldn't see them for the dark tinted windows that were similar to ours. Being that I'm the head of this operation, these guys are basically under my command, and can't take a leak without my permission. Well, they can't move in on the target until I give the go-ahead.

As a precaution, I dispatched one of our agents to the Yarborough's home, to trail Kenneth Yarborough as he went about his daily routine, cleaning toilets or whatnot. The agent was instructed to report back to me when Yarborough retires to his home for the evening, but that didn't mean I couldn't call and inquire on the current location of the target. Hell, my cellular has been in my hand from the moment we left the war room because I was really anticipating the call. So, why the hell not?

"Pearson," Special Agent Pearson's voice boomed through the earpiece.

"Tell me something good," I said, looking out at the light flow of traffic moving in and out of the fairly-new establishment.

"I think the subject is on his way to the destination," he informed.

"You think?"

"We're moving in that direction. Stand by for confirmation."

"Standing by."

Concluding the call, I looked out at Atlanta Road. Though I was watching vehicles zip by, my mind was on the pressure that was put upon me by the Department of Justice to solve the bank robbery case. Reid and I are scheduled to have a conference with Director Hopkins tomorrow in reference to this, in which we'd drawn up a proposal to see if he'd permit us to set up around-the-clock surveillance on Damien Turner. Plus, a wiretap. We feel as though these procedures will better our chances of finding the other two culprits involved in the robbery. Perhaps Turner would lead us to them.

"I'm listening," I answered my phone after checking the caller I.D.

"The bird is secured in its nest," Pearson unnecessarily coded.

"Great! We're seventy-six."

Finally securing my cellular in one of the pockets on my tactical vest, I relayed this to my team. Then, I conducted a radio check to make sure everyone's transmitters were working. Once this was done, our small convoy was back in motion, moving amongst the light traffic on Atlanta Road in silence. In fact, such missions are always conducted in silence. Well, everyone, I've been on. All conversations are made in the war room. Once the units mount up and move out, all fraternizing goes out of the window. Officials from several agencies are always attached, pretty much forming groups of strangers, but it's very rare that someone would use such a time to get acquainted with a person of interest.

After a few minutes of traveling on the main road, we turned onto West Atlanta Street. Immediately upon passing Oakridge Drive, I turned in my seat to peer out of the rear window. Alpha Two's SUV entered the street as instructed. The next entrance was Carruth Drive, our entrance into the neighborhood. The deputy made the turn and pretty much slowed the truck to a snail's pace, in order to give Alpha Two enough time to get into position.

Although it was high noon, and after business hours, I expected to see residents returning home from their jobs or whatever, but the street was deserted, except for a few children frolicking around the front yard of one of the few run-down homes. Special Agent Pearson's *borrowed* car was parked across the street, a couple of houses away from the Yarboroughs. The deputy drove past him and parked directly across the street from the aforementioned residence, shutting off the engine.

Now, looking out at the house with the oddly colored Dodge Ram parked in its driveway, my mind reflected on the bedroom of Bernadine Yarborough. I could actually visualize the little girl sleeping peacefully in her own bed. Then, I could see Mr.

Yarborough and his wife ease into her room like thieves in the night. Yarborough wrapping his massive gloved hands around his daughter's tiny neck. Bernadine's eyes jerking open with terror from the sudden violation, then filling with tears from the realization of who the violation was coming from. As her larynx was being crushed, and her short-lived life was coming to a tragic end, she tried real hard to utter words questioning her daddy's reasoning to no avail, while her own mother watched impassively.

"Alpha Two is in position," a female's voice announced through the transmitter lodged in my right ear. "Over."

"Roger that, Alpha Two. Stand by," I responded, then regarded the rest of the squad. "Let's rollout, Alpha One!"

Everyone donned their helmets. The deputy in the front passenger seat was in possession of the battering ram. Upon dismounting, we all scuttled across the street with handguns at the ready. Although Special Agent Pearson's mission was to trail Kenneth Yarborough all day and report his whereabouts, he also had an imperative to watch out backs while we're inside and to assist with the collecting of evidence once the subject has been apprehended.

Reaching the front door, holding my Glock in my right hand, I eased the shabby, and noisy screen door open with the other, propping it open with my back as the two Fulton County deputies took their positions on either side of the battering ram. Reid stood opposite of me on the other side of the door that I'd noticed on my initial visit was very fragile due to damage caused by an infestation of termites.

After each of them had given a nod, indicating they were ready, I pressed the talk button on my headset. "Alpha Two. Prepare to breach in five—four—three—two—one."

Boom!

The deputies took one swing with the battering ram, and the flimsy, wooden door ripped off its hinges and security fastenings, crashing to the floor. Then, the deputies backed away to discard the steel beam, and to draw their weapons. At that time, with her gun aimed, Reid dashed through the threshold, boots sounding like thunder upon the fallen door. I entered behind her, just as Mrs.

Yarborough cried out from some other part of the house, subsequently being ordered to lie down on the floor by one of the men from Alpha Two.

Reid veered off into the living room, but I kept forward, hearing the two deputies trailing behind me. I was just about to try the knob on the bathroom's door when it swung open. Kenneth Yarborough, who was still in the process of tying a towel around the mid-section of his wet, and naked body, seemed to be in a rush, considering he left the shower on. Clearly, he had heard the commotion of the front and back doors crashing in, plus his wife's cry for help.

Seeing me with my gun now aimed at his temple, Yarborough stopped dead in his tracks. I know he'd never seen me in tactical gear before, nor with a gun in my hand, but I don't think those are the reasons why fear was visibly registering in his enlarged eyes. No, sir. He'd been discovered, and he knew it. Hell, my presence alone gave that away.

Then, suddenly, I became angry all over again as mental pictures of what he'd done to his own daughter re-entered my mind. What happened next was pure impulse. I found myself lunging at Yarborough with my left arm moving like lightning, striking him in his right eye with my closed, gloved hand. While he was in the midst of stumbling backward, I brought the butt of my Glock down on the bridge of his nose, instantly shattering its bone structure. He cried out in pain as he lost his footing. I don't know if I lost my own footing, or was still moving on impulse but, when Yarborough's bareback made contact with the moist tiled floor, I was on top of him.

At this time, I assumed my gun was lying somewhere beside us, because it was no longer in my hand, and I was pretty sure of this because both of my hands were clamped around Yarborough's throat, as I intentionally tried to squeeze the life out of him. Then, I found myself struggling with the pairs of hands that were trying to pull me up. My team was trying to save him. Or was it me they were thinking about? Whatever their reasons were, they finally managed to pull me off a now panting, and hysterical looking Kenneth Yarborough.

Looking back at my team, and seeing the looks on their faces, made me realize that I had let my emotions get the best of me. Yes, I really fucked up this time.

***

After dropping Kenneth Yarborough off at the federal holding facility downtown, all participating parties returned to the James P. Russell building, where we reassembled in the War room to write individual statements on how the apprehension procedure had been conducted.

One statement had to corroborate the next. Any incident, or accident, had to be reported. Any injuries to officials and civilians have to be recorded, including cause of said injuries. So, yes, the injuries Yarborough sustained in the ordeal had to be documented and answered to. Of course, there was no need for me to lie, or try and cover the incident up in my own statement when there were seven others that would utterly differ from mine.

Once all written statements were completed and collected by Director Hopkin's secretary, the other officials made for the elevators to return to their agencies, while Reid and I journeyed off to our office to prepare to retire to our homes for the rest of the day.

Reid had taken a seat behind her desk and begun jotting something down in her small notepad. Anxiety was doing a number on me, so I couldn't sit down even if I wanted to, being that I was too anxious to get out of there, so I could spend some time with Monique and Melody before turning in for the night.

But I wanted to fulfill my promise to Mrs. Rodgers the grandmother of the deceased, Bernadine Yarborough, before leaving the office. Therefore, while standing, I searched through my Rolodex for her phone number, which only took a few seconds. Just as I was about to remove the phone's receiver from its cradle, it rang causing me to pause a bit. Customarily, I waited for it to ring a second time before answering it.

"Special Agent Bishop," I stated through the mouthpiece.

"I wanna see you in my office, right fucking now," Hopkins voiced, then quickly hung up, disallowing me any time to protest.

"What's the matter?" Reid questioned when I replaced the receiver. Clearly, she recognized the pensive expression on my face.

"That was the director," I answered, now regarding her. "He wants to see me right away."

"Did he sound angry?"

I drew a breath. "That would be an understatement."

While en route to the director's office, I thought about how distraught Kenneth Yarborough's wife had appeared through the process of us taking her husband into custody and searching their house for evidence. It was evident that she was frightened. Hell, my team saw that. They figured she was frightened and shocked to find out that her very own husband was responsible for the death of their only daughter.

But I knew better. Hell, it took everything in me to not attack her as I'd done her husband and drag her ass down to the federal building to be booked for murder and abduction also. However, I feel as though she'll get what's coming to her.

As usual, the director's office door was standing wide open as if he was expecting me. Well, he was expecting me. Also, as usual, he had the phone's receiver glued to the side of his face. Plus, his lips were moving, and his visage made it appear as though he was having a serious conversation with someone. I mean, do I really have to tell you that he made a show of concluding his call upon noticing me standing in the doorway? As usual, right?

"Close the door behind you," Hopkins instructed, after waving me in.

I complied, then quietly approached the desk.

"I received a call from a medical-personnel at the housing facility," he said, once I stopped in front of the desk. "Telling me that Yarborough was seriously injured prior to being admitted," I said nothing. "What the fuck did I know about this?" the director posed what I took to be a rhetorical question. "Not a damn thing. Well, not until I went over these written statements."

That's when I noticed the pile of documents in front of him. Still, I remained silent.

Placing his elbows on the desk, Director Hopkins steepled his fingers while drilling his eyes into mine. "I hope you have a perfectly good reason for why you committed the act of assault against the civilian you were in charge of bringing into custody, Bishop. Because neither statement mentioned anything about him resisting arrest."

I shifted my weight from one foot to the other.

"You went against the Code of Conduct like I knew you would," he resumed. "I've warned you about this. Now, there could possibly be a lawsuit against the department, because you allowed your emotions to override your capacity to think rationally."

There was really nothing I could say. I'm guilty as charged.

"I knew it would come down to this," he went on, holding his hand out. "Your gun and shield. As of now, I'm suspending you until further notice."

Playa Ray

Chapter 11

December 11; 2002

Riverdale, Georgia

If you were keeping up with the dates, then you'd know that I was suspended until further notice on the thirteenth of June, which was six months ago. I'm quite sure you're wondering what the hell has happened between then and now, and how long I've been temporarily out of commission. What about the two cases I was working on? The bank robbery? The kidnapping case that resulted in Kenneth Yarborough being arrested for the murder of his own daughter? I'm quite sure you're very anxious to know how those turned out.

Well, here goes, after being on suspension for ninety days, Director Hopkins allowed me to return to the office on the seventeenth of September, although my office had moved, and I was assigned another partner. What happened to my ex-partner, Wilma Reid? Nothing, actually, her office never changed – only her partner. Plus, to further my punishment, Hopkins had taken it upon himself to assign me to miscellaneous details. Lately, I'd been deployed to assist local homicide and robbery detectives, whenever I'm not playing subordinate to my current partner, Special Agent Paul Rucker who's only had his shield for no more than three years.

However, Wilma Reid continued the investigation into the bank robbery. She managed to get Hopkins to grant her request of setting up round-the-clock surveillance on the bank officer, Damien Turner for two weeks, only to run into a brick wall, being that he didn't lead them to anybody who fits the bill as the other two culprits of the robbery. Plus, the court-ordered wiretap served no purpose, being that he'd only called and received calls from his mother and girlfriend. Perhaps he was smart enough to realize the possibility of him being a suspect and chose to move with extreme caution, just in case. I warned you about those lefties. A high percentage of those wrong-handed fuckers are too intelligent for their own good. So, that case has been closed.

The kidnapping case? Well, after a week of being housed at the federal holding facility, Kenneth Yarborough was interrogated by Wilma Reid and another agent from the division, in the presence of a court-appointed lawyer. Believe it or not, but I was surprised when Reid told me how Yarborough sang like a canary. Yes, he'd actually broken down and confessed about the murder of his very own daughter, withholding no details. He even told of his wife's involvement, claiming their lack of income motivated them to commit the selfish act. So, as it went, Tonya Yarborough was subsequently picked up and charged as well, both still awaiting a trial date to be set. I'll put you up to speed on everything else as the story unfolds.

It was a little after two a.m. when I brought my BMW to a halt behind one of the police cruisers that blocked off a section of the street, its strobe lights dancing along with those of the other emergency vehicles, giving the neighborhood that gloomy look which indicated that something bad had happened, and at this time of the morning it was a bit surprising to see what appeared to be the whole neighborhood standing around, trying to figure out what happened at the home of one of their neighbors.

As much as I hated to leave the warm confines of my car, I had a job to do. Therefore, I zipped my blazer all the way up before stepping out into the cold night air that's known to accompany the last month of the year. Unfortunately, after receiving the call from Hopkins, I ended up rushing out of the house without grabbing a skull cap. Therefore, I'll have to get through the night with the wind nipping at my scalp.

Holding only my small notepad in hand, I approached a couple of beat cops who were put in place to keep spectators on the other side of the crime scene tape, although this crowd seemed to have no interest in getting any closer than they already were. Either the two officers had already been apprised of my arrival, or they took the three large letters emblazoned on my windbreaker to be the *Real McCoy* because they were more than obliged to permit me beyond the bright-yellow tape where all the action lied.

The scene of the crime was a white house that was about twenty-five yards from where I parked. Being that residents lined the sidewalk, I chose to stick to the road, zig-zagging between emergency vehicles as the cold wind had a field day on my scalp and gnawed away at my bare ears. Passing two awaiting ambulances, I noticed they were empty, meaning that the bodies were still in the process of being bagged, though I didn't know how many there were. All Hopkins told me to do was to get my ass out of bed, and report to the scene of multiple homicides in Riverdale, Georgia.

Ignoring stares thrown at me for being the only FBI agent on a mere homicide scene, I finally entered the driveway where the crime scene unit seemed to be dissecting a white Mercedes-Benz, and a minivan. I swatted at some of the insects buzzing around the Klieg lights as I continued, entering the front door that stood wide open, pulling out my credentials, which I found myself not having to use.

"It's nice of you to join us, Agent Bishop," Riverdale Chief of Police Richard Barns greeted from the other end of the living room. It appeared as though he was giving the four paramedics last-minute instructions on how to handle the four corpses that were already zipped up in black body bags and ready to be shipped out to the morgue.

"Thanks for having me," I responded, catching a glimpse of a female crime scene technician in the small hallway, shining a fluorescent flashlight along the walls. "What'cha got on your hands?"

The rotund, Caucasian official drew a breath before answering. "A quadruple homicide. All males. Two African Americans. Two Caucasians. Mid to late twenties. All bound before sustaining singular gunshot wounds to the backs of their heads. The possible murder weapon – a forty-four handgun – was found on that sofa. The scene also depicts home invasion from the manner it was found."

"So," I said, brandishing an ink pen, and flipping my notepad open. "You think the perpetrators intentionally left the murder weapon at the scene of the crime?"

"It appears that way," he replied. "Forensics found gun powder on the weapon that suggested it had been fired recently."

I nodded, jotting that bit of information down.

"Let's get out of these guys' way," he resumed, indicating the awaiting paramedics. "I'll show you the rest of the house."

To reach the chief, I had to step over two of the bagged corpses, though I couldn't help but step into the large puddles of blood that stained the burgundy carpet and felt thick and sticky beneath the soles of my boots. While conducting the maneuver, I glanced over at the coffee table, where an empty money counter sat idle.

En route to the first bedroom, we passed the female technician, who didn't even pause for a millisecond to regard us with a mere glance as she continued to scan the walls for usable prints or marks. The first bedroom we reached had been visibly ransacked. There was a police detective, who appeared to be taking his time as he casually moved about the room, searching for clues. I nodded for Chief Barns to move on. Inside the second bedroom, two uniformed officers were documenting their findings. We passed a bathroom before reaching the last bedroom that was as wrecked as the others. The top mattress of the bed had been thrown against the wall. A male forensic inspector was kneeling down, dusting a pistol-grip pump that was lying upon the secondary mattress. For some reason, I took it upon myself to enter.

"I guess that was too much for them to carry, huh?" I said, getting a closer look at the weapon.

"It appears that way." The technician looked up, then furrowed his eyebrows. Apparently, he was wondering about my presence at such a scene, at such an hour.

However, I didn't care to entertain his inquisitive look. Instead, I took a look around the room before crossing over to the dresser where the glare of several pieces of jewelry had caught my attention. There were a sixteen-inch gold chain and matching bracelet, which were accompanied by two gold rings. One of the rings had the shape of a horseshoe on it, emblazoned in diamonds. The other one was plain.

"Perhaps they ransacked the house to make it look like robbery was the motive," I offered, using my ink pen to move the jewelry around. "I mean, why would they leave these items behind?"

"Hell," Barns replied, now standing beside me. "Why would they execute four men who were already bound, and posed no threat?"

"Two perfectly good questions of mystery."

"I assume they were only after money and drugs?" the chief of police let on. "Atlanta had a case like this not too long ago. In September, I believe. They found three men and one woman bound on the living room floor, and a toddler crying his eyes out on the sofa of one home."

"I remember that," I told him, picking up the plain ring with my hand to see *DRSQ* engraved on its flat surface. "But these people weren't murdered, right?"

"Right, but that doesn't exclude those perpetrators from being the same ones to act in this case, Bishop."

"True, indeed." I replaced the ring, then turned to face the big man. "Maybe we should harass APD about that particular case, to see if we could conjure up some kind of lead."

"*We?*" Chief Barns questioned, then placed an avuncular hand on my shoulder. "You're FBI, Bishop. This case belongs to the Riverdale Police Department. I know you fucked up, and Hopkins made the decision to punish you, instead of terminating you, but hasn't he punished you enough?"

I said nothing.

"What he's doing to you," Barnes resumed, "is something I've never heard of. I mean, he actually wakes you up in the middle of the night to accompany local cops in investigating residential burglaries. It's like he hands you off to different relatives to be babysat."

***

The chief of police's words had been echoing in my mind from the moment he'd spoken them. After assisting the responding officer with questioning neighbors, I left the crime scene, making it back to my own residence at 4:51 a.m. There was no need for me to try and get some rest, being that I had to be at the office at eight. Hell, I couldn't bring myself to repose if I wanted to, because my mind was racing. I have to have a sit-down with Director Hopkins today. Instead of wondering how long this *babysitting* thing was going to last, I know I'll have to inquire about it myself.

Once I cleaned my apartment, I showered, then fixed myself some breakfast. By 7:32 a.m., I was back out the door, heading for the office. Of course, I was rehearsing all kinds of scenarios of how I was going to broach the subject with my superior.

As always, Hopkins wasn't there when I arrived, but my partner, Special Agent Paul Rucker was already seated behind his desk, enjoying a cup of coffee and a breakfast sandwich, when I took a seat behind my own desk, which sat in a far corner of the office, opposite of his.

"Morning, Bishop!" Rucker greeted, after washing his food down with a swallow of coffee. At the age of thirty-three, Rucker stood at 5'11, and weighed about a hundred and sixty-five pounds, with sandy-brown hair that was about three inches long and always slicked to the back. The only facial hair he owned was his eyebrows.

"How's it going, Rucker?" I mumbled, powering up my computer.

"I can't complain," he replied, smiling. "Every night, my kids don't forget to remind me of how many days we have left before Christmas. Plus, they want every toy that advertises on television."

"Yeah, I know what you mean." I was now thinking about Melody and her litany of items she didn't *mind* getting for Christmas.

"I hear you went out to that multiple homicide scene in Riverdale."

I typed my password in before answering. "That's true."

"How was it?"

"Like any other multiple homicide scene," I said with a shrug of the shoulders.

"I see," he said slowly. "I also see that you're a bit cranky. Have you had your morning dose of caffeine yet?"

I looked across the room at him. "No, I haven't."

"Then you need to be on your way to the break room," Rucker advised, holding his cup up. "I think Mary finally got it right this time. In fact, there's no telling when we'll get it like this again."

He was right, Mary Joseph, Director Hopkins' secretary was lousy at making coffee. The forty-seven-year-old woman can bake her ass off, but the simplicity of brewing a decent pot of coffee was apparently beyond her range of common sense – if I put that correctly. Hell, sometimes we would throw out a pot of her coffee to make it seem as if us employees had devoured it, which undoubtedly gave Joseph the impression that she was doing something right. We all love her, and wouldn't dream of breaking her precious heart, so if the false sense of hope we give her makes her happy, then we're all happy.

I entered the breakroom and was a bit surprised to see my expartner, Wilmer Reid leaned against the counter, holding a steaming cup of coffee up to her mouth with both hands. Her pocketbook and briefcase were sitting atop the table, and she was wearing her overcoat, indicating that she'd just got in, and had not been to her office yet.

"Morning," I said, moving towards the coffeemaker in which Reid had to scoot over for me to reach.

"Good morning to you," she replied with a smile on her face. "You look haggard."

"That's an understatement." I was now pouring the dark, hot liquid into a Styrofoam cup. "Hopkins roused me from my sleep at one this morning, dispatching me to a multiple homicide scene in Riverdale. I've been up since."

"I can't believe he's still punishing you like that," she sympathized, slowly shaking her head. "If it was me, I would've just fired your ass."

I noticed the smirk on her face and laughed. "Yeah, I just bet you would've. How's the coffee?"

"It's wonderful!" exclaimed Reid. "There may be a hint of vanilla extract. However, I think Ms. Joseph found the right beans this time."

"Found?"

"She gets them from some local coffee bean shop," Reid explained, helping herself to another cup. "You haven't even tried it yet. Try it. I promise you'll like it."

Sighing inwardly, I reluctantly lifted the cup to my mouth, and took a small sip, instantly tasting the faint taste of vanilla extract Reid pointed out. "Mmm!" I expressed, following up with a bigger sip. "This *is* good! I may have to fill my thermos up before everyone gets in."

"You read my mind," Reid said with a giggle. "So, how's the fraud case coming along?"

"To be honest," I started, leaning against the counter, "I have no idea."

"Are you serious!" There was a look of disbelief on her face. "You mean to tell me you don't have a clue as to how the case is going?"

"That's Rucker's case," I countered. "I'm pretty much like a ride-along. While he's interrogating people, I stand off to the side, nodding, looking like a damn bobblehead."

Reid laughed. "I think you'd make a cute bobblehead action figure doll."

"Very funny," I joked. "Anyway, I'm making it my—"

I stopped mid-sentence upon seeing Director Manny Hopkins walk past the breakroom in his leather trench coat and carrying his briefcase. My intention was to have a casual man to man with him about the on-going punishment he's inflicted upon me, but why was I all of a sudden angry?

"Breathe, Bishop!"

I diverted my attention from the empty doorway to Reid and realized I was holding my breath.

"It's too early," she resumed, concern etched across her face. "You know how he is when he first gets in. If you're planning on approaching him about what he's doing to you, then I advise you to at least wait until this afternoon."

"You know I appreciate your advice," I told my ex-partner. "But sometimes it's good to bother people when they're not in the mood to be bothered."

"Bishop!"

I was already crossing the threshold. As I said before, Reid has been keeping me out of trouble ever since we've been knowing each other, and I really do appreciate her for it, but today was not one of those days that I felt the need to be saved.

As always, Hopkins' office door was standing wide open when I approached but, surprisingly, he wasn't pretending to be on the phone this time. No, he was eating a breakfast sandwich, with a napkin tucked into the top of his shirt, which is something I'd only seen done on television shows. So, he was looking pretty ridiculous at this very moment.

However, I was so determined to get this over with, I didn't even wait at the threshold for him to wave me in. No sir! I marched right on in as if it was my very own office and flopped down unusually hard into one of the two chairs in front of his desk, noting the stunned expression he was now regarding me with.

"It's not polite to chew with your mouth open, Director," I spoke, indicating his mouth that was agape.

My supervisor took a swig of his beverage and wiped his mouth before attempting to chew me out. "Bishop, what the hell—"

"How long is this gonna go on?" I cut him off. "Yeah, I fucked up when I assaulted Yarborough, and I accepted my suspension like a man, but what you're putting me through now is beyond reproach. I love my job, but I'm not reporting to any more crime scenes that's below my pay grade, nor requires the presence of the Federal Bureau of Investigation. If you don't believe me – try me!"

Hopkins slowly leaned back in his chair with his eyes still transfixed on me. I don't know if I was reading it right, but it seemed as though his expression had gone from stunned to amused. "It took you this long to grow a pair?" he asked, a smirk appearing on his face. "And, to answer your question, it was going to go on for as long as you allowed it to. Hell, if you didn't mind me using you as a puppet, I didn't mind tugging at the strings at two and three in the morning to have you investigating purse-snatchers. I'm just glad you finally decided to take the issue up with me before the Justice Department caught a whiff of what I was doing, which would've surely cost me my job."

Now, it was *my* turn to take on a stunned expression. What he was doing to me could have cost him his job? So, he was violating one of the Federal Codes of Ethics? Had I known this I would've filed a formal complaint with *his* supervisors.

"As of today," he went on, a smirk still lingering. "You no longer have to commit any acts unbecoming of a federal agent. However, I'm assigning you to the Drop Squad investigation. I've designated North as point, so the sooner you report to him, the sooner he can put you up to date on what he and his team has so far." He leaned forward and retrieved his sandwich off its wrapping. "Now, if you don't mind, I'd like to enjoy my breakfast in peace."

***

After another trip to the breakroom to fill my thermos with the vanilla-tasting coffee, I took an elevator down to the fourth floor, where Agent North's office is located, though the War Room was my destination.

Yes, I notified my partner, Rucker that I would be working on another case, but he didn't seem at all concerned. I mean, I didn't expect him to launch a Million Man March protest about it, but I also didn't expect him to take the news impassively as if I told him I was on my way to the store or something.

Anyway, getting off the elevator, I marched to the War Room and rapped on the metal door before turning the knob, and pushing it open. There were at least a dozen agents present, sitting in chairs, or just standing around. They were all jotting down notes while North, who was standing at the board, went over the developments in the case they were building against the notorious gang known as Drop Squad. Well, that's what they were doing before I barged in. Now, they were all looking at me as if I was out of my jurisdiction by being on the fourth floor, when my office is located on the sixth.

"It's nice of you to join us, Mr. Bishop!" North prompted, re-garding me with a genuine smile. "The director has already in-formed me of your arrival. If you would take a seat, I'd be glad to fill you in on what we have thus far."

Closing the door back, I crossed the room and found a seat at one of the tables. After settling in, I took a long swig of the delicious coffee before pulling out my pen and notepad. Seeing that North was giving me an inquisitive look, I nodded to let him know that I was ready.

"Well, Mr. Bishop," North went on, indicating the large board where multiple photos of people wearing Drop Squad Chains were hanging about. "We're pretty much waist-deep into our investigation. These are some of the photos taken during routine surveillance. This guy here—" He was tapping his pointer on a rather large picture of a younger-looking man wearing cornrows and a Drop Squad chain. "—is one of us. Special Agent Kent hails from the Denver branch and is loaned to us for this mission. So, we're highly responsible for his safety. All of these guys here—"

While North went on with his presentation, I flipped open my notepad, looking for a blank piece of paper to begin new notes on, when I caught a glimpse of the four letters I'd copied from one of the rings found at the murder scene in Riverdale, Georgia this morning *DRSQ*. My eyes quickly shot up to the board once I realized that I had just seen these four characters in one of the surveillance photos.

Right there! This particular photo depicted two guys standing outside of a corner store. One had a cell phone to his ear, and the other one was in the middle of twisting the cap off a bottle that was concealed in a brown paper bag. They were both sporting the Drop Squad chain with its full lettering, but the apparent abbreviation appeared on the front of their shirts.

It took everything in me to not interrupt Agent North with what I've stumbled upon this morning, though I was anxious to do so. Instead, I waited patiently, listening, and taking notes.

"—for the remainder of the week," North was saying. "Now, before we dismiss, are there any questions?"

My arm shot up like a skyrocket.

"Yes, Agent Powell?" he acknowledged one of the others.

"I think we should go ahead and start our surveillance on the bowling alley in East Point this weekend," the stout, Caucasian man insisted from the seat he'd stuffed himself into.

"That's not a question, Powell," North pointed out, prompting snickers from some of the others. "We'll start our surveillance on the bowling alley when *I* feel like it's time." He turned to me. "Your question, Bishop?"

"It's not a question," I assured, then went into what I discovered at the crime scene earlier, in reference to this particular investigation. "So," I resumed. "There could possibly be two funeral services packed with Drop Squad members this weekend."

North said, "I thought you mentioned there were four men murdered."

"Only two of them were possible Drop Squad members."

Agent North seemed to ponder my reply before responding. "I need you to find out the when and where of these services, so we can make a proper reconnaissance before the weekend hits. If they're both held at the same time, but at different locations, we'll split up into two units. The objective is to get as many photos of every member as possible. Then, we'll reconvene here to see if we can identify any of them."

My arm shot up again.

"Yes, Bishop?"

"I can get you the information," I told him. "But I won't be able to tag along, due to prior engagements."

Chapter 12

Saturday

Every week, I'm required to work for six days. Every other week, I have an option to take Saturday off, unless barred by the director, due to some kind of complication in a current case. Or, if I'm working a case that requires additional hours as with in or out-of-town tactical pursuits.

Well, this is my other week, and, lucky for me, I'm not on tactical duty, nor having complications with a case, though I'm not technically working on one at the moment. I'm also lucky that North didn't submit a request to Director Hopkins to have me accompany his team to one of the two funeral services that were being held at the same time, but at separate locations.

"You're up, B," Tyrone announced, after finishing up with another customer.

Getting to my feet, I shed my coat and hung it on the coat rack before taking a seat in Tyrone's chair while he disinfected his utensils. Despite the below-freezing temperature outside, it was comfortably warm inside the barbershop. I don't know why I hadn't taken off my coat the moment I entered, which was over thirty minutes ago.

Plus, the place was pretty much crowded, which was usual for a Saturday, being that this was a day most people found free time from their busy schedules. While people chatted amongst each other, *T.I.'s I'm Serious* album played at a respectable volume through the speakers of the shop's stereo system.

"What have you been up to, my friend?" Tyrone inquired, as he draped the barber's tarp over me.

"Not too much," I answered. "Just taking it one day at a time. What about you?"

"Just trying to keep the lights on," he said, searching for the right guard for his clippers. "You know how it is."

"Sure." I was wondering if he was subliminally reminding me of what he did outside of cutting hair. Or maybe not. "So, how's it going with the salon?"

Tyrone spun me around to face him, then planted a firm grip on my shoulder. "Word to the wise, never buy a business, and let your woman manage it."

"That bad, huh?"

"Is it!" He was slowly shaking his head. "Clarissa is actually parading around as if *she* bought the damn place!"

"Shit, what the hell did you expect?" asked Tank, one of the other barbers. "It's a woman's natural instinct to claim shit they don't have the money to buy."

"Amen to that!" Keith another barber pitched in garnering laughter from the other barbers and customers, even the women in attendance.

"What'd y'all scrubs got going on in this bitch?"

Tyrone was just spinning my chair around as one of their regular customers entered, clad in a black winter one-piece *trap suit* with matching skull cap and boots. All I knew about him is that his name was Steve, and he resided in Deerfield Apartments, which is where I'd grown up at. I only know that because he's here on most of my visits to the shop. Plus, he's extremely talkative.

"Scrubs!" Tyrone responded to Steve's question. "Man, you better sit your Fire Marshall Bill looking-ass down somewhere!"

"Nigga, you look like a retarded chihuahua!" Keith pitch in, aiding his co-worker.

"I know I'm not being double-teamed by Itchy and Scratchy," Steve shot back, taking a seat in the chair I had occupied. "What y'all need to do is get down with his movement I keep telling y'all about."

"Man, ain't nobody even heard of these niggas you're mascotting for," Keith told him.

"Just because *you* haven't heard of them," Steve went into defense mode. "That doesn't mean they're not known. The Kings are about to take this shit over. So, y'all need to drop them Detroit niggas and fuck with the home team."

The Kingz, huh? As Tyrone cut my hair, I pondered the group's title, while listening attentively to Steve, hoping he'd furnish me with a little more information about them, but he didn't. In fact, the conversation veered off into sports, then to some female from the area, who passed genital herpes on to two brothers she was cheating with.

I was still pondering what Steve had said on my drive to College Park. I've never heard of the group, so they were obviously new. Or maybe they weren't. Maybe they'd been in the drug game for some time and were now out to make a name for themselves, which is the biggest mistake any drug dealer can make.

Why? Because, they'll have imbeciles like Steve running around, mouthing off about them to anybody, in the presence of people they shouldn't be speaking like that in front of. People like me, of course. If I haven't learned anything since I've been on the force, I've learned that people like Steve always makes the best informants.

I swear Melody had to have been standing sentry at the window because, before I could find a spot to park, she was dashing from the apartment as if it was on fire, with her coat already buttoned up, and pink skull cap pulled over her head. All I could do was smile as I pulled the BMW in between two other cars and parked.

"Hey, Brian!" Melody exclaimed, climbing into the front passenger seat, closing the door back, and throwing her arms around me as I embraced her back.

"Hey, baby!" I gave her a peck on the cheek. "I assume you saw me pull up?"

"Yes," the now ten-year-old replied with her usual bashful smile.

"Momma said you called and told her that you were on the way. I was bored, so I was just looking out of the window."

"Bored, huh?" I was smiling back at her. "And what's taking that crazy woman so long?"

"I don't know," Melody answered with a shrug. "She was already ready when you called. Is Granddaddy, Dorian going with us?"

"No, baby," I answered her question that was in reference to my father. "He's not too big on parties, but we'll see him tomorrow."

"There's Momma!"

I looked to see Monique strutting towards the car in a white jean suit, white fur boots, and a white mini fur coat that was obviously faux, considering her income. Plus, she was carrying two gift bags with her pocketbook dangling from her shoulder, and a platinum blonde wig atop her head that was a little too much if you ask me, but hey, I am not complaining. Perhaps she has her neighbors under the impression that I'm a drug dealer.

As always, Melody sucked her teeth as she made the transition from the front to the rear seat, leaving the door open for her mother, whose perfume made its entrance before she did.

"Here, child!" Monique said, handing one of the gift bags to her daughter, after climbing in beside me. "You just ran out of the apartment and left you grandma's present on the living room table."

"I forgot, Momma."

"Yeah, I see that." Monique leaned over and kissed me in the mouth. "Did your daughter tell you about the gift swopping thing they're doing at her school?" she asked me.

"No, I didn't hear about that," I said, backing out of the parking spot. "Tell me about it, Mel."

"Next Friday," Melody went on to explain. "We have to pick names out of a hat. The girls have to pick a boy's name, and the boys have to pick a girl's name. Whoever's name we pick, we'll have to buy them a Christmas present, and bring it to school that following Monday."

I smiled. "That's cute! I didn't think they still did that."

"Y'all did that when you were in school?" she asked in amazement.

"Sure, we did, but everyone's names were thrown into one bucket altogether. I ended up picking another boy's name."

"What did you buy him?" Melody wanted to know.

"Nothing," I answered. "My mom wasn't working, and my dad didn't agree with buying a gift for another child when he could barely buy gifts for his own."

"So, what did you do?"

"I explained this to Tyler Beck," I told her. "And was grateful he accepted one of my old toys that were still in good shape. We were best friends from that day forth."

"Wow! Do you think I should take one of my old toys to school?"

"I wouldn't recommend it," I said with a chuckle.

"Why not?"

"Because, if the boy's name you pick isn't into dolls, he may take offense."

"If he *is* into dolls," Monique pitched in. "You two may become best friends forever."

"Monique!"

"I'm just saying," she offered with a smirk. "They're starting pretty young these days."

"I think you were dropped on your head when you were a baby," I said, causing them both to laugh.

Making it to Decatur, Georgia, I pulled up to Monique's mother's house and had to park further down the street for the amount of vehicles that were present, which I assumed belonged to friends and other family members of Gloria's who turned fifty on Wednesday but was celebrating today.

I ended up parking about six houses down from Gloria's, which did not sit well with me. I've never been a victim of car theft, and I hope like hell I didn't become one today, being that I wouldn't have a visual on my ride from Gloria's house.

The aroma of grilled meat greeted us the moment we exited the car, and we could hear rap music playing beyond the front door as we finally neared it. Plus, we could hear a vociferous Gloria yapping away about something incoherent.

"Momma's louder than the radio!" Monique discoursed as she rang the doorbell.

"I'm coming! I'm coming!" Gloria's voice sounded from somewhere inside the house, followed by the sound of heavy footfalls nearing. Then, the door swung abruptly open on its hinges. "Hey, y'all!" she shouted louder than necessary. "Come on in!"

Gloria had a red plastic cup in hand and didn't look any older than she did the last time we'd seen her, but she did look as though she'd put her all into her appearance, considering the brown curly wig, the excessive make-up, and orange lipstick that matched the sweater and snug-fitted jeans she was wearing. Not to mention the extremely long press-on nails on all ten of her fingers.

We all wished her a happy belated birthday as we entered, bestowing her with hugs and the two gift bags, in which she couldn't wait to dig into and marvel at the diamond tennis bracelet that Monique and I bought for her, and the Gucci perfume that Melody had picked out.

"Thanks, y'all!" the fifty-year-old woman cooed.

After collecting our coats to store away in her bedroom with those of the other guests, Gloria disappeared up the stairs, leaving us to mingle with the crowd that wasn't as large as I thought it would be. Melody cheerfully greeted one of her female cousins, and Monique set out to be the surrogate host until her mother returned.

Me? Well, I moved through the house, greeting the few people I was familiar with, though I was in search of Clyde, Gloria's current boyfriend ever since Rico just up and disappeared on her almost three months ago without a goodbye or a Dear Jane letter. It was like he completely fell off the face of the earth because I'd even tried locating him to no avail. It was almost like he was hiding from something or someone. Maybe I should look into all the crimes that were committed around the time he decided to get ghost.

"How's it going, my friend!" Clyde beamed, upon seeing me.

I was just about to enter the kitchen, where groups of people were standing around, drinking and conversating when the older man entered the back door in his overcoat and skull cap. He had to remove one of his gloves to shake my hand.

"I can't call it, Clyde," I responded, returning his greeting. "I see Gloria's got you on the grill."

"Yeah," he said, rolling his eyes. "Who else would she find to stand out in below-zero weather for her? But that's my baby, and it's her day. So, whatever makes her happy."

"That's love for ya'," I offered, smiling at the man who was three years younger than Monique's mother. "So, how did that interview go?"

"The same as the rest." He was slowly shaking his head from side to side. "They said they'll call me, but you know how that goes."

"Yeah."

Well, of course, I know how it goes. Clyde Leslie was released from prison earlier this year, after serving seven years for trafficking and probation violations. Yes, you know I did my own homework on the guy. He claims he's a *new man*, with no intention of going back to prison. I guess we'll see how that works out, huh?

Playa Ray

Chapter 13

Sunday

"Baby?"

I stirred and went into a full-body stretch before I was finally able to force my eyes open to see Monique standing over me with a plate of food in one hand, and a cup of coffee in the other. Her hair was still wrapped up in a scarf, and she was cloaked in her favorite blue robe with the cartoon character, *Betty Boop* on the breasts of it.

After leaving Gloria's house around six-thirty last night, we rode back to Monique's place, where I had already planned to spend the night. She, Melody, and I played Monopoly until Monique sent her daughter off to take her shower before bed. Once Melody retired to her bedroom for the night, Monique and I showered together, then snuck naked back to her bedroom, where we quietly made love for almost an hour, and pillow-talked until we dozed off

"Breakfast," she now announced, placing the cup on the nightstand, and waiting until I sat up before handing me the plate that consisted of grits, eggs, toast, and bacon strips. "I'll be back, baby."

"You have to wake Melody up?" I asked as she made for the door.

"Hell no! Her greedy ass was sitting at the kitchen table before I could cut the damn stove on!"

A mental picture of Melody sitting at the table with that adorable grin on her face, made me smile. By the time Monique made it back and sat beside me with her own plate, I had consumed a large portion of my meal, and half of my coffee.

"Now look at *your* greedy ass!" my girlfriend chided, seeing the damage I'd done. "Your daughter is already on her second plate. Do I need to refill yours before I start on mine?"

"No. I'm good, baby." I leaned over and kissed her on the jaw. "I was just hungry – don't be mad at me."

She regarded me with a seductive grin. Well, if you're still hungry, I got something you can nibble on."

All I could do was shake my head. "I'm not even going to entertain that, right now. Eat your food!"

"Yes sir, baby!" she remarked, laughing.

Of course, I was done with my meal before Monique was finished with hers, and was ready to take my shower, but Melody had beat me to the bathroom. When she was done, I quickly got in, though I wasn't in too much of a hurry to get out, considering I emerged thirty-something minutes later.

By this time, Monique was still in the kitchen, washing dishes, and Melody was holed up in her bedroom, doing God-knows-what. I have clothes hanging up in Monique's closet, so that's where I went to find something to put on. It seemed like the moment I stepped into a pair of jeans my cell phone vibrated atop the nightstand.

Being that this was my personal phone, which not that many people have the number to, I immediately crossed over to it and picked it up. The name and phone number on the screen usually show up once a month or every other month, but it's been almost three months since the last time I'd seen it.

"Hello?" I answered the phone.

"How are you, my son?" my mother's voice pierced the earpiece with little to no enthusiasm.

"I'm fine, Momma." Of course, my voice was analogous to hers. Hell, every time I talk to her, I find myself struggling to keep my true feelings in check. "How are you holding up?"

"I just had an operation on my foot," she replied. "But I'm okay for the most part. Are you and that girl still together? What was her name?"

"Monique," I answered, just as my girlfriend entered the room. "And, yes, we're still together."

"That's great!" Brenda Bishop offered blandly. "What about that little girl you're so crazy about? How's she doing?"

"Her name is Melody, Momma," I said, watching Monique as she gathered her things for her shower. "And they're both doing okay."

"That's good!" There was a pregnant pause before she finally asked, "How's your dad?"

"He's doing better than ever," I replied, hoping to give her the impression that he moved on, and is happy with someone else. "In fact, we're all going to see a movie, then having dinner at the Varsity, which is where he insists on going, claiming he hasn't been there since he was a teenager."

"He took me there on our first date," my mother informed. "That was our favorite restaurant until we started exploring others. So, what movie are you all watching?"

"We'll decide on one when we get there," I answered, now watching Monique leave the room. I sat on the edge of the bed.

She drew a breath. "Well, I don't wanna hold y'all up. I called to see how you're doing, and to share my good news with you."

"What good news?

"Joseph and I have been seeing a fertility doctor," she explained. "It took close to four months, but we finally made it happen."

"Made what happen?" I asked, knowing damn well what she was implying.

"I'm pregnant, Brian."

There it is! This lady is fifty-five years old and doesn't have anything better to do than to force pregnancy upon herself, which should've been one of the *thou-shalt-nots* in the Holy Bible. A fertility doctor, really? I've never questioned why I was the only child, but now I'm under the impression that my mother may have become sterile sometime after my birth. I mean, I'm quite sure they both had dreams of raising more than one child. Could that have been the reason for their split? Because my mother couldn't stand the fact that she couldn't bear my father any more offspring?

I pondered this from the moment I got off the phone with my mother. Hell, I was still pondering this on the drive to Marietta to pick my father up from the nursing home. I knew Monique and Melody wanted to go inside with me, but I asked them to stay in the car.

I figured my father would've been waiting in the lobby, but he wasn't. A male orderly informed me that he hadn't been down, then offered to call up to his room, but I declined, telling him that I would make the trip up, just in case he needed some assistance.

Getting off the elevator, I marched to my father's door and paused. For what? Why was I hesitating? Of course, I'm going to relay to him what my mother revealed to me. I mean, what kind of son would I be if I didn't? It's not like *she* was going to tell him. Hell, they don't talk to each other.

"It's open!" my father yelled from beyond the door, answering my knock.

Just like any other human being who found themselves being the barrel of bad news, I took a deep breath before turning the knob and pushing the door open. Just as I'd expected, my father was not alone. Also, as I expected, his *guest* was none other than the young, female orderly he's so fond of. He was already seated in his wheelchair, fully dressed, and she was perched on the edge of the bed, clearly holding us up.

"Hi, Brian!" the orderly greeted as if we were high school classmates, though she's a bit younger than me.

I only nodded in response.

"Brian, this is Carmen," my father introduced. "She helps me out a lot."

Yeah, I bet she does, I thought, but said, "Thanks, Carmen!"

"I'm just doing my job," she offered. "I guess I'll have to roll you down to the lobby, huh, Mr. Bishop?"

"I'll do it," I intervened, stopping her in her tracks. "I want to discuss something with him before we leave."

"Okay." She patted my father on the knee. "Well, you have a nice time, Mr. Bishop."

"I'll think about it," my father replied, making a face, then locked his eyes on her behind as she sauntered out of the room, giggling. Once she was gone, he turned to me with a glow in his eyes. "She's a wonderful person."

"Yeah, I'm quite sure," I said, taking her spot on the edge of the bed. I found myself drawing another breath before speaking again. "Mom called me earlier."

The old man groaned, turning his head in the other direction.

"She's pregnant," I plunged in, relieved to get it off my chest.

Well, that regained his attention. When my father slowly turned his head to face me, I studied his visage for any sign of hurt, but nothing registered. In fact, his facial expression never changed.

"Are you okay, Dad?" I asked after a while, remembering that Monique and Melody were still waiting outside in the car.

"Of course, I'm okay," Dorian Bishop insisted. "Now get your ass up and take me to this dinner and movie you promised me."

Playa Ray

Chapter 14

Monday

December 16, 2002

"Bishop, I don't give a rat's ass about some local crumb snatchers trying to make a name for themselves!" Director Manny Hopkins blurted out after I purveyed him with what little information I'd learned about the up and coming group known as the Kingz over the weekend.

"You just got out of the doghouse and you're already trying to find your way back. I didn't assign you to go chasing down petty drug dealers. You could've stayed on the police force for that shit! I assigned you to assist North and his team with the Drop Squad case."

"But—"

"No *buts*, Bishop!" he cut me off, banging his fist on the desk for emphasis. "I don't wanna hear another word about these cocksuckers! Now get the fuck out of my office before I write you up for insubordination, and have you recusing kittens out of trees for old, White women!"

I didn't know if I should take that as a racial statement or what, but I left that son of a bitch's office steaming, thinking of all those cases where employees ended up shooting up their workplaces for whatever reasons. Not saying that I was contemplating the act, but I pretty much had an idea of how those people must've felt beforehand.

However, as I said in the beginning, no one controls my emotions, but me. Yes, I want to smash Hopkins' teeth in or pay another co-worker to shoot the place up on my off day, but I have other plans. I'm going to investigate the Kingz anyway. So, if this local group does grow big enough to become a beacon on the FBI's radar, I'll have so much evidence against them, Hopkins will practically beg me to be the lead investigator on the case. I'll show his ass!

"It's nice of you to join us, Agent Bishop!" Agent North spoke when I entered the War Room on the fourth floor. "Please have a seat beside Agent Thomas. There's a criminal photo logbook awaiting you."

My notepad and pen were in my hand as I crossed the room under the stares of every pair of eyes in the room as if I was some kind of extraterrestrial or something. However, I took a seat beside Agent Rhonda Thomas, with who I'm familiar, being that her office is on the same floor as mine. She greeted me with a warm smile, in which I nodded my response before directing my attention back to North who was standing at the front of the room beside the projector screen that had a picture displayed on it by the overhead projector. He was giving me a look as if asking if I was settled in. I nodded.

"Mr. Bishop," North went on. "We're going over the photos taken at both funeral services this past Saturday to see if we can identify the Drop Squad members in attendance by referring to the criminal photo logbooks. Now, keep in mind, we've been investigating the group for a little over a year. So, we already have the four-one-one on some of these guys you're about to see. However, we'll fill you in as we go. He looked to the screen, then back out at the rest of us. "If I'm not mistaken," he said. "Somebody informed me that we already have the identifications of these two?"

"Yes sir," Powell spoke up. "These guys are Cecil Branch and Jamal London."

"Thank you, Agent Powell!" North said, then pressed a button on the remote he was holding to change the picture on the screen. "In this photo," he went on, "we have a visual of four men, with three sporting their gang emblem. Are there any familiars in this bunch?"

That's when I realized that the other agents had stacks of eight-by-ten photos in front of them, which they referred to first to see if they'd already I.D.'d any of these guys before turning to their photo logbooks. Shit, the logbook was all I had.

However, determined to make myself look busy like the others, I flipped the book open and reverted my attention back to the screen. As in the previous picture, the four men were being shown exiting the church at the conclusion of the service, trailing the casket along with the other attendees. Plus, they were all wearing black suits with their Drop Squad chains and medallions visibly on display, except for the third guy.

Not knowing which one to begin my search on, I studied each of their faces, looking for distinctive features that may avail me, when my eyes locked on the face of the one that wasn't sporting the chain and thought my eyes were playing tricks on me.

However, my eyes weren't doing such a thing. After all the time and energy, I put into searching for this piece of shit to no avail, these motherfuckers spot him on a fluke! All I can assume is that he joined Drop Squad, and ditched Gloria before I could find out and link him to whatever investigation the group's name may come up in, although he doesn't appear to have a consortium with them in this picture.

Perhaps he's still waiting for his chain to be issued to him. I mean, I don't think the leader just has those things lying around, ready to be passed out upon every initiation. Or maybe Rico was just a friend of someone at the funeral. Well, whichever one it was, I'm sure as hell going to find out. Right now, my first priority was the Kingz.

Chapter 15

Friday

I need to come up with a way to get taken off this Drop Squad investigation. Before I'd joined North and his team, they had already suspected one guy as being the leader of the notorious gang. Now, thanks to our mole, Special Agent Kent from Colorado it's been confirmed that the man they suspected, is only one of three leaders of the organization.

Trust me, it's an honor being a part of a big investigation such as this one, considering the commission it brings about, but it's interfering with my personal venture, which is the investigation of the Kingz. In just these past five days, I've managed to find out quite a lot about Steven Chambers the extremely talkative guy from the barbershop. I tapped his cellular and had been listening in on his many conversations, which is how I learned that a person by the name of James will be paying him a visit tomorrow.

Why am I so interested in this James person? Well, for one, Steve is worse than a female when it comes to chattering away on the phone about any and everything. However, when James called on yesterday the call lasted no more than two seconds.

All James said was, "I'ma come through Saturday," in an all-business tone, before hanging up, leaving Steve no room to respond.

Plus, right after the call, Steve called some other guy and bragged about soon being *the man* in the Deerfield projects. So, yes, I am highly interested in this guy.

"All eyes on!" Thomas' voice came through my earpiece, pulling me from my reverie.

She, Powell, and myself were assigned to monitoring the movements of Philip Lakes, one of the headmen of Drop Squad. At the age of thirty-four, Lakes was the owner of P.L.'s Limousine Service, and The Royal Suite hotel in Alpharetta, Georgia. On top of monitoring his calls, the three of us have been trailing him in three separate vehicles and staking out his home in shifts. Just last night, we ran eight-hour shifts outside his hotel, where he stayed the night with a fairly-young woman, though he has a wife and two children at home.

Being that Agent Powell was on post when Lakes left the hotel it was his duty to notify Thomas and I, so we could go ahead and set up on our usual, but separate posts. The vehicles loaned to us are from Motor Pool and could be swopped out at our leisure which is something I took full advantage of.

Yesterday, I was driving an immaculately restored seventy-nine Oldsmobile Cutlass. Today, I'm driving a two thousand and one Cadillac Escalade in which I had parked on the side of J.R. Crickets that sat right across the street from the limousine company owned by Philip Lakes. I couldn't see where Thomas was parked from my position, but I knew she was located a little further up the street in a faux Bell South phone company van that's equipped with the soundboard for listening in to Lakes' cellular and office phones.

"I have subject in sight," I said into the micro transmitter attached to the collar of my shirt upon spotting the burgundy Lexus Coupe approach and pull into the parking lot of the limousine company.

Grabbing my binoculars off the front passenger's seat, I zoomed in on the 5'11 man as he emerged from the car, clad in a black leather trench coat. I watched as he entered the establishment and made small talk with the White female receptionist behind the front desk before heading for his office with a stack of papers, she handed to him.

Now, this is where the fun stopped for me. I could see the whole inside of the building through its large, unobscured windows, but I could not see inside Lake's office for the Venetian blinds, in which he seemed to never have open. This is where Thomas comes into the picture. I'm the eyes, she's the ears. From this point on, she'll keep me informed of anything suspicious in his conversations, although everything he says will be recorded.

"The bird has nestled in his nest," I conveyed over the transmitter, before swopping my binoculars for my camera and adjusting the lens on the two men who were already there, washing and detailing the various models of limousines.

"Copy that," Thomas responded.

The only two vehicles in the J.R. Crickets' lot were the Escalade, and some beat-up Toyota I assumed belongs to the shift's manager, or owner, though I was parked on the side of the store. I didn't have the engine running, so it had gotten a bit nippy inside, but I know for sure I'm doing way better than these two, who were probably on the verge of freezing to death.

Click! Hell, a few more pictures of the two Drop Squad members won't hurt a thing. *Click! Click!*

While I was *bird watching*, the other drivers had begun pulling in. The employees of J.R. Crickets had also begun arriving for work which wasn't that many. They seemed to pay me no mind as I snapped away with my camera, though the windows were tinted, and I was parked several yards away from them.

North said that he was working on having a bug planted in Lake's office but, until then, Thomas, Powell, and I are going to have to improvise, which is why Thomas is the ears, I am the eyes, and Powell had retired to his home for eight hours, after following Lakes from the hotel this morning.

"I think we have something!" Thomas exclaimed through the earpiece.

"I'm listening." By this time, we'd been staked out for almost three hours, and I had been watching the traffic across the street through my binoculars again.

"A call just came in on Lakes' cellular," she informed breathlessly. "It's Williams. He's asking Lakes if he'd heard anything pertaining to the death of a person by the name of Rambo. A Luke is also mentioned." There was a long pause before she spoke again in a more hushed tone. "I think the price on someone's head just went up."

***

"Play it back from the beginning," said Agent North.

While still in the midst of staking out the limousine company, Agent Thomas placed a call to the lead investigator, informing him of the call that had garnered her undivided attention, which prompted North to call a meeting with the whole group, with the exception of one agent, who he'd sent to sit outside of Lake's home until we adjourn.

Right now, we were all in the War Room on the fourth floor, where we found out that we weren't the only ones with a discovery. It appeared that one group had captured images of Miles Whitley, one of the three leaders of Drop Squad, in an apparent drug interchange with a known drug dealer but couldn't verify the bandied items.

Once North went through the motions of strategizing a subsequent plan of action for that group, he turned to Thomas for her discovery, although the group he had on Kenny Williams had recorded the same call. Now, after rewinding the audio disc, Thomas pressed play for North and everybody else in attendance to hear the conversation for the second time.

Recorder:

Lakes: *"Talk to me!"*

Williams: *"How's it going, brother?"*

Lakes: *"Everything's well on my side. How 'bout yours?"*

Williams: *"No complaints this way. Have you heard anything on Rambo's murder?"*

Lakes: *"Nothing. And them niggas who did Luke haven't been found, either. In fact, I been thinking about raising the price."*

Williams: *"To what?"*

Lakes: *"Twenty thousand a head."*

Williams: *"So, are you still thinking, or is it official?"*

Lakes: *"It's definitely official."*

Williams: *"Cool. I'll make sure word gets out. Also, the new recruits got their chains yesterday."*

Lakes: *"Hell, it took long enough."*

Williams: *"Yeah, it did. Make sure you hit me up when you hear something."*

Lakes: *"Will do. Peace!"*

Williams: *"Peace!"*

Click!

"I sure as hell hope we know who this Rambo character is," said North, who was now standing with his arms folded over his chest.

"We do, sir," Special Agent Ross insisted. "His name is Marcus Henderson. We attended his funeral this past Saturday."

"We attended two funerals this past Saturday," North pointed out. "So, I assume Luke was the other deceased?"

No one spoke, probably because no one knew.

"His name was Luther Harris," I offered from the wall I was leaning against, gaining everyone's attention. "He was involved in a bank robbery I was investigating back in June, along with two other culprits. They made off with an undisclosed amount of cash. The two unknown suspects, apparently, murdered Harris and made off with his cut."

"Was Harris Drop Squad?" North wanted to know.

"Not according to my investigation," I answered. "But he has a cousin who is."

There was a pensive look on the lead investigator's face as he slowly nodded his head up and down. "That makes sense. Avenged by association. We have to keep our eyes and ears open on this one. I think these guys are about to take us on one hell of a ride."

***

Saturday

"Man, Crime Boss was the hardest nigga to come out in ninety-four!" Tyrone started as I was entering the barbershop. It was now 2002, eight years after the fact.

After leaving our meeting in the War Room yesterday, it was Rhonda Thomas' turn to stake out Lake's residence. However, we both came to an agreement that I'd take her shift, and she would stand in for me today. Hell, I thought it would be a peaceful night of me watching his home, but Lakes had a trick for me.

At 6:39 p.m., Philip Lakes left his home with his wife and two daughters in tow. I followed them from Riverdale, Georgia, to Buckhead, where they dined at Justin's for almost an hour, before migrating to Twin Lanes bowling alley in East Point. Miles Whitley who was the owner of the establishment was present, so I was able to spot the vehicle belonging to the agent assigned to follow him.

Making sure to park in a spot where I could see the interior of the place through its large windows, and not jeopardize the other agent's position. I grabbed my Nikon camera off the passenger seat and adjusted the lens with the intent to focus only on my target, who I saw confabbing with Whitley. Moments later, Lakes and his family were engaged in a bowling competition with Whitley, his wife, and their three children, while I snapped only a few shots. Around 10:37 p.m., I followed the Lakes' back to their abode, where everything was peaceful for the remainder of the night.

Now, while the barbers and some of the awaiting customers carried on with their debate, I copped the last unoccupied chair, making sure to shed my coat before sitting. I don't think anybody even noticed me – not even Tyrone. However, that really didn't matter, because I was there for one reason. Well, two reasons. I was after Steve to find out who this James character is, and I also wanted my hair cut which is why I came earlier than I usually would. At this time, 11:22 a.m. to be exact – Steve is not present. Therefore I'm hoping Tyrone would get me in and out before he arrives *if* he arrives.

"Yeah, I'll give you that," Tank now responded to Tyrone's assertion. "But he wasn't the hardest nigga to come up out of Suave House."

"Bullshit!" Tyrone spat. "Who was harder than Crime Boss? Eight Ball?"

"Tella, nigga!" Tank expressed, sparking laughter from those who disagreed.

"Ain't no way in hell you just said that clown ass shit!" Tyrone shot back. "You couldn't have been a Suave House fan! Nigga, Yella Bone went way harder than Tela!"

"Who the fuck is Yella Bone?" Tank inquired.

Tyrone answered, "Some bitch Crime Boss had on his album."

"Shit, I think South Circle was the hardest in the camp," one of the awaiting customers chimed in.

130

"South Circle wasn't even a factor back then," Tyrone maintained. "I think those niggas were the first on Suave House's roster, before Eight Ball and MJG took the crown, but Crime Boss was a stone-cold beast on the mic!"

This debate went from who was the best lyricist of the nineties, to the best athlete of all times. Hell, even I offered my two cents from time to time. Especially when someone mentioned Michael Jordan and tried to belittle his talents. I entered the barbershop at 11:22 a.m. and exited at 12:12 p.m., relieved that Steve had not shown up.

However, upon exiting the shop, I stopped to gander up and down the road to see if I could spot my target, who could possibly be on his way in, but there were too many people moving about to do so. Therefore, I moved toward the black '91 Lincoln Town car supplied to me by the department. After allowing the engine to warm up, I pulled out of the lot and drove several yards down before entering Deerfield Apartments, making sure to park where I could see Steven Chambers' apartment through the rear window that was tinted as the others, with the exception of the windshield.

Wait, I'm sensing that you're lost. You're probably wondering how I got all this information on Chambers. Well, I could easily say because I'm FBI, and leave it at that, right? Sure, I can, but that would be a snobbish remark.

However, I accessed Chambers' criminal record and found that he was thirty years old, and had recently been placed on probation for battery, whereas he assailed his son's mother for whatever reason. The victim's phone number was the only number in his file, so I jotted it down, and when I found the time, I made a trip to our department's basement, where a lot of broken and outdated equipment was kept.

My intention was to tap the victim's phone in order to get Chambers' number, so the device I was searching for was there. I found one that was outdated, but it worked, so I took it home. There's no need to ask. Yes, I stole the motherfucker! Hell, I had to steal the manual also, because I didn't know a damn think about operating it. That's what the technicians are for.

Now, after watching Chambers' apartment for more than twenty minutes, and seeing no sign of him, I heard loud music, and immediately spotted the vehicle it was coming from. The four-door BMW was purple with chrome wheels and tinted windows, but what stood out to me about the car was the golden emblem on the front-end of it. I only caught a glimpse of it as the car cruised by, but I could tell it wasn't BMW's signature.

My neck had started to cramp again from how I was turned in my seat to survey the area, so I began massaging and rotating it in order to assuage some of the pain while keeping an eye on Chambers' apartment. I just hate the fact that I don't know the exact time James would arrive, which could very well be a late night when most drug dealers conduct business. It was bad enough I didn't get more than five hours of sleep after staking out Lakes' residence last night. Plus, I have the same assignment tonight, being that I'd taken Thomas' shift last night in exchange for her to take my shift today with doing surveillance alongside Powell.

A figure moving in the direction of Chambers' unit, caught my attention. The Black male, who was clad in dark blue jeans and a black sweater, stood at about six feet, and one hundred and ninety pounds. Plus, he was wearing a thick gold chain around his neck, though I couldn't see if it contained any kind of pendant, being that his back was to me.

Of course, this guy was headed for Chambers' place, because Chambers had the front door open before the man was even close enough to knock on it. Once he entered, and Chambers closed the door back, I drew the conclusion that he was the occupant of the BMW that just pulled in. Looking in the direction it had gone, I saw the top of it and estimated that it was parked about four cars away from mine.

After surveying the area to make sure there were no other prying eyes, I stepped out of the car and pretended to stretch, while doing another survey. Seeing that it appeared I wasn't being watched, I moved in the direction of the BMW. Immediately upon passing the rear of it, I stopped and made a show of patting my pockets like I may have forgotten something. You know, for the sake of whoever may be paying me some attention.

Turning on my heels, I was gandering at the license plate when the emblem on the trunk caught my attention. It was a golden crown that had replaced the BMW's emblem. The same crown I'd seen on the front end of the car. Ha! What a better way to proclaim the title of a king, than by driving around with such a royal symbol plastered all over your vehicle?

Returning to the Lincoln, I retrieved my cellular and dialed the number to the Information Center of the James P. Russell building, wondering how could James be dropping off drugs to Chambers, when he had nothing in his hands that suggested anything of the sort. However, this meant nothing. Perhaps he was only supplying Chambers with a very small quantity that could very well fit inside his pants pocket.

"Information Center!" Hoffman's voice boomed through the earpiece.

"Chad, it's Bishop," I spoke fast as if trying to keep him from hanging up. "Are you busy?"

"Hell, I'm always busy," he responded. "It also sounds like *you're* busy. Are you running from someone? It sounds like you're almost out of breath. I mean, I pray to the High Heavens you're not calling me while you're in the middle of doing the nasty!"

I laughed. "Very funny! I need you to run a license plate for me."

"I'm all ears."

I ran the characters down to him from memory. "Can you do it while I'm on the phone?" I asked, looking out the rear window to make sure no one was exiting Chambers' apartment.

"It's a two thousand and one BMW belonging to a James Young," Chad announced to my surprise. "Do you want the address?"

"Yes sir."

After jotting down the address, I thanked my friend, then hung up the phone with a huge smirk on my face. I got the son of a bitch! Hell, this shit was easier than I thought it'd be – well, thanks to

Chambers. As I said, people like him make great informants, intentionally or unintentionally.

Just then, Chambers' apartment door came open. My camera was in my grasp and aimed in their direction before he and James Young could fully exit the apartment, in which they stopped and stood in front of to converse.

Click! Click! The medallion hanging from his chain was another sure sign that this guy's serious about becoming notoriety in the drug game as it read *KINGZ* and was adorned with diamonds.

The two didn't stand there long. They bumped fists, then Young set off to his car. I thought Chambers would step back inside, but he stood there and watched as James drove away. If I'm not reading it wrong, it appeared as though he was marveling at the BMW, hoping he'd someday stack up enough coins to buy one for himself.

"Come on, prick," I urged, still watching Chambers. "Take your ass back inside!"

As if hearing me, Chambers turned and re-entered his apartment, closing the door behind him. I quickly switched on the ignition and backed the Lincoln out of its spot. I didn't know which way Young had gone, so when I approached the entrance of the apartments, I swiveled my head back and forth, looking up and down Campbellton Road, trying to see if I could spot a glimpse of the conspicuous color.

Bingo! To the left of me, the BMW had already gone about a quarter of a mile down the road. Initiating my left turn signal, I moved out onto Campbellton, making sure to stay as far back as possible, while keeping Young in sight, because, another thing I'd learned during my time on the force is that most criminals are naturally paranoid. They spend more time watching their backs more than they do their fronts. My awareness of this has availed me many times when I was surveilling a target, and I pray to God it won't fail me now.

However, I ended up trailing him to a house out in Summer Hill, whereas I parked in front of a house much further from the one he was visiting. My camera was out, and the lens was already focused by the time Young had made it to the door and knocked

Click!

Moments later, the door came open, but I couldn't see who was on the other side from the angle I was positioned. However, I did see the small brown paper bag Young had in his hand before entering. *Click! Click!*

I'm already assuming he's making a drop to another one of his workers. Though I care nothing for the underlings, I still jotted down the address. Hell, whenever I build a solid case against the Kingz perhaps I could use their workers to testify against them in trial, which is what the FBI has been doing for centuries.

Again, Young did not stay long. No longer carrying the package, he made for his car, looking around as if for potential danger, with one hand stuffed into his pants pocket. Yes, the local authorities would have a field day arresting him for the gun he's presumably clutching, which is something we at the bureau consider petty. I've witnessed arms dealers sell truckloads of guns to people, but didn't make a move on them, being that they weren't the original targets.

Now, at 1:31 p.m., I was once again trailing my target along the highway, which was a bit relieving, because I was provided more cover from the congestion of vehicles traveling the multi-lane public road. Besides keeping James Young in sight, I found myself struggling to keep my eyes open, which was a reminder of my lack of sleep, and the many hours of unrest I have ahead of me. It's not the Drop Squad case, and the time and energy I'm putting into it, because I'm used to that. It's just the fact that I'm currently working two cases, which requires a little more extra time and energy. Therefore, I need one of the cases off of my schedule. I just have to find a way to make that happen.

Seeing Young take the Martin Luther King Jr. exit, gave me the impression that he was headed home, which had me wondering if I should continue following him, being that I already have his address. Although I was anxious to see his dwellings, I relinquished my pursuit for the moment, dialing Agent Powell's number on my cellular as I drove past the exit.

***

It was a little after 7:00 p.m. when I was finally able to relieve Powell and Thomas who informed me that Lakes had not left his home all day. They also informed me that Agent North now wants us conducting twelve-hour shifts, with only one agent on post. Well, Powell had told me this over the phone.

After trading the Town car in for a burgundy Mercedes-Benz coupe, I had enough time to share a pizza with Monique and Melody, being that North's new twelve-hour shift rule went into effect today. Hell, I even had enough time to casually drive past James Young's house to see that his car wasn't there.

Now, parked several houses down from Lakes' home, I toyed with the listening device the bureau had set up at North's request, wondering if it worked, because there were no incoming, or outgoing calls on Lakes' cellular since I'd been on post. I mean, I'm quite sure he has more than one mobile phone, but this particular device had been buzzing like a beehive from the moment we've tuned in. I'm not the smartest man in the world, but I think he's on to us, or maybe not. I just can't think of any other reason why he hasn't been outside his home anytime today and why his cell phone seems to be deactivated all of a sudden.

Even if it was their anniversary, and he and his wife made plans to spend it together alone, they would have at least gotten rid of the children but, according to Thomas and Powell. The children had not ventured outside the house any time today, either. This can't be blamed on the weather. It's not like it's below zero. Even if it was people would still be out doing their last-minute Christmas shopping considering we only have three more days before the big day.

I yawned for the umpteenth time today, which was only a constant reminder that I need a whole week of rest. My eyelids were extremely heavy. Trying to figure out what Lakes had going on made them even heavier. Plus, the dazzle of the Christmas lights that decorated most of the homes on the street didn't make the situation any better whereas they seemed to be slowly lulling me into La-La Land."

Chapter 16

Tap! Tap! Tap!

I don't know why, but for some strange reason, my back was hurting like hell. On top of that, my neck had a crook in it, and my legs felt like they were on the verge of cramping. My bed has always been soft, and extremely comfortable, but right now, it was anything other than. If that wasn't enough, it felt as though I had forgotten to turn the heat on because it was freezing.

Tap! Tap! Tap!

There's that tapping noise again but it couldn't be coming from the front door considering the distance between it and my bedroom. Besides, this seemed a lot closer and the material being tapped on sounded like glass. Wait a minute! *Glass?* As in my bedroom window's glass? No way! The only way a person would be anywhere near my window is if they were standing on a scaffold or a lengthy ladder. Either way, they're in violation and well inside the guidelines of the Amendment that gives me the right to use a firearm against any violator of my home. Okay, I got the Amendment all misconstrued. Anyway, it's time I escape the darkness provided by the backs of my heavy eyelids, so I can make some sense of what's going on around me. Well, here goes.

Oh shit! This was one of those times I'd rather face one of the many nightmares I'd forced myself awake to escape. Realizing I wasn't lying in my bed, was bad but it wasn't the worst of it. No, sir. The worst of it was realizing that I was still seated in the Mercedes Benz Coupe a few houses up from Lakes' home and I allowed myself to get caught sleeping on the job.

This is also one of those times I wish I could disappear or turn back the hands of time. Well, since I don't possess those powers I had no choice but to face the music. Turning the ignition to start the car, I press the button to roll the window down, inviting the morning air in to mingle with the cold air that already permeated the interior of the car.

"You weren't answering your phone," Special Agent Powell asserted. He looked like he'd been out jogging, whereas he was clad in a gray sweatsuit, tennis shoes, and a gray skull cap. A disguise, of course. "Thomas and I didn't know what to make of it," he continued. "So, we notified North. He told me to check by here first and to report back to him."

"And I assume you'll tell him you found me asleep," I accused figuring he's more susceptible to be North's golden retriever than Thomas would.

"I think that would be snitching," he pointed out, to my surprise. Plus, he didn't sound offended. "Hell, you're lucky he sent me and not Thomas."

I had no response to that. Instead, I toyed with the knob that operated the heat component, turning it up a notch.

Powell cleared his throat, and looked both ways before continuing, "Anyway, North's called an emergency meeting. Apparently, something's come up."

I now regarded the green-eyed, Caucasian agent. "What was it?" I asked.

"He wouldn't say," Powell offered, with a shrug of his shoulders. "Really, the tone of his voice led me to believe something's come up. However, he wants everyone present in the War Room, like yesterday! I'll see you there."

"Wait!" I stopped Powell in his tracks as he looked as though he was about to break into a run, obviously to maintain his facade. "You still have to report your findings to North. I mean, he's gonna want to know why I haven't been answering my phone."

"Didn't you accidentally cut it off?"

I furrowed my eyebrows in confusion. "I've never accidentally cut my phone off. I don't even think that's—" I stopped mid-sentence when I recognized the look he was giving me. Realizing what it meant, I retrieved my cellular from the cupholder and shut it off. Then, I looked back up at my co-worker. "You know what? I think I did accidentally cut it off."

"Then I guess he'll just have to live with that," Powell said with the wink of an eye before jogging on up the street.

As I rolled the window back up and powered my phone back on, I found myself feeling bad about how I misjudged Special Agent Powell. I know my reference of him being a snitch didn't sit too well with him, but he did a fantastic job of not letting it show. We've spoken to each other on several occasions and held numerous inconsequential conversations over the years but have never gotten the chance to know each other personally. I just hope my little comment didn't dampen my chance of befriending Powell because I now had a strong feeling that he would someday be an asset.

***

Despite how urgent Powell expressed the meeting was, I didn't plan on making it without freshening up. Therefore, I drove back to my place, where I showered, shaved, and put on a fresh suit. See, I'm supposed to have the whole day off, being that Thomas and Powell will each be conducting their twelve-hour shifts today and you already know how my Sundays are spent.

However, it was only 9:17 a.m. when I exited my home, and I didn't plan on picking Monique and Melody up until eleven. So, as of now, it would be safe to say I have enough time, though it would greatly depend on North and this emergency meeting he'd called.

"Hello?" I answered my cell phone. At this time, I was driving the Mercedes along I-285.

"Hey, my son!" Dorian Bishop's voice penetrated my ear with a hint of excitement.

"How are you, Dad?"

"I'm fine," he answered, then cleared his throat. "What time do you think you'll get here?"

"Close to twelve," I told him. "Why?"

He was silent a moment before asserting, "I want to talk to you about something. You know, out of the presence of the girls."

Now, it was my turn to be quiet for a moment while my mind automatically conjured up a million and one possible scenarios of what my father wanted to talk to me about. "Yeah, sure," I finally answered slowly. "I'll meet you in your room before we head out."

"That'll work," my father said, then hung up.

Damn! If it's not one meeting, it's another. It's bad enough I was already racking my brains trying to figure out what North's meeting could possibly be about. Now, my father has planted his own seed of confusion. I think this is too much for a person with an empty stomach, though, I don't think I can bring myself to eat anything. If it wasn't for the fact that I'd driven home instead of heading straight for the James P. Russell building, and knowing North was undoubtedly going to chew my ass out for being late, I would stop for a cup of coffee. Hell, I already had to make one stop, which was at the motor pool to swap the Mercedes back out for my BMW.

It had taken longer than expected at the motor pool, being that they don't operate with a full staff on Sundays, so it was 10:12 a.m. when I finally walked into the War Room, where it seemed that all of the assigned agents were present, with the exception of myself. Even Powell was there, looking refreshed and dapper in a smoke-gray suit, with his jet-black hair oiled and slicked to the back. They were all seated at tables with cups of coffee in front of them, which made me a bit sore that I didn't stop for any.

"I'm glad you could finally join us, Special Agent Bishop." Agent North stood from the chair he was seated in at one table, then slowly strolled in my direction. "I'm sorry to hear about your accident. You know, how you *accidentally* deactivated your cell phone."

There was snickering amongst the other agents but I said nothing as the agent in charge stopped in front of me.

"I guess something like that could happen to Albert Einstein, huh?" he went on, sparking more snickering, as he now moved toward the projector, switching it on. "We've wasted enough time already. If you would have a seat, Mr. Bishop. We can go ahead and get started."

Without a word, I crossed the room under the stares of everybody present and claimed the seat North had occupied, being that it was the only one available. The aroma of various flavors of roasted coffee beans was eminent in this area, even from the cup that sat in front of me in which I'm sure belonged to my predecessor. Talk about torture!

"Special Agent Bishop," North said after I was settled. "You were teamed up with Special Agent Thomas, and Special Agent Powell to conduct surveillance on a subject by the name of Philip Lakes, correct?"

"That's correct," I answered, feeling like I was standing trial at this very moment.

"Were you stationed outside his home last night?"

"Yes, I was."

North's eyebrows went up in anticipation. "Do you have anything to report?"

"There was no movement at the Lakes residence," I offered. "According to my colleagues, Lakes had not ventured outside his home at any time that day. My reportage is the same as theirs. Also, Lakes never received nor made any calls on the cellular we have a tap on."

"And how sure are you that Lakes never left his home last night?"

"Very sure," I answered, still feeling like I was on a witness stand, though I was starting to get the impression that North had a point he was trying to drive home.

"Okay," the agent in charge said, pulling the remote to the projector from his pants pocket and pressing a button on it.

The picture that showed up on the screen didn't spark my interest as it contained an image of the front of some restaurant, I couldn't see the name of. However, I did notice the date and time at the bottom of the photo which was 12-21-02/21:17, which was last night during the course of the time I was on post.

"This picture was taken last night by Special Agent Ross," North informed in his all-business tone. "According to his reportage, Ross had trailed his target, Kenny Williams, out to Clayton County to this very restaurant."

North pressed the button again bringing another picture onto the screen. This particular photo showed a side-view of Kenny

Williams in a large fur coat approaching the entrance of the restaurant flanked by two other men, who were dressed in street attire.

"This is the subject Williams entering the establishment," North went on with his narrative.

When he pressed the button again, I almost shit bricks! On top of blinking my eyes over a dozen times, I checked and re-checked the date at the bottom of the photo, hoping like hell the date differed from that of the other two. It didn't, I was actually seeing Philip Lakes entering this restaurant in Clayton County at the same time I was parked outside his home in Riverdale. Well, there's no need for me to ask myself how is this possible because I know North is just dying to rub my nose in this shit.

"Any idea as to who this guy is, Mr. Bishop?" North posed locking eyes with me from across the room.

My jaws were set. At this time, I didn't think it was anyway possible for me to open my mouth without telling this son of a bitch what part of my body he could wrap his lips around.

"What about you, Mr. Ross?" the agent in charge redirected his attention. "You're the photographer, here. Can you tell me who this person is?"

"That would be Philip Lakes, sir," Ross answered like the true ass kisser I'm getting to know him as. "He's one of the three head figures of the gang known as Drop Squad."

"Thank you, Agent Ross." North directed his attention back to me. "Agent Bishop, do you concur with the delineation of your colleague?"

"Yeah," I answered through clenched teeth, consciously aware that everyone in the room was watching to see how I would weather this storm.

"Any idea how Mr. Lakes managed to slip by you in order to make his meeting with Mr. Williams in Clayton County?"

"Nope," I answered, knowing damn well the cocksucker slipped by me because I'd fallen asleep while watching his residence.

Special Agent North drew a breath before continuing. "Special Agent Bishop, at this time, I have no choice but to drop you from this investigation. A report of this matter will be on Mr. Hopkins' desk tomorrow morning, so you can check in with him once you get in. You are dismissed."

Hell, that didn't go as bad as I thought it would. I mean, I wasn't expecting a public hanging, but I at least thought he would get hostile enough for me to knock his teeth down his throat. Perhaps he was leaving the theatricals to Manny Hopkins knowing he was going to tear me a new asshole, and probably have me doing miscellaneous details again.

However, with my dignity still intact, I raised from my chair and strutted out of the room as if I had not a care in the world, even though tomorrow had its own fruits to bear. It was no reason to get all jittery, though. I'll just have to deal with the director when the time comes. Until then, I had a ritual to keep to.

Despite how I was feeling, I found myself smiling when Monique and Melody emerged from the apartment together, which was a historic Kodak moment. Ever since I'd known Monique, she'd never been prompt. Maybe she was trying to be a *good girl* being that Christmas was a few days away. Yeah, right!

"Hey, Brian!" Melody beamed, climbing into the back seat as her mother gathered in beside me.

"Hey, sweetheart!" I responded, looking back at her. "I see you're wrapped up like a Christmas present back there."

"Momma made me wear this scarf," the now ten-year-old pointed out, turning her nose up. "It smells like old people!"

"And how do old people smell?" I inquired, backing out of my parking spot.

She shrugged her shoulders up and down. "I don't know. It doesn't smell like any of my friends or classmates."

All I could do was laugh.

"I don't care if it smells like *dead* people," said Monique, who wasn't at all amused. "You're gonna wear it! And just for that not-so-funny comment, I ought to make you wear it to school. That way, you'll be the only ten-year-old smelling like an eighty-year-old."

"I think that would be cruelty to children," I pitched in.

My girlfriend regarded me with furrow eyebrows. "Oh, I have another one," she informed. "I can make you wear that one to work."

"Yeah," I responded. "That'll be like trying to get a frog to walk on two legs."

Melody was laughing now.

"Whatever!" Monique expressed, punching me in the arm. "So, how's the investigation going?"

"It's going," I said, knowing she was referring to the Drop Squad case I was just dropped from.

"You've been real vague about your cases lately," she accused. "You know how much we love your stories."

"Yeah, we miss your stories," Melody added.

"Oh, and Melody told me about another gift she wants for Christmas."

"Another one?" I looked into the rearview mirror to see her with that shy grin on her face.

"Don't be acting all shy, Mel!" Monique pressed. "Tell him what you told me last night!"

"You know better than to act shy with me," I encouraged the young girl. "Let me hear it!"

"I, um," she hesitated. "I want you to adopt me as your daughter."

"You're already my daughter."

"She wants you to do it the legal way," Monique pointed out.

"I'm aware of that, Monique," I said. "But we'll have to make the proper arrangements."

"We can do it whenever you're ready," she replied.

Melody was ecstatic about this Christmas gift, although it probably won't be official until February. Not only would this be a special gift to her, but it would be a special gift to me also because I want it officialized just as bad as she does. Who knows? Maybe this would spawn a marriage between Monique and I, *maybe*.

Making it to Marietta, Georgia I parked in the parking lot of the assistant living facility and asked the girls to remain in the car, then entered the building. After signing in at the front desk, I got onto the elevator, and was on my way to my father's unit, still feeling exuberant about Melody's request. I just hope I was still in good spirits after hearing what Dorian Bishop had to say.

"Come on in, Brian," my father answered my knock.

I entered and was surprised to see that he was seated in his wheelchair, fully dressed. I was even more surprised to see that he was alone because I had a strong feeling Carmen the young orderly who appears to be his personal assistant would be present. However, she wasn't present, but the scent of her perfume was, which accounted for him being ready, and the place being squeaky clean.

"Have a seat, son," my father said, regarding me through his famous sunglasses. "This won't take long."

Closing the door, I crossed the room and reluctantly sat on the edge of the neatly-made bed, looking at my dad, who was parked in the middle of the room that resembled those of the many hotels I'd visited. He seemed to study me for an eon before taking a deep breath.

"Carmen is pregnant."

"By who?" The words left my mouth so fast for a second it seemed like someone else had said them.

"What the hell do you mean *by who*?" Dorian Bishop took offense with a scowl on his face. "Who else would she be pregnant by?"

"I apologize, Dad," I offered, trying to assuage some of the hostility, and make sure not to ruin our outing before it even starts. "I didn't mean—"

"I know what you meant, Brian," he cut me off. "I know you don't know much about her, but Carmen's a good woman. No, I don't know for sure if the child is mine, but I truly don't believe in my heart that she would tell me it is when it isn't"

What a fucking coincidence! Just a week ago, my mother called and informed me that she's having a baby. Now, my father just revealed that *he's* having a baby. Well, not him, but this young orderly he'd obviously been pitching woo with for God-knows-how long. What kind of parents are they? Neither one of them had the decency to consult with me before doing something that people over fifty shouldn't be thinking about doing. I mean, I'm quite sure I'm too old to be the big brother of some snotty-nosed, diaper-wearing siblings, right?

"Also," he resumed. "I'll be moving in with her in a couple of weeks. We're making it official between us."

Chapter 17

Monday

December 23, 2002

It was 7:49 a.m. when I pulled into the parking garage of the James P. Russell building. After parking, I thought about sitting in my car a little while longer to prolong the inevitable, but I knew it was only foolish thinking. Therefore, I killed the engine, grabbed my phone and briefcase, then dismounted.

The bottoms of my shoes click-clacked on the concrete as I made for the entrance. I was so caught up on wondering how it was going to go with Hopkins, I didn't pay any attention to the figure climbing from the gray Ford Mustang 5.0 I'd just passed, until he called out my name, causing me to stop in my tracks. I turned to see Special Agent Powell approaching with a book bag slung over his shoulder.

"Are you okay?" he asked, stopping in front of me.

I only nodded, feeling a bit leery of this encounter.

"Look, man," he went on. "I had not the slightest idea about the meeting between Lakes and Williams. Like I said, North called me about the meeting, but gave no details as to what it was about."

"It's cool," I finally spoke. "I appreciate you for sticking up for me."

"Hey," Powell said, with a shrug of his shoulders. "What's the use being part of something if you're not going to stick up for one another?"

"Touché!" I offered. "So, what was the meeting really about? I'm quite sure North didn't gather everyone together, just to witness my fall from grace."

"Definitely not," he responded with a smirk. "The meeting was mainly about what actually transpired at the restaurant in Clayton County that night."

"Which was?"

"Williams ordered for one of their men to be murdered and dis-membered right on the spot."

"In front of customers?"

"No," answered Powell. "Everything took place in a secluded area at the back of the restaurant."

"And how the hell did Ross manage to see all of this from the parking lot?" I asked, incredulous.

"Kent was there."

"The mole?" I inquired of the agent from the Denver branch, who'd infiltrated Drop Squad.

"We saw pictures of him showing up to the restaurant with four other members of the group," Powell told me. "According to Kent, one of the men he'd shown up with had been coming up short with the money from the product he'd been pushing for the organization, but Kent didn't know any of this until they showed that night. As it went, Williams confronted the kid, had one of the other members shoot him dead, then ordered the butcher to knife him, and seal him inside some kind of cannister. Kent and the other three subordinates were responsible for disposing of the body."

"Does Kent remember where they dumped it?" I asked, thinking of a mobster movie I'd recently seen, where someone was butchered and canned in the same fashion.

"I'm quite sure he does."

"And what does North plan on doing about it?"

"He's gonna give it a week," said Powell. "Then anonymously tip off the locals. That way, no one would become suspicious of Kent."

I was nodding my head up and down. "That's clever."

"In the meantime," Powell went on. "He's discontinued our intelligence operations until further notice."

"He didn't say why?"

"Nope."

"I think they know they're being watched," I finally said aloud.

Powell looked off in a distance, as if in deep thought. Seconds later, he drew a breath and said, "Thomas feels the same way."

"What about you?" I posed. "How do *you* feel about it?"

"I've always felt like they knew," he responded. "A blind man can see that these guys are smart. Especially Williams and Lakes.

They've been doing it too long to not know if they're being watched, or to not have someone watching their backs." He turned to face me. "I think North knows this also, which is why he's pulled us back."

I thought about this as Powell and I entered the building and made for the elevators. It felt good to know that someone else shared my notion about the head members of Drop Squad. Maybe they didn't know who – as in which government agency – was watching them, or if they were being targeted by rivals or robbers, but I'll wager anything that they knew they were moving under the watchful eyes of someone.

However, that's no longer my concern, being that I was removed from the investigation, but if Powell finds himself needing my assistance, I definitely won't hesitate to provide it. I just hope I don't have to tell him that.

Powell nodded at me before getting off the elevator on the fourth floor, and I continued to the sixth knowing that we have an unspoken bond between the two of us. Being that Manny Hopkins didn't usually get in until after eight-thirty, I stopped by my office that I share with my partner, Paul Rucker. First, to deposit my briefcase and shed my coat. Then, I grabbed my thermos and made for the breakroom that was as deserted as the hallways and my office.

It seemed like I was the only one to show up to work, although I knew it wasn't true being that a fresh pot of coffee was brewing, and a box of pastries sat atop the counter which indicated that Mrs. Joseph had already made her morning rounds before settling at her cubicle to begin her secretarial duties. It also seemed like she'd added a few more ornaments to the room, when just three weeks ago, there only sat a miniature Christmas tree atop the counter, adorned with colorful lights, candy canes, and small, fake gift-wrapped presents under it. Now, the place was festive of the nearing holiday, but the most talked about item amongst the staff was the mistletoe that hung over the entrance which flaunted Mrs. Joseph's sense of humor. Hell, the shit also made me feel awkward whenever another man was in the vicinity which is why I filled my thermos, grabbed a jelly-filled doughnut, and got the fuck up out of there before someone else arrived.

Back inside my office, I powered my computer up, then took a bite of my doughnut while waiting for the dinosaur to roar to life. Strawberry gelatin. My favorite! I took a couple of small sips of the hot beverage to wash it down. The moment I sat my thermos down, Paul Rucker entered the office with his tote bag over his shoulder, and his coat draped over his arm.

"Good morning," my partner greeted, upon closing the door back and crossing over to his own desk.

"Morning," I responded, typing my password into my computer, seeing that it was ready to do my bidding.

"I hardly see you since you've been working with North and his team," Rucker mentioned. "How's that going?"

"I'm no longer working with them," I admitted. Hell, there was no use in lying, he was going to find out eventually. "I screwed up. North kicked me off the investigation."

"Damn," he expressed, moving toward the door with his thermos. "I gotta hear this, but after I get my morning wake up."

In seconds he was gone. I don't mind telling him what happened, but I'm not really in the mood to talk about it at the moment. It's not like I'm seething about being dropped from the case, because it really worked in my favor. I now have time to work on the Kingz investigation, which is why I was now typing in the name I've been waiting to type in all weekend.

Of course, about a dozen James Youngs popped up on my screen, but I already knew which one I was looking for. Using the scroll button, I scrolled down until I saw him staring back at me from one of his mugshots.

"Let's see what you've been up to, Mr. Young," I said, clicking on his file to view his criminal history.

Well, I wasn't at all surprised to see that he'd been in and out of the Juvenile Detention Center ever since he was ten years old, for charges ranging from vandalism to aggravated assault. His adult criminal record consisted of guns, drugs, and more aggravated assaults. In fact, according to the file, he was currently out on bond for possession of cocaine, possession of a firearm, and – yes, you've guessed it – aggravated assault.

I had begun reading the summary of the recent assault case when Rucker re-entered the office which was at the same time my desk phone started ringing. Though my partner was preoccupied with his cup of coffee, and whatever flavor of doughnut he'd chosen, as he made for his desk, I still put my computer in sleep mode before pulling the phone's receiver from its cradle.

"Bishop," I announced through the device.

"I expected you to be stationed outside my office like one of those Russian guards with the dick head-looking hats when I arrived," Director Hopkins' voice reached my ears with all unpleasantness. "In fact, you have approximately five minutes to show your ugly face in my office. That should be enough time for you to come up with the world's greatest excuse as to why I gotta put up with your bullshit early this morning."

Then, the fucker hung up before I could reply. Not that I had anything to say anyway. The way he talks to me, you probably think he's racist, right? Well, he's not, and I'm not solely basing this on the fact that he's married to a Black woman. It's just that Hopkins like any other person, feels that he'd attained his position through hard work and dedication, and refuses to take crap from anybody he doesn't have to take it from. So, he pretty much talks to all my coworkers in that manner.

"Off so soon?" Rucker inquired when I rose from my seat.

"Yeah," I replied, headed for the door. "I'm off to see the Pope."

At this time, the place was buzzing with early morning activities of the other agents arriving, moving to and from their offices, or the breakroom. As I moved along the corridors, I was kind of hoping to run into Wilma Reid, but I was kind of hoping not to run into her, being that I was on borrowed time, and I was really trying to come up with the world's greatest excuse as to why I'm already back in the hot seat in less than two weeks. I didn't think I would need an excuse for why I should not be fired, but I was working on one of those, too.

"You wanted to see me, sir?" I can't believe I posed this asinine question, upon stopping in the threshold of Hopkins' office.

To my surprise, he wasn't on the phone talking to one of his imaginary associates. In fact, it seemed like he was just sitting there, staring at the entrance awaiting my arrival like a predator lying in wait for its prey. In response to my query, the director scowled at me. Taking it as a warning, I entered, closed the door behind me, then nonchalantly strolled over to the desk, and took a seat in one of the two visitor chairs.

The office bared the aroma of some kind of cooked seasoning, which drew my attention to the partially eaten sandwich atop the desk. Damn! I can almost predict the storm I'm about to face, considering how Hopkins hates to be disturbed before consuming his breakfast, but if I'm not mistaken, he's the one who summoned *me* to his office, right? So, clearly, he can't blame me for ruining his meal, right? Well, I hope he doesn't.

Now, leaning back in his chair with his arms folded over his chest, Hopkins narrowed his eyes at me. "I already read North's report," he stated, "but there's three sides to every story. Let me hear yours."

"I accidentally cut my phone off," I offered, maintaining my excuse, knowing the lead investigator mentioned it in his report.

"Which accidentally impaired your vision, huh?"

I know I must've had the stupidest look on my face right now. "Excuse me, sir?"

Hopkins leaned forward, interlocking his fingers, forearms rested on the desk. "The report claims you allowed your mark to evade you while you were supposedly parked in front of the mark's residence."

"Supposedly?"

"Were you positioned outside of the mark's residence on the date and time in question?" he asked with raised eyebrows.

"Of course, I was," I took offense once again feeling like I was on the witness stand.

"I assume you don't have any proof of this," said Hopkins. "No photos?"

"There wasn't anything to photograph," I protested through clenched teeth, fighting the urge to dive across the desk on him, even though I was in the wrong. "Lakes remained inside his home all day Saturday."

"What about Saturday night, Bishop?" The accusatory tone was thick now. "How did Lakes manage to sneak by you, and make a meeting with another leader in their organization in Clayton County?"

It was my turn to lean back in my own chair. I exhaled before saying, "I have no idea."

"Are you on the take, Bishop?"

"What!" I moved up to the edge of my seat as if pushed from behind.

"Are these guys paying you to—"

"Why would you ask me something like that?" I cut him off, surprised that he came at me like that, but highly aware of how such an accusation was detrimental to the career and/or freedom of any government official. "You've known me too long to even *think* I'd pull such a stunt."

"Is that so?" He leaned back in his chair again. "If I can recall, I've known quite a few agents for a long time before they went rogue. Some very close friends, if I may."

"You know I can't refuse a polygraph," I pointed out, knowing this was my only defense.

The director just stared at me.

"You can set that up at any time," I pushed.

"Or, I can just have you hand over your gun and shield," Hopkins finally replied.

Now it was my turn to stare and say nothing.

"Get the fuck out of my office before I have you doing security at the city Zoo!" he bristled.

A pass? The Pope was giving me a pass? I couldn't believe this shit! Hell, I was half expecting him to actually confiscate my gun and badge. Especially after the remark about me being on the take. Shit, I thought this would be my last day as Special Agent Brian Bishop.

I should've been like one of those cartoon characters when their legs start running in place before their bodies actually move in the direction in which they're running in. However, I played it cool.

I gave a simple, "Yes, sir," then casually strolled out the same way I strolled in.

***

Okay, listen up! From here on out, I want you to forget everything you know about my personal life. If I don't mention anything about it that means either it's not important, or it's none of your business. Mainly, it's none of your business.

Right now, I'm on a very important mission, which is to build a solid case against the up-and-coming group known as the Kingz. At this point, you're either in or out. If you're in, welcome aboard. If you're out, it was a pleasure having you along this far. Be safe, and don't forget to look both ways before crossing the street.

To my nonquitters, I need you to understand that this is not going to be a pleasant journey. This is not the time to be judgmental, nor question any actions I may take because I can pretty much assure you that some acts I commit will be unethical, and unbecoming an FBI agent. Whether you hate me or not at the conclusion of this story, frankly, I don't give a shit! In fact, I've done enough talking. Welcome to the Investigation!

Chapter 18

Thursday

December 26, 2002

My Christmas with my father, Monique, and Melody, which was spent at Monique's mother's home was wonderful, but believe it or not, I couldn't wait for it to end. North had done me a huge favor by banishing me from the Drop Squad investigation, so I was extremely anxious to get my hands dirty with my own, which is why I shot Monique a line about having to be back on post today to get out of spending another night with her, so I could get an early jumpstart on what I had to do.

No, I had not told Monique about my weekend faux pas yet, but I will eventually. Anyway, I managed to pull myself out of bed a little after 7:00 a.m. this morning. Well, even though the government gave us the rest of the week off, I forgot to adjust my alarm clock, which is how I was able to do so.

After showering, I got dressed, donning a pair of black jeans, a black turtleneck, and a pair of Nike running shoes. My black Nike hat, and black leather coat, completed my ensemble. I had intended to fix myself a light breakfast, but my mind was so preoccupied with my mission, I fled my abode without doing so. I didn't think about my stomach until it grumbled, pretty much accusing me of negligence. Denny's was my option.

It was almost 10:00 when I turned my BMW onto Mitchell Street and cruised past James Young's house, where his BMW was parked at the curb, being that the home builder had forgotten to include such a place in their blueprint. In fact, it seemed like every house on this particular street had been constructed without driveways.

I wasn't at all surprised to see that the street was deserted, even though it was common for children who'd received brand new bikes, go-carts, etcetera, on Christmas day, would usually be out bright and early the next day, riding them just as hard as they'd done on the previous day. Maybe the children in this neighborhood didn't receive any of the aforementioned items.

Whatever the reason was, I wasn't complaining. Thankful for the abandonment, I drove halfway up the street, then made a U-turn, parking in front of a house that had no vehicles in front of it, which was on the same side, but five houses away from Young's. Shutting off the engine, I grabbed my camera off the passenger seat, making sure it was loaded and ready.

I couldn't see Young's car from where I was parked, but I had a decent view of the front of his house. As I watched the place, I began to wonder if he lived alone, or if he has more than one vehicle. If he didn't live alone, or have more than one vehicle, then there was a possible chance that he wasn't in. It's the holidays, true enough, but I don't think drug dealers take days off.

Well, it didn't matter, because I was going to wait out here all night for this scum bag. People like him doesn't stay in all day. Therefore, I reclined my seat just a little and listened to the wind as it whistled and beat against the exterior of my car. The weatherman had predicted snow, but all we'd gotten were ephemeral snowflakes which was okay with me, because snow brings icy roads, and icy roads were bad for business. Especially when a person is doing something they have no business doing.

I can't believe it was after 4:00 p.m., and there had been no sign of Young. Leather seats are comfortable, but after almost seven hours, they begin to feel like boulders. Not only had the interior become cold, but I had to piss like a racehorse. Sure, I could drive off to the nearest restaurant, and use their lavatory, but I was not going to take a chance at missing my mark just in case he decides to take a joyride in my absence.

Just then, a dark green BMW of the same make and model as Young's and my own entered the street. The chrome wheels stood out, but so did the gold emblem attached to the front end of it. I've already assumed this was one of the Kingz, and I was prepared to stoop low, figuring he'd drive this far in order to make a proper U-turn, but he didn't. The occupant parked directly across the street from Young's house, where there was only a small tract of grassy land. No houses lined that side of the street.

My trusty camera was already in my grasp and aimed at the car that was about forty yards out before he could extinguish the engine. The driver's door swung open, and a light-skinned male who stood at about 5'10 to 5'11, emerged, wearing a smoke-gray jean suit, and black ball cap.

Click! Click!

He crossed the street and was momentarily blocked by the line of vehicles, as he made for Young's house. Reaching the front door, he knocked, then looked around as he awaited an answer. *Click!* That's when I was able to get a good shot of his face. Momentarily, the door came open, and the man entered. I couldn't see who answered the door but I did notice the newcomer wasn't wearing the KINGZ medallion I'd seen Young sporting the other day.

Three minutes hadn't passed by, when another BMW pulled onto the street, matching the others, except for its color, which was black. Parking behind the green one, the driver dismounted, wearing blue jeans, a black leather coat, and a blue Kangol hat atop his head, from which I could see the tail end of cornrows hanging from under it.

This guy was also light-skinned. *Click!* I couldn't really see his face for the sunglasses he had on, but I did get a few good shots of him before he disappeared inside the house as well. He also wasn't wearing the medallion.

A meeting! That's what this has to be. After fifteen minutes went by and no one else showed, I concluded that these three were the heads of operations. Just like Drop Squad. Is that how street organizations are spearheaded now? By three individuals? Well, if these guys intended to rival, or duplicate Drop Squad, they have a long way to go, and I'd be there every step of the way.

Other than the handful of children frolicking around, or riding their bikes up and down the street, there was no other movement, so I decided to send Monique and Melody a text:

//: Hello, my favorite girls in the world! I'm on post. Really boring. Miss you both!

In under a minute, their reply came back: *//: Miss U 2 babe! Your daughter wants 2 know when U R coming over. Wants 2 hear stories.*

I smiled, texting back: *//: Soon. Love you both!*

Reply: *//: Luv U 2! SYS.*

I shook my head, ever since texting was invented, it's like people just forgot how to spell, and have adopted the tradition of substituting words for numbers and creating their own acronyms. I mean, what the hell does *SYS* mean?

A dark SUV driving past my car pulled me from my reverie. That's when I looked up and caught the tail-end of the black Chevy Suburban that had begun to slow down. Though I could only see the top of it at this point, I could tell it had stopped in front of Young's home. I quickly grabbed my camera, more than eager to snap pictures of anybody, after being dormant for another thirty-two minutes.

However, nothing happened for another four minutes. At that time, Kangol Hat emerged from the house, followed by Ball Cap, both moving in the direction of the Suburban. A quarter of a minute later, Young exited, with a brown bookbag hanging off one shoulder. After locking up the house, he also moved towards the truck, though I still could only see the roof of it.

Moments later, the SUV moved toward Martin Luther King Drive. Losing sight of the truck, I started my car, rolled the driver's window down, and cautiously stuck my head out, to see which turn it would make. That's when I saw that it was trailing Young's BMW, which made a right turn onto MLK. Once the Suburban was out of sight, I pulled out of my spot, and followed, more than happy to roll my window back up as the heating system sputtered out the last of its cold air, and began to warm up the interior.

Approaching the main road, I stopped and watched the two vehicles as they came to a halt at the traffic light at the intersection of Martin Luther King Jr. Drive, and Ashby Street, which was about two hundred yards out. Initiating my right turn signal, I turned onto MLK, and drove as normal as possible, but fast enough to make the light when it turns green.

Just so happens, the light turned green just as I was about a hundred and thirty yards away. I knew I was taking a risk of getting pulled over by some local shit head, but I had the gas pedal to the floor as I watched BMW and Suburban cross Ashby Street behind two other vehicles. I was eighty yards out now. Seventy. Sixty. Fifty. The light turned yellow. Thirty. Twenty. Red light. I slammed down on the brake pedal, bringing the car to a screeching halt.

"Fuck!" I bellowed, bringing my fists down on the steering wheel.

I was beyond pissed as I watched my targets slip away, but not pissed to the point where I didn't survey my surroundings to make sure there were no cops in the vicinity. There weren't any. Well, as far as I could tell, there wasn't any driving around in squad cars. I made sure to analyze the BP gas station to my right, which is a known hangout spot for beat cops.

Finally, the light turned green again. Of course, I pulled off at a regular pace, but you better believe I was inching down on the gas pedal, slowly increasing the speed. Hell, in thirty seconds, I was already doing forty-five miles per hour. I got over the hill and was able to spot my targets. They were half a mile out, approaching Northside Drive.

To make a long story short, I ended up trailing them to Metropolitan Avenue. I was a good eighty yards behind them when they turned into the parking lot of Kroger City. By the time I entered the lot, the BMW was parking in front of a white Lexus that was parked at a distance from the other vehicles belonging to shoppers and employees, and the Suburban was moving further down, parking alone.

All too familiar with the set-up, I knew that a drug transaction was about to take place. I also knew that drug dealers are extremely vigilant at their rendezvous spots, so I had to look extremely normal, but I had to park in a spot that afforded me a great vantage point.

Therefore, I kind of circled the semi-crowded lot until I found a spot, I was content with. From where I sat, I could see the BMW and Lexus. I knew where the SUV sat, with its dark-tinted windows, but couldn't actually see it.

It was dark out, but the grocery store's multiple arrays of street lamps had the parcel lit like Klieg lights at a crime scene. The windows of the Lexus weren't tinted, so looking through the lens of my Nikkon, I could see there were two occupants, a female at the wheel, and a male beside her. I couldn't get any shots of their faces, being that I was pretty much looking at the backs of their heads.

Just then, Kangol Hat emerged from the back seat of Young's car and approached the Lexus. *Click! Click!* He casually looked around before climbing into the back seat. He didn't have anything in his hands, but that meant nothing. By the movement of their heads, I could tell that Kangol Hat and the male passenger were talking.

Shortly, the car started, but Kangol Hat didn't dismount for another minute or so. When he did, the Lexus pulled out. If I was operating with a full unit someone would be dispatched to tail them for identification purposes but being that I'm a one-man show at the moment, I had to stay focused on the Kingz.

Therefore, I ended up trailing them from place to place, meeting to meeting, as each one of them conducted business with their customers. In the midst of this, I placed a call to Chad Hoffman from Information, to see if he was at home. He was. Plus, he was on his computer as always and was more than happy to run the plates on the Suburban for me. Not only did he inform me that the truck belonged to a Jesse Bridges, but he went as far as running down Bridges' criminal history to me, which consisted of a couple of armed robberies, and aggravated assaults. Birds of a feather, huh?

It was well after eight when the Kingz made it back to Young's home. The BMW turned onto Mitchell Street, but the Suburban continued down MLK. I did likewise, parking where I had a view of the street Young lived on.

I'd already identified James Young. Now, it was time I learn about the other two confederates, which is why I called myself playing Russian roulette at the moment. The first one to exit the street would be my assignment for tonight.

Just then, the black BMW belonging to Kangol Hat emerged. Being that there weren't many vehicles traveling along MLK at this time of the night, I waited until he rounded the bend before switching on my lights and following at a considerably long distance. On the expressway, taking advantage of the evening traffic, I got close enough to read the license plate, in which I logged into my cellular, before dropping back.

I wanted to phone Hoffman, and have him to run the plate for me but thought against it. Though I knew he would do it, I didn't want to wear out my welcome. Besides, there would be plenty of other things I'd need his immediate assistance on in the near future.

Kangol Hat got off on the Bankhead Highway exit and made a right turn. By the time I made it to the main road, I spotted him entering the lot of a truck stop. He'd already parked and was headed inside, when I entered the lot, making sure to park where I could see the entrance of the one-story building.

I'd never been inside the place. However, I could tell that there was an arcade just beyond the diner, which I was looking through the large windows at. It was packed with people. Just then, I saw a customer waving as if flagging down a waiter. However, it wasn't a waiter they were flagging down, but Kangol Hat, who strolled into view, and slid into the booth across from them.

Aha! Perhaps this is another drug transaction. Last one of the day? I powered on my camera. I had a great view of the two as they talked. That's when I realized that the awaiting customer was a woman. It was hard to tell at first because her hair was as short as mine, maybe shorter. I saw the bulge of her stomach under the table, which could be accountable for the plumpness of her face. *Click!* There was no food on the table, and it seemed that neither one of them were interested in ordering. Just talk.

Maybe this wasn't a drug transaction after all. Maybe this was Kangol Hat's mistress. My theory, he'd been stepping out on his woman with her, got her pregnant, and they're still secretly seeing each other. Nine times out of ten, this is someone his wife is highly familiar with. Trust me, I am not judging – just theorizing.

Kangol Hat looked at his watch, apparently ready to depart. They talked a little longer, before he dug into his pants pocket, and handed her a wad of bills across the table. *Click!* A little hush money, perhaps? They talked some more. She then, handed her cell phone to Kangol Hat who punched in a series of numbers before handing it back.

Well, that concluded their tryst, because, without a hug, kiss, or handshake, Kangol Hat made his exit. Just as I followed him here, I followed him a little further down Bankhead, and then down Bolton Road, until he entered some apartments that had a rooted sign out front that advertised them as Maple Creek Apartments, headed home.

Chapter 19

Tuesday

January 7, 2003

After following Ray Young to his apartment that night, I made a promise to myself that I would remit my investigation of the Kingz until after the new year, and I did. Up until now, I'd learned quite a lot about the four of them. Yes, there are four of them, and they have six bodyguards, known to them as *Kingzmen*. Plus, they have a warehouse on Fulton Industrial, which I doubt is packed with Kilos of cocaine, or whatnot. Maybe they have high hopes of this happening. Who knows?

However, I still hadn't come up with anything substantial to present to Hopkins in order to get his approval, but I will eventually. I did find out that one of their workers was murdered on Christmas evening, along with a known prostitute. As reported, the prostitute was performing oral sex on the male inside of a parked car when the vehicle was riddled with bullets on both sides in which I assume was a grave message to the renowned clique.

Of course, the Kingz paid their last respects, and my devoted ass was right there at the graveside snapping away with my camera. There weren't that many people present, but there was one guy who seemed to cling to the group. He wasn't wearing the Kingz' chain, but he gave the impression of somebody of importance. I later identified him as Eric Mills the other brother of one of the King, Frederick Mills. He also has a history of drugs and assaults.

"Bishop," I answered my new business cell phone I purchased last week.

At this time, my head was hurting from reading over tons of documents on Gerald Osborne, a multi-millionaire businessman, who allegedly embezzled millions of dollars from people to set up fraudulent banking accounts. My partner, Rucker was seated across from me, at his own desk, nose-deep in another mountain of documents pertaining to the same case.

"Detective McCoy," the female caller announced

"I'm listening," I say, casting a glance at my partner, who stopped what he was doing to be nosey.

"A body has just been discovered behind an auto parts store on Bankhead Highway," she explained. "Female. Early to mid-twenties."

"What's the cause?" I inquired, hoping my partner didn't catch on that I was asking the cause of someone's death.

"Strangulation," McCoy answered, "and possibly rape. She was with child, so she was rushed to the hospital to see if the baby still had a chance."

"Is that possible?" I asked, wondering why *with child* played over and over in my mind. "Could the child still be alive?"

"It's rare," she said, "but it's possible. I'm not a doctor, so I really can't explain it, but it has something to do with the remaining oxygen inside the womb."

With child. Bankhead Highway. I wonder if— "Did you manage to take a picture with your phone?" I asked, knowing this was something she does in her cases, in which she downloads to her computer when she returns to her office.

"Yes, I did," she answered slowly and hesitant.

"Could you send me a facial?"

She was quiet on the other end. All I could hear was indistinct police chatter from her radio. Finally, she said, "In confidentiality."

"I'd have it no other way," I told her, verbally signing my John Hancock.

"Stand by."

It took almost a minute for the message indicator to show up on my screen. I opened it and almost swore out loud. I don't know why, but I couldn't believe this woman had been strangled, and possibly raped, which was probably not in that exact order unless some sick fucker preferred having his way with carcasses. I've only viewed her through the lens of my camera just that one night, but there was no mistaking that this was the same woman I'd seen meeting with Ray Young at the truck stop, a couple of weeks ago. I remembered how she looked then, compared to now, lying on the granite pebbles, blank eyes staring up at nothing, with irregular imprints on her neck, caused by whatever weapon was used to asphyxiate her.

"Did you get it?" McCoy's voice came at me in almost a whisper, being that I didn't have the phone up to my ear.

Pulling my eyes away from the screen, I put the phone up to my ear, clearing my throat. "Ah, yeah, I got it. Where are you, right now?"

"I'm still at the crime scene," she answered.

"Could you be more specific?"

"Auto Zone. Bankhead Highway."

Auto Zone! If I'm not mistaking, that's just right up the street from the truck stop. "How long will you be there?" I asked.

She sighed. "I just got here, so it may be a while."

"I'll call you right back."

"Okay."

"I need a break," I said to Rucker, as I stood, donning my coat. "A few more minutes of this, and *I'll* be under investigation for embezzlement."

Rucker laughed. "Yeah, I hear you. I'm about to take a break myself. Will you be taking the unmarked car?

"Definitely."

Retrieving my cellular, and the keys to the Crown Vic, I exited the office, heading for the elevators. I waited until I made it to the parking garage before calling McCoy back.

She answered with the announcement of her name.

"Meet me at Petro in about twenty minutes," I told her.

"Why Petro?"

"It's a hunch," I said, "but it might help you with this case."

It took me no time to reach Bankhead Highway, being that I had the siren wailing like a new-born baby, all the way to the west side of Atlanta. Like most nightspots, Petro didn't look all too alluring in the daytime, although business was in full swing as usual, with tractor-trailers roaring in and out, and regular travelers stopping in for breakfast at the diner.

I spotted the black unmarked Dodge Challenger, parked in the far corner of the lot, which was close to the main road, but far as hell away from the building. This made me think of my ex-partner, Wilma Reid who has a knack for doing the same thing. Why women do this? A man may never know.

As soon as I pulled the Ford alongside the Dodge, Homicide Detective Kowanda McCoy emerged wearing a long, black, leather trench coat, khaki pants, and black Reebok running shoes. Standing at 5'10, and 155 pounds, she had flawless mocha skin, brown eyes, and jet-black, shoulder-length hair that parted in the middle, and cascaded down the sides of her head. At the age of thirty-two, she was a devoted Christian, who's married to an author and screenwriter.

"Detective," I said, as I dismounted, extending my hand.

"Special Agent," she responded, shaking my hand in a firm, feminine grip. "Again, why here?"

"Let's take a walk," I told her, then moved in the direction of the building, with her falling in step beside me. "So, how's Mr. McCoy?"

A broad smile spread across her face. "He's fine. In fact, he and his team are about to shoot their first movie. Right now, they're doing casting calls."

"That's great!" I commended, genuinely. "This could make you two rich."

"No," she contended. "This could make *him* rich. I make my own money."

"But you know he's gonna spoil you."

"He does that now," she offered. "I mean, I'm not complaining about having four cars, a big house, and enough jewelry and clothes to start my own Macy's, but he knows I'm not materialistic. I donate the allowance he gives me to my church, and children's hospitals."

See? Devoted Christian. We entered Petro and were hit by the aroma of cooked foods, and the natural noises of a way station in full swing. Passing the diner, we came upon a steel door with a plastic sign that read: *Management*. I took it upon myself to rap on the door with my knuckles. Seconds later, the door squeaked open, and there stood a short, pudgy White woman in a dingy gray shirt with *Petro* on its left breast, and *Manager* on the right. Her blonde hair was pulled into a discreditable ponytail and her eyes showed signs of a person lacking proper rest.

"What's the problem?" she asked, agitation lining her tone.

I shoved my credentials in her face. "I'm Special Agent Bishop, and this is Detective McCoy." I refused to say, *homicide* detective, which would've made her more nervous, and tip her off that someone had been murdered. That's none of her business. "May we come in?" I asked, retracting my credentials.

The 5'5 manager looked as if she was considering telling us to take a hike. Then, reluctantly, she stepped aside, allowing us entrance. Just as I expected, the place was a mess. The desk was cluttered with documents, food, drinking containers from the diner, and empty potato chip bags. The small, plastic container was also full of trash that spewed out onto the stained carpet. There were no windows, and the small office reeked of stale food and sweat.

"How may I be of some assistance to the FBI?" the woman asked in a more gentle tone, closing the door.

"We need to view your cameras footage of last night," I told her.

"Wouldn't you need a warrant for that?"

"Only if we were investigating *you*," I lied, ready to pile lies on top of lies. "We received a tip that a fugitive had stopped in and dined at your diner last night. We're just following up on the tip to see if it's true. Then we're out of your hair. I promise."

She chewed on her bottom lip for a few seconds before asking, "Which cameras are you interested in?"

"The front parking lot."

"There's only one."

"That's fine."

Moving over to her desk, the manager had to brush away debris to get to the keyboard. Tapping a few keys, she managed to pull the sole footage up on the screen, then turned to face us.

"Could you give us a minute?" I asked her.

Now, she was really looking like she was considering telling us to fuck off and I was half expecting her to do so, but she complied, closing the door behind her. McCoy and I exchanged a look before

I stepped behind the desk and looked down at the frozen image on the monitor. To my surprise, the detective had taken a seat in the chair as if it didn't need to be disinfected. Okay, maybe it didn't.

The angle of the screen showed that the camera was mounted on the right side of the building, and tilted leftward, where I couldn't see the entrance of the lot, but the far corner, which is where McCoy and I are were parked now, all the way up to the entrance of the building. Yesterday's date was at the bottom of the screen, but the time was 14:07.

"What are we looking for?" asked McCoy.

"As I said," I answered, "this is a hunch. Just bear with me."

I punched keys, fast-forwarding the image on the screen. I know you're wondering about the history between me and Detective McCoy? Well, you know the FBI periodically works with local police departments to solve cases, which is how we met. We've worked together on many cases. Especially when Hopkins had me on *punishment*, forcing me to accompany the locals on cases that are considered demeaning to a person of my caliber.

Why did she contact me about this case she's working on? Because she's one of the detectives I'd contacted and informed that I was investigating an up-and-coming drug cartel out of Atlanta and that I would like to be consulted whenever there's a homicide to see if we could connect a few dots. One hand washes the other. You know how it is.

"Bingo!" I said, slowing the footage to its normal pace, when I spied the familiar BMW on chrome wheels come into view, searching for a spot to park.

"And who might this be?" McCoy inquired.

"One of my subjects."

"How is this gonna—"

"Just be patient," I cut her off. "This is gonna be quite interesting."

Sighing, she leaned back in the chair, and we watched as Ray Young got out, clad in a gray dress suit, and strolled into the building. I hadn't seen his assumed mistress show up yet, but if their date was set for eight o'clock, then she should be on the way, being that the time on the screen was 19:56.

I stifled a yawn but stretched my limbs to the ceiling while keeping my eyes on the movement on the monitor. When there was no movement for several minutes, I closely inspected the cluttered desk again, using a ballpoint pen to move items around. Then, out of curiosity, I pulled the top drawers open and immediately realized why the manager was reluctant to leave us in here alone.

There was a saucer, containing what appeared to be cocaine, a rolled-up bill, and a razor. McCoy was also looking at the contents. When she gave me a knowing look, I regarded her with a benign smile, while pushing the drawer shut.

"You're Homicide," I reminded her in a low tone, "not Narcotics. Besides, doesn't the Bible say something about turning the other cheek?"

"That's not what it means," she contended.

"Well, that's what it means today," I said, turning my attention back to the screen. "Here's your girl right here."

Though it was dark, I was able to spot the short-haired woman as she climbed from the passenger side of some dark, older model sedan, in a dark coat that seemed to bear down on her protruding stomach. We watched as she wobbled across the lot and entered the building. The driver of the car didn't get out.

"Okay," McCoy said, making a *T* with her hands. "Time out! I'm lost, right now. How did you—"

"She's my subject's mistress," I explained. "This is where they meet up and talk."

"Just talk?"

I shrugged my shoulders. "That's all I've seen them do so far."

"The unborn child," she said, still watching the monitor. "Is it his?"

"It's possible," I answered. "I've seen him give her money. Perhaps to keep the news from his current woman. Who knows?"

"God knows," McCoy stated as if to convince me of something I'm already aware of. Then, as if drawing some kind of conclusion, she looked up and asked, "Do you think he did it?"

"No, I do not."

"Oh?"

"It wouldn't make sense for him to do it."

"You mean, to murder her to keep her from spilling the beans?"

"To *rape* and murder her to keep her from spilling the beans," I rectified, watching a white SUV park not far away.

McCoy slowly nodded her head up and down. "You may have a point, Bishop. What about the driver of the car she arrived in?"

Damn! I didn't think of that. Tapping more keys on the keypad, I managed to zoom in on the sedan, but it was parked directly under a lamp post that cast a reflection on the driver's window, making it look like a mirror. Plus, the glass protection over the camera was in dire need of dusting.

"That sucks," said McCoy, also seeing the obstruction.

"Yeah," I agreed, refocusing the camera to its normal view.

Just then, Young exited the establishment and appeared to be looking around as he made for his car. When he pulled away, another minute and forty-eight seconds had elapsed before his mistress emerged, also looking around. *For what?* I wondered, watching her approach the driver's side of the car she arrived in. After handing something to the driver, she walked off, moving toward the corner of the lot, toward the white SUV!

I tried to zoom in on the truck, but it was futile. The range was too far and the picture was too grainy. The driver of the Sedan had pulled on, and I watched the woman climb into the passenger side of the SUV, a bit upset that I couldn't get a view of the driver, due to the ancient surveillance system. However, being good at identifying most vehicles I was able to make out the white truck with its matching rims, as it pulled out of the lot.

"It's a Chevy Tahoe," I informed Detective McCoy. "White. Matching wheels. I'm quite sure there aren't that many in this area of the same customization. If you put out an APB, you'll have to lie saying the tip came from a witness."

She sighed, pushing herself up from the chair. "May God forgive me!"

"Oh, He will," I said, smiling, patting her on the back. "Now, let's give this woman back her office before she goes into withdrawal."

Playa Ray

Chapter 20

Saturday

January 11, 2003

I've been investigating the Kingz since the twenty-first of December, and have learned a great deal about them, but I still don't have anything concrete enough to present to the director. I know twenty-two days is not a long time, but I'm starting to feel like I'm barking up the wrong tree. It may take forever for the Kingz to reach fed status. Or maybe they never will. Maybe I should use them to find out who their supplier is, then employ my talents to take the supplier down.

No! Fuck that! The Kingz are *my* project! I started this investigation, and I'm going to finish it, no matter how long it takes. Yes, I'm anxious as hell, but I know I have to proceed with a leveled head and have patience. Yeah, picture that. My impatient ass proceeding with a leveled head – whatever the fuck that means!

I entered the barbershop a little after 10:00 a.m. It wasn't packed, but there were enough people for me to be the third person to occupy Tyrone's chair, and the moment my bottom made contact with the seat, guess who made a grand entrance, boasting, bragging, and talking loud as usual? Yes, *that* fucker! I know I sound as though I wasn't happy to see him, but I was extremely happy he'd shown up, sporting a Kingz chain like he was one of the head honchos, though I knew better. Hell, the shit didn't even look metallic.

"Y'all niggas ain't getting no real money!" he was now saying, now seated in the waiting area. By this time, I'd been in the chair for over five minutes. "Before long," Steve continued. "y'all won't have no choice but to get with this shit. Or take up shop somewhere else."

"That sounds like a threat," Tyrone acknowledged.

"That definitely sounds like a threat," Keith pitched in.

"Them niggas ain't making no noise," Tyrone said, maintaining his composure while putting the finishing touch on my *normal* haircut. "I heard of 'em, but they ain't taking over niggas' trap n' shit. Everybody ain't pushovers."

"Shit, these niggas ain't no hoes!" Steve carried on his representation. "They got bodyguards, who they call Kingzmen. They just knocked two niggas off Wednesday. One nigga came up short with that paper. Mike had introduced this nigga to the Kingz. They told Mike he could either knock the nigga off or die with him. They even gave Mike the pistol to off the nigga with."

"Shit, what did Mike do?" inquired Tank.

"He went out bad," Steve replied, shaking his head from side to side. "They gave him sixty seconds to make a decision, and he froze. Those were the last sixty seconds of his life. Real talk, I ain't never seen a nigga get killed until then. They fucked them niggas up, then told the Kingzmen to chop Greg's dick off."

"They chopped the man's dick off?" Keith asked in disbelief.

"Man, these niggas *been* chopping niggas up!"

For some reason, I had a feeling that Chambers was exaggerating, though it made me think about what Agent Powell had told me of the meeting with Philip Lakes and Kenny Williams, where they had ordered that one of their subordinates be minced. If what Chamber was saying is true, did it mean that the Kings were mimicking Drop Squad? Or is this brutal act adopted by all street organizations?

I ruminated this as I pushed the rented Ford Explorer along the expressway, hoping to catch the funeral service of Sylvia Baker the woman who was raped and strangled to death earlier this week. Detective McCoy phoned me on Wednesday, informing me that Baker's unborn child had survived the ordeal, and will be released to Baker's aunt. McCoy was ecstatic about the news, said she'd even taken pictures with the premature child, and some of Baker's friends, at the hospital. Of course, she sent images to my phone.

Making it to the church, I saw that I had missed the first part of the service, being that the attendees were now outside at the burial site, as the reverend gave the final eulogy. There were only nine vehicles present, and I was highly familiar with two of them, which were the dark blue, customized BMW belonging to Keith Daniels, and the black, customized BMW belonging to Ray Young, although Young's car wasn't parked with the others.

Making it seem as though I was there to visit one of the other graves, I parked on the far side of the circular land, which put me at about one hundred and fifty yards away from the mourners, and that much distance away from a guy in a long trench coat and round-brimmed hat, who appeared to be visiting someone's plot, but his posture seemed all too familiar to me.

Leaving the engine running, I grabbed my camera off the seat beside me and focused on the man that was standing off to himself. Well, shit! The large hat and sunglasses almost threw me for a loop, but why the hell was Ray Young standing further away from Baker's plot? Probably because her boyfriend was present, and he was trying to circumvent an unwanted quarrel with him. Or he didn't know any of Baker's family members and wanted to avoid the *who, why,* and *what* questions they would pummel him with if he approached. However, I commended him for paying his last respects.

Click! Panning my camera, I focused on the small group of mourners, who had just begun to disperse, headed for their vehicles as the groundskeepers shoveled dirt onto Baker's casket that had been lowered into the earth. Keith Daniels was amongst them, which really had me confused as to why Young wasn't being that they're both parts of the same organization.

Just then, Daniels and three women changed their course and were moving in Young's direction. I don't know why, but the women looked vaguely familiar as if I'd recently seen them in passing, or something. *Click! Click!*

Upon approaching Young, Daniels and him seemed to have an awkward exchange, like they were total strangers before one of the women pitched in. As she and Young conversed, she seemed to become upset, rolling her neck like women do for emphasis, though she seemed more tomboyish.

Perhaps what the woman was saying had rubbed Young the wrong way, because he turned and walked away, leaving the four of them standing in disbelief. As Young made for his car, I thought of following him, being that he hadn't been to his apartment since Baker's murder, but for some reason, I thought I'd better stick with his brother for a while. Maybe he'll end up providing me with enough evidence to get approval from Hopkins to launch a full-scale investigation on them, being that he seems like the most active of the four.

***

I found myself parked on Mitchell Street again, watching James Young's house, where there were no vehicles present. This made me wish that I'd journey out here after leaving the barbershop, instead of the gravesite. Maybe I would've caught Young before he disappeared. It's Saturday, so there's no telling where he could be at this moment. He didn't strike me as the type who would be snuggled up with the warm body of a female companion on such a cold day. Nope. I'd bet anything he was out somewhere, distributing that poison to'his underlings.

As I watched the house, and the children play up and down the street, I thought about the phone-tapping device I *borrowed* from my workplace. At first, I knew nothing about it, which is why it had taken forever for me to set it up, and I definitely didn't know, being that it was connected to my phone jack, that it would run my phone bill close to a thousand dollars. Hell, ever since receiving the bill, I hadn't even thought about powering it back up. However, the device is a necessity, so maybe I'll get Hoffman to help me figure something out.

I was so caught up in my thoughts, I hadn't realized it had gotten dark until headlights shone through the windshield of the Explorer, interrupting them. It seemed that all the children had been called inside, which also made me realize how easy it would be for someone to abduct a child from this area because I'd camped out on this street several times, and not once had I been accosted by a suspicious parent, nor a police officer, summoned by a suspicious parent. Would I be wrong for using the word *careless*?

The time on the dashboard was 6:21 p.m., and Young still hadn't made it home. Figuring I'd call it quits for tonight, I waited until the car that interrupted my thoughts, drove by, before starting the engine, giving it a couple of minutes to warm up. The moment I pressed down on the brake pedal and reached for the gear, the purple BMW came into view, moving at a fast pace. I quickly snatched my foot off the pedal to extinguish the brake lights and stoop low to avoid being seen as the car zipped by.

I already knew he was about to make a U-turn, so I didn't come back up until I heard the car roar by again. James Young appeared to be in a rush as he exited the vehicle and moved briskly toward his house. He didn't have anything worth noting in his hands, so I didn't bother with the camera. Just then, approaching from my rear, another car drove by with its lights off.

This was a black Ford Crown Victoria. It stopped in front of Young's home, which first had me thinking it was a robbing crew. Then, almost instantly, I thought some local government agents – perhaps GBI – were about to lunge from the vehicle, and arrest Young, but it just remained idle in its spot. Hell, I figured there was no threat when Young regarded the car with a mere glance before entering his home.

About seven minutes later, Young now wearing a black cargo, pants suit and boots, re-emerged, locking his house up. As he neared the Ford, the front-passenger door came open, and a man dressed in the same attire as him got out and climbed into the back seat. Once Young climbed into the front seat, the car drove off.

Familiar with the dress code, I already knew that the guy who climbed from the front-passengers seat was a Kingzman. Therefore, I automatically assumed another one was at the wheel. How many occupants in all? I have no idea, being that the windows were dark.

However, I ended up trailing them to Coweta County, periodically allowing myself to lose sight of them, which is a technique I mastered over the years, to keep from getting made. I especially had to actuate this tactic, when the driver exited the expressway and began turning onto streets I didn't bother getting the names of.

Finally, we came out on a main road that seemed deserted of vehicles but was lined with occasional mom-and-pop businesses such as tire shops, gas stations, cleaning services, and non-franchised restaurants. Considering the vacancy of the road, I dropped back to the point where the Crown Victoria's taillights looked like a tiny red dot up ahead.

Then, suddenly, the red dot disappeared. I didn't panic, because that's not something I'm good at doing. Instead, I maintained the speed limit, just in case these guys had made me and were lying in wait, preparing an ambush. Thinking this, I unholstered my gun and sat it in my lap. I'm also not good at cracking under pressure when it comes to handling my weapon.

Another quarter of a mile up the road, I spotted the Ford off to my right, sitting in the empty parking lot of some non-descript restaurant, facing the road. As I came upon it, I couldn't tell if anyone was still inside the car for its dark windows, but being duly aware that my windows were as clear as a champagne glass, I kept my head straight as I passed the car, only regarding it from the corners of my eyes, and was prepared to smash the gas if they lunged from the car in attack mode. However, I was able to scuttle by unscathed, and I was able to tell that they were still inside the car. Now, as I watched them from the rearview mirror, my mind was racing. They were parked in the parking lot of a restaurant that probably didn't bring in anything near five hundred dollars a day, so certainly they were not going to pull off this petty break-in.

However, their car was facing the street. Facing whatever it was *across* the street. I shifted my gaze, but I was too far out to make out what kind of establishment it was sitting across from the restaurant, but I could tell there was a dark-colored Ford Bronco parked there.

As far as I could tell, I wasn't nearing any residential area, and I knew that I shouldn't go too far if I was going to photograph whatever these guys were up to. Well, of course, I'm going to document these fuckers. How else am I going to get this investigation legitimized?

Coming up on a self-service car wash to my left, I decided I would post up there. Entering the lot, I pulled up to the vacuum dock, and immediately extinguished the lights, then killed the engine. Despite the cold weather, I grabbed my camera off the seat beside me, and dismounted, positioning myself between the two, huge vacuum canisters, thankful that the lighting conditions were very poor in this area.

Eyeing the distance between them and myself, I took an educated guess that they were about six hundred yards out. I checked the film compartment of my camera, just as a car rode by. Shit! I can't believe I'm out of film. Climbing back inside the Explorer, I checked my investigation kit to no avail. Fuck! I can't believe I hadn't bought any film. I hadn't signed any out at work, because it required a signed withdrawal form from the director, and I haven't turned in any film to receive any.

Inhale. Exhale.

However, with or without film, I was not going to miss whatever was going down here tonight. Slipping on my gloves, I dismounted again, and re-took my same position between the canisters, adjusting the lens on my unarmed camera, hating the fact that I didn't have my binoculars.

Considering the distance, I wasn't able to zoom in on the Ford like I wanted to, but I had a decent view. I could tell that Young and his men hadn't budged. Switching my view, I caught sight of the sign of the store across the street from them. I couldn't make out the name, but it had a picture of two revolvers pointing at each other. A gun shop! I realized as another car rode by. Now, *this* store would be worth breaching.

James Young, you piece of shit. I always knew you'd be the one to provide me with the evidence I need to bring down your whole organization.

Just then, a squad car drove by, and I was surprised the officer didn't stop to question my presence. Or maybe it wasn't illegal to use the self-service car wash at this time of night. However, I was sure the cop was going to be suspicious of the Crown Victoria sitting in the lot of the closed restaurant and go into super cop mode.

Instead, he turned into the lot of the gun shop and sounded the siren as if to get the attention of someone inside the store.

Then, everything was silent again. I kept my eye on the gun shop, expecting someone to exit, but no one did. I switched my attention back to the Ford. Young and his men were still stationed, probably scared shit less. Whatever they had planned, they were not going to initiate it while this local dick head was sitting there. No matter how ruthless a person may think they are, the presence of a badge always— *Hold the fuck up!*

I'm not the type of person who would question what I see with my own eyes, but that's not to say that I wasn't surprised to see Young and four other men dressed in the same manner as himself, step out of the Crown Victoria, with ski masks on. As if it was all planned out, the five men marched across the two-lane street, carry handguns. I don't know why, but as I watched them move with a purpose, I thought about the movie *Heat*.

"Don't let yourself get attached to anything you're not willing to walk out on in thirty seconds flat if you feel the heat around the corner," I could hear Robert De Niro's character say to Al Pachino's, as the gang approached the squad car, seemingly undetected, one man, aiming his weapon at the driver's window. By this time, the gun shop owner had locked the place up and was about to head for the Bronco. His body language showed that he'd spotted the masked men.

Pow!

I saw the flash from the weapon a millisecond before the window exploded. The sound reached my ears like a firecracker going off in a distance. The owner looked to be reaching for a weapon, but one of the men quick-stepped, gun raised, causing the old, White man to reconsider, and put his hands up in surrender. The gunman, then, pulled the owner's gun from his shoulder holster and motioned with it clearly giving him some kind of instruction.

Complying, the older man turned back to the entrance of the store and used his key to unlock it. When the owner entered, with his aggressor at his heels, they stopped just inside the doorway, presumably to discern the alarm. *Pow!* This one sounded a bit muffled, but I knew what it was, and what had happened.

These ruthless motherfuckers just murdered two people in cold blood! A fucking cop! I don't give a shit about local shiteaters, but we're still part of some kind of brotherhood. What the fuck am I supposed to do, though? I can't just roll up on them, show them my shield, and demand that they stop raiding the shop. I mean, I *could* do that, but it'll only add another body to their count, and I'm quite sure they're content with two. Besides, I'm out of my jurisdiction, right?

However, I could place an anonymous call to the local police department from a payphone and have them send a cavalry over, but if Young is arrested, or murdered, that would screw up my investigation, and I would never intentionally do anything to screw up my investigation.

Playa Ray

Chapter 21

Monday

"Let me get this straight," Hopkins said, leaning back in his chair, with his arms folded. "You watched these street punks murder two people, and burglarize a gun shop?"

"It was on the news, sir," I replied, struggling to maintain my composure, as I sat across the desk from him.

"I saw the damn news, Bishop!" he retorted. "My issue with this story is that you *watched* these fuckers kill a cop and his father, clean a whole gun shop out, and you did absolutely *nothing*. Plus, you have no evidence to back up this allegation, while you were *supposedly* investigating these hoodlums, which, by the way, is still illegal without my consent."

"Like I said," I spoke through clenched teeth now. "I didn't know I was out of film until that night, and I did call the police department from a payphone, anonymously."

Yes, I called the local authorities, but it was after Young and his men had departed and I had gotten a closer look at the crime scene, mainly the bodies making sure to steer clear of any surveillance cameras unaware that the culprits had made off with the recordings. It's just too bad I didn't have any film to record the gruesome scene.

The director narrowed his eyes. "And what about this illegal investigation you're carrying on with?"

"You told me I'll need substantial evidence in order for me to get your permission to launch a full-scale investigation," I reminded.

"And you still haven't brought any back," he pointed out.

I remained silent.

"Just stick to your assignments, Bishop," he went on, leaning forward, and resting his elbows on the desk. "Too many agents have ruined their careers, and their lives trying to prove points that weren't worth proving. Don't be a statistic."

I left the director's office, knowing exactly what I needed to do, which may very well ruin my career—or my life. However, it's time for me to step it up, and apply pressure where it needs to be applied. From here on out, I'm holding no more punches, and no one's exempt!

"Good morning, Bishop!"

I stopped in my tracks at the sound of my name and realized that I was so caught up in my thoughts, I passed Wilma Reid without even noticing her. Laying eyes on my ex-partner now, I realized she was as gorgeous as ever, even though her dark hair was pulled back into her regular ponytail and there were no facial cosmetics to speak on. However, the pants of her dark blue suit were a bit snug-fitting, showing off her toned and shapely legs.

"Oh! Good morning, Reid!" I responded. "I'm sorry, I didn't see you."

She smiled. "Obviously, studying for a college exam?"

"It damn sure feels like it," I offered with a forced smile. "What's on *your* agenda?"

"Still working the missing child case with Palmer."

"And how's that going?"

She rolled her eyes. "If I hear another word about how his father helped solve the Wayne Williams case back in the eighties, I'm gonna turn in my shield."

"He helped arrest the bogeyman?" I asked, thinking of how parents used to scare their children by telling them that Wayne Williams the child murderer would get them if they were not in the house before dark.

"So, he says," Reid replied, with the wave of a hand. "Anyway, how's Monique and Melody?"

"They're great!" I answered, just as my business phone vibrated in my pants pocket. Pulling it out, I saw Detective McCoy's number on the screen. "I have to take this," I told Reid.

"Okay," she said. "I'll catch you later."

"Talk to me," I said through my phone as I made for my office.

"We found two bodies wrapped in a tarp," McCoy informed. "Both male, early to mid-twenties. One died from multiple gunshot wounds, and the other only sustained a fatal gunshot wound to the back of the head."

"No mutilations?" I asked, remembering what Chambers had said about the Kingz murdering and chopping up two men last week.

"Well," she said slowly, "one was found with his male component cut off and shoved into his mouth."

I smiled, wondering if she'd ever used the word *dick*. "Did you actually see it?" I asked, hoping God doesn't write me a one-way ticket to hell for taunting her.

"Of course, I actually saw it!" There was disgust in her voice.

"Does it change the way you view the male organ?" I persisted, still smiling like a mischievous child.

"Is there anything you can tell me about these men?" she disregarded my question, using her all-business tone.

"Not at the moment." I was standing just outside my office now. "How's that strangulation case going?"

"The ME found semen inside Baker," the detective informed. "Samples had been sent to the crime lab, so I should hear something by tomorrow."

"That's great!" I commended. "Is there an APB out for the truck?"

"Not yet. I wanna see what tomorrow brings."

"Keep me posted."

"I will."

I don't know why, but Mondays always seemed to drag by. However, once the day was finally over, I left for the day, opting to leave the rented Explorer, and take the Crown Victoria. Plus, instead of heading home, I drove out to Campbellton Road. Being that the Ford is too conspicuous, and could easily be identified as government-issued, I didn't enter Deerfield Apartments but chose to stake out at the gas station across the street. The locals are known for doing this, so whoever sees me, will only assume that the locals are just being nosey as usual.

At 5:57 p.m., it wasn't quite dark out yet, which didn't matter to me. Today, I was out to apply pressure by any means necessary.

Plus, I came equipped with my binoculars, fully-loaded camera, and extra rolls of film I'd purchased myself, although I didn't intend to use any of these items, but you never know what may transpire on a stakeout. Saturday proved that, right?

I couldn't see Chambers' apartment door from where I sat, but I could see the tail end of his green Buick Regal sitting in the lot. This was good because there was a possible chance that he was either inside his apartment or somewhere in the vicinity, selling his product. I was just hoping he planned on driving somewhere tonight, which would be more suitable for the only plan I devised.

As I yawned, my mind reverted to the dinner I had with my father yesterday at the apartment he now shares with Carmen, his young, pregnant girlfriend, who still works at the nursing home. I kinda feel sorry for her because no matter how hard she tries to be nice to me, I still carry on like I have something against her. She senses it. My father senses it. Hell, even Monique and Melody can sense it and they're crazy about her.

I'm highly aware of how I've been acting toward Carmen. I just can't figure out the origin of my deportment. What my mother and father had, ended long before it actually came to an official end. Surely, I couldn't be tripping off that. I'm supposed to be happy that my old man's happy. I mean, I am, right?

A group of men rounding one apartment building caught my attention. I couldn't make out their features without my *spyware*, but the large, bright medallion hanging from the chain of one of the men, could be spotted, and identified from a mile away. Chambers and the three men walked over to the green Regal. Two of them sat upon the trunk, Chambers and the other guy stood around.

Deciding I'll get a few shots, I grabbed my camera, and made sure to get perfect angles of each of the men's faces as they talked and passed a blunt around. Then, I just watched them. Being the most talkative person I've ever encountered, I wasn't at all surprised to see that Chambers was doing all the talking, probably boasting and bragging about the Kingz.

Suddenly, Chambers pulled a cell phone from his pants pocket and held it to the side of his face. Then, as if the conversation was private, he stepped away from his friends but remained in my sights. Concluding the call that only lasted a little over two minutes, Chambers walked back over to his friends. They talked for another minute or so before Chambers dapped them up. As the three men departed, Chambers climbed into the Regal.

Yes! The fucker's about to fall right into my hands. I just hope he plans on driving far away from this area, which would be more appropriate for what I have in mind. I adjusted the knob on my heating condition as Chambers pulled from his parking spot and drove toward the entrance of the apartments. Without using his turn indicator, he made a left on Campbellton Road, which made me smile to myself.

After waiting a good thirty seconds, I pulled out of the gas station, and followed, half caring if he spotted me. Chambers knew nothing of my occupation but things are about to change tonight, and it's totally up to him how drastic that change would be. I already knew I was jeopardizing my visits to Tyrone's barbershop, but this is something that has to be done. Besides, there are thousands of other barbershops in Atlanta.

Whoever Chambers was off to meet, he didn't have to access the expressway to do so. After fifteen minutes of driving, he turned onto some dim-lit residential street. By this time, I was pretty much on his bumper, still not caring if he noticed. We passed rows of houses on each side before he made another right turn onto another street with me still on his ass. I didn't immediately see any houses, just trees, and undergrowth on both sides. Perfect!

I activated my emergency lights and sounded the siren once watching the blue and red lights flashing from the grille of the Ford dance all over the rear of the Buick, visibly distorting its dark green hue, and make a disco scene out of the interior through its clear windows. To be honest, I thought Chambers was going to take me on a high-speed chase, in which I would not indulge, but he didn't. Like a law-abiding citizen, he immediately pulled to the curb and stopped which had me on high alert. Drug dealers didn't usually pull over if they were dirty, unless they were confident that they would come out unscathed, or they intended to *go out with a bang.*

My trench coat was already unbuttoned which gave me easy access to the Glock in my shoulder holster. After putting the Ford in park, and sliding my hands inside my black gloves, I waited until Chambers put his car into park, and let his foot off the break, before pulling my gun and dismounting.

"Cut the car off!" I voiced, inching closer, gun at my side.

Chambers complied, though he didn't roll his window down. Reaching the car, I noticed he had both hands on the steering wheel, which was something else I did not expect. He wasn't wearing a seatbelt, so I hope he's not stupid enough to ask me why I pulled him over. Well, I'm about to find out, with my gun in my right hand, I pulled the driver's door open with my left, getting a faint whiff of the marijuana he'd just burned with his buddies.

"Why'd you pull me over, officer?" he questioned, squinting his eyes against the bright flashing lights.

"Step out of the car, Chambers!"

"What the fuck!" he mumbled, stepping out, now standing with his face just inches away from mine. "Man, you're not the fucking police!"

I slammed the car door. "Shut the fuck up and turn around!"

When he complied, I pushed him up against the car and patted him down with my free hand, finding a .22 revolver in his right pants pocket in which I dropped into a pocket of my coat.

"I don't have no cash on me," Chambers offered. "Despite what I be saying at the shop, I ain't getting it in like that."

"Clearly," I said, holstering my gun, and brandishing my handcuffs, "but this is not a robbery. You're under arrest."

"For what?"

Of course, I didn't answer. Cuffing him, I walked him to the Ford and planted him in the back seat. Climbing in behind the wheel, I shut the flashers off and pressed play on the recorder sitting in the slot beneath the radio, sure that Chambers hadn't seen it.

"What am I being arrested for?" Chambers tried again.

Pulling out the revolver, I held it up for him to see. "Didn't I just get this off you?"

He didn't answer.

"Possession of a firearm is five years in prison, right?" I resumed. "Are you ready to serve that kind of time?"

"I still don't believe you're a cop," he finally responded. "This car ain't even outfitted like a cop's car."

"You would know, huh?" Dropping the gun on the passenger seat, I shoved my credentials in his face. "You're right about me not being a cop. I'm FBI – something far worse than a cop, which means you're in *deeper* shit."

"You be at the barbershop, though."

"We like to stay groomed, too," I told him retracting my credentials.

"So, the FBI had me under investigation?" Chambers asked, incredulously.

"Yeah, right," I remarked with sarcasm, now watching him through the rearview mirror. "I wanna know more about the Kingz."

"I don't know what you're talking about."

I smiled. *Now* this son of a bitch wants to keep his trap closed. It's all a front, though. I'm all too familiar with his type. It won't take much to make him sing. He's already a canary. This fucker is probably dying to tell me what I want to know. All he needs is a little push.

"As I understand, Mr. Chambers," I started, "you're on probation for assaulting a Ms. Lynda Joyce who as I understand, is your son's mother. The judge granted her petition for a restraining order, and you violated that on several occasions by driving out to her apartment on Carter Street and harassing her."

"That's a lie!" he contested with anger. "I haven't been harassing her!"

I had anticipated this reply, which is why I was already reaching for the manila envelope in the glove compartment. Switching on the interior lights, I extracted large photos I'd taken of Chambers and his son's mother, standing outside of her apartment door, talking on three different occasions.

"The FBI doesn't make accusations," I said, holding the photos so he could see them. "Unless we can validate them."

"I wasn't harassing her," Chambers stood his ground. "We were talking like civilized adults."

"These photos show that you're in violation of a court-ordered restraining order." I placed the photos back inside the envelope, then shut the interior lights off. "That, plus the gun, equals ten years. I mean, I can think of some more shit if that's not enough."

I turned my attention to a minivan that rode by with a female behind the wheel. Other than that, the street was quiet. The only noise that could be heard inside the car was the low hum of its engine, and Chambers' concentrated breathing. I already knew he was mentally fighting to make a decision but didn't have to guess what that decision would be.

Suddenly, he exhaled sharply. "I don't know a whole lot about them."

"I know the basic stuff about them," I said, still watching him through the rearview mirror. "Like, their names, where they live, and certain places they visit."

"If you know all of that," Chambers replied. "What the hell do you expect for *me* to tell you?"

"You can start off by telling me about the two men they executed last Wednesday. What were their names? Where did it happen?"

"Greg and Mike," he offered. "I didn't know them niggas. The Kingz called all their workers to the warehouse that night. I've never seen any of their other workers until then."

"So, they called you all in to witness the fatality of a couple of violators?"

"Yep," he replied. "That was the first and last time I'd been there. The first and last time I'd seen the other workers."

"Is this the same warehouse on Fulton Industrial?" I asked, knowing the place.

"Yeah."

"What's inside this warehouse?" I wanted to know. "Is it completely empty?"

"It's not empty, at all," answered Chambers. "I really can't explain it, but it has an office and several rooms. The room we went

190

into was large and had four real thrones, in which the Kingz sat in. We sat in metal folding chairs."

"Do you know anything about any other murders they'd committed or orchestrated?"

"None."

"I think you're lying, Steve."

"I'm not. They don't tell us shit like that."

"Well, from here on out," I said, "you'll be my eyes and ears. If you hear anything about any up-and-coming shipments of drugs, or murders, I want all the details."

"What if I don't comply?"

"Then you'll serve ten years in prison," I answered. "I have a gun with your prints on it. Plus, photos of you violating a court order." Now, I turned in my seat to face him. "You can play the tough-guy role all you want – I know better. By your second year in prison, you'll be somebody's bitch. You'll probably get raped in intake. If you think I'm bluffing, try me. I'll drive you down to the police station and have you booked, right now."

Sighing, he directed his attention out the window to his left, slowly shaking his head from side to side. Then, after another expel of air, Chambers asked, "So, how do I contact you?"

Playa Ray

Chapter 22

Tuesday

"Bishop," I answered my cell phone as I watched a gray Mercedes-Benz G-Wagon pull into the driveway of the house next door to the one I was parked in front of.

I know I said I would follow James Young for a while but, for some reason, I could not stop thinking about Ray Young, and his mistress, Sylvia Baker. No, I don't believe Young murdered her himself, despite seeing her on video, leaving with someone in a white truck that night. However, though I'm not completely committed to the notion, it's possible that Young could have had her murdered for whatever reason, but the guy he hired, had taken it too far by giving in to his sexual impulse. Makes perfect sense, right?

"His name is Keyonne Sharpe," Homicide Detective McCoy said through the earpiece.

I was confused. "Whose name?"

"The suspect," she answered. "The one in Baker's case. The semen found, belongs to Keyonne Sharpe. I contacted DMV about the white Chevy Tahoe. It's registered in his wife's name. Her house is being watched at this moment."

"What about the media?" I inquired.

"It's in the morning's paper," she said. "But the news stations will broadcast it at six o'clock tonight."

"Which would let him know that he's a wanted man," I stated, still not understanding why the locals did that. They should know by now that once a person is put on notice they are wanted by the law it gives them a head start for the border.

"We'll catch him, Bishop," McCoy said with much confidence.

"I sure hope so, Lieutenant."

Ringing off, I looked at the clock on the dashboard of the Ford Explorer, seeing that it was only 10:41 a.m. At eight o'clock I had driven out to Gerald Osborne's mansion, to question him about some of his finances that weren't lining up, but he wasn't home. Rucker was off, investigating another case, which is why the drive was solo, but, instead of returning to the office, I drove out to Riverdale, Georgia, and had been casing out Ray Young's home ever since, hoping he would lead me to Keyonne Sharpe, or whoever he hired to murder his mistress.

After another twelve minutes, Young emerged from his home, wearing a dark blue suit, a gold crown atop his head, and carrying another outfit enclosed in stain-proof plastic, slung over his shoulder, with something resembling a small treasure chest in his other hand. After placing everything, including the crown, in the rear seat of the BMW that was parked in the driveway, behind his Oldsmobile, he climbed in behind the wheel, and immediately pulled out, being that the car was already running before he came out.

I was parked five houses down from his which was in the opposite direction of the way he had to go in order to reach the main road. Once he made a left on the main road, I put the SUV into gear and followed him to the expressway. When he got off on Fulton Industrial, I pretty much knew where he was headed. So, as always, when he pulled up to the gate of their non-operational warehouse, I pulled into the lot of the Colonial warehouse, which was right across the street.

It was still business hours for the Colonial workers, but I was able to obtain a parking spot that gave me a good vantage point of the building across the street. However, by the time I parked, Young had already cleared the gate and was driving toward the entrance. I had my binoculars out by the time he parked beside his brother's car and began pulling his things from the rear seat, before heading inside.

I still couldn't figure out why these idiots would purchase this big ass building on Fulton Industrial. One of the most known areas frequented by law enforcers of every agency in the Atlanta region. It's not like they're moving truckloads of drugs, but hell, they could at least buy or steal a few tractor-trailers to make the warehouse *look* legit. Right now, the only vehicles present were the two BMWs belonging to James and Ray Young, and a dark blue van parked to the left of the entrance, with its rear-facing the building.

At this time, my personal cell phone rang.

"Tell me something good," I answered, seeing that it was Rucker's number on the screen.

"How'd it go with Osborne?" he inquired.

"He wasn't home."

"Are you waiting him out?"

"Shit no!" I answered as the dark blue BMW belonging to Keith Daniels entered the lot of the warehouse across the street. "Right now, I'm just out and about. Do you need my assistance on something?"

He cleared his throat. "No, but we do need to get this Osborne case over with."

"True." I was watching Daniels enter the building with what appeared to be the same items Young was carrying. "I think he knows he's going to prison."

"I'm quite sure he does."

"You think he'll skip town.?"

Rucker laughed. "I sure hope so. I haven't ridden shotgun with the U.S. Marshals in forever."

"Yeah, I wouldn't mind the trip," I told him. "In fact, I'm making a B-line back to Osborne's place, right now."

"Great! Let me know how it turns out."

"Sure."

Placing the phone back onto its clip on my belt, I was back to peering through my binoculars, assuming Frederick Mills will soon show up, being that his comrades have. I was also wondering about the items they were carrying. I was sure that the small treasure chests held their chains with the *KINGZ* medallions, but why the crowns? Why the extra outfits or dress suits covered in plastic covers? All this for a meeting? Or maybe they were meeting up here and planned on heading out together in the van. A group date with four women, perhaps?

No, that didn't fit. The date did, but not the van. I couldn't decipher the construction of its interior, but I couldn't see these guys traveling together in that considering the *royal* image they were endeavoring with the chains, crowns, and—

Wait a minute! It's not a date and it's definitely not one of their meetings, like the first one I encountered them having at James Young's home. They weren't wearing crowns, nor carrying small treasure chests and extra clothing then.

Now, as I watched Mills pull up to the warehouse, it all started to dawn on me. What I was thinking was probably wrong, but I'm rarely ever wrong when I think like this in investigations. However, there's only one way to find out if I was halfway right in this case. I dialed Chambers' number.

"Already?" This is how he answered the phone, clearly checking the caller's ID beforehand.

I got straight to business. "On the night Greg and Mike were murdered. How were the Kingz dressed?"

"They had on crowns and robes," Chambers answered as if describing something he encounters daily.

"Robes?"

"Yeah," he said. "Just like the ones the kings wore back in the Biblical days n' shit."

"Have you ever seen them dressed up like that before?" I asked, trying not to jump the gun too soon.

"Not with my own eyes," he answered. "But I heard they were dressed like that at the New Year Eve's party they threw at Club Strokers."

"That's the only time you've heard of it?"

"That's it."

Shit! This only means there's a possible chance that I'm right about what's about to take place inside the building across the street from where I'm parked. From what I understand, the crowns and robes are for special occasions, such as grand parties, and assuming the role of magistrates. However, it's twelve in the afternoon, which is too damn early for a grand party, but not too early to pass down the death sentence to a violator of the Crown.

Even if an execution was actually about to take place. What the hell could I do to prevent it? Notify the locals? Please! Again, I will not jeopardize my investigation, because my subjects like to engage in extracurricular activities like anybody else. If a fucker violated and must be punished, so be it. People are murdered every day, right?

I did want to stick around to see how many bodies would be brought out to the van, but I have Rucker under the impression that I was on my way back to Gerald Osborne's mansion, which is something I have no intention of doing. Well, not today, but I know I can't stay out here for too long. I had to report back to the bureau. In fact, that's exactly what I'm going to do.

"Rucker," my partner answered on the third ring.

"I'm at Osborne's," I lied. "He's still not in. Should I wait, or try again tomorrow?"

"That's really up to you," he told me. "Whichever you choose, I'll document it, and send it up."

"Are you back at the bureau?"

"I'm en route."

"Okay," I said slowly, watching the Kingzman who'd stepped out of the security booth at the gate, to fire up a cigarette. "I haven't had lunch yet, so I'll grab a bite, then give Osborne another hour and a half to show."

"Great! I'll document it as soon as I get back in."

"Thanks, Ruck!"

"No problem."

Okay. Now I have spare time on my hands. I just hope it's enough for me to find out what I need to find out. If this is what I think it is, then I'm sure the Kingzmen will be responsible for disposing the bodies. If I could just get a few pictures of them with the corpses, and a few close-up pictures of the corpses and their dispatched locations, I'm pretty sure Hopkins would grant me this investigation. If he doesn't, then I'll have no choice but to assume *he's* on the take.

I didn't see any more movement until twelve minutes before one o'clock. That was when Mills and Daniels exited the warehouse, carrying the same items they carried inside, and heading for their cars. At this time, I was holding my camera, focusing the lens, although it was almost a blur from this distance. I managed to snapshots of the two before they climbed into their cars and pretty much drove off together.

Ray Young emerged almost five minutes later. As I snapped shots of him, I felt my Adrenalin rushing a little. I mean, I felt like I was real close to having my shot at nailing these hoodlums. Three Kingz were already out. I didn't see any reason for James Young and the Kingzmen to stay any longer, other than to prep the bodies for transport.

As Ray Young's BMW reached the security booth, a Kingzman emerged from the building and approached the rear of the van. When he opened the rear doors, I was able to see him through its windshield, and he appeared to be moving things around as if making room. Just then, James Young emerged, carrying his own regalia. After saying a few words to the Kingzman, he got into his car and drove off. The man re-entered the building, leaving the rear of the van open.

"I'll catch you some other time, my friend," I said, as I watched Young drive off down Fulton Industrial.

Then, my eyes reverted to the warehouse. Seeing movement, I lifted my camera for a better view and saw the same Kingzman holding the door to the entrance open. At that time, another one exited, walking backward, holding onto something I couldn't see until he and the person he was carrying it with were in full view.

A body!

Click! Click!

I knew this shape pretty well, though I could barely make out the material it was wrapped in. Cellophane, perhaps? Once the two men shoved the body into the rear of the van, they shut the doors, which pretty much indicated that there were no more. The one who was holding the door, locked it, then crossed over to a caged-in shed to free the two Rottweilers, while the other two men climbed into the van. Only taking a few seconds to show the dogs some affection, the third man climbed into the side door of the van, and it sped toward the entry gate, with the dogs frolicking behind.

The Kingzman in the security booth, let the gate open for them. The dogs had made it to the gate while it was in the process of closing but were obedient enough to not venture outside of it. After securing it with a lock and chain, the fourth man joined the others in the van, and they made off down Fulton Industrial.

Well, that was my cue. I backed out of my spot and drove to the edge of Colonial's parking lot. The main road was busy with mainly tractor-trailers, which made it uneasy for me to pull out, so when I was finally able to, I spied the van ahead of me at about a quarter of a mile. I had to close the gap a little, so I maneuvered in and out of lanes, passing other motorists in the process. These fuckers are not getting away from me today.

Whoop! Whoop!

The reflex action of anyone hearing a siren is to glance into the rearview mirror, which is what I did, and I'd be damned if the squad car of a local bonehead was on my tail. Being that I was in the middle of the three lanes, I ignited my right turn signal, and moved into the far right lane, when opportunity presented itself, hoping he'd just drive by me, but he didn't. Exhaling sharply, I took another look up ahead at the van that was gradually getting away as I brought the Explorer to a halt and got out my credentials.

Now, as I kept my eyes glued to the rearview, I expected the officer to step out of his vehicle, so we could get this over with, but he wasn't budging. Perhaps he was awaiting a response from dispatch on my license plate. After what seemed like an eon, the dark-complexioned, 5'11, 165-pound male climbed from his vehicle. As he took his precious time moving toward the SUV with his left hand rested on his sidearm, I was half hoping a semi plowed into him, and knocked his stupid ass into outer space. Yeah, I know I'm wrong for thinking like that, but this fucker couldn't have picked a worse time to pull me over. I rolled down the window when he approached.

"Illegal lane change," he explained as if assuming I was going to question the stop, which I wasn't.

"I've already concluded that," I answered, handing my credentials over to him. "I'm on a stakeout and was trailing a few of my subjects."

"Were you now?" He looked over his left shoulder as if he was capable of figuring out which vehicle I was after. Looking back at my credentials, then back at me, he said, "FBI or not, I still have to run you in. If everything checks out, the ticket's on me. Oh, and I apologize for interfering with your investigation, but I got a job to do also."

***

Wednesday

"Please enlighten me on how you fucked *this* one up, Bishop," Director Manny Hopkins said, looking through the photos of yesterday that I had digitally enhanced by one of our data analysts.

"It wasn't my fault this time," I argued, still pissed about yesterday's ordeal. "Some cocksucker pulled me over while I was trailing them to wherever they were going to dispose of the body."

"Did you get this cocksucker's name?" There was a smirk on his face.

"Of course, I got his name *and* badge number."

"Well," he said, placing the photos atop his desk. "If you were doing this legally, you could've cited him for interfering with a federal investigation."

Is he implying what I think he's implying? "Are you gonna grant me permission to—"

"You don't even know where the fucking body is!" Hopkins cut me off. "In fact, you don't know *who* the body is. As far as we know, the fucker could be from Utah or some shit!"

"So, you're agreeing with me that they were carrying a body?" I asked, trying a different tact

He picked up the photos and sifted through them again. "Hell, it doesn't take a rocket scientist. Yes, I agree, but these guys are their henchmen, right?"

"Right." I think I know where this is going.

"You want my permission to investigate the Kingz?" Hopkins went on, "But in your photos, they're not the ones carrying a dead body. Who's to say the Kingz even knew about the body? Maybe the Kingzmen had the body stashed somewhere in the warehouse and waited until the coast was clear before disposing of it. This is the scenario of your photos project, considering the time of departure on each one, and I'm quite sure the Justice Department will draw the same conclusion."

"But you could make this decision without them," I reminded him. "You'll only need their permission to move in on the Kingz, once I gather enough intelligence on them, and I'm quite sure I can do a more thorough investigation if I had a team."

He said nothing as he continued sifting through the photographs. Finally setting them down, he leaned back in his chair, and just stared at me, which is something I've always hated. It made me nervous. Especially when I'm trying to get his approval on a case. However, to avoid eye contact, I pulled out my cellular and feigned to be searching for something. I believe Hopkins knew he made people nervous when he stared at them, but I refused to give him the pleasure of knowing he did the same to Special Agent Brian Bishop. Poker face, bitches!

"I'll tell you what," he finally said. "Let me sleep on it. In the meantime, compose a list of agents you'll like to have working under you."

"You'll let me run lead?" I posed, making sure to solidify the position I rightfully deserve.

"'If' I give my approval," he stressed, "I'll let you run lead. However, if you fuck this up, it'll be a cold day in hell before you get my blessing again. But, like I said, *if* I give my approval. Now, get the fuck out of my office! I've seen enough of you for one day."

I can't remember the last time I left Hopkins' office in good spirits. Fuck that! I was ecstatic! Sure, he said to let him sleep on it, but I know he'd already made his decision, and the first two agents on my *wish* list would be Wilma Reid and Powell. Plus, I'll jot down the names of a few good agents I've had the pleasure of working with in the past.

"Bishop?"

Speak of the devil! Special Agent Powell stood before me in stonewashed jeans, a black sweater, white dilapidated running shoes, and a black skull cap pulled low over his head, which is one of the perks of being an FBI agent because we can pretty much dress however we feel like dressing unless an assignment called for formal or tactical wear.

"Powell!" I greeted, extending my hand. "How's it going?"

"Great!" He took my hand in a firm grip. "How are you holding up?"

"No complaints on my end."

"That's good to hear," he replied, looking around as if biding for time. Then, he asked, "Are you doing anything right now?"

Well, I was about to compile a list with your name on it. "No, not at the moment. What's up?"

"I have to meet with Agent Kent," Powell explained. "Thomas would usually tag along and pose as one of his side chicks in public, but she's out sick, and I'm not trying to go alone."

"What about the other guys on the squad?"

He was shaking his head. "They have their own assignments. Besides, I don't want just anybody riding with me, but if you have other plans—"

"I'll meet you in the garage," I said, cutting him off. "Once I grab my coat, and log it in, I'll be right down. Where's the destination, anyway?"

"Gwinnett County."

Just as promised, I logged in my movement, grabbed my coat and keys, then took the elevator down to the parking garage, where Powell was waiting in the confines of a white Isuzu Rodeo with the engine running. As I climbed in beside him, I immediately caught a whiff of strawberry scent, which wafted off the rubbery air freshener dangling from the rear-view mirror, although it didn't rid the car of the smell of cigarettes that was barely noticeable.

We pretty much rode in silence for the first fifteen minutes or so, although the radio was playing alternative songs at a low volume. It wasn't until we were traveling along the expressway when Powell turned the radio up for a song that must've been one of his favorites, because he drummed on the steering wheel, and sung along as if he was the only one in the truck. All I could do was smile to myself.

"Who was that?" I inquired when the song had gone off.

"That was Creed!" He said this with much reverence. "These guys are one of the best rock groups to ever do it!"

"Your favorite, huh?"

"One of 'em," he answered, stifling a yawn.

"So, is there anything particular I need to know about this meeting?" I questioned, seeing that I was about to enter unfamiliar territory. "Is there a certain role I'll have to play, being that Thomas is out?"

"No, you're good," he told me. "After finding out Thomas was sick, North and I rearranged the meeting, picking a whole new location. He figured it was safe enough for me to go alone, which is why he didn't appoint anyone to join me. So, really, all you have to do is sit back and enjoy the ride."

Well, that's exactly what I did. We arrived in Lawrenceville, Georgia, at a little after twelve in the afternoon. I've journeyed out here on several occasions, but still wasn't conversant with the city's terrain, although a few places stood out to me. By now, I had shed my coat to acclimatize to the car's temperature and found myself drumming my fingers on my thigh, and bobbing my head to the awkward-sounding music coming from the speakers.

Shortly, Powell pulled the Isuzu into the parking lot of a Publix grocery store, which was pretty much empty. I immediately spotted a green Buick Regal on chrome wheels, sitting off to the side, and occupied by one individual at the wheel. Exhaust fumes billowing from the rear of the car indicated the engine was running. I was hoping the guy wasn't Agent Kent, and that this was not the way they arranged their meeting, because it was too conspicuous, but I was wrong.

Powell parked a short distance from the Regal. Seconds later, Kent emerged from the car, clad in blue jeans and gray sweater. As if the scene wasn't already suggestive, the Denver agent was sporting him ominous *Drop Squad* chain and carrying a briefcase. Plus, he suspiciously looked around as he crossed over toward us.

"This looks more like a drug transaction," I remarked on the scene.

"Which is the look we were going for," Powell admitted. "You know, just in case he was being followed."

"By Drop Squad members?"

"Or some other agency."

"I see."

"Agent Kent," Powell spoke, when the guy climbed in behind me. "This is Agent Bishop, my tag along for today."

"How's it going, brother?" Kent extended his hand.

"Pretty good," I replied, shaking his hand.

"Whatcha got for me?" Powell got straight to business.

"Right now," Kent said. "They got me playing bodyguard to Miles Whitley. He owns the Twin Lanes bowling alley in East Point and has a Caucasian girlfriend by the name of Reese Blanchard. She's thirty-six, and resides in Dalton, Georgia, although she crashes at his place a lot. Here," he said, handing Powell a notepad. "Her address is in there, along with other things I've recorded."

"The Kingz?" Powell inquired, upon glancing through the pad This definitely had my attention.

"They're some new group he was raving about," Kent explained. "I heard him question their come up as if he had reasons to believe they're responsible for hitting one of their drug houses last year and knocking off their men."

"Did Whitley say anything that led you to believe he's going to retaliate on this group?" I asked, clearly intervening.

"Not directly, but I wouldn't put it past this dude. He's a wolf in sheep's clothing."

I thought about this during the drive back to Atlanta, and I definitely remember the home invasion Kent had referred to, which happened in early December, at a house out in Riverdale, Georgia, where two of their men had become casualties. I also remember listening to the recorded exchange between Williams and Lakes about the price going up on the culprits' heads.

If Whitley had an inkling that the Kingz were responsible, did it mean that Lakes and Williams shared his sentiment? If so, this meant that the Kingz' lives could be in grave danger. Or maybe Whitley was just going down his list of usual suspects and ended up mentioning the Kingz way too many times in front of Kent, but it was good that the agent had thought to document it.

"So, what's one of your favorite past times?" I asked Powell once the radio station had taken a commercial break.

"I don't have many," he answered. "But I do enjoy playing canasta with the fellas on my days off."

"Canasta?" I inquired.

"It's almost like rummy," he explained. "But you use two decks of cards. It's actually fun. You'd like it."

"Maybe." I directed my attention out my side window. "What about family outings? I'm quite sure there's something you like to do with the wife and kids. You do have kids, right?"

"Not that I know of," the hurt in Powell's voice, was evident. Or was I imagining it? "I've never had a wife," he continued, "or anybody worth holding that title. What about you? You seem like a family man."

The thought of Monique and Melody made me smile. "I do have a girlfriend and daughter," I told him. "Well, Melody is my girlfriend's daughter, and I plan on adopting her."

"Through nuptial?"

Shit no! "We're exploring that option, also," I lied, retrieving my business cellular from my pants pocket. "Bishop," I announced.

"I managed to sneak down to the basement on my break," Chad Hoffman said through the phone in almost a whisper.

"Okay," I pressed, knowing he was about to tell me about a conversation he'd heard on the recorder from the wiretapping machine I snuck back into the building, and now had secretly running in the basement, with the help of Hoffman, who changes the films whenever he can.

"There was a conversation about some trucks being delivered to the Palace on Saturday," Hoffman informed. "Do you know where this place is?"

"No," I replied, thinking of Chambers. "But I'll find out."

Chapter 23

Saturday

January 18, 2003

It was my off day, and I had planned to spend it with Monique and Melody, but once again, I found myself parked across the street from the Kingz' warehouse which I was informed by Chambers is known as the Palace. Also, as of today, Director Hopkins still hasn't gotten back to me about approving or disapproving my investigation into the Kingz, though I turned my team request list into him on Thursday.

Now, as my BMW sat idling amongst the other vehicles belonging to the Colonial employees at 11:29 a.m., I had my binoculars glued to my face, watching the goings-on at the warehouse belonging to the Kingz which wasn't much. I've been in this exact spot ever since eight o'clock, even though the Kingz and Kingzmen hadn't begun arriving until after ten-thirty, and I still haven't seen any signs of any kind of trucks that were supposed to be delivered.

On Wednesday, after returning to the building from my tagging along with Powell, I journeyed down to the basement and listened to the recorded phone conversation between James Young and Frederick Mills myself. All Mills had told Young is that the trucks would be delivered to the Palace on Saturday. No set time was ever mentioned.

"Bishop," I answered my ringing cell phone, after placing my binoculars on the seat beside me.

"Detective McCoy," my caller identified herself.

"How's it going, Lieutenant?"

"Oh, the usual," she replied with a sigh. "If it's not one murder, it's another."

"Who's on the slab now?" I inquired, thinking about the body I saw the Kingzmen with this past Tuesday.

"Leslie Sharpe," she answered. "Wife of Keyonne Sharpe."

"Are you serious?" Well, of course, she's serious. "I thought the house was being watched by Cobb County's finest."

"Not last night, apparently," the detective spoke with sarcasm. "Someone disfigured their alarm system and breached the back door to get in. The children found her this morning with her throat slit. They were unharmed."

"Now that's sad," I expressed, as I watched a tractor-trailer pull up to the gate of the warehouse across the street, followed by a blue Mazda Protegé. "It's one thing when your home alarm can't protect your family. It's another thing when your children wake up and find you dead in your own bed after an apparent burglary."

McCoy sighed. "Yeah, I feel sorry for those kids."

"What's the word on Sharpe?" I inquired. By this time, the truck was driving toward the building, with the Mazda still trailing.

"We're still banging on doors or whatnot," she responded. "Right now, both the governor and commissioner are in talks of issuing a reward for his capture. How long that'll take, I have no idea."

"If I stumble upon some information that could assist you," I said. "You know I won't hesitate to call."

"Thanks, Bishop."

"No problem."

Tossing the phone on the passenger seat, I grabbed my binoculars and peered through them just in time to see the truck backing its trailer into one of the loading docks on the side of the building, under the watchful eyes of three of the Kingzmen. The Mazda sat in wait, the occupant was still inside.

As I watched the truck, I struggled with the asinine thought that the trailer contained a large shipment of drugs, although I heard with my own ears that *trucks* would be delivered – not drugs.

At this time, the truck driver, after parking perfectly into the loading dock, was walking toward the Mazda, where he climbed into the passenger side. It made a wide U-turn, headed back down toward the entry gate that was already mechanically sliding open as it neared. As it made its way down Fulton Industrial, one of the Kingzmen entered the building, leaving the other two standing with the two guard dogs. I was half expecting the Kingz to exit, but after four minutes had gone by, my expectations diminished.

This is when I realized what was going on. Maybe these guys are smart after all and decorating the warehouse with tractor-trailers is quite genius if I may. Hell, this was my reason for being out here today – to find out about the delivered trucks. I could head on out to Monique's place now, right? Yeah, I could, but I think I'll stick around a little while longer.

Approximately forty-seven minutes had elapsed by the time another rig arrived at the Palace, followed by the same Mazda. At this time, I swapped my binoculars for my camera, deciding I'll get a few pics of the truck driver, but first I got a shot of the car's license plate before it cleared the entry gate. I'll get the alphanumerics to Hoffman some other time.

Today, I came prepared with a new extended snap-on lens that had a view tantamount to that of my binoculars. Therefore, when the driver of the truck had finally docked it beside the other one and was headed back to the Mazda, I managed to get a couple of clear shots of him. I'll run them through our face recognition data system next week.

Once again, the Mazda eased on down Fulton Industrial, which had me wondering if they'd return with another one. If so, how many more? Although both rigs boasted the *Ryder* logo, I'm one hundred percent sure they're stolen. I can run this by Atlanta Chief of Police Darrel Manning who could contact surrounding Ryder truck rental dealers to see who's missing some property, but that would garner questions from the chief that I won't be too enthused to entertain. To do so, would only cause him to send cavalry to the Palace, and—no, I won't mention this to Manning, or anybody else for that matter.

It was 2:07 p.m. when the man backed a fourth truck into the loading dock. This time, after parking the rig, he crossed over to the Mazda and leaned against it. Just then, the driver of the car, a female, got out and joined him. I managed to get a facial shot of her as they cuddled against the car. You know, just in case.

The Kingzman that had entered the building while the guy was parking the last truck, now emerged from the building, rejoining the other two with the dogs. Okay, *now* I was expecting for the Kingz to show themselves which is something they had not done since they arrived.

My camera was at the ready when the entrance door swung open, and only three of the Kingz emerged. As I snapped shots of them, I realized Ray Young was the missing link. Maybe he stopped by the restroom to relieve his bladder. God knows I'm in dire need to do so myself.

Upon approaching the truck driver, Mills handed him a brown paper bag in exchange for what appeared to be the keys to the trucks. From my vantage point, it seemed like the man was trying to explain something to them, but Mills was showing impatience toward him as if trying to rush the man along. Plus, I noticed the Kingz kept looking over their shoulders at the entrance as if hoping Ray Young didn't come out just yet. As if he and this guy are mutual enemies.

Hmm! Interesting!

Suddenly, the three Kingz simultaneously looked back at the entrance. Following their gazes, I saw that Ray Young had exited. The whole scene was uncanny, seeing they all just froze, and how the younger brother seemed to pay them no mind as he moved toward his BMW where he leaned against the trunk and looked out at them with disinterest.

Click!

Then, as if someone un-paused a movie, everyone resumed. The man and his companion got into the Mazda and rode off, and the other Kingz crossed over to Ray. After a few seconds of exchanging words, they all climbed into their own cars. At this point, I was thinking of trailing behind the Mazda, to see what all I could find out about this guy, because if he's a threat to either King, then he probably need to be eliminated, which caused me to think about what Agent Kent said about Whitley's suspicions. The same applies to him and his group also.

***

One Week Later

"Sir, that bus is set to arrive around eleven fifteen this morning," the receptionist informed me over the phone.

"Thank you, ma'am!"

"You're welcome, sir."

I placed the receiver into its cradle, then checked my watch as I walked away from the payphone. Lucky for me, I had approximately twenty-nine minutes before the ETA of the Greyhound bus that was on its way from Bibb County, though I didn't intend to leave the Greyhound station that merged with Marta's Garnett transit station, and sat right across from the Pretrial Detention/Municipal Court building.

The sharp wind that perpetually swept throughout the atmosphere, had my ears frozen numb, considering I didn't have on earmuffs, and I'd chosen a ball cap, in lieu of a skull cap. However, I was greatly depending on the bib of my cap, and the dark lenses of my sunglasses to conceal eighty percent of my face from any and all visual recording devices, and people with photographic memories, because I don't need anything, or anyone being able to place me anywhere near this place after today.

Well, another week had gone by and I still can't believe Director Hopkins hadn't said a word to me about the Kingz investigation. Not even in passing. I wanted to inquire on it, but I had the feeling that Hopkins was waiting for me to do so, so he could throw a fit and deny my request. No sir, I'll wait his ass out.

Now, with my hands stuffed into my pants pockets, I was standing at the Greyhound's information board, pretending to be checking the bus schedules. Just this past Thursday, according to the phone conversation Hoffman and I had recorded, Ray Young had driven out to Cordele, Georgia to meet with some drug trafficker who'd driven up from Miami, and the other Kingz had secretly followed him to make sure he was well protected. I would have nosed around but Rucker, myself, and several other agents were out at

Gerald Osborne's mansion arresting him for embezzlement. Plus, it had taken forever to document all of Osborne's assets as they were being confiscated.

I usually didn't participate in that part of an arrest, but Rucker was point, and he insisted. Tackling that project, and momentarily playing comforter to Osborne's distressed wife, who was subsequently escorted to her mother's home by one of our agents, had us tied up until after eight that night. Then, we had to do more paperwork upon returning to the office, which had me returning home at a quarter to ten. I was exhausted but still managed to call and check up on Monique and Melody.

Yes, I missed that drug deal in Crisp County on Thursday but didn't plan on missing the one the Kingz was set to attend in Lithonia today. Well, that depends on how things will play out within the next hour or so because I've been anticipating this day for five years.

A Greyhound bus pulling into the terminal caught my attention. I managed to read the digital sign that read *New York* before it parked amid the other four buses that were already docked and watched as people shuffled towards it with their belongings. Then, by instinct, I slowly scanned the crowded bus terminal to see if anyone was watching me specifically. You know, one could never be too careful these days.

At this time, another bus roared into the terminal, the noise of its diesel-operated engine commingled with that of the others as it choked and coughed out dark exhaust fumes, adding to the already polluted atmosphere, but that wasn't my focus right now. I was more focused on the digital sign that advertised the bus as hailing from Bibb County.

As people gathered their things and moved in its direction, I only inched forward, hoping to blend in with the crowd of people who were expecting someone to dismount. However, the person I'm waiting on doesn't have a clue as to what I look like, or that I was even awaiting them, but I'd committed his identification to memory after hours of staring at the photo in his criminal file.

There was a loud hiss from the bus before the service door creaked open, and a handful of people slowly poured out, some gathering things from the compartment beneath the bus. Then, I spotted him. The brown khaki pants, blue light-fabric coat, and the cheap, black and white shoes that looked like knockoff versions of low-cut All-Stars, were definitely not hard to miss.

Despite the photo and description on Criminal Records, Leonard Watts seemed to have gained quite a few pounds. Whereas his face had appeared shrunken in on the photo, it was now more proportioned, and I doubt if he still weighs one hundred and sixty-eight pounds. He looked more like two hundred and twenty, especially in the upper body, which was barely noticeable through the small jacket. Perhaps this came from spending large amounts of time working out like most criminals do to intimidate other prisoners, or to impress the female guards. Plus, with his box-style haircut, his complexion had gotten darker.

A brown paper bag was tucked under his arm, Watts stepped down from the bus, looking around, but not as though he was looking for someone. He was taking in the scenery, happy to be home. Even without the prison-issued release clothing, a person could see it in his eyes that he'd been away for a while. Hell, I was almost happy for him myself. *Almost.*

Moving on, Watts walked in the direction of the Pretrial Detention building, which is also in the direction of the parking lot I'd parked the unmark in. I devised this plan years ago, although the beginning of it will pretty much be whimsical and is solely dependent upon this guy's movements.

Making it to the corner, Watts made a left, keeping to the sidewalk, and I was about thirty yards behind him, with my hands stuffed into my pockets for warmth. As I passed the parking lot, I looked over at the departmental Crown Victoria, wondering if I should go ahead and climb behind the wheel, but I had no clue as to where he was headed.

Suddenly, Watts ducked into a check-cashing place. That's when I realized he was about to cash the twenty-five-dollar check given to him by the Department of Corrections upon being released.

However, if he plans to take the train, he'd have to retrace his steps and pass me in the process. I stopped in my tracks and found myself looking over at the roof of the Ford again. Yes, it was time to make an executive decision.

"Fuck it!" I mumbled to myself, now moving towards the un-mark.

There was no telling how long Watts was going to be inside the store, so I managed to pull from my parking spot in record-breaking time. Now, I had to make something of a horseshoe on Broad Street to enter the small lot of the cashing place, but there were too many vehicles passing by putting me in the mind of Fulton Industrial. However, I was not in a civilian vehicle this time.

Considering that, I switched on my emergency lights, and sounded my siren. Oh yeah! That won me major respect. Drivers began to realize that their vehicles were equipped with brakes and used them to make a hole for me. Taking advantage, I pulled out, made a left turn, then completed the horseshoe by making another quick left turn, but another hole had to be made for me, in order for me to gain access to the store's lot.

The moment the hole was made, I quickly disengaged the emergency lights, and pulled to the far right of the small building, hoping I was out of view of their exterior camera, though I didn't see any. There were only three other cars present. I slapped the gear into park but left the engine running, and donned my black gloves.

Just then, the store's entrance door swung open, but a woman exited, stuffing bills into her large pocketbook as she approached a white Toyota Camry. Not once did she look in my direction, which indicated that she was unaware of the small disturbance I just made in the middle of the street before pulling in. I was a bit relieved that she got into her car and immediately pulled out, eliminating herself as a witness.

Momentarily, the door came open again. The glass on it was tinted, but not dark enough for me not to spy the khaki pants, and black and white shoes before Watts came into full view. That's when I made my move, lunging from the car, but not fast enough to draw unwanted attention. To match his stride, I circled a Chevy Malibu and met him head-on.

"Leonard Watts?" I spoke, blocking his path.

He regarded me sideways. "Um, yeah."

"I'm Special Agent Michael Callahan," I said, flashing my credentials for half a second. "From the Federal Bureau of Investigation."

"I just got out," Watts stated, apprehension now registering on his face. "I ain't did shit. I *just* got off the Greyhound."

"We know this," I assured, taking a casual look around. "What I'm doing, right now is only routine. Could you, please, step over to my car?"

He wavered, only taking a mere glance over at the Crown Victoria.

"There are no new charges against you, Watts," I resumed. "However, if you don't comply. I was given direct orders to take you in for obstruction. Trust me, a federal obstruction is way worse than a regular obstruction. Plus, it'll be a violation of parole. Back to prison, you go."

I turned and headed back to my car, leaving Watts to weigh his options. I mean, I already knew what he would pick. The human mind is so easy to manipulate, especially when it came to the law. It doesn't matter how much a person may *think* they know about the law they can still be duped. So, you better believe I just pulled the wool over this fucker's eyes.

Did I look back to see if he was following me? Shit no! I nonchalantly climbed behind the wheel, closed the door, and waited. At that time, an SUV pulled in. Before the driver could get out, Watts appeared beside my car, looking like a man who'd just accepted his fate. I rolled the window down.

"Do I have to sit in the back?" he asked.

"That's up to you," I responded, rolling the window back up.

He seemed to cogitate this for a moment, before circling the rear of the car and climbing in beside me, placing his paper bag at his feet. I backed out, ready to take on the traffic on Broad Street again, but this time, I waited for an opening, then casually pulled out of the lot.

"I thought the James P. Russell building was that way," Watts said, gesturing with his thumb.

"We're not going to the James P. Russell building."

"Apparently," he sneered.

"You paroled out at your aunt's house, right?" I changed the subject. "Olivia Bryant?"

"Yeah." He was giving me a suspicious look. "Is that where you're taking me?"

"Nope," I answered. "You'll get there on your own time. How did you spend your time in prison? Pick up any trades?"

"Not really," Watts answered. "But I did get my GED. Other than that, I worked out, watched TV, and read books."

"What kind of books?"

"Street shit mostly. I fucks with Stuart Woods and John Grisham, too."

"Did you join a gang while you were in?" I asked, already knowing the answer.

He looked at me but didn't answer.

"You have no reason to lie to me, Watts," I pressed. "As I said, no new charges are being brought against you, but I want you to know that we kept tabs on you. So, there isn't too much we don't know about you."

"Yeah, I joined a gang," he finally admitted. "But I did that shit to survive. Niggas were actually getting raped in that motherfucker. If you were alone, you were a target."

Keeping one hand still on the wheel, I threw the other up in mock surrender. "Hey, I'm not judging you. You did what you had to do."

"I'm not bringing that shit back to the streets if that's what the FBI's worried about," Watts stated. "That was some prison shit. It's over."

"Trust me," I replied. "The bureau's never worried a group of hoodlums. That's what the Gangs Task Force is for."

"So, why am I talking to the FBI?"

"Because we're investigating the officer you were accused of shooting," I said, quoting what I'd rehearsed over the years. "I've read his report. Now, we're trying to get *your* side of what went down on that day."

"You want me to write a statement?"

"A verbal statement would do."

"Aren't you gonna record it?"

Smart fucker! "There's no need for a recording."

"A'ight" he replied with a shrug. "That day, I was driving my mom's car, because she had gone shopping for a mattress in my truck. When dude pulled me over, I had just left my girl's apartment on Cleveland Avenue. The car smelled like weed because I had just burned the last of the blunt, I'd been smoking. Something told me to hit the gas, but I didn't. I stopped. When he got to the car, he didn't ask for my license and registration, nor tell me what he pulled me over for. He just opened the door and told me to step out."

"Did you have on a seatbelt?" I inquired.

"Of course, I had on a seatbelt."

"His report said you didn't."

"His report was false."

I nodded. "Go on. What happened next?"

"Hell, I got out," he resumed. "I didn't think about the three-eighty in my pocket until he put me up against the car and started patting me down. Before he could reach inside my pocket for the gun, I pushed off the car, did a quick spin, then took off. That old man was on my ass, though. My mind was so preoccupied with ditching the gun, I had pulled it from my pocket as I ran—" Watts paused to clear his throat. "That's when I heard the first two shots," he went on. "And I knew these weren't warning shots because I could actually feel the bullets fly past me. I saw my life flash before my eyes, and I was scared as fuck thinking I was about to be the next nigga killed by a cop."

"Go on," I urged after he paused for a good ten seconds.

"He killed somebody," Watts assumed. "That's why the FBI's investigating him, huh?"

"Continue with your side of the story."

"Yeah," he mumbled, diverting his attention out the side window. "Anyway, by this time, I was running through McDonald's parking lot. On instinct, when I heard the first two shots, I ducked. When I looked back, I saw him running with his gun up as if he was trying to get a good aim. Shit, I was so scared, I just swung my arm back, and let my shit rip. I can't say I was trying to hit the old man but I was trying to get him up off me by any means necessary. But I *did* hit him. I didn't know where at the time, but I found out I caught him once in the chest, and once in both legs. Like I said, I was just trying to get him off me."

"You accomplished that, right?" I asked, struggling to maintain my emotions.

He shrugged. "Yeah, you can say that."

"So, how'd you get caught?"

"Shit, I made it halfway down Metropolitan," he said, proudly. "But, instead of using back streets, my stupid ass stuck to the main road, and fucked around and got picked up by two cops who were already en route to the scene. I had already ditched the gun by then, though."

He paused, once realizing we'd stopped behind the remains of a fire-damaged liquor store. I watched him as he took stock of his surroundings before regarding me with an inquisitive look. That's when I removed my sunglasses and stared into his soul. That same glint he had in his eyes upon stepping down from the Greyhound bus, was no more. In fact, it had been replaced with genuine fear.

"W-what's going on?" Watts stammered.

Maintaining eye contact, I reached my left hand down into the umbrella holder and pulled out the .22 Revolver I'd taken off Steve Chambers, holding it by my abdomen with the barrel pointed at Watt's upper body.

"That officer you shot," I spoke through clenched teeth. "Is my dad. Oh, I'm not mad at you for shooting him. Hell, that shit comes with being a cop. However, I do place full blame on you for my parents' separation."

"Your par—"

"Yeah, nigga!" I cut him off. "My dad's in a wheelchair, para-lyzed from the waist down. He'll never walk again. My mom got tired of waiting on him, hand and foot, and skipped town with his so-called best friend which left me in the middle of this hatred they now have for each other."

"Yo, man—"

"Shut the fuck up!" I snarled. "I guess you assumed you'd do your time, get out, and go on about your happy life, huh?"

He didn't respond.

"Any last words?"

"Man, I'm sor—"

Pow! Pow!

I fired two slugs into Watt's' chest cavity, clipping his ingenu-ine apology. On impact, his eyes went wide with the realization of his fate, and he sucked in a sharp breath as if trying to hold on to the last of it to no avail. Now, clutching at his chest, as the life slowly drained from him, Watt's' enlarged eyes remained locked onto mine until his head finally dropped forward, chin resting on his chest.

Thanks to the proximity of the shot, the caliber of the gun, and the clothes he was wearing. I didn't have to worry about blood splat-tering anywhere inside the car, but I still had to hurry and get him out before it seeped through his garment.

First, I discarded one of my gloves and felt for a pulse. Seeing that he didn't have one, I unbuckled his seatbelt before pushing open the door on his side and shoving him out onto the debris-lit-tered ground, making sure to toss his bag out behind him. Taking one last look at the deceased man, I pulled the door closed, and made my way back to the main road, thinking how easy it would be to pin Watts' murder on Chambers, being that his prints are still on the revolver.

***

"I'm here," Chad Hoffman answered his phone.

"And where's *here*, exactly?" I inquired.

At this time, I was in the parking lot of Burger King, on Northside Drive, using the payphone being that I intentionally left both of my cell phones at home to avoid being traced to the location I'd just left. You know just in case the investigation takes a wrong turn.

"Fulton Industrial," Hoffman answered my question. "I'm still parked across the street from the warehouse. All Kingz are present, but I still haven't seen anyone resembling what you described as a Kingzman."

"Perhaps the Kingz are awaiting their arrival," I offered, hoping I was right. "Anything else?"

"Um, yeah." He seemed to linger a few seconds. "It may not mean a thing, but only three of the guys showed up in the BMWs you mentioned. The fourth guy showed up in a newer-model Cadillac."

"That's got to be a rental," I told him. "Listen, I'm on my way. I told you I'd left my phone at home, so if you're not there when I arrive, I'll call you from another payphone to get your location."

"Okey-dokey!"

All I could do was shake my head as I placed the receiver into its cradle and headed back to the car I parked amongst those of the Burger King's employees and customers. Although I'd been anticipating Leonard Watts' release date, not once had I thought about the possibility of me being in the middle of an investigation on that date, until yesterday.

Finding out who's supplying the Kingz isn't as important as murdering Watts but it's important, nonetheless. However, I knew I couldn't be in two places at one time, physically, and that I would need a dependable accomplice. I really wanted to call upon Agent Powell, but knew Hoffman was a better choice, considering everything he knows and has contributed to the investigation. Plus, he was surprisingly free today. After shooting him a curve about having to take my father to a doctor's appointment, he was more than happy to keep an eye on the Kingz until I was available.

It was shortly after 12:00 p.m., when I made it to Fulton Industrial, cutting off my siren and emergency lights just before exiting the expressway. I was relieved to see that Hoffman was still stationed in Colonial's parking lot, although his orange Chevy Astro van stood out like a sore thumb amongst the other vehicles. Entering the lot, I parked where I could watch the warehouse across the street, then got out and headed for the highly conspicuous vehicle.

"I forgot you had this bright ass van," I said, as I climbed in beside Hoffman, who resembled a nerd with those large eyeglasses glued to his freckled face. Plus, he was clad in gray slacks and a matching cardigan. "There's no way in hell you would've been able to trail them in this shit," I told him.

"Well, thank God I didn't have to," he replied, laughing. "So, how's the old man?"

"He'll live," I mumbled, looking across the street at the warehouse. "You still haven't seen any Kingzmen?"

"None."

"It doesn't make any sense," I said, almost to myself. "Why show up this early, then have to wait for security, when they usually get here first?"

"Maybe the Kingz are still putting the money together for the purchase," Hoffman offered. "And don't want the Kingzmen there until that's complete."

"Perhaps," I responded, now realizing that it's possible they may have a safe inside the warehouse. "But like I said, the Kingzmen are usually here first with one occupying the booth out front, operating the gate."

"There they are!"

I was already looking toward the warehouse, when four figures exited the building, one carrying what appeared to be a briefcase, though I could barely tell who was who, being that Hoffman had no binoculars in the van. Well, except for those glued to his face. He could probably see the *back* of the warehouse with those things.

"I'm gonna follow them," I told Hoffman, watching the Kingz climb into the Cadillac. "Wait until we're long gone before you move this miniature school bus."

"Very funny."

"And thanks." I offered my hand.

"Glad I could be of some assistance," he said, shaking my hand. "If you need me again, you know I'm just one call away."

"I'll remember that."

I was out of the van and headed for the Crown Victoria as the Cadillac made its way to the entrance gate of the warehouse. I was inside the car by the time they reached it, now watching Ray Young remove the chain and push the gate open to let the Cadillac through. After pushing the gate shut, then reapplying the chain and lock, he climbed back into the rear, and they made off down Fulton Industrial.

By the time I was able to turn onto the main road, I spotted the car getting onto the expressway, which was about one hundred and eighty yards out. It was a good thing I knew which exit they were headed for, so I could pretty much maintain a good distance behind them until making it to Lithonia, Georgia, although I wanted to get close enough to get the plate's number. However, like I said, drug dealers are extremely cautious on transaction days. Therefore, the Kingz wouldn't have a hard time spotting the Crown Victoria, which just may as well have strobe lights on top of it.

As I traveled along the expressway, trying my best to be invisible, my mind reverted to the look Leonard Watts had in his eyes before his soul drained from his body. This was something I'd never witnessed first-hand, until today. I mean, I've killed before. It's just that I've never had the chance to actually watch a person die like that, which was quite disturbing, and would probably haunt me for a long period of time.

We reached Lithonia in no time. Despite how cautious these guys are assumed to be, I had no choice but to move a little closer to the Cadillac as it exited, lest I lose sight of them on the city streets. There were three vehicles between us, in which the one in the middle was a cargo truck – the perfect buffer!

Reaching the main road that I didn't bother getting the name of the Cadillac made a right turn onto it, followed by the other three vehicles with me bringing up the rear. Gas stations and restaurants were flanking the four-lane road for a good mile or so before I found myself surrounded by a gamut of trees, kudzu, and underbrush that seemed impenetrable. Despite the cold weather, the sun was beaming, which caused me to pull down the overhead sun-visor.

The Cadillac kept to the far-right lane. The other two cars had moved into the left lane to pass the truck that was a good forty-five yards behind the Cadillac, and I was still using the truck as a shield to prevent being made by the Kingz.

Momentarily, I passed an opening in the forest on the right, in which the Cadillac had entered, and was treading slow upon the gravel. Knowing better than to enter no man's land, I continued behind the truck. Hell, as far as I knew, they could have spotted the Crown Victoria and made a bogus turn to see if I would follow. Maybe some other fool would have given them confirmation by making the turn. Not *this* fool.

Several yards up, I came upon a Shell gas station to my right, and I could see a gated apartment building further up on the left. The apartments were too far, so I opted for the gas station, and chose to dock in front of the payphone that was located closer to the road.

Parking, I shut the engine off, grabbed my camera off the passenger seat, and threw the secure strap over my head, letting it hang just below my chest. Placing the extended lens into my coat's pocket, I hurriedly exited the car, figuring if that was a bogus turn the Kingz made, then they would be driving by any minute now, and I don't want to be anywhere near the unmark when they did.

As I moved toward the store, zipping up my coat to conceal the camera, I kept my ears perked up, listening for the sound of passing vehicles, whereas only two had driven by before I reached the front door, headed in the direction from whence I'd come. I made sure to memorize the make and model of the two cars, just in case the plug was occupying one of them.

However, when I reached the entrance, I stopped and turned around as if I had forgotten something. That's when I heard metallic rattling to my left and saw a scraggly-dressed White man rounding the building, pushing a shopping cart filled with a variety of junk. An idea formed in my mind, instantly, and I approached, blocking his path.

"Excuse me, sir," I said politely as I could, trying my best not to wrinkle my nose up for the pungent odor wafting off him. "I was wondering if I could borrow your cart for a few."

"Are you fucking kidding me!" he exclaimed with wide eyes, revealing badly stained, and missing teeth. "This is everything I own, and I collect my cans fair and square. Steal you a cart from the grocery store and collect your own damn cans!"

Looking down at the contents of the cart, I saw several plastic shopping bags filled with beer and soda cans. Plus, there were folded blankets and a pillow on the bottom rack of it.

"I'll tell you what," I said, pulling a wad of bills from my pants pocket, flipping through them. "You can keep your personal stuff, and I'll pay you fifty dollars for the cans and cart. I'm quite sure you can get another cart for free."

"Deal!" He snatched the offered bills from my hands, marveling at them while broadcasting that gruesome smile of his.

"I have another deal for you."

Just when I thought his eyes couldn't get any larger, and his smile couldn't get any scarier, they did. "Yeah?" he asked, stuffing the bills into his pocket as if worried I would ask for them back.

"Of course," I said. "I'll give you another twenty bucks for your coat and hat."

"Sure!"

He didn't hesitate to hand me the filthy brown skull cap, before peeling off the large, multi-stained gray coat, which was only one of the few he had on, and handing it over. Trust me, the smell of those items had my stomach churning something awful, but this was important. Therefore, I removed my ball cap and sunglasses and began donning the fetid items, while the old man retrieved his bedding accessories from the bottom of the cart.

"Are you going undercover?" he asked, now studying me with the last of his belongings clutched to his chest.

"Perhaps," I answered, taking hold of the cart, and pushing it towards the main road.

There were no sidewalks, so I found myself pushing the shopping cart along the edge of the road, against the traffic, hoping like hell no one in this area was driving while under the influence of any kind of substances.

Just then, two white Cadillac Escalades passed me in tandem, on the opposite side of the street. Call it instinct, but I kept my eyes on them until they both turned onto the same dirt road the Kingz had, which was about one hundred and eighty yards out. So, this was the plug. Apparently, he didn't know that moving with a convoy drew more attention than with one unit.

Not wanting to miss out on identifying this guy, and possibly members of his entourage, I pushed the cart faster, with no definite plan in mind, but hoped my seventy-dollar disguise prompted no more than a mere glance from the subjects I was endeavoring to get precariously close to.

My legs and thighs ached from a lack of exercising, I was about a hundred and thirty yards from the opening when I heard a succession of gunfire as if there was a gun range up ahead. However, I knew damn well there was no gun range in the same exact area the Kingz was supposedly meeting with their supplier. By the sounds of it, somebody had been lured into an ambush.

I found myself slowing down when I heard the shots intensify as if one side was returning fire. The shit sounded like a fucking war zone! Why couldn't these fuckers just conduct a decent drug transaction, and everyone returned home safely to their families? Well, I can't save the world, so all I could do was root for the Kingz and hope they came out on top. For the sake of my investigation, of course.

Now, I was about a hundred and ten yards from my destination, when I saw a dark-colored van moving fast in my direction, its engine revved up to its highest peak. Perhaps this was one of those intoxicated motorists I was worried about encountering, which is why I readied myself to dive out of the way at the first sign of impact, but the van slowed upon reaching the dirt road, then turned onto it, and sped out of sight, leaving a cloud of dust in its wake. Did someone summon backup?

At this time, I realized the gunfire had ceased, but anticipated it to start back up once the van reached the scene. Still moving in that direction, I tried to ignore the rattling of the steel cart and aluminum cans while listening out for the shoot-out finale. After a minute or so, all I could hear was the annoying sounds of the shopping cart and worthless cans. Perhaps there wasn't a shootout finale. Maybe the opposing team had already been wiped out, which had me wondering which team that could be, because I definitely didn't remember seeing the van trailing behind myself, or the Kingz, on our way out here.

Speaking of the van, just as I was a little under a hundred yards out, I saw the nose of it peek from the opening of the forest, before pulling out into the road and moving casually in the other directions. This left the Cadillac CTS, and both Escalades. However, as I got within fifty yards out, there had been no sign of either vehicle.

Boom!

Oh shit! The explosion came from the area in which I was headed, and I had automatically assumed it was one of the vehicles, way before the faint smell of burnt gasoline reached my nostrils. I kind of slowed down a bit, while anticipating two more explosions, being that there were two more vehicles.

The wind was blowing quite hard, which made the cloud of dark smoke almost invisible, so the motorists periodically passing by wouldn't see it if they were keeping their eyes on the road ahead of them.

Finally reaching the opening, I turned the cart onto the dirt road, and instantly caught hell with rocks getting caught under the tires, hampering their movements, though I kept trudging along. At this time, I was highly convinced that no one else was leaving the area, and there would be no more explosions. Plus, I'd become confident in my smelly disguise.

The dirt road seemed to go as far as eighty yards before branching off to the right, cutting through another part of the forest, which is where I assumed, I'd find what I was looking for. More agitated with pushing the cart now, I got it as far as I needed it to be from the main road and shoved it into some underbrush to conceal it a bit. Then, I grabbed one of the shopping bags full of cans, and continued along the trail, pretending to be in search of more cans, just in case someone did pop up out of nowhere.

So far, it appeared that I was alone, as I reached the second opening of the forest. The thick array of trees parried most of the wind, so the smoke from the fire was prominent, though it didn't surmount the foul odor wafting off the coat I had on.

Cautiously moving along the adjacent dirt road, I immediately spotted the exploded vehicle, which was the Cadillac CTS – the same car the Kingz arrived in! By now, it was charred beyond recognition as it blazed away in the sunlight that was partially blocked by the tall trees.

The two Escalades were parked further away from it. Plus, there were bodies strewn about the place, most of them clad in Army fatigues. I searched for dress suits as I neared, being that the Kingz were dressed in such, but only spotted one. From the distance I was at, the one in the suit appeared to be a White man. The supplier, no doubt.

Well, it didn't take long to put the pieces to *this* puzzle together. The Kingz had set their supplier up. Perhaps they had the Kingzmen already in position, which is why they didn't show up at the warehouse to escort them here. Truth be told, I underestimated them. These ruthless motherfuckers are really trying to build their own empire and prove they're not to be fucked with!

Nearing the burning car, I tossed the bag of cans into the brushes, and undid both of the coats, freeing my camera. Powering it up, I snapped a shot of the CTS making sure to get one of the license plates. Then, I moved toward the Escalades, taking pictures of the military-dressed corpses, surprised to see a woman amongst them, but noting that she was the only one without an assault weapon lying beside her. Looking around, I spotted an AK-47 lying afar off and wondered how her gun ended up that far from her body.

Making it to the White male in the trench coat and dark suit, I stood over him for a few seconds, studying his face to see if it was familiar to me. His head was turned to the side, and there was a puddle of blood there indicating where he sustained his gunshot wound. Though his eyes were closed, there still wasn't an ounce of recognition there.

Just as I was about to raise my camera to seize a picture of him, I thought I saw the slight rise and fall of his chest. Pausing, I watched to make sure I wasn't seeing things. Then, I saw it again. This piece of shit was actually still alive. I mean, there's nothing I can do for him. I'm not even supposed to be here. Hell, at this very moment, I was contaminating a multiple murder scene, and could easily become an accessory to it. Shit, I already have one murder under my belt for the day.

Making it back to the Shell gas station, I pushed the cart to the side of the store, looking for the guy I purchased the things from, but he was nowhere to be found. Therefore, I parked it on the side of the dumpster and was glad to relieve myself of the man's coat and hat, though my leather coat still assumed the stench.

Moving towards the unmarked, I redonned my ball cap and sunglasses for the sake of the few customers that were milling about. Reaching the car, I stopped and looked over at the payphone, thinking about the man who was slowly dying beyond the thick walls of the forest. Maybe I *could* do something to save him.

"Nine-one-one!" a female's voice announced through the earpiece of the payphone. "What's your emergency?"

"Yes," I said, disguising my voice the best I could. "There's been a shooting near the Shell gas station off McClendon Highway. I've found bodies beyond the wooded area nearby. Some could still be alive."

I hung up and climbed behind the wheel of the Ford, hoping the emergency response operator didn't take the call as a ruse, and knowing Lithonia Chief of Police John Moody was going to have a field day with this case if she didn't.

Chapter 24

The red brick house wasn't much to wow at, as it pretty much resembled the other houses lining both sides of the street, but the lawn looked as though it had recently been tended to, and the flower bed beneath the front windows, looked like something out of a Home Gardening magazine. In the driveway sat a Harley Davidson motorcycle that was blocked in by the white Isuzu Rodeo. Parked at the curb was a blue Nissan Maxima, in which I parked behind, pretty much blocking the mailbox, though I figured the mailman had already run, being that it was now 6:37 p.m.

Upon leaving Lithonia, Georgia, I journey back to my place, where I showered and shampooed for more than an hour while reflecting on my *awesome* day. To my knowledge, nine people lost their lives today. Well, make that eight and a possible, because the supplier probably made it. Who knows? However, I was expecting to get calls on both of these incidents by Monday.

After showering, I dumped some clothes into a trash bag, right along with the clothes I had on earlier, and took them to the dry cleaners next door to my locale. While en route to Marietta, I placed a call to Monique and had a long and pleasant conversation with her and Melody, which seemed to put my mind at ease for the time being. God knows I needed that!

Now, I climbed from the Ford, carrying a plastic bag from a corner store just up the street from here. Walking along the concrete walkway, I studied the small, neatly, trimmed shrubs, and well-placed lights that lined it, which could make a person feel like they're off to see the Wizard. You know, the Wizard of Oz? The yellow brick road? Aw, fuck it!

There were three steps before reaching the porch. After climbing those steps, I pounded on the door with my fist, hoping to be heard over the funny-sounding music coming from beyond it. While awaiting a response, I looked down at the flower bed of assorted flowers, and couldn't name one of them if my life depended on it. Maybe there were a few dandelions?

Momentarily, the front door came open, and Special Agent Dan Powell stood there, clad in blue jeans, house shoes, and a blue sweater with *FBI* stenciled in the center of it. The aroma of pot-pourri wafted from inside the home, along with that alternative rock music Powell is so fond of. No, I'm not against that kind of music. It's just not the kind of music I grew up listening to.

"You have a beautiful garden!" I said to Powell.

"I see you came bearing gifts." He nodded at the bag in my hand, blatantly disregarding my comment. "Whatcha got"

"Chips and dip," I answered. "You said you already have beer."

"Hell, I have chips and dip, too." He stepped aside, allowing me to enter. "But it's the thought that counts, right? Come on in."

It felt good to step in out of that cold weather. Especially since I was wearing a windbreaker that was pretty much a misnomer, be-ing that it didn't prove to be impervious to the cold wind that was kicking ass and taking names at this very moment.

Just as I expected, the living room was quite tidy, from the ar-rangement of the furniture and entertainment system to the miscel-laneous items, such as wall paintings, ashtrays, coasters, etc. Powell took my jacket and hung it up on a coat rack beside the front door. Then, we entered the kitchen, where two other Caucasian men were seated across from each other at the table. Powell introduced them as Lester and Stuart, before relieving me of the bag I was carrying.

"Another FBI agent, huh?" said the one who was introduced to me as Stuart. Clad in a red shirt that boasted *Georgia University,* he looked to be in his mid-thirties, with his dirt blond hair snipped into a crew cut. He was shuffling and reshuffling a deck of cards with his boney hands that were attached to his skeletal body.

"I suppose I am," I answered Stuart's inquiry, as I took a seat in one of the two empty chairs at the table. "I take it you guys are on the force?"

"Shit no!" Stuart exclaimed. At this time, Powell placed an opened bottle of Corona on a coaster in front of me, then returned to the counter. "I work for UPS," Stuart went on to explain, "and Lester bags groceries at Publix."

"I'm the assistant manager," Lester spoke in his own defense. He also appeared to be in his mid-thirties, with green eyes, and dark hair that was slicked back. Plus, his voice was notably soft, as if it belonged to an adolescent.

"You still bag groceries," Powell chimed in, returning to the table. He placed a bowl of tortilla chips, and a bowl of salsa dip on top of the table before taking his seat across from me.

"Don't be trying to marginalize my title, Dan!" Lester retorted, taking a tortilla chip from the bowl, throwing it at Powell, which made us all laugh.

"So," Stuart finally said, taking control of the conversation, still shuffling the cards, "I hear you wanna learn how to play canasta."

"Dan told me about it," I replied, taking a sip of my chilled beer. "He said it's like rummy but played with two decks of cards."

"That's true," he said. "Tonight was supposed to be poker night, but we're changing our—"

"Whoa!" I cut him off. "Don't break your ritual for me. If it's poker night, then, by all means, let's play poker. In fact, I'd rather play poker."

"Great!" Lester let out, then looked to Powell. "Dan, why don't you be a good boy and fetch the poker chips?"

"And what's in it for me?" Powell wanted to know.

"This." Lester dipped one of the chips into the salsa and fed it to him.

Powell crunched on the chip with his eyes closed, as if savoring it.

After swallowing, he opened his eyes and said, "That'll work," then exited the kitchen.

"So, Bishop," Lester started. "How close are you and Dan?"

"How close are we?" I asked, confused.

He and Stuart exchanged a glance.

"Have you two ever worked as partners on a case?" Stuart took the reins.

"Just recently," I answered, sipping my beer. "Well, actually, it was a multiple agent case, where we were all split into three-man groups. Dan and I ended up in the same group."

"The Drop Squad case?" asked Lester.

"Yeah," I answered slowly, somewhat surprised to hear the assistant manager of Publix, speak such words

"I thought that case was still under investigation," Stuart joined in.

"It is," Powell said, upon re-entering the kitchen, carrying the box of poker chips. "And stop trying to pry confidential information out of my partner," he told his friends before retaking his seat and handing the chips over to Lester to divvy up.

"You act like you don't trust us, Dan," Lester accused.

"Everything's not meant to be shared," Powell stated, seriously. "I've told you guys that. Now, what are we playing for? And, no strip poker, Lester."

Lester seemed to instantly turn red with blush. "Now, why on Earth would you think I'd suggest such a thing, Dan? That hurt my feelings."

"We can play for shots," Stuart suggested.

"I'm up for that," Powell agreed, then looked across at me. "What about you, Brian? You up for taking shots?"

"I guess so."

Powell retrieved a bottle of Vodka and four shot glasses, and our game commenced. The rock music coming from the stereo in the living room proved to be great for the background as we played our hands and made small talk, which seemed to mainly be about me.

Now, I don't consider myself to be the best poker player in the world, but I've been known to beat the socks off some of the greatest of the greats. Tonight, just wasn't one of those nights. Hell, I didn't win a hand until the fifth deal, which means I was already four shots in by then. Plus, I was halfway through my second Corona, which was not such a good mix with the Vodka.

I don't know if it was the alcohol, or what, but as the night went on, I could've sworn I'd caught Stuart and Lester shooting furtive glances in my direction. It had to be the alcohol, because, in order to penetrate a person's poker face, you have to evaluate it, right? That's what I was trying to do, which is how I was able to catch them watching me. But what about the periodic touching of the feet? Surely, I couldn't ascribe *that* to the alcohol. I know what I felt. I just couldn't discern which of the two was playing footsie with me under the table.

"I think that's enough for tonight," Lester said, after winning another hand, while the rest of us downed our last shots.

I had to blink away the film in my eyes to see the digits on my watch. It was 10:57 p.m., which meant we'd been playing for over four hours. I couldn't recall how many shots of Vodka I'd taken within that amount of time, but I knew it was way more than I'd ever consumed all at once.

"Yeah," Powell now replied, stifling a yawn. "I think I'm beyond inebriated. I can't remember the last time I'd lost that many hands while playing for shots."

"A couple of weeks ago," Stuart assisted. "At Gertrude's place."

"Shut the hell up, Stuart!" Powell said, sparking laughter. "You're like a damn walking floppy disc."

"I'm just making sure you remember the ass-whipping I put on you a couple of weeks ago," said Stuart, as he gingerly pulled himself up from his seat. Looking down at his friend, he said, "Come on, Lester. You'll have to be the designated driver."

"Shit, I'm always the designated driver." Lester stood, prompting Powell and me to do likewise. Then, he held his hand out to me. "It was good to meet you, Brian."

"Same here," I replied, shaking his hand, though the alcohol had me thinking he held my hand a little too long.

"I hope we didn't make a bad impression on you," Stuart intervened, offering his own hand. "I mean, we should've at least let you win most of the hands. That way, we could expect you to come back."

"No, it's okay," I told him, shaking his boney hand. "You win some, you lose some. Everything played out how it was supposed to play out. No hard feelings on my end.

"Come on, you two," Powell said, ushering his friends out of the kitchen. Looking back at me, he said, "Once I get Uncle Fester and Cousin It on their way, I'll be right back."

"I have to drain the weasel again," I replied, moving in the opposite direction of the three.

I'd been to the bathroom two times tonight, with no difficulties. Now, my head was spinning, my vision was a bit blurry, and I was pretty much tottering through the corridor, brushing up against the walls. Hell, I had to hold onto the sink to maintain my balance over the toilet, though I did manage to lose control of my aim a couple of times. 'Sorry about that, Powell!'

On my way to the living room, I began to wonder if I was competent to operate a motor vehicle in this condition. Me being an FBI agent won't keep my ass out of jail if I'm stopped by a local piece of shit, but I had to try.

Making it to the living room, I encountered Powell, who was seated in the recliner, strolling through his cell phone. The stereo was now playing at a low volume. I knew I was drunk, and my appearance corroborated it, according to the bathroom mirror, but Powell didn't look as though he'd consumed a drop of alcohol. He didn't look up until he heard the sound of me bumping into one of his tall speakers.

"You okay, Brian?" he asked, a concerned look on his face.

"Yeah, sure," I lied, stopping in my tracks, and trying to stand as normal as possible.

"Are you well enough to drive?" he tried again.

I had the answer in my head but, for some reason, it wouldn't come out.

"Have a seat," Powell told me. "I put on some coffee. Maybe that'll wake you up a little."

"Perhaps," I said, crossing the room to the sofa.

"Stuart and Lester really enjoyed your company," Powell admitted. "And this came from two guys who are not too fond of meeting new people. That says a lot. Believe me."

"They're cool, too," I muttered, extracting my phone from its clip, and checking it for missed calls. Perhaps from detective McCoy or Chief Barns, but there weren't any.

"Let me check on the coffee."

Powell disappeared into the kitchen. After replacing my cell phone, I found myself shaking my head, as though I could shake the drunkness away. Silly me. I haven't been in this state since the first party I went to in college, where I was pressured by my peers to join in on a game of Truth and Dare.

"Here we go!" Powell said, re-entering the living room, carrying two coffee mugs. "This should help take the edge off."

Handing one cup to me, he took a seat beside me on the love seat, which seemed a bit awkward. Well, at least that's how my alcohol-induced mind conceived it. However, it didn't matter, because my intentions were to sober up a little and be on my way. Therefore, I immediately began sipping at the extremely hot beverage, burning my tongue. Powell seemed to only take a few sips of his before placing the cup on the coffee table in front of us.

"Maybe I should've let it cool a bit," he said, planting his back against the cushion. "Or dropped in a couple of ice cubes."

"It's fine," I lied, now feeling uncomfortable with the closeness, but kept sipping, hoping to regain a large amount of common sense I'd lost during the night.

"You know you can chill here for the night," he offered. "Don't let the alcohol trick you into thinking you can make that drive safely. Friends don't let friends drive drunk, you know?"

Sighing inwardly, I put my cup down beside his, and planted my back against the cushion of the sofa, feeling defeated. I mean, who was I kidding? I knew damn well I was in no condition to drive. I didn't mind staying over with my new-found friend, but something just didn't sit well with me at this very moment.

"I have two guest rooms," he went on, "but only one is suitable to sleep in. Should I prepare it for you?"

"You don't have to," I said, looking at my watch, but thinking about the small garden outside. "What time does your wife gets home?"

"My wife?" He was looking at me as if I'd spoken in a language, he was not familiar with.

"Or girlfriend," I offered with a shrug. "I'm quite sure you don't live in this cozy home alone."

"I already told you I don't have one of those," he answered, scooting forward to retrieve his cup of coffee. "It's not that bad, though," he offered, taking a sip. "When I come home from a hard day at work, I know peace and quietness awaits me. I don't have to deal with someone else's problems while trying to cope with my own. So, I guess you got the family thing going on at your place, huh?"

"Shit no!" I exclaimed, retrieving my own cup. "I love Monique and my step-daughter true enough, but I enjoy peace and quiet just as much as you do."

"Cheers to that!" Powell held his mug out, and we clinked glasses, laughing.

After taking sips of the beverage, we simultaneously sat our cups down. Then, something seemed to be happening at that very moment, because we found ourselves staring into each other's eyes. I'm no fool – I knew it was the alcohol. All of a sudden, as if in slow motion, Powell began leaning into me. My body was numb and wasn't doing anything my brain cells were commanding it to do, so his lips managed to meet mine with no resistance.

It was a peck, in which I'm not really sure I'd participated in. He pulled his face back just inches away from mine, still looking into my eyes. At this point, my brain cells were going haywire with commands, but my body seemed like it had completely shut off. Hell, even my eyelids seemed like they were on strike because they hadn't blinked once during this ordeal.

Assuming I was comfortable with the introductory kiss, he closed the gap between us to deliver the full report. I found myself parting my lips to allow his tongue access to mine, which clearly constituted full participation. Then, I felt his hand enter under my shirt and began caressing my chest, which sparked a tingling sensation between my legs. Slowly, my rod erected until it was pressing against the fabric of my jeans. Powell must've sensed it, because he withdrew his hand from under my shirt, and gripped it. That's when I broke the kiss.

"I'm sorry!" he apologized, withdrawing his hand.

I got to my feet. "I need to be on my way."

"Are you sure you can make it?" he inquired. "At least take the coffee with you."

"I'll manage," I said, retrieving my windbreaker off the coat rack, putting it on. "Thanks anyway."

I was out the door, staggering along the lighted walkway toward the Crown Victoria. It was now darker out, and much colder than it was when I arrived. When I started the car, the cold air flushing from the vent, made me wish I'd took Powell up on his offer, and brought the coffee with me, but the cold air was the least of my worries. Hell, my head was hurting, and my vision was at least thirty percent impaired. Fuck that! Drunk or not, I gotta get the fuck away from here!

As I drove, I found myself questioning my sexual preference for the first time in my life. Am I gay? Bi-sexual? Surely, I couldn't be either of those, because I have no interest in men, though I did get an erection while making out with Powell, but that had something to do with pheromones, right? Any mammal could be sexually aroused if touched in their most sensitive spots, no matter as to whom or what touches them. Ha! A person doesn't need a degree in biology to figure *that* shit out.

I don't know how I did it, perhaps by the grace of God, but I managed to make it to College Park Projects in one piece. Hell, parking the car between two other vehicles, proved to be a much harder task, which I swear had taken every bit of five minutes. Finally docked, I shut off the engine, and pushed the driver's door open, accidentally striking the side of the Volvo station wagon beside me.

Despite the weather, and the present time, people were out and about. Mainly, drug dealers and users, I assume. However, I was just hoping neither of the ones watching me was the owner of the Volvo I just assaulted. However, no one said a word to me as I tottered along, thinking about my gun in the glove compartment of the Ford.

I used my key to gain entrance to the apartment that was quiet, and relatively dark, being that everything was off in the living room, and the only light visible, was reflecting from the adjacent kitchen. Easing the door back up, and locking it, I moved silently through the living room with alcohol-induced tunnel vision, which had me feeling like I was in a horror movie.

The light in the bathroom was off, but the door was wide open. Melody's bedroom was next. I peered in to see that she was asleep with the covers up over her head. Monique's bedroom was ajar, and I could see the constant flickering of light from her television, though I couldn't hear it.

I entered and saw that my girlfriend was asleep with the covers pulled up to her chest. I could only see the left side of her face, being that it was turned in the opposite direction. Plus, her head was wrapped in a scarf, as always, presumably to keep from messing up her hairdo while she slept.

I wasn't worried about Melody waking up and coming into the room, but I still eased the door shut, and pressed the button on the knob to lock it, anyway. Then, without as much as a mere glance at the muted television, I crossed over, and stood at the foot of the bed, glancing down at my woman who was clearly sleeping peacefully. It was just too bad I was about to interrupt her, and for my own selfish reasons.

So, with this mental bullshit going through my mind, I began undressing, feeling like a fucking pervert who'd just crawled through the window of some woman I'd been preying on. Now, down to nothing but a pair of socks, I started at the foot of the bed, crawling atop Monique, who didn't budge. Only taking a few seconds to look down at her still sleeping form, I began kissing her gently on the neck. That's when she awoke with eyes the size of half dollars.

Before she could say or ask whatever it is, she was about to say or ask, I clamped my mouth down on hers, and began osculating her, though it didn't last long. She broke the kiss by clamping both hands on my face.

"You've been drinking!" Monique expressed in a hushed tone, making a face.

"I know, baby," I said, trying to get back to the kiss, but she held me at bay.

"Did you at least lock the door?" she inquired.

"Of course, I did."

Accepting my answer, Monique lifted the blanket, allowing me to join her underneath it. I was back on top of her, although she was clothed in pajama pants and a T-shirt, I was already pulling the shirt over her head, being careful not to mess up her hair, which would definitely get me cursed out, and spoil the mood.

Once her shirt was off, instead of resuming the kiss, I moved down and started kissing and sucking on her B-cup breasts with their dark nipples that were already swollen with anticipation. Hell, my rod was also swollen, as it lied, wedged between her thigh and my stomach.

I had moved further beneath the covers now, slobbering down her belly button for a few seconds before helping her out of the pajama pants, which was the last item of clothing she had on, besides her socks. Then, I attacked her clitoris with my lips, tongue, and teeth, while trying hard to fight off the image of what transpired between Agent Powell and myself.

"Ouch, baby!" Monique exclaimed. "You're biting it too hard!"

Okay, so I let up with the teeth, but I was still licking and sucking her little love button like it was the Last Supper. I could tell it had started to feel good, because Monique arched her back, and sucked in her breath like she usually does, although I think my performance level was through the roof at this moment. She loves it when I go down on her because I usually wouldn't let up until I bring her to an orgasm.

Well, tonight, I was going to have to take a rain check, because this was not what I took that dangerous drive over here for. So, raining on her laconic parade, I drew myself up and took position between her legs. At this time, her facial expression was part surprising, and part questioning, but I already knew why: I always put on a condom before entering her.

Again, things are a little different tonight. The mind state I was currently babysitting, was telling me to just plunge into her deep hole, and wreak havoc on the pussy, but I didn't want to deprive Monique of the way she likes me to tease her beforehand. So, I took hold of my rock hard dick and began rubbing the tip of it against her labia, prompting her to gyrate her mid-section to pretty much tease herself as always, but there was no way I could keep at this for too long.

"Ooh, shit!" Monique cried out, when I unceremoniously dived into her abyss with every inch of me, colliding my pelvis against hers.

Feeling her hot, and extremely wet juices on my handle, seemed to sober me up a little more and turned me into a human jackhammer because I was putting the pound game down. Hell, I had the bed springs testifying, and the headboard singing *hallelujah* against the wall!

"Baby!" Monique got out between breaths. "You're gonna wake Melody!"

Yeah, I heard her plea, but I continued handling business. In fact, I only stopped long enough to lift her right leg over my left shoulder. With the image of Powell still taunting me, I felt compelled to thrust deeper, using long strokes, which did soften some of the noise coming from the bed.

As much as I wanted to close my eyes and enjoy the true wetness of Monique's love mound, I couldn't. I felt the only way to shake those thoughts, was to stare into her eyes as I tried to touch her rib cage with the tip of my dick. Her favorite position is doggy style, but she wouldn't be assuming that position tonight, though she doesn't know it yet. She'll find out when I—

"Ooh shit!" we both sputtered in unison.

I was reaching my climax, and I knew Monique was reaching hers also, because her nails were now digging into my back, and she was working her hips, meeting me thrust for thrust. I could actually feel her walls tightening around my rod, which made me come quicker than I ever have. After exploding what felt like a pint of semen inside of her, I released her right leg, and collapsed right there on top of her, both of us panting, and satisfied for the moment.

There! I did it! I knew I wasn't gay. There's no way in hell I would trade my love for pussy, for another dick. I mean, who really does that? Not me. Now, I won't be bias toward Powell and his life-style, but he'll have to find some other guy to work his moves on because this guy here is pro-pussy!

Chapter 25

Monday

January 27, 2002

"Reid came looking for you," Rucker announced, the moment I re-entered the office.

I had just returned from the fifth floor, where I was assisting a few agents with a project they were working on, which had me occupied from 9:30 this morning, up until now. Surprisingly, I had no encounter with Agent Powell, though I wasn't intentionally dodging him. I also wasn't looking for him, either.

On yesterday, I received a call from Detective McCoy, informing me of a body that was found behind the burned liquor store on Saturday night, just off McDaniel Street. According to her, Forensics were still working the scene, and there were no witnesses to the homicide. However, I do intend on periodically checking in with her on the progress of that investigation.

Later that night, I also received a call from Decatur Chief of Police, John Moody, giving me the rundown on the multiple homicide scene the Kingz had left behind. According to his reportage, the Lithonia Police Department had received an anonymous call about the murders. Upon dispatching to the scene, officers discovered one survivor and had him rushed to the hospital, where he still lies in stable condition. The investigation is still ongoing, and I'm most definitely going to keep track of this one.

"What'd she say?" I now responded to Rucker's announcement, taking a seat behind my desk, and switching on my computer.

"She just stuck her head in," he responded from behind his desk. "Hell, I knew she wasn't looking for *me* unless her fine ass is ready to duck off in one of these mop closets."

"You would take a fine ass woman like Wilma Reid to a mop closet?" I bantered.

"Shit, I'd take a fine-ass woman like Jennifer Lopez to a mop closet!" Rucker shot back, laughing. "I don't discriminate!"

"Now I know," I responded, laughing. After checking my watch to see that it was 11:41 a.m., I asked, "What do you have planned for lunch?"

"I'll be eating in, today," he said. "The wife stuffed my lunch pail with last night's leftovers. In fact, there's enough for two, if you're interested."

"No thanks!" I told him. "I'll be going out, but it'll be to clear my head – not for food."

"A titty bar, huh?"

I shot an incredulous look across the room at Rucker. "What!" He burst into laughter.

"You know what?" I went on. "You're fucked up in the head. You really need to get that checked out."

As planned, on my break, I exited the office, leaving my partner to his leftovers. Still thinking about Reid, and wondering what she could've wanted earlier, I stopped by her office, only to be told by another female agent that she and her partner were out on errands. Making a mental note to check back later, I made my way down to the parking garage.

At about fifteen minutes later, I was pulling my BMW into the parking lot of Bell South, bypassing the lot of any restaurant, which would've only galvanized my appetite, when I had more important things on my mind. Parking, and leaving the car running, I grabbed my cell phone and scrolled through my list of contacts. Selecting the first person I'd planned to reach, I found myself tolerating some gospel ringtone by Kirk Franklin before the recipient finally answered.

"Detective McCoy," she announced through the earpiece, sounding as though she was not in the mood to be bothered.

"Are you busy?" I asked, foolishly.

"Is that a trick question?" she shot back.

"Perhaps I called at the wrong time."

"I'm going over a case file," McCoy told me. "But I believe I could spare a few minutes for my friend at the Federal Bureau of Investigations. Whatcha got?"

"I was just wondering about that homicide you called me about, yesterday," I said, hoping I didn't sound suspicious.

"What about it?" she inquired.

"Any new developments?"

"Nothing substantial," McCoy answered with a sigh. "A CSI conjured a theory that the vic may have been murdered inside a vehicle, then shoved out of it."

Shit! "And how were they able to draw *that* conclusion?" I asked, all of a sudden feeling hot.

"From the positioning of the body," my question was answered. "Well, that's how it was explained to me over the phone. I didn't actually visit the crime scene, nor view the crime scene photos."

"What about the identification?"

"He was I.D.'d as a Leonard Watts if I'm saying it right."

"Sounds to me like you haven't begun to scratch the surface on this investigation yet," I acknowledged. "I assume this guy's family hasn't been notified."

"And your assumption is right," said the lieutenant. "However, I'm passing this case down to Miller. He'll have to handle all of that."

"Oh!" was all I could say, while realizing how great her choice was because, if she wasn't working the case, then she wouldn't be the one to uncover that Watts was just released from prison after serving time for assaulting my father and tie me in to his murder.

"You seem quite interested in this case, Bishop," McCoy pointed out. "You don't suspect your boys of having their hands in this, do you?"

"It wouldn't surprise me if they did," I responded, shooting a curveball. "Now, I have to find out if Watts had any ties to the Kingz. However, if I do find out anything, I guess I'd have to report it to Miller, right?"

"Please do," she implored. "I have enough going on as it is."

"I understand."

"And speaking of which," Detective McCoy went on, "I'm going back over Sharpe's case, right now. The wife."

"Okay."

"I still can't fathom how someone was able to break into her home and murder her," she started. "While Clayton County was stationed outside her house. They're definitely under investigation for that. I also can't understand why she had to suffer for something her husband did. And I can only imagine what those children are going through, after finding their mother dead, then finding that their father had also been murdered."

"I think you're too attached to the case."

"I'm human, Bishop."

"So, am I," I replied, now thinking of how I went about the Bernadine Yarborough case. "Look, I have to get back to the office. If you need anything, you know my number."

"Okay."

Ringing off, I hit the Lithonia Chief of Police.

"Moody," the older man barked through the earpiece.

"It's Bishop," I promulgated. "Anything new on that weekend case?"

"It's coming along," he answered. "As bizarre as it is, we're trying to put the pieces together, right now."

Figuring he was on borrowed time, I plunged right in. "Did you get an I.D. on the survivor?"

"Francisco Franco," Moody recited. "An ex-soldier, who served in Desert Storm, and own a used car dealership, amongst other businesses. The deceased were all soldiers and based at Fort McPhearson. What they had going on in that remote area, is a mystery within a mystery. The scene was set up like a drug transaction, or a ransom drop, but no drugs or money was recovered."

"What about the burning car you mentioned?" I pushed on. "Surely, it belongs to someone. A missing party, perhaps?"

"Missing indeed!" he replied, humor ringing in his tone. "The car belonged to an Enterprise rental outfit in the Atlanta area but was rented out to a Michael Nolan of Dublin. My investigator checked the Dublin address, which belonged to some pet clinic."

"Didn't Enterprise get a photocopy of his driver's license?" I inquired, jogging my memory for a Michael Nolan, but coming up short.

"Yep. I'm looking at that as we speak."

"Could you send a picture of it to my phone?" I was anxious to see who the Kingz had duped into renting the Cadillac for them.

"You're familiar with the name, huh?"

"It sounds familiar," I lied, checking my watch, seeing that it was now 12:22 p.m.

"Okay," Moody gave in. "I'll send it, but if you come up with anything—"

"You'll be the first to know," I cut him off.

Concluding the call, I pulled out of the phone company's lot and headed back toward the James P. Russell building. Moody's text came in just as I was about five minutes out from my destination, so I waited until I reclaimed my parking spot, before opening the text and staring at the all too familiar face on my screen.

Oh shit! Frederick Mills' face was the last face I expected to see staring back at me from my screen. Hell, I didn't expect to see the face of *any* King staring back at me from my screen. It's obvious that Mills had used a fake I.D. to rent the car, but why would he risk his face being plastered all over the News after burning the car, knowing there would be a mass investigation behind such a scene they'd left behind? Perhaps they're not as smart as I think they are.

Upon returning to the sixth floor, I journeyed off to the break room to see if there were any doughnuts left from this morning. To my luck, there were a few bear claws. I heated one up in the microwave, filled a Styrofoam cup with coffee, then made for my office.

I wanted to stop by Reid's office to see if she'd made it back but figured I'd do it later. Making it to my office, I unlocked the door and entered to see that Rucker was not in, but I could see the red message indicator on my desk phone from the door. I'm a man of business, true enough, but I was not going to check my messages until after I finished my bear claw and coffee, which took about eight minutes. Now, it was time to find out who this one message had come from.

"Get your ass to my office, right now!" Director Hopkins' voice boomed through my phone's speaker.

There was no telling what time he left the message, but I didn't plan on making him wait any longer, just in case this visit was meant to play out in my favor. Therefore, I hightailed it out of there and moved along the hallway in long strides.

As always, Director Manny Hopkins' door was standing wide open, and he had the phone's receiver glued to the side of his face, looking well-engaged in conversation. Spotting me, he scowled at me for a few seconds before bidding me to enter, by gesturing toward the chair before his desk.

Closing the door, I found myself now taking shorter strides as I neared the desk and took a seat across from Hopkins, who was dapper in a dark blue suit and red tie. His desk was usually neat, but it was now a bit cluttered with several documents strewn about, ink pens of various colors, and a half-eaten bear claw that made me think of the one I consumed minutes ago.

"Just do it the way I told you to!" Hopkins said to whoever he was conversing with on the phone. "Yes, I'm aware of that. You just do as you're told! Let *me* worry about any after effects!" Slamming the receiver down into its cradle, he glowered across the desk at me as if anticipating the wrong thing to come out of my mouth, so he would have a perfectly good reason to leap across it. "Where the fuck have you been all day?" he barked.

"I was assisting Lee and Williams with their case, earlier," I explained. "I left for lunch around eleven-fifty, and just returned about ten minutes ago."

The director now regarded me with narrowed eyes, as if trying to discern if I was lying or not. "Here!" he finally said, handing me a piece of paper from his desk.

Receiving the paper, I saw that it was a signed and stamped document, granting my request to investigate the Kingz. I looked up, but before I could say anything, he was handing me another piece of paper, which was the typed list of agents I'd turned in to him. Well, it wasn't the full list, because Wilma Reid's name had a line drawn through it, as if by a red ink pen. I looked up.

"Is there a reason why Reid is excluded from my team?" I asked, trying not to sound disappointed.

"Of course, there is," Hopkins answered, leaning back in his chair. "She's transferring."

"Transferring!"

"Papers came in this morning," he said. "Like I told her, it's out of my hands. When the heads pull that random bullshit, there's no appealing it. It's either go or resign. Hell, I'm surprised she didn't tell you about it, out of all people."

So, *that's* why she was looking for me, earlier. To be the bearer of bad news, because this is definitely some news, I am not too fond of. Oh, well. I won't get to work with Special Agent Wilma Reid again, but I will get to put an end to the reign of the Kingz.

Chapter 26

July 4; 2003

Friday

"I can't believe you're still in here on the phone, Brian!" my fiance, Monique spat, upon entering the living room, where I was perched on the arm of her mother's love seat. "Everybody's outside, enjoying themselves, and you're hiding in here on the fucking phone! Probably talking to some skank!"

My cellular was held to my chest to cover the mouthpiece, I regarded Monique, who was wearing sandals, khaki capri pants, and a purple maternity top that didn't do much justice for her bulging stomach, which was the result of her moving into her sixth month of pregnancy. Both of her hands were poised on her hips and the 12 karat diamond engagement ring I'd presented her with, three months ago, glistened beautifully from the sun rays pouring in through the windows.

"I'm talking to Agent Simmons, baby," I told her. By now, she was familiar with the name of every agent working under me. "You know he had to report his findings to me. Once he's done, I'll be right out. I promise."

"Well, tell him to wrap that shit up!" she said, then headed back outside, where the barbeque was taking place in the back yard.

"Go ahead, Simmons," I said through the phone, getting back to business.

"Are you sure it's safe?" he asked. "Queen Latifah sound like she's about to *Set It Off* on your ass over there!"

"Fuck you!" I shot back, laughing. "Who else is there?"

"Norris Boyd had just shown up with some blonde babe," Simmons informed. "Right now, he's speaking with Daniels and a few of the Kingz' underlings."

"Do we have any intel on the blonde?" I asked, thinking of the many women we'd encountered Boyd with, ever since I'd added him to this investigation. Including the Asian woman, he's married to.

"It's hard to say," Simmons answered. "I don't have a photographic memory, so I can't say for sure I recall a picture of her on the bulletin board in the War Room."

"Well, if you can," I started, "get a clear shot of her. She could be somebody of importance."

"Will do."

"And are you sure Richard is not the other D.J.?" I asked of Norris Boyd's brother, who goes by *D.J. Goldfinger*, a local, but well-known D.J. in Atlanta. So far, we haven't been able to determine if he was doing anything other than spinning records at clubs, being that his brother is pretty much a kingpin.

"It's not him, Bishop," answered Simmons.

"Says the man who doesn't have a photographic memory."

"I'm positive about this one," he persisted. "However, I did get a picture of him."

"My man!" I said, smiling. "Is there anyone else I need to know about?"

"Not at the moment. If anybody else shows up, I'll make sure to document it."

"Thanks, Simmons!" I got to my feet, stretching. "And I appreciate you for doing this for me."

"No problem," he told me. "Like I said, I would've just been sitting at home, drinking beer, and masturbating off my ancient Playboy magazine with Pamala Anderson on the front cover."

"That's too much information, my friend!" I said, laughing. "Just be careful out there. We'll rendezvous the first chance I get."

"Roger that."

Fastening my cell phone back into its clip, I exited the living room, thinking of how notorious the Kingz have become over the past five months. On top of linking up with other drug dealers in New York, Virginia, and Florida they had opened up a BMW dealership in Marietta, Georgia and Ray Young had pitched in chips with two other men, opening their own customs shop, in which I'm sure is just another trap spot.

Immediately after obtaining the director's permission to investigate the Kingz, I pulled rank on John Moody, the Lithonia Chief of Police, to gain jurisdiction over the Francisco Franco case, and was able to prevent Frederick Mills' face from being plastered over the news for the false identification he used to rent the car that was found at the multiple homicide scene in Lithonia. No, I'm not sweeping that case under the rug, I just don't want the Kingz to know that they are not as evasive as they think they are.

"Well, look who's decided to rejoin the festivities!" Gloria, Monique's mother blurted when I stepped out into the backyard, where she and a group of her contemporaries were doing the Bus Stop to McFadden and Whitehead's *Ain't No Stopping Us Now*, that was playing from the portable stereo on the porch, where Clyde, Gloria's boyfriend was still showing off his skills on the grill.

Slipping my sunglasses back onto my face, I stepped off the porch and approached the table I was sharing with Monique, my father, and Carmen my father's girlfriend. Yes, Dorian Bishop's grumpy ass was in attendance, looking like an older version of me, seated in his wheelchair, with his own sunglasses glued to his face.

Re-taking my seat, I took a sip of my beer that was still cold. Right now, it was just my father and me at the table, because our women were part of the *Thriller* scene playing out in front of us. Why they dubbed this dance the *Bus Stop*, I may never know. However, I did find it funny to see Melody and other children in the midst, hesitantly trying to keep up with the steps to a dance that was probably made popular in the nineteen sixties.

***

After dropping Monique and Melody off at our house in Smyrna, Georgia which is not too far from the studio apartment I'm still holding on to, I phoned Agent Al Simmons who informed me that he'd trailed the Kingz from the barbeque they'd thrown at Maddox Park in Atlanta to some small club in Buckhead, where he was now parked in the parking lot, watching the entrance. He also told me that the four of them had traveled in one of their company's SUVs, minus their Kingzmen, which had come as a surprise to me, considering their current status.

It was 9:12 p.m., by the time I'd made it to the club. The first vehicle I spotted upon entering the lot, was the black Cadillac Escalade belonging to the Kingz. The blue Dodge Intrepid that was occupied by Simmons, was parked across the lot from it. I drove past him, parking my BMW five slots away, with the rear-facing the club, then dismounted.

For it to be the Fourth of July, the place was packed as if it was any other regular Friday with people moving about as if they didn't have a care in the world. As I moved in the direction of the Intrepid, my attention was drawn to the large number of people occupying the outside deck and the ones crowded around it. There was a drinking contest going on, which sparked boisterous cheers and applause. However, the night was warm, like the sun was still lingering in the sky.

"Anything new?" I asked once I slid in beside Simmons.

"Nope," he answered. "They're still inside."

Al Simmons was thirty-three years old and had transferred to the Atlanta Division on the day Wilma Reid was transferred to the Oakland Division, which is where Simmons had come from. As the Kingz' investigation evolved, I found myself needing more agents, and quickly recruited, being that he was Reid's replacement, though I knew nothing about him. However, he turned out to be the most ambitious of all the other agents working under me, which is why I wasn't surprised when he decided to work today, instead of taking advantage of the break I allowed everyone.

"Great," I said, looking toward the entrance of the small club. "Go home and get some rest. I'll take it from here."

"By yourself?"

"Of course." I was now regarding him. "It's the Fourth of July. I don't think they'll do anything extra tonight. They're probably in there drinking and discussing their next shipment, before returning to their respective homes. So, like I said, go home and get some rest. That's an order!"

I dismounted and headed back toward my car. Instead of climbing in, I pulled out my cell phone and sat up on the trunk. After pretending to dial a number, I put it up to my ear, just as the Dodge

Intrepid was pulling out of the lot. This particular crowd was predominately White, which probably made it seem normal for Simmons to be seated in his car alone. I mean, it's not like people were paying me any attention, but I still maintained my ploy, moving my lips, and periodically gesturing like I was actually talking to someone.

About eight minutes into this act, Keith Daniels exited the club, flanked by two White women, who both looked to be in their mid-thirties. They were both holding on to him and giggling as though they were under the influence of multiple substances. I was expecting the other Kingz to emerge at any moment now. Switching my gaze, I saw Daniels and the women walk past the Kingz' company truck, and climb into a white Chevy Suburban, with Daniels climbing into the front-passenger side.

My memory is pretty good, but I don't remember seeing photos of these women on our bulletin board. Pulling the phone away from my face, I pretended to dial another number but was typing in the Suburban's license plate numbers as it pulled out.

Seconds later, I spotted the other three Kingz emerging from the building. All of a sudden feeling like I was jeopardizing my identity, I eased off the hood of my car and climbed in behind the wheel, where I continued monitoring them through my rearview mirror until they were out of my line of vision. It took almost two minutes for them to pull out of the lot.

No, I did not intend to follow them. I was too inquisitive about what went on inside the place. Therefore, I got out and crossed the lot. Lucky for me, only three people were waiting to get inside, which took no time. Once I paid the doorman five dollars, it was showtime.

For the club to be small, the inside was elegantly laid out with oak wood tables and chairs. There was also a dance floor, where a handful of people were dancing to some classic rock music coming from several speakers hanging from the walls.

I was so engrossed with the activities on the dance floor to the right of me, I wasn't minding my twelve until I felt the impact to my left shoulder, causing me to stop, turn, and face the Caucasian male, who apparently wasn't paying attention as well. He was clad in a white button-up that boasted palm trees, green cargo shorts, and black dress shoes with no socks. The three top buttons on his shirt were unbuttoned, revealing three small gold chains.

"Hey, man!" he growled. "Watch where you're going!"

"Yes, sir!" I replied with a nod, not wanting to draw unnecessary attention to myself.

Clearly content with this small victory, he peacocked right out the front door, which was fine by me. Continuing on my way, I surveyed the rest of the atmosphere and found what I was looking for before reaching the bar, where two men were fulfilling the orders of their customers. Finding an empty stool, I perched up on it and waited for one of them to approach, which didn't take long, because these guys were professionally mixing and serving drinks as quick as vending machines could process the amount inserted, and comply with the push of a button.

"What'll it be, sir?" asked the smaller one with the extremely large eyeglasses that took up half his face.

"I need to speak with whoever's in charge," I spoke in my all-business tone, gently placing my credentials atop the bar.

"Um," he stammered, eyes glued to my badge and identification card, "I guess that would be me."

"You guess?" I inquired, recovering my credentials for the sake of wandering eyes.

"Well, that *is* me," he rectified. "I'm Milton. Co-owner and manager. How can I be of service?"

"Can we speak in your office?

"Sure." He looked over at the other bartender. "Carl, I'm gonna need you to hold it down for a few. I'll be right back."

In the midst of doing some kind of juggling trick while mixing a drink, Carl gave a mere nod without even looking in our direction. I followed Milton to a small office that was just beyond the bar. I don't know why I expected the place to be unkempt, but it wasn't. Plus, it only consisted of a desk, chair, and a small, cheap-looking file cabinet in one corner. The place also had a sweet smell to it.

"I would offer you to have a seat," Milton said, "but, as you can see, there's only one chair."

"Which is all I need," I asserted, rounding the desk, and planting my bottom in the black, soft-cushioned chair. See, in this business, you have to be a little aggressive, or some people will challenge your authority. "I need to view your surveillance tape," I told him.

"Are we under investigation?" he asked, closing the door. He was already giving me a look for how I commandeered his private space

"Perhaps."

"Wouldn't you need a warrant to access our surveillance?"

Exhaling sharply, I leaned back in the chair with my arms on the rest, drilling my eyes into his. "Sir, if you make me call in for a warrant, I'll have it delivered by the Fire Marshall, and you and I both know what happens when the Fire Marshall gets involved."

The club owner was pensive. Of course, he knows what kind of business a Fire Marshall would bring to his establishment, but what he didn't know is that I was blowing smoke, and was inconclusive to have a warrant produced at this moment, let alone have a Fire Marshall shut his club down for the night. Now, I was thinking about the lie I'd told the manager at Petro.

"To fully answer your question," I resumed, breaking the silence, "no, you're not under investigation. We're tracking a fugitive, and the bureau just received an anonymous tip that she was seen inside your establishment tonight. I didn't see her when I came in."

"Do you have a picture of her?"

"Not on me," I told the smart fucker, "but I'll know her when I see her."

"Alright." He rounded the desk and typed in his password.

"I'll take it from here," I said, once the live images of their three cameras appeared on the screen.

"Sure."

When Milton stepped back to maintain a view over my shoulder, I went to work on the keys, dismissing the exterior camera and cropping the two interior cameras to both take up half the screen. Then, I took the time frame back to 7:00 p.m., figuring it to be a respectable time to open the doors for club hoppers. Besides, Simmons informed me that the Kingz made it to the club after eight, so it wouldn't be long before I discover what they were really up to.

The left side of the screen was a diagonal view of the bar, whereas I could see the full length of it. Right now, I was seeing Milton with a clipboard in hand, taking stock of the beverages, and Carl along with the two bouncers I encountered at the entrance, were occupying stools at the bar, engaged in conversation. The right side gave me a visual of the rest of the club, from the direction of the bar to the entrance. It was deserted.

Working my fingers again, I pushed the images forward, until I saw the first sign of people entering the club. By this time, the two bouncers were standing out front, and Carl was behind the bar with Milton ready to grant their customer's wishes. Of course, I was feigning interest in every female that appeared, for the sake of the story, I told Milton, who was still lingering behind me, presumably intrigued by the thought of a fugitive showing up at his establishment.

However, it wasn't hard to spot the two women I'd seen Keith Daniels leave with, as they approached the bar, and were visibly flirting with Carl as he fixed and served their drinks, in which they chose to sip right there at the bar while occupying two of the stools. When Carl had become busy with serving other customers and was no longer paying them any attention, they both spun around and looked out at the growing crowd.

I tinkered with the keys some more, moving the timeframe forward a little, until I saw all four Kingz enter, with their medallions prominently on display. The place wasn't packed, so they were able to find an empty table to sit at. Neither one of them made any effort to approach the bar, which had me under the impression that they were here on business with an outsider.

By this time, Milton had journeyed off to his office. Upon returning, I saw him grab a rag, and began wiping down the bar. At that instance, James Young got up from the table and approached.

Thanks to the closeness of the camera, I had a perfect view of the faces of both, bartenders, and customers, as if I was actually standing there myself. Young said something to Milton, who hadn't looked up when he approached. Then, Milton looked up and—hold the fuck up! He wasn't just smiling, he was *beaming* at Young as though they were old classmates or something. While they talked, on the right side of the screen, I saw Daniels get up, and head for the restroom, which was adjacent to the office. Suddenly, Milton pointed towards something or someone, causing Young to look over his shoulder. After another second of exchange between the two, Young moved back in the direction of their table, only to bypass it, and stop at one that was two tables away from theirs.

The two women who'd taken up post at the bar simultaneously got off their stools and headed in the direction of the restrooms. Directing my attention back to Young, I saw he was conversating with the group at the table, which consisted of two White women, and—

Oh shit! It was the same fucker who bumped into me upon exiting the place. How could he, Milton, and Young be connected?

As I continued to watch, it appeared that James Young had said something offensive to the two women, because they grabbed their things, got up, and stormed off angrily. Young sat down across from the guy, and they continued with whatever the hell they were discussing. Ray Young and Frederick Mills were still seated at their table, and Keith Daniels had not returned from the restroom, which I could see his two, late-night flames standing at.

Already pretty much knowing how things were going to play out, I pushed the images forward until the last of the Kingz had exited. After seeing my handsome self, stroll in, I quickly stopped the video, so Milton wouldn't get a glimpse of the unpleasant encounter I had with his friend, who'd made it his business to stop by the bar and chat him up before leaving.

"Another prank call," I said, now getting to my feet.

"Prank call?" Milton asked. "You mean to tell me people actually call in, claiming to see fugitives?"

"You'd be surprised," I told him, holding my hand out. "Thanks for your time, sir."

"Glad I could help," he responded, shaking my hand.

I was on my way, trying not to give him the impression that I was in a rush, although I was. Exiting the club, I tried not to draw attention to myself as I slowly strolled along the parking lot, pretending to be searching through my phone, but was furtively scanning for this Mystery Man. He wasn't amongst the crowd gathered around the outside deck, nor seated in any of the parked vehicles. He'd gotten away for now, but the moment he and James attempt to contact one another, I'll have that fucker by the hairs of his ass.

Chapter 27

Sunday

10:52 p.m.

Sunday dinner, which was prepared by Monique, and her mother, Gloria, was at our home. Carmen, who's now seven months pregnant, had driven my father out. You know, by now, I'd gotten over being angry at my parents for waiting until they were almost one hundred years old, to compete with each other in a child-bearing competition. In fact, I am more than happy to have two brothers and a son on the way. Plus, my mother and I are speaking more frequently now. I can't say the same about her and my father, but I chose to not let what happened between the two of them, interfere with my own personal life.

After dinner, we all engaged in several games of UNO, and casual talks about future events. When our house cleared a little after eight, Monique retired to the bedroom, complaining of stomach cramps, and Melody and I took on the task of cleaning up before I sent her off to bed. I took a good twenty-something minute shower before climbing in beside my fiancée, who was already snoring up a storm. Giving her a peck on the cheek, I laid back and settled into my thoughts of nothingness, until I'd fallen asleep, only to be awakened by the constant vibrating of one of my two cell phones atop the nightstand on my side of the bed.

Rolling over and seeing that it was my business phone, I quickly, but cautiously, threw the covers off me and climbed out of bed. Disregarding my loafers, I swiped the phone off the stand, and padded towards the door, casting a glance at Monique who was still dead to the world. Finally, on the other side of the bedroom door, I looked at the screen and instantly became elated, knowing I was about to receive information I've been anticipating for the past two days.

"I'm listening," I said through the device.

"Young just received a call from Daniels," Special Agent Carlos Moreno announced. Ever since Friday, I'd kept around-the-clock surveillance on James Young just in case he meets up, or contacts Milton Long, or the other guy he met with at the club that night.

"Okay," I urged, a bit upset he wasn't telling me what I expected to hear.

"Daniels was pretty upset," Moreno went on to explain. "Said something about killing some guy for putting his hands on his child. They're calling an emergency Kingz meeting."

Oh shit! Keith Daniels has four children by three different women. I've never heard of him being in contact with the one in Virginia, and the one who made a living by dancing and selling her body didn't have a steady companion to speak of. Besides, Felicia Gibson didn't seem like the type who would let someone violate her or her son, and not take action herself. Therefore, the emergency meeting has to be in reference to Nicole Lane who resides in Florida with her boyfriend, Willie Carswell. Perhaps Carswell doesn't know with who he's dealing with, but if he's done some stupid shit like violating one of those children, then he has definitely sealed his fate.

"Just stay on his ass, Moreno!" I now hissed through the phone. "If you even *think* those fuckers are about to do something, ring me up!"

"You got it, Boss!"

Concluding the call, I eased back inside the bedroom, where Monique was still sound asleep, with one hand resting protectively on her bulging stomach, and donned a pair of shorts over my boxers. Leaving back out, I peered in on Melody before heading for the living room, where I placed my phone on the coffee table, then reposed on the sofa to see if I could catch a few more Zs while awaiting a follow-up call from Moreno.

To be honest, I don't think the Kingz would do something stupid, like drive all the way to Florida, to settle a score with Carswell on this very night. They would at least take a few days to plan everything out, which would give me sufficient time to obtain the director's approval to assemble a small group of agents to trail the Kingz to the Orange State, where domestic agents will intercept and assist us. Well, they'll Birddog us the entire time we're on their territory. Then, we'll have to wrestle for jurisdiction over whatever crime the Kingz decide to commit in Florida. However, if I *don't* run this by the director, and decide to do it myself, I would have to worry about all that extra bullshit.

Anyway, Moreno's call came in a little after two a.m., waking me from my beauty rest again. The coffee table wasn't exactly in arm's reach, so I had to sit up in order to retrieve my phone.

"Come on with it," I said, upon answering.

"They're on the move."

"I need you to be more specific than that, Moreno."

"After getting off the phone with you," he went on to explain. "I followed Young to some abandoned warehouse, where he convened with the others in the parking lot."

"Were you able to get pictures of them?" I wanted to know.

"I couldn't get close enough without being made," Moreno answered. "It was impossible."

I sighed. "Go ahead.

"They talked for a good thirty minutes or so," he resumed. "Then adjourned, I thought they were calling it a night but, while en route to his home, Young placed a call to Maurice Griffin telling him to grab another Kingzman, and to meet him at the Palace in thirty. Young wasn't back inside his home no longer than twenty minutes before heading for the Palace. He used one of their company's trucks to pick up his comrades, while Griffin and another Kingzman followed in the other SUV. Right now, I'm trailing them along I-Seventy-Five South."

"Pull back!" I told him, already knowing where this convoy was headed.

Sometimes, it pays to have common sense. It also pays to be equipped with sense that's uncommon to most, because I'd wager anything that it hadn't dawned on Moreno that these fuckers were on their way to Florida. Of course, I wanted to tell Moreno to continue with his pursuit, but that would be a clear case of career suicide. Hopkins would definitely have my ass for it. Hell, Moreno's ass also.

"Are you sure you want me to pull back?" Moreno now asked. "I'm not at the end of my shift yet."

"Go home, Moreno!" I said, moved by his devotion and ignorance. "Get some sleep and take tomorrow off. That's an order!"

"Yes, sir!"

***

Tuesday

"Okay people," I started, looking out at my team of agents seated before me in the War Room. "As we already know, this is gonna be a very busy day. You all have been constantly briefed and trained for these multiple tasks. Each agent has his or her own role to play. Does anybody need to be reminded of what their role is?" No one spoke up. "Are there any questions at all?"

"What if someone attempts to elude us?" asked Agent Powell, who I'd kept at a distance ever since what happened between us at his home that Saturday night.

"Attempt to apprehend them, Agent Powell," I said, not trying to hide the sarcasm in my tone. "As I said, the thing is not to harm them, and definitely not ourselves. There are no warrants out for these people. All we want is signed affidavits. However, if anybody does flee, then the next time they see us, they *will* be arrested. Any other questions?"

There were no other questions.

"Alright, let's move this shit out," I commanded. "Pierce, I'll meet you in the garage. Also, I want to be kept abreast of everyone's movements."

As everyone filed out, I turned to face the board I was standing in front of, where we had photos and brief information on everybody, we'd found to be in association with the Kingz. Right now, I was focused on the photo of Blake Jones, aka B.J. who's close to the Kingz, but is extremely close to King Ray according to my source.

I don't know why, but I feel that no matter how much of a bond he has with Ray Young Jones would get on the stand and sing like a canary against the notorious group. He's fairly young, and I haven't encountered many guys his age, who wouldn't squeal on their very own mother, once being put under the kind of pressure I'm capable of producing. Or I could be wrong about him. If I approach him, there's a possible chance that he'd tip off the Kingz that the FBI are seeking them out, which could be bad, but not detrimental to this investigation, considering the substantial evidence we already have stacked up against them.

At this time, I was the only somebody left in the War Room. After checking my cellular phone to see that it was 11:48 a.m., I selected a phone number from my contacts list.

"Hello?" Agent Carlos Moreno's voice sounded in my ear.

"How's the weather?"

"I haven't heard anything yet," he answered. "Right now, I'm tuned in to the World News, waiting for the new developments at twelve."

"How long have you been up?" I asked, exiting the War Room, heading for my office.

"Since seven o'clock," he told me. "Honestly, I didn't need any days off. I actually wanted to come in today. I've been anticipating this day for weeks. I wanted to be a part of this."

"Technically, you're not off today," I assured. "You're just working from home. What we're doing today, is minor. You have a delicate role in Saturday's mission. Just stay focused on *that*.

"Yes, sir."

"And ring me up the moment you hear something."

"Will do."

The only thing I had to retrieve from my office, was the blazer to my dress suit, which is something I'm not a fan of wearing, especially in the summertime. When I made it to the parking garage, Pierce was waiting in front of the elevator in the black Chevy Tahoe I signed out from Motor Pool, with the engine idling.

"Did you check with the tag?" I asked, upon sliding in beside the Caucasian man, who was a couple of years younger than me.

"I sure did," he answered. "He's parked outside their apartment, right now. As far as he knows, neither one of them has left it today."

"Good," I said, reclining my seat, and donning my sunglasses. "Break a few traffic laws. I wanna catch them together."

As Pierce did what I told him to do, I was silently hoping a local dick head would pull us over, so I could flex my muscles, but we made it to Allen Temple Apartments unscathed. Checking in with our tag man, we discovered that our subjects were still cooped up inside their apartment. Once we parked, I ordered our man to cover the back door of their apartment, just in case, someone decides to try out for the Olympic Track and Field.

"Should I bring the folder?" Pierce asked, after shutting off the engine.

"Leave it," I told him. "I'll send you back out here for it if they decide to play hardball. You ready?"

"Let's do it!"

Forgive me for exaggerating a little, but when I got out of the truck, it felt like I had walked right into a desert, with the sun showing no mercy, and the heat index above abnormal. I was just glad we didn't have to walk too far to reach the apartment we were headed for. I was also glad that there weren't that many people out and about, and the small amount that was wasn't paying us too much attention. Reaching apartment twelve, I took the initiative and knocked on the door.

"Who is it?" a feminine voice answered, almost instantly.

"FBI, ma'am." I tried to sound as easy going as possible, though I had one hand rested on my Glock and my credentials in the other.

Now, it was quiet beyond the door, except for the sound of a television that was barely audible. I inched closer, listening for any sounds of anyone trying to access the back door, but heard nothing. Then, there came the sound of security locks being disengaged before the door slowly opened to the thirty-one-year-old woman, who was clad in dark blue capri pants, a red blouse, and white tennis shoes. She wasn't much to look at in the face, but from the neck down she was a head turner!

"Ms. Trina Holt?" I questioned, already knowing it was her.

She darted her eyes back and forth from my partner and I, before answering. "That's me."

I held up my credentials. "I'm Special Agent Bishop, and this is Special Agent Pierce. Do you mind if we come in?"

"Um," she lingered, looking as though I told her to assume the position or something of that nature.

"We're not here to arrest you or your fiancé," I said, making sure to indicate that I knew her husband-to-be was also there. "We also won't confiscate, nor charge you with whatever contraband we may encounter while partaking as guests in your home. That's my word. We just need both of you to cooperate with us."

That same skeptical look still plastered on her face, Holt, once again, visibly evaluated Pierce and I, before stepping aside to allow us entrance. I entered the small apartment first, immediately taking stock of the living room that only consisted of a sofa, coffee table, a plasma television, stereo system, and other miscellaneous items you may find in the average person's home.

However, Bobby Johnston wasn't in this particular room, and I was on high alert, with my hand still resting on my gun, attentively watching the narrow hallway that led to the other rooms. Despite the sunlight filtering through the windows, the hallway was dark, which had me wondering if he was lying in wait, thinking we were here to arrest him.

"Bobby Johnston!" I called out. "We already know you're here. We also know you have warrants, but we're not here about those. However, if you don't comply, then I'll be more than happy to notify the police department of your whereabouts and keep you cornered until they get here. It's your call."

There was no immediate response. I cast a glance back at Holt who was still standing by the front door that was now closed, wearing a frightened expression on her face. I noticed Pierce had drawn his weapon but held it down by his side.

Suddenly, there came the sound of a door creaking open. I didn't draw my gun, because I had faith that my highly trained partner would get the drop on Johnston if he even *looked* like he wanted to harm us. However, that was not the case. The 6'1, 210-pound man slowly emerged from the semi-darkness, with his hands out, palms up, pretty much letting it be known that he wasn't planning on dying, or going to jail today. Plus, he was already fully dressed just in case he had to make a run for it, I presume.

"I'm Special Agent Bishop," I announced, holding my credentials up for him to see. "And this is Special Agent Pierce. Like I said, we know about your warrants, but we're not here on that business. We need you and Ms. Holt to accompany us to the James P. Russell building downtown, on another matter."

"Do we *have* to go to the James P. Russell building?" asked Johnston. Clearly, he was skeptical about my promise.

"Again," I spoke slowly, struggling to maintain my composure, "no one is being arrested, and yes, you both will have to go with us. I don't have all day to debate this."

"Do we have to ride in the back of y'all police car?" Holt wanted to know.

"We're FBI agents," Pierce answered, obviously offended. "The word *police* is an insult to what we stand for."

"Can we trust you to follow us?" I intervened, hoping Pierce wasn't about to shoot the woman for her ignorance.

"We can do that," Johnston agreed.

As we made our way back downtown, with Johnston and Holt trailing us in their green Mazda Protegé, I phoned and checked in on the other members of my team. So far, everything was going well. Progress was being made. Director Hopkins wasn't pressuring me about concluding this investigation, but I had a feeling it wouldn't be long before he does, which is why I plan on wrapping it up within the next two weeks and taking down the Kingz by next month.

Before entering the parking garage that's for personnel only, I instructed Holt to park her car at one of the parking meters nearby and informed them that Pierce would collect them in the lobby.

Before Pierce could find a spot to park inside the garage, I had taken off my blazer, preparing myself for the heat that seemed to linger in this particular area.

"I want them separated," I told my teammate once we entered the elevator.

"Yes, sir!" he answered. "After I get them situated, do you mind if I take a small lunch break?"

"It doesn't have to be a *small* break, Pierce," I told him. "Take as long as you want. We'll get started when you're done."

A couple of agents got onto the elevator on the Ground floor, as Pierce was getting off. Just as the shaft cleared the fourth floor, my business cellular vibrated on my hip. Retrieving it, I looked at the screen and smiled. There was no reason for this person to call me, except to bestow some good news upon me.

"Come on with it," I said through the device, stepping off on the sixth floor.

"Willie Carswell was found murdered in his driveway," Moreno informed. "According to the news, he sustained multiple gunshot wounds to the face."

"No lead on any suspects, huh?" I was entering my office now. Rucker wasn't in.

"As always," Moreno replied sarcastically. "There's something else. It may not be connected, but—"

"Just spill it, Moreno!" I urged, taking a seat behind my desk.

"A Caucasian female was found dead in her own bathtub," he went on to explain. "Authorities are suspecting foul play because she was found fully dressed, even though the place didn't seem disturbed."

"What's the proximity of the two incidents?" I asked, feeling there could very well be some kind of connection between the two.

"They didn't give the precise locations," said Moreno, "but they both occurred in Miami."

Of course, they both happened in the exact same city. I'd wager anything that they're both connected somehow. I already know the Kingz are responsible for Carswell's demise, but I can't prove it, substantially. Especially to the Department of Justice, who would only brush it off as mere speculation. There's only one way I'd be able to link them to these murders, and that would entail a trip to Miami.

A rap on my office door, which was standing wide open, brought me from my reverie. Seeing that it was Pierce, I looked at my watch and realized I had been in my own little world for more than thirty minutes, which is something I'm known to do whenever I'm working a big case, such as this one.

"What's the word?" I asked Pierce, who remained standing in the threshold, holding a dark brown folder.

"I separated the couple," he told me. "They're in rooms One and Two. Also, Delta Team has returned with their subject. I think they've already started."

"Well," I said, getting to my feet, "perhaps we need to get started also."

There were six interrogation rooms on our floor. At this moment, Johnston occupied one, and his wife-to-be occupied another. Being that Delta Team had not come back empty-handed, this meant that one of the Kingz' workers was also held up in one.

Holt was in Interrogation Room One, so Pierce and I entered the observation booth of Interrogation Room Two, where the bureau records and monitors the interrogations. Looking out through the large mirror-tinted glass, I took a few seconds to evaluate Bobby Johnston who was seated in one of the two steel chairs at the steel table. In front of him was his cell phone, a pack of Newport cigarettes, and one of our complimentary ashtrays.

As he smoked one of his cancer sticks, Johnston appeared to have not a care in the world, but it was a facade. He was beyond worried. He was only putting up this front because he knew there was a possible chance that someone could be watching him from behind the glass, he could only see his reflection in. Yeah, sure. Like we, busy FBI agents, had nothing better to do than to stare at him for over thirty minutes.

I turned to Agent Pierce. "You're up," I told him.

He regarded me with a stunned expression. "Y-you letting *me* interrogate him?" he stammered.

"We don't have all day," I said, moving over to the controls, pretty much letting him know that my decision was final.

"Yes, sir!" he deferred, then quickly left the control room with the folder in hand.

I didn't bother taking a seat. After buzzing Pierce into the interrogation room, I waited until the door slammed shut, before initiating the audio recording device and opting for the speaker, instead of the headphones. Now, standing with my arms folded over my chest, I looked out at my protegé, anxious to see how he'd handle himself.

"Sorry for the wait, Mr. Johnston," Pierce offered, before placing the folder on top of the table and taking a seat across from him. "Would you like anything to drink?"

"How long do we have to be here?" Johnston inquired, disregarding the agent's hospitality while grounding out his cigarette in the ashtray.

"That's totally up to you, sir."

"How's that?"

"Well," Pierce started, placing a document from the folder, in front of Johnston, "the sooner you write and sign this affidavit, the sooner you and your sweetheart can be walking right out of the front door."

"Write an affidavit saying what?" asked Johnston.

"That you will testify against the Kingz if subpoenaed by a judge to do so."

Shit! I'm smiling from ear to ear right now. Agent Pierce got straight to the point, and he delivered it so fucking good! Hell, I don't think I could've done a better job at doing it as calmly as he did. This isn't something that's taught to us in training. It's developed through time and experience. So, yes, I'm very proud of Special Agent Pierce, right now.

"The Kingz!" Johnston exclaimed, shooting a glance in my direction as if a dozen agents were prepared to dive through the glass if he shows any signs of aggressiveness. "I don't know any Kingz!"

"Figure you'd say that."

Pierce opened the folder up and began placing large photos, one at a time in front of Johnston whose cool facade seemed to fade instantly. They were the same photographs I'd taken of him going back and forth, dropping off stolen tractor-trailers to the Kingz, at their warehouse on Fulton Industrial, with Holt trailing behind in her Mazda.

"I think these photographs contradict your claim, Mr. Johnston," Pierce went on, resting his elbows on the table, now making direct eye contact with the subject. "I know the lead investigator promised you wouldn't be arrested for the warrants you have out for you at this time, but you *can* be arrested for lying to a federal agent. In fact—" Pierce began collecting the photos. "—the only way you'll walk out of this building without restraints, is if you complete that affidavit. You have ten minutes to do so."

Pierce got up and headed for the door. I buzzed him out, shut off the recording device, then buzzed him into the control room, where I was still smiling.

"I didn't think you had it in you," I commented. "Good job!"

"Thanks!" He was also beaming. "Do you think he'll do it?"

"There's no doubt in my mind," I replied, checking my watch. "Now we have to deal with the woman."

"I take it you'll do the honors?"

"Sure will."

He handed over the folder. Making it to Interrogation Room Two, Pierce entered the observation booth, then buzzed me into the room, where Trina Holt was seated at the table, engrossed in whatever she was doing on her cellular. She concluded whatever it was as I sat opposite of her, placing the folder before me.

"Is he going to jail?" she asked, placing her phone into her pocketbook atop the table.

"That has yet to be determined," I answered, regarding her with narrow eyes. One may think her question was out of concern, but it sounded to me like she was *hoping* her boyfriend was hauled off to the clink. "You and Ray Young were an item at one time, am I right?"

"We dated," she said with a shrug.

"King Ray, right?"

"That's what he calls himself now."

I leaned forward, resting my elbows on the cool, steel table. "What can you tell me about the Kingz?"

"Nothing," answered Holt, brushing at the bang of her synthetic hair with her hand. "Ray and I broke up way before he called himself a King or joined it. However, that works."

"Do you still love him?"

She made a face. "I ain't never loved him! Men are incapable of love, so I keep my heart to myself."

"What about Johnston?" I pried, already getting a sense of what kind of woman she is.

"He's my fiancé," she reminded me.

"Do you love him?"

"You made me take a trip downtown just to question my sex life?" she caught an attitude.

"No, I did not." I fished the other statement form from the folder and placed it in front of her with an ink pen. "I brought you here to fill out an affidavit, saying you'll testify against the Kingz if called upon to do so in the court of law."

"I can't testify about something I don't know," she stated, matter-of-factly. "I don't even be around them. Like I said—"

She stopped mid-sentence when I began spreading the photos out in front of her. Yes, Trina Holt now conveyed the same facial expression Bobby Johnston had when Agent Pierce conducted this same tact that's famous amongst investigators all over the world.

"Are you sure you don't have any ties to the Kingz?" I pressed. "I mean, I'm not the smartest agent in the world, but I'm quite positive that's you and your fiancé at the warehouse on Fulton Industrial, that's owned by the Kingz. In fact, on this very day, you and Johnston delivered four stolen tractor-trailers to this building, where the Kingz not only distribute drugs but murder and mutilates human beings. As far as the bureau knows, those trailers could be used to distribute drugs *and* body parts, to which you and Johnston are accomplices to."

"Not me!" Holt protested, now on the brink of tears. "I didn't steal those trucks. I was just there."

"Being *just there* could get you life without parole," I said, getting to my feet. "And that's only if you take a plea. You said you never loved Young – prove it! Write the statement!"

While in the midst of the investigation, an idea came to me, which is why I told Pierce to retrieve the photos and statements. I head for my office, dialing a number on my cellular.

"Information Desk!" a familiar male's voice answered. "Chad Hoffman speaking."

"Chad, I've got some homework for you," I told him.

"Fire away!" he said.

"I need you to contact every hotel and motel in the city of Miami," I began. "And see if any of them had a Michael Nolan check in any time yesterday."

"That could be more than a dozen lodges!" Hoffman let out. "But you know I love investigatory work. Hell, I can get started on that, right now, if you want. I'm not doing a damn thing at this very moment."

"The sooner, the better," I said. "There's a possible chance that this guy may have rented a vehicle, also."

"Say no more!" Hoffman was animated now. "With luck, I'll have this info back to you in a jiffy."

"Thanks, Chad!"

"No problemo, amigo!"

I was slowly shaking my head from side to side as I concluded the call. Just as I was to place the phone back into its case on my hip, I literally ran into Mary Joseph, Director Manny Hopkins' assistant.

"Oh! I'm sorry, Mrs. Joseph!" I said to the older woman, who was quite stunning in her blue skirt and matching pumps, with her afro neatly blown out.

"No harm, no foul, baby!" she replied, showing all thirty-two of her perfectly white teeth. "Have you been to Mr. Hopkins' office?"

"No," I answered. "Is he—"

"Yes," she cut me off. "Like yesterday."

Shit! What the fuck could the Grinch possibly want with me? As if I haven't been dealing with him long enough to not be able to make an educated guess, right? Hell, he only calls me to his office whenever he wants to chew my ass out for something I'd done or didn't do. Well, I'm about to find out whichever one it is.

"Come on in, Bishop!" Hopkins asserted when I made it to his office. Once I took a seat, he asked, "How long do you have before you wrap this investigation up?"

"I'm estimating about two more months from now," I answered, already knowing where this was going.

"Negative!" he said, pounding a fist on his desk for emphasis. "You now have two weeks to present something to me, or I'm shutting down the whole operation! Now get the fuck out of my office!"

Well, damn! That was the briefest meeting I'd ever had with the director. He didn't seem to be in a foul mood, but that didn't mean he wasn't serious about what he said about putting the kibosh on my investigation, which is something I can't afford right now.

By the time I made it to my office, I received a call from Bravo Unit, informing me that they arrived with their subject. Being that I had already made it clear that I'd be interrogating her, the unit secured her in one of the interrogation rooms and was awaiting my arrival. Therefore, I detoured and made my way back to the East Wing of the building, where I came across Agent Pierce, who was leaning against the wall in the hallway, reading over some documents

"Did they complete 'em?" I inquired, upon approaching.

"Yes, sir," he answered, placing the affidavits inside the folder. "Are they free to go?"

"That was the deal," I told him. "Once you escort them to the lobby, you're done for the day. Feel free to leave if you want."

"Thanks, sir!"

He handed me the folder, then set out to retrieve Johnston and Holt. I made for Interrogation Room Three, but stopped by the observation booth of Interrogation Room Four, to see if my agents have made any progress with Jarvis Clay, aka Killah, a subordinate of the Kingz, who sales drugs for them in the Carver Homes community. By doing so, I was informed that Clay was illiterate, which is why it was taking so long, but one of the agents was assisting him with writing the affidavit.

Hey! That was music to my ears! I don't care if it took his dumb ass all night to write the statement, I'm just glad I already have three people to testify against the Kingz in court. Well, make that four, because Steven Chambers will have his ass there also.

I finally entered the observation booth of Interrogation Room Three, where the two agents that made up the Bravo company, were lounging around, engaged in conversation. They became quiet upon my entrance, but I disregarded them and looked out at Kimberly Ellis who was seated at the table, nervously picking at her fingernails, with a worried expression on her face.

"Did anybody say anything to her?" I asked, now realizing there were a statement form and ink pen in front of her, right beside her pocketbook.

"Not pertaining to why she's here," one of them answered from behind me. "You told us not to."

"Good!" I said, still watching James Young's ex-girlfriend. "Let's get this over with!"

Chapter 28

Saturday

July 12, 2003

"The eagle has landed," I said through my radio transmitter, when the Greyhound bus arriving from Virginia, pulled into the station. "I repeat, the eagle has landed. All units stand by."

I was seated in the front passenger seat of a black Chevy Tahoe, accompanied by three of my agents, who were all dressed in full tactical gear, though I chose to stick with the casual look, sporting a gray, two-piece suit and burgundy tie. Plus, I had my *Highway Patrols* on my face, which made me think about Wilma Reid, who arrived Wednesday on a leave and wouldn't be returning to California until the following Wednesday.

It was now 11:33 a.m., and we had been parked in the parking lot of the Greyhound station ever since 10:00 a.m. We already knew what time this particular bus came in, but we arrived early to make sure we got into position before Keith Daniels showed up, though he got here a little after eleven, like he does every other week to meet with this person, who'd just stepped down from the bus, clad in black shorts, a T-shirt, and an Oakland Raiders ball cap, with a book bag, slung over one shoulder.

Thanks to our fellow agents in Virginia we were able to identify the man as twenty-three-year-old, Terrence Mann a college student with no criminal background. That would have changed the moment he returned to his native state. However, I asked the Virginia boys to spare him but to keep him on their radar.

Without the least bit of interest in his surroundings, Mann crossed the lot, headed for Daniels' BMW. He definitely didn't pay any attention to Special Agents Carlos Moreno, and Rhonda Thomas who were both standing amongst the crowd of awaiting people, looking like a cute, interracial couple with their arms around each other. I also had four more agents positioned in the parking lot of Club Magic City, which was less than fifty yards out from our current location.

To my knowledge, and maybe I'm surmising a bit, but these Greyhound buses don't stay docked no more than thirty minutes, which means we have twenty-something minutes before engaging. Therefore, I kept my eyes on Daniels' car that I couldn't see the inside of for the dark tinted windows while wondering how I was going to collect enough evidence, or something substantial enough to tie the Kingz to the two murders that came about in Miami while they were there.

According to Chad Hoffman, Frederick Mills had used the same false identification he'd used to rent the burning car found at the multiple homicide scene in Lithonia, to rent a hotel room and Ford pickup in Miami, but that only places *him* closer to the scene of the crime, not the other three, which is why I'll be taking the next three days off. Yeah, I'm quite sure I have enough evidence stacked up against the Kingz to have them sentenced to life without parole but I want more than that. I'm pushing for the D.A. to file a Notice of Aggravating Circumstances which would surely have them sentenced to death, once found guilty.

"Alpha Two, load up!" I barked through my transmitter, upon seeing Mann climb from Daniels' BMW, slinging the bag over his shoulder.

"Roger that!" Moreno's voice sounded through my earpiece.

I watched as Moreno and Thomas boarded the Virginia bus, both carry backpacks. Their orders were to position themselves at Mann's six and to subdue him upon extraction, if necessary. By the looks of the small crowd still loitering nearby, it didn't seem like the bus would be pulling out any time soon, although Mann always boarded right after concluding his transactions with Daniels, which was pretty smart.

"Alpha Three, you have a bogus seventy-six," I announced through the wire when the bus to Detroit began to depart. "Do you copy?"

"Alpha Three copy," came the response from Agent Powell, who was positioned with the other agents in the parking lot of Magic City, one of Atlanta's most prestigious strip clubs.

Now, watching Daniels' BMW exit the parking lot, I eyed the chrome wheels, thinking how good they would look on my own BMW. Ha! Maybe I'll lay claim to them after all the Kingz' assets are confiscated upon their arrests. Or maybe I'll just get the whole car at the auction and grab one for Monique also.

"The eagle is leaving its nest," I announced, as the Virginia bus slowly pulled away. "I repeat, the eagle is leaving its nest."

"Alpha Three copy," came my response.

I looked over at Agent Andrew Pierce, who was seated behind the wheel of the SUV that was already running. He put the gear in drive, and pulled out onto Gwinnett Street, making sure to get directly behind the bus, when it exited the terminal. Usually, during takedowns, other agencies are involved, but I didn't plan on taking Mann down unless he doesn't comply, which I highly doubt.

Club Magic City was coming up on our right. Suddenly, I saw the black Chevy Tahoe with its red and blue lights flashing from its grill, pull out in front of the bus, causing its driver to bear down on the brakes. The four, tactical-dressed agents, were out of the vehicle, carrying handguns before the bus could come to a complete stop. Once our SUV halted, my company lunged from it, but Alpha Three had already boarded the bus.

This was like a scene from a movie, so people who were driving, walking by, or just standing around, were heavily engrossed in what was going down in front of the famous club.

"Subject is secured," I heard through my earpiece, just as I reached the entrance of the bus. I didn't have my gun out, because I didn't feel the need for it.

"You're green-lighted for extraction," I relayed, then stepped back to give Alpha Three room to bring Mann off.

I watched as the four agents backed out, one at a time, with their guns still aimed, before Mann came into view, walking with his hands atop his head. Then came Thomas and Moreno with their weapons out. Thomas was carrying Mann's backpack. As they escorted Mann to my awaiting SUV, I turned to the older White man sitting at the wheel of the bus.

"This shouldn't take long," I told him. "We just need to ask this guy a few questions."

"I have a deadline, sir," he protested.

"So, do I," I replied, thinking about what Director Manny Hopkins told me. "If you don't want to be hauled off to jail for interfering with a federal investigation, then I suggest you sit tight. Like I said, this shouldn't take long."

Making it back to the truck, I saw that Thomas had dumped the contents of Mann's bag onto the hood, which were a brick of cocaine wrapped in cellophane, and a chrome-plated Colt Python .357 Magnum. Two of my agents had Mann sandwiched in, in the rear seats of the SUV, while the others stood around, awaiting my next command.

"This traffic needs to be decongested," I told them, seeing that motorists were having a hard time moving around us on the two-lane street. When they dispersed upon my suggestion, I climbed into the front passenger seat, closing the door back. After a few seconds of letting the subject's mind wonder about his fate, I said, "How's it going, Terrance?" He didn't respond. "The silent treatment, huh?" I went on, now looking back at him. "You're not restrained, nor on your way to the county jail, and this is how you show your gratitude? I don't know about Virginia, but a kilo of cocaine, and a loaded gun, can get you life in prison down here. Especially dealing with the Feds."

"So, what do y'all want?" Mann finally asked.

"We already know you're getting your work from the Kingz," I plunged in. "You take the bus down here every two weeks, and meet up with Keith Daniels, aka King Black."

"If y'all already—"

"There's a reason why that bus is still there," I cut him off. "By law, I can only hold it for a certain amount of time without probable cause. Whether or not you're on it when it pulls off, is totally up to you."

"And what do I have to do?" asked Mann.

"All you have to do is write a statement saying you'll testify against the Kingz if called upon to do so by a court of law."

"Then, I'm free to go?" he sounded skeptical.

"Of course," I answered. "Plus, you get to keep your cocaine."

"What about my pistol?"

"Don't press your luck!"

***

After having my agents fill out and sign Mission Report documents, I dismissed them, giving them a whole week off. Once I filed everything away, I left the building, placing a call to Wilma Reid, explaining that I'd pick her up from her hotel the moment I leave from my late barber's appointment.

Actually, I had planned on driving to Miami alone, but, when I told Reid where I was going, and why, she couldn't help but include herself, saying I'd better have her back in time to catch her bus back home on Wednesday morning. Of course, I didn't turn her down. In fact, she's the only person I would rather have accompany me. Perhaps we could catch up on old times.

It was well after 7:00 p.m., when I pulled my BMW into the parking lot of Tyrone's barbershop, parking beside his burnt-orange '79 Chevy Impala on chrome wheels, which was the only other vehicle present. It was at Tyrone's behest that I show up after hours, which was a first, and I didn't like it one bit. I didn't think he would try something, but one may never know.

"Come on in, my friend," Tyrone said, upon unlocking the door to let me into the empty barbershop, making sure to lock it back.

The place was empty, but it wasn't completely quiet, as *Too Short* and *Lil Kim's Call Me* played at a low volume from the stereo. The vacant stations, including Tyrone's, were clean, with utensils hanging in their proper places. Even the floor was spotless.

"So, why the late appointment?" I asked, taking a seat in Tyrone's chair, but keeping a wary eye on the restroom door that was closed, which was usually open when unoccupied.

"I wanted to pull your coattail about some shit," he said, stepping behind me, and grabbing the barber's tarp.

"I'm listening."

"You know we've been knowing each other ever since we were kids."

"Get to the point, Tyrone!"

"Right." Tyrone draped the tarp over me and fastened it. "There's a rumor that Steve has been feeding you information about the Kingz."

"Really?" I watched the restroom door from the corners of my eyes, and, thanks to the tarp, Tyrone couldn't see that I had my right hand rested on my gun in my holster that was unfastened.

"That's the word on the streets," answered Tyrone. "It's an ongoing topic in here also."

"So, the other barbers found out about me, huh?"

"I don't know how," he said, switching his clippers, "but they did. That's why I told you to come late."

"Are you sure you didn't confirm this?" I asked, accusingly. "They do know about our history."

"Hell no!" Tyrone spat. "I told them I didn't know what you did for a living. That you were very secretive about your personal life."

I cleared my throat. "So, I guess you're trying to find out if the rumor is true."

"I'm not prying," he professed, "but you know what those dudes would do to him if they found out. Whether it's true or not."

"We put ourselves in certain predicaments, Tyrone," I said slowly. "I'm an FBI agent. If a person wants to volunteer information about some criminal activities, they're aware of, that's between them and the individuals they're volunteering the information on."

"We're all from the same spot, Brian."

"Tyrone, you have a good thing going for yourself," I pointed out, ready to nip this conversation in the bud. "You run a legitimate business, *and* sell drugs without interference. It would be a shame if your luck just changed all of a sudden."

He continued cutting my hair without a word.

"Chambers chose to be a snitch," I resumed, "and snitches get stitches. Isn't that how it goes?"

Chapter 29

"Mmm!"

I heard myself moan, and I definitely felt something wet and warm going up and down the length of my swollen manhood. Hearing the sound of someone gagging, caused me to force my eyes open to see Wilma Reid on her hands and knees, trying to take every inch of me down her throat.

Upon leaving the barbershop, I met Reid at her hotel, then we made off to Florida in her rented Dodge Magnum, reaching our destination a little after 2:00 a.m. I had already made reservations at a hotel beforehand, so all I had to do was show my I.D. and collect the room key.

Being that there were no doubles, I insisted that Reid take the bed, and I made a pallet on the floor. Now, I didn't have the slightest clue as to what time it was, as the sun shined brightly through the thin curtains, and Reid attempted to swallow me whole while drilling those seductively green eyes into mine. Plus, she was completely naked.

This was all a surprise to me, because, during our drive down, neither one of us had mentioned anything about having sex with each other, although I'd always wanted to tap that white ass. Also, I had to have been pretty exhausted in order for me to not feel her peel the covers off me and pull my dick through the opening of my boxer shorts.

Well, now that I'm wide awake, I may as well participate, right? Grabbing Reid by her shoulders, I pulled her up towards me, then took her by her waist, moving her into the sixty-nine position. She didn't hesitate to fill her mouth back up with my still throbbing cock. Of course, I didn't just lie there, staring at her neatly shaved pussy that had no kind of smell to it, by the way. I, first, toyed with her clitoris, using my tongue. Then, once she started gyrating her hips in ecstasy, I took it into my mouth like a hungry infant does the nipple of its mother's breasts.

We were both moaning now. Her head game was superb, and I'm quite sure I was stirring up the juices in her vines, summoning them to the forefront. Then, feeling the urge to unleash a freakier side of me, I relocated my mouth to the crack of her ass and found myself repetitiously licking, kissing, and blowing on the entrance of her dark abyss.

I usually like to have some kind of mood music playing in the background, during sexual intercourse, but this was abruptly engaged by Wilma Reid which pretty much left me optionless if that's even a word. Therefore, the only sounds that could be heard were slurping, and occasional moaning. However, at this very moment, I was a little too thirsty to find myself inside her, so I put an end to the foreplay.

When we got to our feet, I came out of my T-shirt and boxers, so that we were both naked. I didn't bring any condoms, and I assume she didn't either because she didn't protest when I scooped her 5'5 frame off the floor with both hands gripping her ass cheeks. She wrapped her arms around my neck, legs around my waist, and smothered me in a kiss, as I eased her down onto my rod, entering her with no guidance.

At first, standing right there in the middle of the hotel room, I began slow grinding, while kissing her back. Then, I was grinding harder. The next thing I knew, I had picked up the pace, eventually breaking the kiss. Reid threw her head back and let out the sexiest woman grown I'd ever heard.

"That's right, baby!" she urged. "Give me that long, black dick! Tear this pussy up!"

By this time, with my fingers dug into her soft ass cheeks, I was plunging as deep as I could go inside her. The sound of our bodies clashing into each other was loud and I could feel her juices dripping down my right thigh, which brought me close to climaxing. As bad as I wanted to shoot off in that tight pussy of hers, I couldn't, hell, a mental image of Monique, made sure I didn't.

Stopping mid-stroke, I turned and took a couple of steps to the bed, where I laid her on the edge of it while staying penetrated. To subside my orgasm a bit, I began kissing her, and slow grinding, using short strokes. Once I felt it was safe to get back to business, I folded her short, well-defined legs back, with her feet above her head, and *really* put the pound game down!

The surprisingly flexible bitch wasn't begging for me to tear the pussy up now. No sir! She was trying to buck up out of the position, but I wasn't having it. She went from begging me to give her all the dick, to take some of it out, which only galvanized me to pitch harder and deeper. Now her eyes were rolled up in her head, and the cheap-ass headboard was banging against the thin wall like I was trying to drive the whole bed through it.

"Ooh, shit, Brian!" she let out, now rubbing her clitoris. "I'm— I'm about to come!"

"You better come all over this dick," I urged, feeling her muscles tighten around my pole. "Make that pussy skeet!"

"Ahh!" Reid cried out, doing exactly what she said she was going to do, drowning me in her hot liquid.

I kept stroking, until her body stopped quivering, making sure she got it all out, before rolling her onto her stomach and diving back in, with my feet still planted on the floor. While continuing my assault, I couldn't help but stare down at her perfectly round, and flawless ass that vibrated from the impact of every thrust, which was enough to push me to my peak again. This time, I didn't hold back. The moment I felt myself about to explode, I pulled out, stood erect, and began jerking off.

"Ahh!" I expressed, as my warm load shot out onto her back, her ass, the bed, and the already stained carpet.

After taking separate showers, Reid and I headed for a nearby Denny's, where we ate in, and had a light conversation, mainly about the case I'm working on, and how things are going for her back in Oakland. Leaving there, we made it to Enterprise, the car rental dealership Mills had used upon their visit here earlier this week.

"Hi!" the White woman behind the front desk greeted us, once we entered. "Welcome to Enterprise! How may I help you guys?"

"I'm Special Agent Bishop," I said, flashing my credentials, "and this is my partner, Special Agent Williams. We're here to see the manager, Mr. Wayne Todd. If you would ring him up for us. I told him I'd stop by today."

The woman let out a sharp breath. "Well, unfortunately, Mr. Todd's wife went into labor in the middle of the night, so he didn't show up today. I mean, it's not like we were expecting him to being that it's his first child, and we are just as excited for him as he is, I tell ya! However, our assistant manager, Mrs. Sandy Beck is the active manager, if you'd like a word with her."

"Sure," I said, hoping this wouldn't turn out to be a blank trip.

The clerk picked up the receiver, punched in a few numbers, then waited. "Yes, Mrs. Beck? There are a pair of FBI agents here to see Mr. Todd but would like to speak with you. Okay." Hanging up, she regarded us and asserted: "She'll be out in a sec."

"Thanks!"

"No problem."

Being that there were customers behind us, Reid and I stepped aside to wait on the assistant manager, who didn't have us waiting for long. Sandy Beck, a White woman in her late-thirties, emerged from the back, carrying a CD case in her hand. She took one look at us and came right over.

"May I have your name, sir?" she asked.

I showed my credentials. "Special Agent Bishop."

"Mr. Todd called my home from the hospital early this morning," Beck explained. "First, to give me the news on the birth of his firstborn. Then, to inform me that he'd left this for you."

"Thanks!" I said, receiving the clear case that had *FBI Bishop* written on it in black marker.

"You're welcome," she responded. "I hope it helps out."

"So, do I," I told her, then lead the way toward the exit.

"Special Agent Williams, huh?" Reid said as we emerged from the building.

"Just protecting your identity," I told her. "Just in case shit takes a wrong turn. Now we need to find a library, so I can view this disk."

"Why didn't you ask the manager?"

"Then, she would've known we were out-of-towners," I answered. "If she's smarter than what I give her credit for, she would've deduced that we were out of our jurisdiction and asked to see a warrant."

"Smart man!" she commented. Once we were back inside the rental, she said, "So, I guess we're off to the nearest library, huh?"

"Not yet," I said, securing the disc inside the glove compartment. "There's a Days Inn just up the road from here. We'll search for a library once we leave from there."

It had only taken seven minutes to reach the low-budget motel. After instructing Reid to park in front of the small office, and to wait, I was back out in the ninety-degree weather again. Hell, the office may as well not have an air conditioner unit, because it did nothing to reprieve anyone of what's waiting on the other side of those doors. It's like I started to perspire more, the moment I approached the desk, where a balding, middle-aged White man was down on his knees, fumbling with a bundle of cable cords.

"Excuse me, sir!" I interrupted. "Are you Mr. Douglas?"

"I sure am," he responded, getting to his feet, and regarding me with a gap-toothed grin. "And you must be from the bureau?"

"Yes, I am." I didn't bother showing him my credentials because, clearly, he didn't think I was Special Agent Bishop, being that I had Chad Hoffman make the phone calls for me, which gave him the impression that I'm Caucasian.

Looking into one of his counter drawers, he produced a sheet of white paper, with a photocopy of the faux identification card Frederick Mills used. "I don't know why Agent Bishop didn't want me to fax this to him," Douglas said, handing it to me. "I assume it must be Top Secret. This guy some kind of serial killer, or something?"

"Shit no!" I said, hoping I sounded convincing. "As far as we know, this guy is harmless. He's just a known car thief, who transports stolen vehicles to chop shops in different states. Seven vehicles were reported stolen from this area, this past weekend, which prompted us to check the local lodgings to see if it was our guy."

"And he stole all seven vehicles by himself?" The old man seemed impressed.

"He has an entourage," I added to my lie.

"If I see him again," the old fart said, "should I notify you guys?"

"You won't see him in this area again."

"What makes you so sure of that?"

"He doesn't have a reputation for frequenting the same scene," I answered. "However, thanks for the photo."

Upon leaving the hotel, I concluded that a trip to a library would be time-consuming, being that I already know what I'll see upon viewing the disc. Therefore, I gave Reid the address to a home out in Dade County, which was the last destination on my itinerary, and hoped to God that somebody was there.

Well, there was a blue Ford Mustang, and a gray Honda Pilot parked in the driveway of the red brick home, with its picture-perfect landscape, and white picket fence, which gave the place such a surreal look. In fact, every house lining the street gave off the same impression.

"Do I stay in the car?" Reid asked, after docking the car at the curb in front of the house.

"Of course not!" I answered, pushing my door open, and getting out. "Besides, two or more agents always makes a visit seem more—*important*, if I may."

"How about more *intimidating*?" Reid offered, as she also got out.

I rounded the car, tugging on my blazer, despite the irritable heat index. "That too," I replied. "Now, let's see who we'll be *intimidating* on this Sunday afternoon."

"Isn't it time for a new pair of Highway Patrols?" she asked, as we trailed the winding concrete walkway to the house.

"Nope," I answered, adjusting the sunglasses on my face. "When I retire, I'm gonna have these in a glass case, like an artifact at a museum."

"I swear you remind me of Mike Lawry from the movie, *Bad Boys*!" Reid said, laughing.

"So, you think I look like Will Smith, huh?"

"Please!" she expressed, making a face. "You look more like Emmet Smith."

"Emmet Smith!" I exclaimed, ringing the doorbell, upon approaching the door. Reid was laughing. "I see you got jokes," I told her. "We'll have to talk about this later."

"Oh, you don't like the—"

Reid stopped mid-sentence when the front door began to open slowly. On instinct, we both reached for our sidearms but didn't unholster them. Momentarily, we were looking at a woman, who appeared to be in her mid-forties, and clad in light fabric capri pants and blouse, with sandals on her feet. Gray strands of hair decorated the left side of her ponytail, and the bags under her eyes were sure signs of heavy drinking, drug abuse, lack of sleep, or all the above.

"Mrs. Rochelle Lane?" I asked, already knowing it was her.

"Um," she lingered, eyes darting from me to Reid. "Yes, that's me."

"I'm Special Agent Bishop," I said, showing my credentials, "and this is Special Agent Williams. Are you on your way out?"

"No," she answered, stepping aside. "Come on in."

I followed Reid into the home, which was a great representation of the exterior, as the living room was moderately decorated, and looked as though no one spent any amount of time in it. For that reason, I stopped short of the door. Reid did likewise.

"Does this have something to do with Willie?" Mrs. Lane inquired, upon closing the door. "I've already told the police officers what I know about him, which isn't much. My daughter dated him."

"Which is something we're aware of," I said, grateful that she was the one to break the ice. "Have you spoken to Nicole since the incident?"

"She called me to let me know that she and the kids were back in Atlanta," Lane answered. "That they were safe."

"Safe from who?" I pried.

The older woman shrugged her shoulders. "I don't know. Maybe she was letting me know that they'd made it safely to Atlanta. It *is* a long drive, you know."

"Yes, it is," I concurred. "You and your husband live in this house alone, right?"

"Yes. He's out visiting his mother at this moment."

"So, Nicole and the kids were staying with Willie Carswell?"

"Yes."

"Could you tell me what day it was that Nicole decided to move back to Atlanta?"

Mrs. Lane just stared at me.

"I'm not implying that she had anything to do with Carswell's murder," I tried to reason.

"It sure as hell sounds like it!" She was on the defense. "Like I said, I didn't know much about Willie, and my daughter had nothing to do with his murder. But, if it makes you feel any better, she left the night before he was killed."

"Thanks a lot, ma'am!" I offered. "We're sorry to have bothered you, but it's all routine."

"I understand."

"Have a nice day!"

"Y'all do the same."

She seemed relieved to let us out, and I was a bit relieved to be out of there, although there were questions, I didn't get to ask. I thought about this on our way to the car, but I was focused on the two White men emerging from a black Crown Victoria parked across the street, both clad in suits and ties, with visible sidearms, and all-too-familiar badges clipped to their belts. Plus, like yours truly, they were both wearing sunglasses.

"I can spot an FBI agent with my eyes closed," the first one asserted, as they met us by our car. He was of medium height, late-thirties, clean-shaven, with brown hair matted to his scalp.

"I would like to believe that I'm highly familiar with every agent in our department," he went on, "but I've never seen either of you. Do you mind telling me where you guys hail from?"

"Atlanta," I took the initiative.

The other agent let out a long whistle. He was slightly shorter, and a bit heavier than his partner, with jet black hair barely peaking from his scalp, and a full goatee.

"Atlanta, Georgia!" the first agent carried on. "The Peach State! Surely, you guys don't have business here, or I would have known all about that. So, I'm assuming you're some kin, or friends to the resident of this home. I mean, I can just ask Mr. and Mrs. Lane myself."

I didn't care to reply, neither did Reid.

"So, you guys are here on official business," he concluded. "Out of your jurisdiction. I've never had a fellow agent cited for interfering with a federal investigation, but there's a first time for everything, right? Who's your handler, anyway?"

"Manny Hopkins," I answered, reluctantly, seeing that all his accusations and questions were aimed directly at me.

"Does Manny Hopkins know that two of his underlings are sticking their noses where they don't belong?" he pushed. "Perhaps you were questioning Mrs. Lane about her daughter, Nicole Lane, who hauled ass to Atlanta on the night prior to the day her boyfriend was murdered."

Damn! This fucker is on his game! My delay of response brought a huge grin to his face.

"Unless you people are here on *official* business," the agent proceeded, minus the grin. "I suggest you climb back into your contraption and head back to the place where you're most welcomed."

Chapter 30

Thursday

July 17, 2003

"I think you may have something here, Bishop," Director Hopkins expressed, as he looked over the evidence I'd accumulated in my investigation on the Kingz, which were photos, copies of phone records, compact discs containing video surveillance footages and recorded phone conversations, written affidavits, and other miscellaneous items that were sprawled atop his desk.

Being that I'd given my team the week off, I had dedicated my time preparing everything to be presented to the Department of Justice for their approval to proceed, or disapproval. Even with all the evidence I have, I still feel it's not sufficient. Like there's something missing. I always feel this way when it's time to turn in my findings, but this was different somehow.

"It's all adding up to me," Hopkins now admitted, "except for the gun shop job, and the deal in Miami, Florida."

"I know I'm going out on a limb with the gun shop heist," I said, hating the fact that James Young could get away with murdering the gun shop owner and an officer of the law. "But I have substantial evidence that places Frederick Mills in Miami, around the time the two murders occurred. Also, Nokia's mobile phone towers place Keith Daniels not only in Miami but right at the home of Willie Carswell."

"What about the other two?"

"The brothers were smart," I was loath to admit. "They left their cell phones here. So, did Mills."

"I'm telling you how the Justice Department will view it, Bishop."

My jaws were set, I didn't answer.

"Anyway," the director said with a sigh, leaning back in his chair. "Let's say they grant you permission to move in on the Kingz. What's your POA?"

"I wanna take them down on the twelfth of next month," I answered, replaying my plan of action over in my head like I'd been doing for weeks now.

"Why the twelfth?"

"According to my source," I said, speaking of Steven Chambers, "there's a huge, annual DJ battle going on that night at Club Warehouse. They'll be judging the event."

"A *huge* DJ battle," he replied, emphasizing on *huge*, "means there will be a *huge* crowd, bringing about a *huge* possibility for casualties, which could result in a *huge* lawsuit."

"Which is why I'll be equipping the auxiliary unit with rubber bullets," I went on to explain. "They'll be the ones on crowd control just in case a couple of zealots decides to show their asses. My primary unit will engage the Kings and their guards. Plus, we'll be ready to deploy tear gas if necessary."

"And I assume this will take place *outside* the club?"

"Of course."

"You still didn't tell me why you chose this date and location."

I couldn't say, because I really didn't have an exact reason. However, it seemed logical, being that I'll be able to apprehend both, Kingz and Kingzmen, on the same night, right?

"Embarrassment!" Hopkins blurted out at a length.

I was baffled. "Excuse me?"

"You're looking to embarrass them in front of all those people," he went on, leaning forward, and resting his elbows on the desk. "To set an example for the next group of thugs, who decides to make a name for themselves."

"Well—"

"I like it!" he cut me off, smiling from ear to ear. "Show those fuckers who's in charge!"

What the fuck just happened! I can't even remember the last time Manny Hopkins – the fucking Grinch – agreed with anything I had to say. Was he mocking me, knowing that the DOJ wouldn't grant me permission to take further action? No, that can't be it. I have too much evidence stacked up against the Kingz. Surely, they'll be more than happy to grant me permission to put these scumbags away. However, I still don't know what I'm gonna do with Steven Chambers when this is all over. Speaking of the son of a bitch, I haven't heard anything from him in over a week.

Playa Ray

Chapter 31

Tuesday

August 12, 2003

"Okay. Listen up, ladies and gentlemen!" I said, upon entering the room and positioning myself behind the podium. "Now that we're all here, I wanna run through the POA once more, before we head out."

It was 6:48 p.m., and our briefing was being held inside the small building of the Zone Five Police Department's shooting range. As I said before, multiple agencies are involved during takedowns, which is why I was now looking out at personnel from the GBI, AFT, Fulton County Sheriff's Department, and our very own Gangs Task Force Unit.

Figuring the Battle of the DJs event would bring about a pre-dominately Black crowd, I requested that these agencies provide me with people of the same ethnic, to keep down suspicion. Anybody of the opposite hue was a part of my cardinal unit and will be well secluded with me until it was time to converge on our targets, which is something I'd been anticipating from the moment I first heard of the Kingz.

"As we already know," I went on, "two Fulton County deputies are moonlighting at the club, who are components of this operation. You other two deputies, along with the three appointed GBI agents, will linger amongst the crowd lined up out front. You'll be on crowd control, and won't reveal yourselves unless the crowd becomes boisterous, and attempts to move in on us."

"How do we engage?" asked one of the deputies, who was a female.

"Your guns and additional cartridges are loaded with rubber bullets," I reminded her. "Shoot the fuckers! Can you handle that?"

She nodded her head up and down.

"ATF?" I turned to the group of four, who looked more like two couples on a double date, than agents who were about to participate in a takedown. "If y'all don't mind me asking, what kind of vehicle did you get from Motor Pool?"

"An eighty-five model Cadillac Seville," one of the men answered. "White in color, chrome wheels."

"Great!" I commented. "You all will position yourselves *outside* of the vehicle. Appear normal. Laugh and joke a little but stay sharp. You're also on crowd control, but you'll be watching our six. Try to keep the full parking lot in your peripheral. Once the scene becomes active, you'll be responsible for keeping anyone in that particular area from interrupting it. Any questions?" There weren't any. "The final two GBI agents will be stationed two blocks down, in the transport vehicle, and will move in on-call, which would be once all subjects are detained. Now, I'm almost certain that no one in my unit has any questions, right?" There were no replies. "Alright, let's gear up and roll out!"

It wasn't obligatory that we all left in tandem, or traveled in a convoy, so everyone pretty much moved out in their appointed group, after conducting their own weapons check. My cardinal unit, and the FBI Gangs Task Force agents, were the only components of this operation, dressed in full tactical gear, carrying assault rifles, and would be concealed until I as point call the scene to action.

There were two, customized cargo vans outwardly promoting two different FM radio stations, but outfitted with two steel benches across from each other, and support bars mounted to the roof, to transport both heavily armed groups. Accompanying me in the rear of the van that falsely claimed to belong to the 96.7 FM station, were Agents Simmons, Powell, Moreno, Pearson, and Thomas. The members of the GTF piled into the other. Plus, two plainclothes agents were driving the vehicles.

Being the last to climb in, I closed the double doors that were equipped with limousine tinted windows, before positioning my M-16 between my legs, barrel to the floor, letting it hang loosely from the strap draped over my shoulder, and clutching my safety helmet on my lap.

We rode in silence for the ride that only took about seven minutes, being that the Zone Five precinct was just right up the street from our destination. However, I couldn't see anything, until our driver found a spot, parking with the rear of the van facing the club. At only a little after seven, there looked to be about twelve people waiting in line, while others, apparently participating DJs, and event staff flashed some kind of card to the three bouncers standing around out front and headed on in. I identified two of the bouncers as the Fulton County Deputies, who are assigned to this case. They were ordered to remain out front once the rest of us entered the vicinity.

"How's it looking out there, Floyd?" I asked, now looking toward the small slit in the steel partition wall that separated us from the front seats.

"Vehicles are slowly rolling in," Special Agent Floyd's voice came back to me through the opening. "A handful of people are just milling about, apparently wasting time before the event kicks off."

"Roger that," I replied, then spoke into my radio transceiver: "Alpha Two, what's your twenty?"

"Ten yards to your nine," came the response from our Task Force Unit.

"Copy that. Bravo One, check-in!"

"We're already in position," responded one of the ATF agents, who were to station outside the government issued Cadillac.

"Got you," I said. "Bravo Two?"

"Approaching the line now." This was the group that would be positioned in the line outside the club.

"Sing me a song, Charlie," I finally checked in with the two GBI agents occupying the transport vehicle.

"We're here, sir," came the reply.

"Roger that," I asserted, then drew my cell phone from a pocket on my vest and selecting a phone number from my list of contacts. While waiting for the lines to connect, I looked out the rear window just in time to see a man approaching the entrance of the club, dressed in black shorts, with *D.J. Goldfinger* in gold letters, on the back of his black shirt.

Well, I'd be damned! If it isn't Martin Richard the young brother of one of Atlanta's known drug dealers, Norris Boyd. That

Boyd is one slick, and cautious motherfucker, which is why I'm willing to wager anything that Richard was dipping and dabbling in the drug game somehow. Even if he was just a trafficker.

"Towns!" the agent I had trailing the Kingz' limousine, answered.

"Tell me something good!"

"They made a brief stop at the warehouse on Fulton Industrial," he informed, "but are now back on the highway. All Kingz are onboard, except for Ray Young, so I assume they're headed to Riverdale to pick him up. The Kingzmen are trailing them in one of the black Escalades."

"Good!" I told him. "Phone me once the last King is onboard, and on their way."

"Yes, sir!"

Concluding the call, I was just about to drop the phone back into the pocket of my vest when it vibrated in my hand. Now, Monique knew better than to call me while I'm on duty. In fact, she knew it was prohibited, unless it was an emergency, but what kind of— "Hello!" I answered, sensing something terrible was wrong.

"Brian, we're on our way to the hospital!" Monique got out in one millisecond, sounding like she was out of breath.

"What's wrong?" I asked, hoping nothing was wrong with our unborn child.

"Carmen's water broke," she explained. "Your dad called me from the hospital. She's going into labor, right now. Melody and I are on our way out the door now."

"Well, y'all be careful!" I told her. "I'll get there when I can."

Now, how about *that* shit! I didn't actually plan on being right there in the Emergency Room while my father's girlfriend was giving birth to their child, but I did want to show my support by showing up at the hospital. Hell, who would've known she would go into labor on the night I had chosen to take the Kingz down? Who knows? Maybe this would be a great story to tell Dorian Bishop Jr. when he gets older. Lucky for me, Monique has another month before bringing Brian Freeman Bishop Jr. into this world, which is why after tonight, I won't be working heavy caseloads and will be spending more time at home, so I can be there to drive her to the hospital when that time comes.

Now, looking out of the rear window, I found myself studying the faces of the people standing in the rapidly growing line, and instantly locked in on a tall, light-complexioned woman with brown micro braids. She was definitely a sight to see, but that's not why I was staring at her. This was Shonda Watson girlfriend of James Young. I can't say if they're still together, because she no longer lives with him, though she was still the secretary of Kingz BMWs before it was burned down just a few weeks ago. I mean, if she and Young were still together, she and her friends wouldn't have to wait in line, right?

"I'm listening," I said, upon answering my cell phone

"All Kingz are onboard," Agent Towns announced. "The calvary is seventy-six."

"Great!" I told him. "I need about a ten-minute notice."

"Yes, sir!"

Ringing off, I looked back out at Watson, but my mind was on Yvonne Miller one of Frederick Mills' *playthings*, who was handcuffed to one of the chairs inside her salon and set on fire. Perhaps Young had realized what he and his comrades were up against, and let Watson go for her own safety, which made me think about the warning from the movie *Heat* again, *"Don't let yourself get attached to anything you're not willing to walk out on in thirty seconds flat if you feel the heat around the corner."*

Maybe I'll be doing the Kingz a favor by taking them off the streets, because, from my vantage point, it seems like they're up against a force much greater than what they would ever be considered. They've bitten off more than they can chew, as the older generation puts it. So, yes, I'm looking at it like I'm saving their lives, although I'll still be pushing for the death penalty for all the hard work and dedication I put into this investigation. Does that make me a spiteful person? Who cares?

"I don't care about any other stops they make, Towns!" I answered my phone again. "Like I said, call me when you're ten-minutes out!"

"Sir, this shit just took a drastic turn!" Towns let out, sounding as animated as Monique had when telling me of Carmen going into labor.

"Speak English, Towns!"

"I'm still stuck at the stoplight," he went on. "Man, four Hummers pulled up, two on each side. They just shot the fucking limousine up! I've never seen no shit like this in real life!"

"I need to know if they survived the attack," I told him, seeing this investigation going down the drain.

"It doesn't appear that way from where I'm sitting," responded Towns. "These guys really did a number on that truck. It would be a miracle if any of them survived that."

"Well, I want you to stay on the scene until you get confirmation," I ordered. "And call me the moment you do!"

Hanging up, I couldn't help but sit there like a frog on a log, though I was feeling more like the log. It took about a good three minutes for me to pull myself together, and radio for my team to stand down, but I didn't give any reason until we reassembled at the building of the Zone Five shooting range.

After dismissing the auxiliary unit, my primary unit, and the Gangs Task Force Unit made for the James P. Russell building in the two vans we'd staked out in. We weren't on the road for no more than five minutes, when the call came in from Towns, who confirmed the fatalities of the Kingz claiming he witnessed the coroners pull the men's lifeless bodies from the limousine, take pictures, then zip them up the body bags.

To Be Continued

KINGZ OF THE GAME 6

COMING SOON

Submission Guideline

Submit the first three chapters of your completed manuscript to ldpsubmissions@gmail.com, subject line: Your book's title. The manuscript must be in a .doc file and sent as an attachment. Document should be in Times New Roman, double spaced and in size 12 font. Also, provide your synopsis and full contact information. If sending multiple submissions, they must each be in a separate email.

Have a story but no way to send it electronically? You can still submit to LDP/Ca$h Presents. Send in the first three chapters, written or typed, of your completed manuscript to:

LDP: Submissions Dept
Po Box 944
Stockbridge, Ga 30281

DO NOT send original manuscript. Must be a duplicate.

Provide your synopsis and a cover letter containing your full contact information.

Thanks for considering LDP and Ca$h Presents.

<u>Coming Soon from Lock Down Publications/Ca$h Presents</u>

BOW DOWN TO MY GANGSTA

By **Ca$h**

TORN BETWEEN TWO

By **Coffee**

THE STREETS STAINED MY SOUL **II**

By **Marcellus Allen**

BLOOD OF A BOSS **VI**

SHADOWS OF THE GAME II

By **Askari**

LOYAL TO THE GAME **IV**

By **T.J. & Jelissa**

A DOPEBOY'S PRAYER **II**

By **Eddie "Wolf" Lee**

IF LOVING YOU IS WRONG… **III**

By **Jelissa**

TRUE SAVAGE **VII**

MIDNIGHT CARTEL III

DOPE BOY MAGIC IV

CITY OF KINGZ II

By **Chris Green**

BLAST FOR ME **III**

A SAVAGE DOPEBOY III

CUTTHROAT MAFIA III

By **Ghost**

A HUSTLER'S DECEIT III

KILL ZONE **II**

BAE BELONGS TO ME III

A DOPE BOY'S QUEEN III

Kingz of the Game 5

By **Aryanna**
COKE KINGS V
KING OF THE TRAP II
By **T.J. Edwards**
GORILLAZ IN THE BAY V
De'Kari
THE STREETS ARE CALLING II
Duquie Wilson
KINGPIN KILLAZ IV
STREET KINGS III
PAID IN BLOOD III
CARTEL KILLAZ IV
DOPE GODS III
Hood Rich
SINS OF A HUSTLA II
ASAD
KINGZ OF THE GAME VI
Playa Ray
SLAUGHTER GANG IV
RUTHLESS HEART IV
By Willie Slaughter
THE HEART OF A SAVAGE III
By Jibril Williams
FUK SHYT II
By Blakk Diamond
THE REALEST KILLAZ III
By Tranay Adams
TRAP GOD III
By Troublesome
YAYO IV

A SHOOTER'S AMBITION III

By S. Allen

GHOST MOB

Stilloan Robinson

KINGPIN DREAMS III

By Paper Boi Rari

CREAM II

By Yolanda Moore

SON OF A DOPE FIEND III

By Renta

FOREVER GANGSTA II

GLOCKS ON SATIN SHEETS III

By Adrian Dulan

LOYALTY AIN'T PROMISED II

By Keith Williams

THE PRICE YOU PAY FOR LOVE II

By Destiny Skai

CONFESSIONS OF A GANGSTA II

By Nicholas Lock

I'M NOTHING WITHOUT HIS LOVE II

SINS OF A THUG II

By Monet Dragun

LIFE OF A SAVAGE IV

A GANGSTA'S QUR'AN III

MURDA SEASON III

GANGLAND CARTEL II

By **Romell Tukes**

QUIET MONEY III

THUG LIFE II

By **Trai'Quan**

THE STREETS MADE ME III

By **Larry D. Wright**

THE ULTIMATE SACRIFICE VI

IF YOU CROSS ME ONCE II

ANGEL III

By **Anthony Fields**

THE LIFE OF A HOOD STAR

By Ca$h & Rashia Wilson

FRIEND OR FOE II

By **Mimi**

SAVAGE STORMS II

By **Meesha**

BLOOD ON THE MONEY II

By J-Blunt

THE STREETS WILL NEVER CLOSE II

By K'ajji

NIGHTMARES OF A HUSTLA II

By King Dream

Available Now

RESTRAINING ORDER **I & II**

By **CA$H & Coffee**

LOVE KNOWS NO BOUNDARIES **I II & III**

By **Coffee**

RAISED AS A GOON I, II, III & IV

BRED BY THE SLUMS I, II, III

BLAST FOR ME I & II

ROTTEN TO THE CORE I II III

A BRONX TALE I, II, III

DUFFEL BAG CARTEL I II III IV

HEARTLESS GOON I II III IV

A SAVAGE DOPEBOY I II

HEARTLESS GOON I II III

DRUG LORDS I II III

CUTTHROAT MAFIA I II

By **Ghost**

LAY IT DOWN **I & II**

LAST OF A DYING BREED

BLOOD STAINS OF A SHOTTA I & II III

By **Jamaica**

LOYAL TO THE GAME I II III

LIFE OF SIN I, II III

By **TJ & Jelissa**

BLOODY COMMAS I & II

SKI MASK CARTEL I II & III

KING OF NEW YORK I II,III IV V

RISE TO POWER I II III

COKE KINGS I II III IV

BORN HEARTLESS I II III IV

KING OF THE TRAP

By **T.J. Edwards**

IF LOVING HIM IS WRONG…I & II

LOVE ME EVEN WHEN IT HURTS I II III

By **Jelissa**

WHEN THE STREETS CLAP BACK I & II III

THE HEART OF A SAVAGE I II

By **Jibril Williams**

A DISTINGUISHED THUG STOLE MY HEART I II & III

LOVE SHOULDN'T HURT I II III IV

RENEGADE BOYS I II III IV

PAID IN KARMA I II III

SAVAGE STORMS

By **Meesha**

A GANGSTER'S CODE I &, II III

A GANGSTER'S SYN I II III

THE SAVAGE LIFE I II III

CHAINED TO THE STREETS I II III

BLOOD ON THE MONEY

By J-Blunt

PUSH IT TO THE LIMIT

By **Bre' Hayes**

BLOOD OF A BOSS **I, II, III, IV, V**

SHADOWS OF THE GAME

By **Askari**

THE STREETS BLEED MURDER **I, II & III**

THE HEART OF A GANGSTA I II& III

By **Jerry Jackson**

CUM FOR ME I II III IV V VI

An **LDP Erotica Collaboration**

BRIDE OF A HUSTLA **I II & II**

THE FETTI GIRLS **I, II& III**

CORRUPTED BY A GANGSTA I, II III, IV

BLINDED BY HIS LOVE

THE PRICE YOU PAY FOR LOVE

DOPE GIRL MAGIC I II III

By **Destiny Skai**

WHEN A GOOD GIRL GOES BAD

By **Adrienne**

THE COST OF LOYALTY I II III

By Kweli

A GANGSTER'S REVENGE **I II III & IV**

THE BOSS MAN'S DAUGHTERS I II III IV V

A SAVAGE LOVE **I & II**

BAE BELONGS TO ME I II

A HUSTLER'S DECEIT I, II, III

WHAT BAD BITCHES DO I, II, III

SOUL OF A MONSTER I II III

KILL ZONE

A DOPE BOY'S QUEEN I II

By **Aryanna**

A KINGPIN'S AMBITON

A KINGPIN'S AMBITION **II**

I MURDER FOR THE DOUGH

By **Ambitious**

TRUE SAVAGE I II III IV V VI

DOPE BOY MAGIC I, II, III

MIDNIGHT CARTEL I II

CITY OF KINGZ

By **Chris Green**

A DOPEBOY'S PRAYER

By **Eddie "Wolf" Lee**

THE KING CARTEL **I, II & III**

By **Frank Gresham**

THESE NIGGAS AIN'T LOYAL **I, II & III**

By **Nikki Tee**

GANGSTA SHYT **I II &III**

By **CATO**

THE ULTIMATE BETRAYAL

By **Phoenix**

BOSS'N UP **I , II & III**

By **Royal Nicole**
I LOVE YOU TO DEATH
By Destiny J
I RIDE FOR MY HITTA
I STILL RIDE FOR MY HITTA
By **Misty Holt**
LOVE & CHASIN' PAPER
By **Qay Crockett**
TO DIE IN VAIN
SINS OF A HUSTLA
By **ASAD**
BROOKLYN HUSTLAZ
By **Boogsy Morina**
BROOKLYN ON LOCK I & II
By **Sonovia**
GANGSTA CITY
By **Teddy Duke**
A DRUG KING AND HIS DIAMOND I & II III
A DOPEMAN'S RICHES
HER MAN, MINE'S TOO I, II
CASH MONEY HO'S
By Nicole Goosby
TRAPHOUSE KING **I II & III**
KINGPIN KILLAZ I II III
STREET KINGS I II
PAID IN BLOOD **I II**
CARTEL KILLAZ I II III
DOPE GODS I II
By **Hood Rich**
LIPSTICK KILLAH **I, II, III**

CRIME OF PASSION I II & III

FRIEND OR FOE

By **Mimi**

STEADY MOBBN' **I, II, III**

THE STREETS STAINED MY SOUL

By **Marcellus Allen**

WHO SHOT YA **I, II, III**

SON OF A DOPE FIEND I II

Renta

GORILLAZ IN THE BAY **I II III IV**

TEARS OF A GANGSTA I II

DE'KARI

TRIGGADALE I II III

Elijah R. Freeman

GOD BLESS THE TRAPPERS I, II, III

THESE SCANDALOUS STREETS I, II, III

FEAR MY GANGSTA I, II, III IV, V

THESE STREETS DON'T LOVE NOBODY I, II

BURY ME A G I, II, III, IV, V

A GANGSTA'S EMPIRE I, II, III, IV

THE DOPEMAN'S BODYGAURD I II

THE REALEST KILLAZ I II

Tranay Adams

THE STREETS ARE CALLING

Duquie Wilson

MARRIED TO A BOSS… I II III

By Destiny Skai & Chris Green

KINGZ OF THE GAME I II III IV V

Playa Ray

SLAUGHTER GANG I II III

RUTHLESS HEART I II III
By Willie Slaughter
FUK SHYT
By Blakk Diamond
DON'T F#CK WITH MY HEART I II
By Linnea
ADDICTED TO THE DRAMA I II III
By Jamila
YAYO I II III
A SHOOTER'S AMBITION I II
By S. Allen
TRAP GOD I II
By Troublesome
FOREVER GANGSTA
GLOCKS ON SATIN SHEETS I II
By Adrian Dulan
TOE TAGZ I II III
By Ah'Million
KINGPIN DREAMS I II
By Paper Boi Rari
CONFESSIONS OF A GANGSTA
By Nicholas Lock
I'M NOTHING WITHOUT HIS LOVE
SINS OF A THUG
By Monet Dragun
CAUGHT UP IN THE LIFE I II III
By Robert Baptiste
NEW TO THE GAME I II III
By **Malik D. Rice**
LIFE OF A SAVAGE I II III

A GANGSTA'S QUR'AN I II

MURDA SEASON I II

GANGLAND CARTEL

By **Romell Tukes**

LOYALTY AIN'T PROMISED

By Keith Williams

QUIET MONEY I II

THUG LIFE

By **Trai'Quan**

THE STREETS MADE ME I II

By **Larry D. Wright**

THE ULTIMATE SACRIFICE I, II, III, IV, V

KHADIFI

IF YOU CROSS ME ONCE

ANGEL I II

By **Anthony Fields**

THE LIFE OF A HOOD STAR

By Ca$h & Rashia Wilson

THE STREETS WILL NEVER CLOSE

By K'ajji

CREAM

By Yolanda Moore

NIGHTMARES OF A HUSTLA

By King Dream

<u>BOOKS BY LDP'S CEO, CA$H</u>

<u>TRUST IN NO MAN</u>
<u>TRUST IN NO MAN 2</u>
<u>TRUST IN NO MAN 3</u>
<u>BONDED BY BLOOD</u>
<u>SHORTY GOT A THUG</u>
<u>THUGS CRY</u>
<u>THUGS CRY 2</u>
<u>THUGS CRY 3</u>
<u>TRUST NO BITCH</u>
<u>TRUST NO BITCH 2</u>
<u>TRUST NO BITCH 3</u>
<u>TIL MY CASKET DROPS</u>
<u>RESTRAINING ORDER</u>
<u>RESTRAINING ORDER 2</u>
<u>IN LOVE WITH A CONVICT</u>
<u>LIFE OF A HOOD STAR</u>

<u>Coming Soon</u>
BONDED BY BLOOD 2
BOW DOWN TO MY GANGSTA